THE DEVIL'S PAINTBOX

EMBER

VICTORIA McKERNAN

Text copyright © 2009 by Victoria McKernan
Photographs on cover and pp. i, ii, iii copyright © 2009 by Eva Kolenko

All rights reserved. Published in the United States by Ember, an imprint of Random House Children's Books, a division of Random House LLC, a Penguin Random House Company, New York. Originally published in hardcover in the United States by Alfred A. Knopf, an imprint of Random House Children's Books, New York, in 2009.

Ember and the E colophon are registered trademarks of Random House LLC.

Visit us on the Web! randomhouse.com/teens

Educators and librarians, for a variety of teaching tools, visit us at RHTeachersLibrarians.com

The Library of Congress has cataloged the hardcover edition of this work as follows:
McKernan, Victoria.
The devil's paintbox / Victoria McKernan.
p. cm.
Summary: In 1865, fifteen-year-old Aiden and his thirteen-year-old sister Maddy, penniless orphans, leave drought-stricken Kansas on a wagon train hoping for a better life in Seattle, but find there are still many hardships to be faced.
ISBN 978-0-375-83750-0 (trade) — ISBN 978-0-375-93750-7 (lib. bdg.) —
ISBN 978-0-375-89162-5 (ebook)
[1. Frontier and pioneer life—West (U.S.)—Fiction. 2. Overland journeys to the Pacific—Fiction. 3. Brothers and sisters—Fiction. 4. Orphans—Fiction. 5. West (U.S.)—History—1860–1890—Fiction. 6. Seattle (Wash.)—History—19th century—Fiction.] I. Title.
PZ7.M4786767Dev 2009 [Fic]—dc22 2008004749

ISBN 978-0-449-81655-4 (pbk.)

Printed in the United States of America
10 9 8 7 6 5 4 3 2 1
First Ember Edition 2013

Random House Children's Books supports the First Amendment and celebrates the right to read.

To my nephews
Peter Michael Thomas, U.S. Army
John Stephen Thomas, U.S. Marine Corps

Also by Victoria McKernan

Shackleton's Stowaway

Son of Fortune

Aiden Lynch slid down the steep creek bank, dirt crumbling beneath his bare feet and dust rising in a cloud behind him. He eyed the muddy trickle of water at the bottom and decided not to drink. Strange how a person could be so particular about drinking muddy water when he had come down to the creek to eat dirt, but nothing else made much sense in his life anymore, so why should that?

Heavy rains three years ago had carved the creek bed down so far that standing here, he was on eye level with the surrounding prairie. It was late April, but the land was still black from the autumn fires, and the low clouds of morning fog made it look as if it were smoldering. It was an eerie, hellish vista. The only thing left for miles around was his family's house, isolated now on a little island of unburned ground. But unlike a real island, which at least offered the bounty of the surrounding sea, the blackened earth of central Kansas was barren and sterile as the moon.

Tiny green blades of grass were starting to poke up, but it would be months before anything could really live here again, even a rabbit. Aiden's stomach growled at the thought of a rabbit, all nicely stewed or fried in bacon grease, but since the fire had wiped out every living thing for six miles around, none was likely to come hopping by anytime soon.

Say a rabbit could jump a yard at a time: how many yards

were in six miles, and how many miles would it hop in a single day? Aiden's brain had never been good with math. His mother used to give them problems to solve like that. If you plant 2 bushels of seed on 100 acres and get 600 bushels of wheat, how many bushels do you need to plant 180 acres, and how much wheat will you reap? His sister Maddy would figure it out in no time, but Aiden got distracted by the story behind the numbers. What if the rains came too heavy, like they did that one year, or not at all, like they had done for two, or the grasshoppers came and devoured the whole crop, or a hailstorm smashed everything? How could you ever know how many bushels? And why were you planting 180 acres anyway? That was twice what any family could handle! Was another family unable to work all their land and leasing some out? Did they lose a son to the war? It was 1865, and the Civil War had taken many men by now.

"It's 3.6 bushels of seed, and 1,080 bushels of wheat!" Maddy would declare while Aiden was hopelessly lost in his thoughts. But it didn't matter anymore; there was no more math these days since their mother was dead.

"Maddy?" he called. "Maddy, are you there?"

He knew where she was, but sometimes, when he got to thinking about all this, he felt a little bit crazy and had to hear her voice and know that she was still alive.

"I'm here." She was downstream and around a bend, where he couldn't see her, but Aiden didn't worry. For one thing, she could swim, and for another, there wasn't enough water in the creek now to drown a mouse. Maddy had gone around the bend because the clay there was soft and smooth. She liked to mash it up on her palm with a little water and lick it. Aiden preferred the harder clay from this part of the bank. It crumbled in his mouth, almost like a biscuit. He chipped a piece out of the bank with his knife and bit off a corner. It didn't taste bad, really; mostly like nothing, though he did miss having something to chew.

For a month now he and Maddy had been living on corn-meal mush. Every three days Aiden would take a few patties of dried cow dung out of the shrinking pile in the shed and build a tiny fire. They would huddle by the stove, enjoying the rare warmth, waiting for the water to boil, then pour a cup of cornmeal into the pot. When it was cooked, they would each eat two spoonfuls while it was warm, then pour the rest into a pan. It set when it cooled, and they would cut it into squares to eat for the next two days. Maddy called it "corn jelly meat." It wasn't so bad when they'd still had salt. Although it meant spending the days hungry, they saved the mush for evening. It helped push back the awfulness of the night. But now there was only one square each, the size of a baby's palm, left for tonight. Aiden took another bite of clay. It was taking far longer to starve to death than he had ever expected.

He had thought a lot about other solutions, but there didn't seem to be any. The army wouldn't take him until he was eighteen. He would have lied about his age—he was al-most sixteen, and he knew that after four years of war, the army wasn't picky these days—but there was still the prob-lem of what to do with Maddy. There were no relatives to send her to, not even a sympathetic neighbor. There were no neighbors at all now. Every farm and homestead around was abandoned. The nearest town was only about four miles away, but the harsh years had driven almost everyone off even before the fire. There were other small towns, but no guarantee that anyone would be left there either, except a few desperate survivors like themselves. It was over a hundred miles to the nearest railhead in Independence, Missouri, and traveling was dangerous enough for a lone man. There were outlaws all over the state, and deserters from the war. There were leftover bushwhackers, proslavery guerilla bands who had ridden the countryside terrorizing the population. There were Indians, wolves, tornados, blizzards and lightning, an endless list of danger. Each day, he decided the next day they would leave; then the next day came and he found another reason not to go. And then the cold came for good and they were stuck as the brutal winter starved on.

A sudden buzz caught his attention. A grasshopper! He dropped the piece of clay, climbed back up the creek bank and picked up the net. It was actually a tablecloth his mother had brought from Ireland. Once beautiful clean white lace, now it was dirty and torn. Aiden held the center in one hand and gathered the edges in the other. Maddy had sewn small stones into the hem for weight. He crouched silently, waiting to get a fix on the grasshopper. Sweat beaded on his chest, but he did not move. Finally, the grasshopper gave another chirp. Aiden flung the tablecloth so it spread out and fell neatly over the insect.

"Damn, boy. What the hell you doing?"

Aiden jumped up, his heart pounding. He spun around to see a man on a horse. He had appeared out of nowhere, on the other side of the creek. This was the first other human being he had seen in five months.

"What're you doing here?" Aiden said, his hand going quickly to the knife at his belt.

"Nothing you need to kill me for, boy." The man laughed.

"Your mama know you're out here messing with her fine tablecloth?"

"Who're you?"

"Jefferson J. Jackson."

"What's your business?"

"Looking for strays." The man leaned back in his saddle. He was old, fifty at least, with gray hair roughly cut and a short gray beard. His face was deeply creased, tanned dark as a boot. He was stringy in the arms and legs, long in the back and a little paunchy in the middle, like a man starting to live easy after a long time living hard.

"They said back in town was a pack of men out here. Any more but you?"

"Who said?"

"Shopkeeper rode out with us from Missouri, some Swedish name, ran the dry-goods store in Sweetwater before the hard times. He said might be sodbusters still out here with two or three grown sons."

"What do you care who lives here?"

"You don't need to be so prickly, boy. Wears you out. Take my word."

Jackson looked him up and down with a hard, piercing gaze. Aiden felt like the man could see right through him, could hear his pounding heart, might even be reading his mind.

"I'm guiding a wagon train west," Jackson said. "To Washington Territory, that's all. Looking for men might want to come along. There's a need for loggers up there. Lot of busted farmers out here might be wanting to start a new life."

"My life is fine, thank you very much," Aiden said in a

shaky voice. His heart was thudding and he feared his knees might give out.

"Well, that's good, then." Jackson shifted in his saddle and looked out over the burned prairie. "Most around here have it desperate. You fish with grasshoppers?" he asked, glancing doubtfully at the small trickle of water in the creek.

"Eat 'em," Aiden said, defiantly. "You never eat a grasshopper? They're delicacies in many foreign countries."

"Is that so?" Jackson had spent many years as a fur trapper, living in the mountains, and had eaten his share of insects. He'd eaten worms once—so hungry he didn't even brush all the dirt off, so it crunched in his teeth. He'd eaten parts of a dead deer, raw, that he'd had to chase away vultures to get to. But the idea of a kid doing it made him feel strangely awful. The boy was tall, with the strangled, spindly kind of height that hadn't keep flesh in pace with bones. He looked like a marionette. His dark brown eyes were watery and overbig in his sunken face. His hair was frizzy, brittle and the reddish brown color of bad health. Aiden blushed under the scrutiny.

"You think up that particular capture technique yourself?"

Aiden hesitated. The idea had actually come straight from an illustration in his favorite book, *The Atlas of the World*. The caption said: *Native Polynesian fishing technique.*

"Wasn't much to think up," he said. That wasn't a lie.

"No. Guess not." Jackson nodded. "You the only one living here, then?"

Aiden forced himself not to glance downstream. Maddy might have heard the man coming and thought to be quiet and hide.

"No," Aiden said. "My brothers went over to the Tollorsen place." He waved a hand toward the west. If Jackson had ridden in from Sweetwater, he wouldn't have passed the Tollorsen place and wouldn't know that they were long gone.

"My two *grown* brothers," he added. "Pa too. Gone *hunting*. Probably on their way back by now."

"So that must be the pack of men he was telling me about, eh?"

"Yes," Aiden said. "That'd be right."

If Jackson was intimidated by the idea of three armed men returning soon, he didn't show it.

"How old'r you, boy?"

"Sixteen. Nearly." He wiped his clay-covered fingers on his pants. Then Maddy appeared out of the mist, silently, like an angel in a dream. She was startled to see the stranger on the horse.

"So like I said, I'm the only one here right now," Aiden said loudly, praying she'd be quiet. "You must be tired, riding all this way," he added quickly. "Why don't you come on up to the house and have some breakfast." Jackson never turned his head even a bit.

"Who's behind me now, boy?" he said evenly. "I ain't looking for no trouble."

"No one's behind you." The grasshopper jumped under the tablecloth and Maddy made a little gasp. In an instant Jefferson J. Jackson drew his pistol, turned in his saddle, cocked and aimed. In half an instant more he raised the barrel and hissed a string of curses.

"Dammit, boy, I told you I ain't out here for trouble! I don't want to shoot no little girls or grandmas or cross-eyed kitty cats! I'll ride off right now, but not with spooks hiding out in the grass. So tell me straight—anyone else out here?"

"No," Aiden said.

"They're all dead," Maddy added in a faint voice. Aiden flinched; so much for his story of father and brothers riding up any moment. But Jackson didn't appear surprised.

"All right, then." He put the pistol back in his holster and got off his horse. Aiden grabbed his sister and pushed her behind him.

"Go to the house now," he said to her, still looking at Jackson. "Point the shotgun out the window in this direction."

"But, Aiden—"

"Go now!" he interrupted. "Shoot this man if he comes near the house. Don't be afraid, go."

"Son." Jackson took his hat off and wiped his brow. "Be easy. No one needs to shoot anybody."

Maddy leaned out from behind Aiden; her dark blue eyes were wide in her thin face.

"Who are you?" she asked.

"Jefferson J. Jackson."

"What name does the J stand for?"

Jackson was taken aback. "Well, ah . . . nothing, exactly." He shrugged, a bit sheepishly. "I just liked the symmetry of it. Who're you?"

"Madeline Lynch, called Maddy. This is my brother, Aiden. Pleased to meet you."

"You two out here alone, then?" Jackson said.

"Pa died last springtime. He fell dead behind the plow." Aiden squeezed her arm hard, but she went on. "Ma was left awhile, but passed in November just after the fire. The flames were higher than any time before, and the wind so hard." She talked in a rush, like she had almost forgotten how. "We had to widen the firebreak so not to burn, but the work of all that plowing did kill her. She bled from inside. It was too soon after the baby. That baby didn't live a day. Came early and was born blue. We rubbed it with vinegar and burned sage but it died anyway. Turned out a good thing."

Aiden saw the smudges of clay at the corners of her mouth, the hard knot of elbows in her stick-thin arms, the dark watery eyes in her sunken face. He felt ashamed.

"The rest went before," she went on, sweeping a thin arm toward the crosses on the hillside, "of various fevers and causes; one to the war and some just for being babies."

There was a long, heavy silence.

"Will you come rest at the house?" Maddy went on. "The tea's just run out, I'm afraid," she lied. "But we filter the muck out of the water through a cloth."

"We don't want to delay Mr. Jackson," Aiden said. "He's got business to tend to."

"Reckon it's on my way back to town," Jackson grunted. Damn nuisance children looked about two days from death. If he saw where they lived, he could send someone back to get them. No one might come, times being what they were, but at least his conscience would be clear. He took his horse by the reins and followed them.

The house was small, about twelve by twelve feet, and made of sod, like most of the houses out here where there was no wood for building. In front was the ring of plowed ground that made the firebreak. On the rise behind the house, the row of seven crosses was stark against the morning sky. Most families had a row of graves, but this one seemed especially unlucky.

Inside, the light was dim, even with the door wide open. The two small windows were covered with oiled paper. There was an iron stove in the middle of the room, but not a stick of furniture in the place. Two thin grass-stuffed mattresses lay on the ground, with a stack of folded quilts on top. In the rest of the room there was nothing but a couple of stoneware jars, a washtub and a tin pail with a piece of cloth over the top. An old shotgun was propped in one corner. Hanging on the wall were a bow and quiver of arrows.

"That's an Indian bow, ain't it?" Jackson said as he examined it more closely. "A nice one." It wasn't a child's toy, but a true warrior's weapon made of smoothly polished ash.

"It's mine," Aiden said, taking the bow out of the man's hand. "For hunting." He flushed with embarrassment, for he knew that he probably lacked the strength now to even string it, let alone draw and shoot.

"Sioux used to come around," Maddy explained, squeezing his hand as if she sensed his feelings. "Ma fixed one up from a buffalo trampling on him. Aiden found him hurt and brought him home. He gave Aiden the bow and arrows."

"I see."

Jackson's eyes swept the rest of the room and rested on a small stack of books. They sat on a bed of stones to keep them off the dirt floor.

"Nice library you got there."

"Oh, we once had a whole shelf full of books," Maddy said. "Any time our pa ever saw a book, he traded for it somehow. He dug a well for *Gulliver's Travels*. We even bought some through the mail at the times we had a bit of money. We had Jane Austen and Mary Shelley's *Frankenstein* and *The Swiss Family Robinson*, and *Aesop's Fables*. But most went for trade again, and the mice got to Aesop."

She knelt down by the pail and poured the creek water over the cloth. "It won't take long to strain out." She got up, went to the flour canister and took out a pair of spectacles.

"Don't do that now!" Aiden whispered fiercely.

"Why not?" Maddy whispered back. "I don't like grasshoppers raw!" She smiled at Jackson. "These were my grandma's," she explained, holding up the thick lenses. "In Ireland. She died in the famine. You heard of the famine? When all the potatoes went bad?"

"I have."

"Our ma and pa came over then so not to starve, and brought the glasses along. The print in some of the books is real small, especially the Shakespeare one."

"You got a book of Shakespeare?" Jackson's face brightened.

"That big one." She nodded at the pile. "Ma stole it."

"She didn't steal it," Aiden snapped. "Took it for wages

due. Before we came west." He looked steadily at Jackson. "My parents were indentured servants in Virginia. They worked off their time." It felt important to him that Jackson understood this. "Regular seven years, plus two extra for the children they brought over with them, though those boys worked from the first day. My parents had skills. The owner asked them to stay on but then cheated their wages."

"Said more was owing for Ma having three more babies," Maddy added. "So we took all of Shakespeare."

"Sounds like a fair trade to me," Jackson agreed easily.

"The people never had read it anyway, pages weren't even cut. We took the *Atlas of the World* too. That's our favorite."

"Was a lot of wages," Aiden said defiantly.

"No doubt."

"We read from it every night," Maddy went on. "It is 'a complete survey of all the geographical divisions of the world and all the various peoples comprised therein,' " she said, easily quoting the subtitle from memory.

"Well, I guess that's nice to know," Jackson said.

"There are illustrations, maps and exceptional rare photographs of native peoples. Would you like to see the curious custom of Chinese foot binding?"

"Maybe later," he sighed.

Maddy led them back outside to a flat rock, where she squatted down, held the grasshopper in one hand, then neatly pinched off its head. She laid it out on the rock as if at some kind of pagan altar, then held the spectacles so the sun shone through the lens, focusing a white-hot beam of light on the insect. The ray first made a tiny scorch on the grasshopper's wing; then there was a sizzling sound, and dark bubbles boiled up out of the headless body and around the leg joints. She picked up the roasted insect by a hind leg.

"Careful, it's hot," she said as she offered it to Jackson.

"Thanks, but I ate my breakfast," he replied.

Maddy broke the grasshopper in half and handed one piece to her brother. Jackson, who had seen all kinds of murder and mayhem in his life, shut his eyes.

"Look, you two're bad off," he said. "That's clear. I'll take you into Sweetwater. There's missionaries there now will feed you, and a government man signing up relief. Half the state is bad off and starving."

"We don't need relief," Aiden said. "I mean to join the army."

"War is over," Jackson said.

"Over?" Aiden knew he should be glad, but it felt like the last step had been kicked out from under him.

"Who won?" Maddy asked excitedly.

"Union Army and General Grant," Jackson said. "A couple of weeks ago, April ninth. They signed a treaty at a place called Appomattox."

Aiden, unsure where the man's loyalties lay, just nodded, but Maddy clapped her hands and gave a cry of delight.

"That means all the slaves are free now?"

"Suppose so."

"So they can go home?"

"Home?" Jackson frowned. Aiden kicked her ankle. There had been massacres in Kansas over the slavery issue.

"To Africa. To their homes," Maddy went on, oblivious.

"Reckon so," Jackson said slowly. "I suppose. Far way back to Africa, though."

"But there must be some like you ready to take them.

Must be logging in Africa too. There's plenty of jungle. I can show you in the *Atlas of the World*."

This child could talk the bark off a tree, Jackson thought as he tipped his hat back to let the sweat cool on his brow. If he couldn't find some decent men, why couldn't they just be ordinary children?

"Look, I don't know about Africa, but I'll take you into town," he said. "Missionaries or whoever, you can sort it out yourselves from there."

"I'll go for the logging," Aiden said.

"You?" Jackson laughed. "I don't recall making you that offer."

"I can swing an axe."

"Boy, you'll do good to swing a full spoon to your mouth."

"Don't you mock me." Aiden's hands curled into fists.

"I ain't, son," Jackson said. "I don't mean no insult, and do say I apologize." Jackson looked at Maddy almost kindly. "What's he look like when he ain't all starving? Strong?"

Maddy nodded. "He beat our grown brothers half the time they fought. I sewed them up, though Ma guided how I did. See there under his eye, that pretty scar? Was split this big"—she held her fingers an inch apart—"and deep to the bone. We sewed up all the fights, but Pa was surely mad that time—"

"That's enough!" Aiden said. "Man doesn't need to hear our business."

"You aim to fight everyone you meet?" Jackson asked.

"Only those asking for it."

"Well, I certainly ain't asking," Jackson said. "Just offering a ride into town. The horse will carry the two of you easy enough, and the walk will do me good."

"What will it take to join with your wagon train?" Aiden pressed. He felt dizzy and urgent, like the earth had stopped spinning for a minute just to give him one more chance. A wagon train would be safe for Maddy. Someone would surely need a girl to help with chores and children. They might even keep her hired on at the other end.

"Boy, I ain't talking about a buggy ride to Sunday school. We're walking two thousand miles across some of the roughest country in the world."

"You been all around the world?" Maddy asked eagerly. "What's it like?"

Jackson squeezed his eyes in exasperation. When he got back to town, he was going to smack hell out of the man who told him there were three or four grown men out here.

"Costs money to travel that far. You got any money?"

"No."

"Got any livestock?"

Aiden shook his head.

"Mule?"

"No."

"We ate it," Maddy said. "Boiled."

"What about the hide?" Jackson looked around hopefully.

"Wasn't so good. Real hard to chew."

Jackson sighed. He didn't need a couple of starving orphans, and he certainly didn't want penniless ones.

"You got any tools?"

"Yeah, we got tools," Aiden said. "Plow. Shovel, axe, some hoes."

"Don't have handles, though," Maddy added unhelpfully. "We burned them in the stove over the winter after the furniture was gone."

"Got a stove," Aiden pressed. "We could sell that."

Jackson laughed.

"It's a good stove."

"Boy, there's fifty stoves sitting out here, left behind by busted homesteaders. There's stoves took root out here and *growing* by now. What you got is called scrap metal."

"Handles are easy enough," Aiden said. "All I need is some wood."

"So you got nothing. What you're telling me—you got nothing."

"I can sell the land. It ain't a homestead—we bought it clear."

"No one's buying land out here, son. God himself wouldn't buy this land now."

"I can teach you all the foreign countries of the world," Maddy offered.

"Well, I ain't moving to any foreign country any time soon," Jackson said wearily.

"I can doctor some," Maddy said.

"So you said."

"I can get a fishhook out of you," she said. "There's a trick to it." She paused, looked down in serious thought. "Well, I *will* tell you, because sometime you might need to know when I'm not around."

"I know how to get a fishhook out," Jackson said. "Don't need any doctoring." What he needed was to get back to town and ease this damn mess in a drink of whiskey.

"Here's what I got," he said, rushing the offer before he had a chance to get his sense back. "Timber company outside of Seattle will pay me one hundred dollars for every man I bring in." He looked the skinny boy over again and hoped he wasn't going to regret this. "Once there, you're bound to work it off. It's hard work. Rough living. Plus cost of your passage owed to me. That's another hundred dollars. Each. It takes most men a year to work it off and you got her to keep, so figure two."

"I can work too," Maddy said.

"No decent women in the camps or anywhere nearby. Men do the cooking, and there's Chinamen for the laundry." He looked her over more closely. "How old are you?"

"Fourteen. Nearly."

"Thirteen, eh? Old enough by the time we get there. There's a mighty lack of women up there, so men'll marry the ugly ones. Fatten up some and learn to keep your mouth shut and someone'll take you. Maybe even pay off your passage." He turned back to Aiden. "You understand my deal?"

"Yes." Aiden burned with the insult to his sister but worked to keep his temper. "You'll take us to Seattle. I'll work off our passage. Might take two years."

"Lot of people don't make it. There's a hundred ways to die on this journey."

"Well," Aiden said, "I do appreciate some novelty."

Jackson almost smiled. "All right," he said. "You've lived hard enough so far; you might do for something yet. If you want to come, I'll take you. But if one of you dies, the other still owes me their keep, got that?"

"Yes, sir."

"I ain't a charity-type man. But I'm fair. I'll figure it out to the day," Jackson went on somberly. "You die halfway, for instance, it's only fifty dollars. But you will owe it—whoever's left. The hundred dollars is for your food and travel only. Anything extra you need, clothes, boots and such, I'll put on your account."

He looked at their bare feet.

"You got any boots?"

"I do," Aiden said. "And I'll buy her some, on my account."

"All right, then." Jefferson J. Jackson was starting to respect this proud kid. "Let's get moving. Bring them books along. I ain't read nothing new for a while, and I'm partial to Shakespeare."

The town had an official name, Sweetwater, but no one ever used it, few even remembered it and the water had never been sweet anyway. The prairie soil out here was alkaline, and even the springs and deep wells had a bitter taste. Most of the homesteaders had simply called it "town" or "The Wood," after the grove of precious cottonwood trees that grew around the spring.

It never had been much of a town, with only a dozen buildings, but now it was grim and crumbling. Last time Aiden had come, soon after the fire in November, the last shopkeeper was packing up to leave. Outside the empty dry-goods store had been a box of ribbon scraps and bits of lace with a note that said *Free. Sorry. Good luck.*

They heard fiddle music as they approached.

"They're having a party," Jackson said. "We've been ten days traveling since we started in Independence. Good grass and water here, so we're taking a day to graze the cattle, shore up the wagons and lighten the loads. Folks always start out with too much. And had a cripple-legged calf born yesterday, so might as well cook that up while it's still fresh and plenty of wood around for a fire." The rich aroma of the roasting meat made Aiden feel slightly insane.

It was late afternoon, and the sun cast deep golden shadows across the ground. As they got closer, they could see the swirl of dresses as people danced beneath the trees.

Aiden remembered the dancing eight years ago, the night before they'd left Virginia. All the other servants, and some of the slaves from miles around, had gathered in a barn for a grand party. He remembered the giddy whirl of the reels and the fierce stomping of jigs. His mother's cheeks were flushed, and his father, twice her size, danced so wildly he lifted her off the floor. His older brothers, who were thirteen and fourteen then, swung little Maddy around until she screamed with laughter. How excited and hopeful they had all been. They would leave in the morning and start the journey west. They would work in the coal mines for a year or two and save some money, then go to the frontier and build a home where land could be had for pennies an acre. But the land hadn't cared about their hard work and grand hopes. The land had claimed them, one by one.

Aiden helped Maddy off the horse. She was trembling. For all her bold chatter back at the farm, he knew how terrified she must be right now. He was feeling pretty much the same way, though he would not show it. He took her hand. It was like a little bundle of twigs. She was all he had left of his family, all he had left in the world.

"Are they all going with us?" Maddy asked Jackson in an awed whisper. "All these people?"

"Reckon so," Jackson said.

"There must be a hundred!"

"One hundred and eight," Jackson replied. "Counting you two. There's probably five or six thousand going west this season, maybe more with the war being over."

"All on the same trail?" Aiden asked.

"Mostly. But I take a small wagon train, specially for live-stock. People are willing to pay for less aggravation, more grass and water. I know the side routes, and we keep off the main trail for as much as we can, until we get to the Continental Divide."

"Where do they come from?" Maddy asked.

"All over."

"Why?"

"All kinds of reasons, I suppose. I don't ask. As long as they have the money to pay me and supply themselves for the journey, and don't seem too loco, I'll take 'em. My job's just to get 'em there."

The emigrants had taken tables and empty barrels out of the abandoned shops and set them up under the cottonwood trees. Women were putting out bowls of apples and radishes and pickles, plates of corn bread and kettles of beans. Most of the people didn't seem to notice Aiden and Maddy, but some stared at the raggedy pair as they followed Jackson to the well. Two young men leaned on the back of one wagon. They looked like brothers, tall, with fair blond hair, square jaws, blue eyes and good teeth. They were in their early twenties, Aiden guessed, and looked prosperous. It wasn't just the new store-bought clothes and good boots, but the way they held themselves, confident and easy.

"We do what you say, Herr Jackson." One of them lifted a large pewter mug as they passed. "We lighten the load like you say!" He pointed to a small beer cask on the tailgate of the adjoining wagon. "It is very good brew, dis one! Come haf some!"

"Germans," Jackson said by way of explanation. "From

Wisconsin. They think they're taking fifteen fancy milk cows to Oregon. Look at 'em." He nodded toward a small herd. "Girly cows. Be lucky if they make it there with five." Aiden saw Jackson look longingly at the beer but then turn back to his horse. The tired animal stood quietly as Jackson pulled off the saddlebags. Aiden and Maddy's meager possessions barely filled one; the books took up all of the other.

"You're welcome to keep them with you to read," Maddy offered. "Except, if you don't mind, for the *Atlas of the World*. We read from that one every night."

"Thank you, miss." Jackson smiled the first easy smile she had seen. "I'm looking forward to Mr. Shakespeare."

"Some of *Aesop's Fables* you can still read too," she offered. "We know them by heart and can fill in the parts around the mouse holes."

"I'll keep that in mind if I feel in need of a moral."

Aiden drew water from the well, marveling at how easy it was to get a full bucket of clear water. Despite the bitter taste, they all drank thirstily, then poured the rest into a trough for the horse. Jackson unfastened the girth and slid the saddle off. Aiden picked up a rag to help wipe down the sweating horse, but Jackson waved them off.

"Go on, get yourselves something to eat."

"Can we really?" Maddy asked, her voice trembling as she stared at all the food. The music had stopped and everyone was crowding around the tables.

"It's a party, ain't it? Looks like plenty enough." He didn't seem to be in much hurry to join in himself, though he did glance back to see that the Germans and their beer were still waiting. "Just watch you don't make yourselves sick."

Maddy took their two tin plates, mugs and spoons out of

their sack. Aiden pulled up another bucket of water and they washed their hands and faces. There was not much they could do about their dirty clothing. With no soap and little water for laundry, none of their other clothes were any better. Maddy tied a bit of ribbon on her braid and made Aiden roll up his frayed shirt cuffs. They walked slowly over to the food tables. Aiden's legs felt jittery, from hunger and nerves, but Maddy's bold spirit was quickly reviving.

"Oh, Aiden, look, there's jam!" she whispered. A blue enamel bowl of strawberry jam shimmered in the sun like a pot of melted rubies. "And butter!" The butter was freshly churned, and the soft yellow peaks glistened with tiny droplets of moisture. Maddy clutched her plate to her chest, suddenly frozen. Her eyes filled with tears that spilled down her cheeks.

"It's okay, Maddy." Aiden put an arm around her. "Starving times are done." He picked up a piece of corn bread, covered it with butter and jam and held it out to her, but she still couldn't move. Aiden held the bread up to her lips and she took a tiny bite. Her shoulders began to shake and he pressed her tight to his side.

"Listen now, I mean it. We got a way to live now. We got a way out. So take a bite. Look." He took a bite himself. He almost gagged. It was shockingly sweet and rich. It seemed to fill up his entire mouth so he wasn't sure he could even swallow it. He picked up a pitcher of fresh milk and poured them both a cup. The milk was warm and rich, with golden gobs of fat floating on top. Maddy clutched the cup and gulped it down.

"Careful," Aiden said. "Let's don't get sick." But once they got started they couldn't help themselves. They moved along the tables, eating pickles and radishes and more bread and butter and slices of ham.

"What's that?" Maddy pointed to a bowl of orange globes in syrup.

"Peaches!" Aiden whispered, unbelieving. "Do you remember peaches? We had 'em once. Pa brought a tin from town one Christmas."

"I don't remember. No."

"Careful, they're real slippery."

Maddy gingerly picked up a piece and took a little bite. Her lips shone with the sugary juice. "Oh, Aiden—it's like— I don't know what it's like!" Her eyes were enormous with delight. "It's like—like eating a cherub!"

"A cherub?"

"Those fat babies—from the Bible pictures!"

"What are you doing!" A high, sharp voice snapped beside them. Aiden looked up to see a girl, about his own age and almost as tall, in a very fine dress with pounds of ruffles. She wore a velvet ribbon at her throat and a fountain of curls on her shoulders.

"You're filthy!" the girl declared. "What are you doing here? Are you beggars? Look at them—" She spun around and squealed at her sister, equally dressed up in ribbons and bows, carrying a ruffled parasol.

"Shall I get Father?" the other girl said.

"We're with the wagon train." Aiden put an arm around Maddy's shoulders and tried to stand like the confident Germans.

"Hmmph." The girl tossed her curls imperiously. "Since when?"

"We just arrived," Aiden said.

"Where's your wagon?"

"We don't have one," he replied. "Um—we don't need one."

"We're nomads," Maddy broke in. "Like the Mongols from the steppes of Asia. Nomads sleep under the stars."

The girl frowned uncertainly at her sister. "Well, we don't mind feeding beggars," she said. "But you mustn't take the nice things. Not the peaches, not the cherries, certainly not the cake. There's plenty of beans and bread."

"Oh, let them have an apple," her sister said arrogantly. "There are some with spots." They both laughed.

Suddenly there was a swish of skirts behind them and Aiden felt a light hand land on his shoulder.

"There you are, at last!" A woman bent and kissed Maddy on the cheek. Aiden caught a whiff of perfume. "Mr. Jackson said you would be coming today. I was so looking forward to meeting you!"

She was the most beautiful woman Aiden had ever seen, even in a magazine. She was small but not skinny. Not plump either. Aiden didn't know what to call it, just all round and soft-looking and beautiful in a way that made him strangely embarrassed to notice. She wore a dark green dress that looked finer than a regular dress but not show-off rich. She had sparkling blue eyes and thick brown hair that was caught up in a twist at the back of her head, from which little strands had escaped and curled around her face. She spoke with an accent he had never heard before.

"Forgive me," she laughed, holding out one soft little hand. "I'm Mrs. Gabriel True; Marguerite True." The silence hung just a little too long before Maddy spoke up.

"Pleased to meet you, Mrs. True." Maddy curtsied. "I'm

Madeline Lynch, called Maddy, and this is my brother Aiden." She nudged him.

"Pleased to make—to meet you, ma'am," Aiden stammered.

"The pleasure is mine." Marguerite turned smoothly from the dumbstruck Aiden. "Annie, Polly." She nodded at the two girls. "How nice you both look in your fine things! Let me introduce you to Miss Maddy Lynch and Mr. Aiden Lynch. They have come to join our wagon train." She beamed at Maddy and stroked the girl's brittle hair. "You must be tired. Have you come a long way?"

"Yes, ma'am. From Madagascar," Maddy said. Aiden kicked her ankle. The food had obviously restored her chatty ways. Marguerite blinked but barely missed a step.

"Yes. Well. Ah—and how is the weather there this time of year?"

"Torrid," Maddy said earnestly. "Quite torrid."

"Oh." Marguerite smiled. "Well, then, you should like Washington Territory very much, I imagine, for the change."

"Yes, that's why we're going." Maddy smiled and Aiden saw that she too had fallen in love with Marguerite.

"Well, there you are!" A booming voice worked its way through a crowd of people and a giant of a man followed. He was six feet tall, broad-shouldered and handsome, with thick curly reddish brown hair. It was cut a little too long and slicked back with pomade in a way that didn't seem to go with his somber preacher's coat.

"Hello, girls." He nodded at Polly and Annie. "You do look divine. May I have the pleasure of reserving a dance with you?"

"I don't believe preachers are supposed to dance." Polly frowned.

26

"Only in front of golden calves they're not," the man said easily. "Under the cottonwoods, they are certainly allowed." He gave them a deep sweeping bow. "And who are your new friends, my dear?" He smiled at Marguerite, reached out and squeezed her little hand. Aiden saw her eyes brighten. It stabbed him in some queer place inside. He had seen his parents look at each other like that.

"Madeline and Aiden Lynch," she purred. "This is my husband, the Reverend Gabriel True."

"Pleased to meet you." He shook Aiden's hand and bowed to Maddy.

"They've come a terribly long way," Marguerite crooned in her lovely accent. "And now they're going west with us."

"Well, that's grand!" If the Reverend True was confused as to why these urchin scarecrows were suddenly under his wife's wing, he didn't show it.

"Will you excuse us, girls?" Marguerite nodded at Annie and Polly. "I think our new friends will need a glass of lemonade after such a journey." With a firm hand, she steered Aiden and Maddy away.

Aiden woke the next morning with the sour taste of vomit in his mouth, the hard ground beneath him and the rough scratch of a wool blanket against his skin. For a moment he had no idea where he was or what had happened to him; then reality came rushing in and he sat up with a jerk.

"Maddy?" The earth lurched beneath him and the sky swirled around so fast he toppled back to the ground, landing face-first in the damp grass. He had never felt so sick and weak in his life. "Maddy?"

He heard someone moving under the cottonwood tree nearby. A gray coat rustled and a man slowly unfolded himself from beneath its shelter.

"Shush," he said hoarsely. "She's fine. Don't wake the entire camp." Aiden leaned up on one elbow. The man stretched out a pair of long legs, rubbed his face and coughed.

"Where is she?"

"In the preacher's wagon. His little French wife is looking after her."

"Marguerite?"

"Is that the one?"

"Yes. Don't you know her?"

"I've seen her."

He was a foreign-looking man, though Aiden couldn't say

exactly what made him look different. He had very dark eyes and black hair, but his skin was no browner than a farmer's. He was taller than average, maybe six feet, but very thin. Aiden couldn't tell whether he was young or old. There were circles under his eyes and his hands trembled like an old man's, but his face was unlined and his hair had no gray. He wore blue wool pants from which a stripe on the leg had recently been torn.

"Are you a soldier?" Aiden asked.

"I'm a doctor." The man reached into the pocket of his coat, pulled out a small brown medicine bottle, uncorked it and took a drink. One of his legs moved restlessly, the heel of his boot carving a little trench in the ground. Aiden didn't remember seeing him at the party, but all of the party felt like a dream right now. He remembered food and music, swirling dresses and Marguerite's blue eyes. He felt the coarse wool of the blanket against his legs and realized he was half-naked.

"Where are my pants?"

"There." The stranger nodded toward the tree, where Aiden's trousers hung from a branch. "You had diarrhea every ten minutes, it was easier to leave them off."

Aiden felt his face go hot. "Is Maddy all right?"

"Yes. She lost it all much quicker than you. People die this way, you know, eating too much after extreme starvation."

"We were careful—about eating. I thought we were. I tried to be."

"Careful for you would be a week of porridge and sweet tea, then maybe a potato and some broth," the man said without emotion. He spoke perfect English, and with a Yankee accent. "How do you feel now?"

"Fine," Aiden lied. He felt as if he had been turned inside out and dragged behind a horse. The man came over, squatted beside him and pressed his bony fingers to the inside of Aiden's wrist to check his pulse.

"Who are you?" Aiden asked. "Why are you tending me?"

"I told you, I'm a doctor. I had nothing else to do last night. I don't like parties. And you vomited on my boots."

"I'm sorry."

"My name is Carlos Javier Perez." The man bowed his head slightly with an incongruous formality.

"I'm Aiden Lynch. Thank you for tending me. But I'm fine now." Aiden struggled to get up.

"The sun has just come up, and it takes an hour to get all the wagons moving. You can rest."

"I can't."

"Why not?"

"Mr. Jackson won't take me if I'm not strong."

"Mr. Jackson fully intends to take you. He offered me fifty cents to keep you alive."

"What—damn! Sorry—"

"What's the matter? You think you're worth more?"

"No—"

"You don't want me to keep you alive?"

"No! I mean yes."

"Then what's wrong?"

"He'll charge it to my account is what's wrong!"

Carlos laughed.

"It isn't funny!" Aiden staggered to his feet, pulling the blanket around him. He snatched his pants off the tree.

"No. I'm sorry, it isn't. But fifty cents—it's quite a fortune for one man's life." Carlos wiped his eyes and sat back down under the tree. He fished in the pocket of his coat and took out a copper penny.

"That is what it costs, lad." He tossed the penny at Aiden's feet. "A penny's worth of shot and powder to kill one man dead." He took another swallow from the medicine bottle. "I've seen a thousand men die at a penny apiece, so you're a fair bargain." This time the medicine seemed to do him some good. His shoulders relaxed, he took a deep breath and his hands stopped twitching.

Aiden pulled his pants on and buttoned them up.

"Thank you, Doctor. I'm obliged. But I'll go now." Doctor or not, this man was far too strange.

"I was serious about the porridge. Eat nothing else for a few days, maybe a bit of bread and honey. And rest. Ride in the wagon. I left some lemons with the preacher's wife, for you both have the scurvy as well."

"What's that?"

"It's why your gums are bleeding."

"Everyone bleeds by end of winter," Aiden said. "Cress and purslane come up and that's the cure." What kind of doctor was he if he didn't know a simple thing like that?

"Fine. I don't care if you do die." Carlos closed his eyes. "But it's easy enough to stay alive now if you're not a complete idiot, so you might as well give it a try. Saves everyone the trouble of digging a grave."

When he got to the group of wagons, Aiden realized he had no idea which one belonged to the Reverend Gabriel True. A couple of them he could rule out right away, as they looked far too rich to be a preacher's wagon, but the rest seemed pretty much the same. All around him Aiden saw and heard the morning come to life. Babies wailed, a rooster crowed, mules stamped and snuffled. Children tumbled from wagons, bigger ones handing down the smaller ones.

The morning sun shone through the canvases, and he saw shadows of people inside, arms thin and spiderlike, made long by the slanted sun. He heard quiet murmurs, the rustle of clothing, the clomp of boots and the swish of oiled laces. The wagons were only feet apart, so every sound was heard. After living so long in isolation, Aiden found the closeness particularly strange. But for the next five or six months, this would be his world: all these people, a whole town on the march to a new world, with their chickens and children, pots and pans and clattering pails. Aiden felt a mix of thrill and horror.

Then he saw Jefferson J. Jackson heading toward the well. He walked with a slow, creaky shuffle that betrayed no specific ailment, just a lifetime of cold ground and numerous small woundings. His eyes were red and foggy, and Aiden suspected the liquor jug had not passed him by last night.

"Mr. Jackson." Aiden walked toward him. Jackson stopped and squinted over at him.

"Oh. You." He gave a racking wet cough, churned up something thick and spat.

"Just want to say I can keep myself alive well enough," Aiden said. "I don't need you putting fifty cents to any doctor on my account."

"What the hell you talkin' about?"

"The doc—the foreign doctor said you gave him fifty cents to tend me last night. I am sorry that I got myself sick, but I want to get it straight with you about the money part before we go on."

Jackson wiped his mouth on his sleeve. "I thought fifty cents might be fair. I know what doctoring costs."

"I would've made do."

"Well, I'm sure you're right."

"It's just I know how bosses will pile it up on you. The owing. You work and work and then comes payday but the money is all gone to rent and goods at the company store, which is three times the normal price, and suddenly there's nothing left. I won't have it. Sorry. But I won't. We worked the coal mines between Virginia and here. Stone quarry too, same bad deal."

Jackson rubbed a hand across his tired eyes. "Well. That's a whole lot of woeful history for my brain first thing in the morning."

"I just mean to be straight, sir," Aiden said. "To be upfront about things. Anything goes on my account, I need to agree to it first."

"Fair enough. I promise in the future I'll consult you, son. If you're not passed out and twitching in the dirt like a stepped-on lizard like you were last night!" Jackson snapped. "Now will you let me go do my business 'fore I crap my own pants?"

Aiden jumped. "Yes. Sorry."

"And so you know," Jackson growled. "No fifty cents on your account. That doc turned back the money."

"What do you mean?"

"Just that. Said not to mind it. He's gone a little crazy in the mind, I think, on account of the war, but that's what he said, no charge, so why would I argue against that?"

"So no money charged to me?"

"Not one penny. But you better calm down your attitude

or I'll start chargin' you for sheer annoyance." Jackson pulled himself up and stretched a little. "Boy—you're spending a lot of energy being mad and turned-up over everything. I know you ain't had the best of it before now, but all you can do is go on from here. So my advice, and I won't charge a penny for it, is that you go easy."

One week and a hundred miles later, the ever-gregarious Maddy knew the life story of just about everybody in the wagon train. "People come from everywhere!" she told Aiden as they walked along one bright afternoon. "From Boston and New York and even Sweden. Annie and Polly Hollingford, those fancy-dressed girls? They come from a plantation in South Carolina," Maddy chatted on, swiping hair off her sweaty forehead. "But they've been living in St. Louis for the war. Their uncle is sending the whole family to Seattle to build a factory for canning salmon. Like canned peaches!" she explained, as if her brother were dim and hadn't heard about canning. She stopped to pick up a buffalo chip and add it to the pile in her sack. Most of the older children spent the days gathering the dried buffalo dung that made their nightly cooking fires. They fanned out on either side of the wagon train, filling burlap sacks and dragging them back to empty them whenever they got too heavy.

Aiden usually kept to the far outside of the group, his bow slung over one shoulder, the quiver of arrows on the other. Twenty-seven wagons and a hundred and eight people scared off most living things, but out here he might hunt up a few rabbits or prairie chickens. He was still feeble enough that he needed Maddy's help to string the bow at the start of each day, but he could draw well enough to kill small game.

He was starting to feel at ease in the wagon train, though he knew he would never fit in as easily as his sister. There were four other "strays" like him, traveling on Jefferson J. Jackson's ticket to work as loggers. Two of the other men were in their twenties, friends from eastern Kansas seeking adventure in the West. Another man was a widower of thirty-two who had left his three children behind with his sister. The fourth was a big man named William Buck. He talked a lot, mostly about all the great things he had done, most of which Aiden thought pretty suspicious. Buck fussed like a child when he didn't get his way and bullied the others, though in the sneaky way of a coward. They all shared meals and slept under Jackson's wagons when it rained, but Aiden didn't feel like any of them would be his lifelong friend. The Kansas boys kept their own company, the widower was too morose and William Buck just plain got on his nerves. So far, the men had light work. They took turns driving Jackson's two wagons, which carried their meager personal gear, food for the six of them and Jackson's store of trade goods. They helped with the cattle, hunted game and dug the latrines for the camp. They took turns standing guard during the night.

Maddy was still staying in the Reverend True's wagon, and it seemed that it would be her permanent home. The Trues had sheltered her the first few days out of charity, but that soon changed.

The Reverend Gabriel and Marguerite True appeared to have no idea of the simplest housekeeping tasks one needed to survive in general, let alone in a wagon train crossing the continent. Marguerite had never even seen a campfire, certainly never cooked over one. She had a book called *The Pioneers' Guide to the Oregon Trail* that told how to bake biscuits in a Dutch oven, but she didn't even know how to make biscuit dough. "A minister's wife has so many other duties to attend to," Marguerite explained vaguely. The first time Aiden brought her a pheasant he had shot, she took great delight in the beautiful feathers, apparently without realizing there was actual meat under the hat decorations.

And so the misplaced pair was completely willing to let a thirteen-year-old girl take over their care. Maddy built the fires, cooked the meals, plucked the pheasants, carried water and mended the reverend's clothes. He tore something every other day, for he was as awkward with the ox and wagon as his wife was with the domestic chores. There was barely enough room in the little wagon for the couple to sleep, so Marguerite piled up a nest of quilts underneath each night for Maddy.

"Those quilts smell so good, Aiden," she said as she picked up another buffalo chip. "Everything in her chest smells of perfume."

Aiden also slept outside, though the blankets Jackson provided were not so plush and hardly perfumed. He didn't mind. He liked falling asleep under the stars. After just this one week of simple food, corn bread and porridge and salt pork, Aiden was starting to feel strong in a way he could barely remember. Jackson led them to creeks or springs each day, so there were wild greens to be had, which quickly cured his bleeding gums. The aches in his knees and shoulders were almost gone too; so much for the scurvy. Maddy's face was filling out and there was color in her cheeks. The skin around her fingernails, which had been split and bleeding all winter, was now smooth. She looked like a girl who might even be pretty someday.

"Oh, and listen," Maddy went on as she slung the bag over her shoulder. "You know those Thompsons? In the two blue painted wagons, with all those children? They have no dead ones at all! Isn't that amazing? Ten alive—Therese, Peter, John, Joseph, Rose, Paul, Monica, Matthew, Catherine and Andrew. Not even any born dead!"

"There's only ten?" Aiden laughed. Children swarmed around those two wagons like a mess of tadpoles. It really was amazing, though. Aiden didn't know of a single family, even rich people back east, whose children had all lived. Two out of three was thought lucky.

He saw Doc Carlos walking alone up ahead. Aiden had not talked to him since the first morning they'd met. Carlos hardly spoke to anyone. He traveled with a man named Joby, and the two of them always camped some distance from the rest.

"What do you know about him?" Aiden asked, nodding in the doctor's direction.

"Nothing much except that he hates dogs." Maddy frowned. "The Thompsons' dog—you know, that spotted hound—was just sniffing round his feet and he went and kicked it clear into yesterday."

"That isn't much to know."

"I tried to talk to him. I asked him could I read his medical books, but he didn't seem like he was even hearing me."

"What about his friend? The one that drives the cart?" Carlos didn't have a proper wagon, just a two-wheeled cart pulled by a pair of mules.

"That man Joby? Likes to talk well enough but has a brain deficiency."

"Like a slow mind? Like the shopkeeper's boy was?"

"Not bad as that. Just off some. He injured his brain in the war. He's really good with the animals, though. He shows Reverend True how to work the oxen. And I tell him things about the world. Mostly he wants to know about the animals—do they have mules in China and so on. He was very enamored with the llamas of Peru."

Maddy stopped to pick up two buffalo patties. Her sack was bulging and Aiden took it from her. A warm breeze ruffled through the tall grass with a low swishing sound. Grasshoppers jumped all around them like popping corn. Aiden still sometimes had to hold back from catching them. Maddy went on about all the people in the wagon train. He didn't mind her endless chatter; it was comforting, the only thing the same from their old lives. It was a beautiful day, the first of May, with the sky so blue it almost hurt to look at. He felt strange, and it took him a while to realize why. He felt strange because he felt happy.

"See them there?" Maddy pointed at an older couple. "They've been married twenty years, and they're going to run a sawmill in Seattle for her brother who got pulled into a machine. He lost parts of both his arms and almost his entire head, just enough left to keep his brain in. Will you not work with the machines, Aiden? When we get there? Please promise."

"Yes. If you'll please to God ease off the holding-in-the-brain kind of talk."

"I bet he looks like Dr. Frankenstein's monster, all stitched together!" Maddy giggled.

"Stop!"

She made a gruesome face at him and ran her finger in a harsh zigzag down one side of her skull. Aiden lunged at her and she darted away. She screeched with laughter as he chased her through the grass.

That day Jackson decided to make camp earlier than usual. He figured they were about in the middle of Kansas and making good time. They were following the Smoky Hill River, but it was about to swing away into a big curve for about ten miles. The wagons would keep on traveling in a straight line the next day, so they would camp before the bend to have water for the night. It was three o'clock and the sun was warm. The women decided it was a good chance to do some washing. Soon the afternoon rang with laughter and singing. Children splashed in the shallow water as the women beat clothes clean on the rocks. The men were banished to the high ground so the women could bathe, and the air filled with shrieks as they waded into the cold water. The men kept themselves busy mending harnesses and shoring up the wagons.

After the women bathed, the men had a chance to wash, and some of them even did. That evening the whole camp smelled like soap, and a lot of the married people disappeared into their wagons right after supper, sending their children to play down by the riverbank. Marguerite, with a shine in her eyes and a blush in her cheeks, gave Maddy a novel to read and suggested she might find the light better down by the river. It was a slim "ladies' novel," which Maddy had never been fond of, but she knew when she was being asked to make herself scarce. Her parents used to send all the children out to the creek to "catch some bluefish" when they wanted some privacy. There were never any bluefish in the creek.

Aiden decided to explore the river bluffs around the bend. It was just after sunset, and there was a low stripe of bright red along the horizon, with a deep blue sky just above, like a field of cornflowers. The water below was silver in the fading light. He was glad to be alone for a little while. The twilight coaxed out feelings and memories that he rarely allowed himself. He thought about the past and the lost, wondered about the future and simply enjoyed the miracle of being alive. Right now, the starving winter almost seemed like a bad dream.

Suddenly the peace was disturbed by a sound in the bushes below. He slid the bow off his shoulder and crouched down. The bushes rustled again, far too vigorously to be caused by any small animal or bird. He heard a snort, then a whine. What could be that big and sound that odd? An injured buffalo?

"Hello?" Aiden called out as he crept up to the edge of the bluff. "Is someone there?"

Now he was answered with a vigorous sob—reassuringly human. He stood up and saw Polly Hollingford, crying like she had been stabbed through the heart.

"What's wrong? Are you all right?" Aiden slid down the little hill but stopped a cautious distance from the girl.

"Of course," Polly sniffed. "Go away."

"You're not hurt?"

"No, I just want to be alone!"

Aiden had never thought of Polly as the type for contemplative solitude.

"Um, this isn't the best place for that, really," he said awkwardly. "It's getting dark."

"Thank you. I would never have noticed that," she snapped.

"It's just—it isn't safe."

"You're alone."

"Well, yes, but you're a girl."

"Just go away." Polly started to cry harder. Her shoulders heaved as she drew great snuffling breaths. Aiden glanced around for her sister, Annie, or anyone else better suited to fix a crying girl, but there was no one in sight.

"What's the matter?" he asked warily.

"Everything!" Polly sobbed. "Everything's the matter! I hate it out here! It's horrible. Everything is filthy and dull and dusty and awful."

Aiden squatted down on his heels, careful to keep well away. He was pretty sure he would be included in the filthy, dusty and awful part.

"Mr. Jackson says the Rocky Mountains are grand."

"I don't want mountains! I want my friends and nice things again. I want dancing and parties and musical concerts."

"There's probably a music hall in Seattle."

"Oh, you are such a stupid boy!" She wiped her eyes on her skirt. "This is the worst place in the world."

"We—um, we have some books you can borrow," he offered. "The *Atlas of the World* is very good. It takes your mind different places."

Polly looked as if she were going to bite his head off, but then just started crying again. Aiden sighed.

"Well, at any rate, it won't last forever." He stood up. "Come on, I'll walk with you back to camp." He offered his hand to help her up, but she sniffed haughtily and took hold of a little shrub instead. Aiden had to turn his face and work not to laugh as the roots ripped right out of the crumbly hillside, sprinkling a shower of dirt on her. She brushed angrily at her dress and hair.

"Oh!" Polly scrambled awkwardly to her feet.

"Shush!" Aiden said suddenly.

"Don't tell me to—"

"Quiet!"

"What is it?" Polly asked, her voice rising with fear.

"Not sure," Aiden said quietly. All around him the twilight felt electrified, like the air just before a storm. "Don't get nervous, but it could be wolves." He couldn't pick out a specific sound, but all around there were little noises that didn't belong to a calm prairie night.

"Wolves!" Polly screeched. Aiden quickly threw his hand across her mouth.

"Quiet!"

Polly shoved his arm with surprising strength.

"No one will hear us down here." Aiden's heart was beating hard, but he tried to keep calm. "If you scream you'll just sound like some wounded animal and get the wolves all fired up."

In the gathering darkness, he saw three pairs of glowing yellow eyes appear in the riverbed. Likely there were more on the bluff above them. Wolves were smart hunters who surrounded their prey and attacked from all sides.

"I'll tell you when to scream," he whispered. Polly nodded slowly, her eyes wide with fright. Aiden took his hand off her mouth.

"Why don't you have a gun?" Polly whispered angrily.

"I'm good with the bow."

"You should have a gun!"

"Well, I don't."

"Can you kill them?" Polly's voice was high and strained.

Aiden swallowed. He was a good shot, but five good shots wouldn't get all these wolves. "Some," he said. "One, yes, maybe two. After that, no, not likely. You have to shoot right through the lung or heart to kill it dead."

"Stupid boy!" She slapped him across the face. "Can you not just tell a lie when it's needed?"

Aiden was startled. "Sorry." He fumbled for reassurance. "We'll be all right," he offered lamely. "They might just go away. Wolves don't regularly tend to kill people." That was true, but wolves would be hungry right now, after the long winter. It was too early for pronghorn or buffalo calves. The two of them out here alone were vulnerable. Might as well have brought along the gravy. He could hear the hot panting on the bluff above them. Aiden picked up a rock.

"See that crack in the bluff just there?" He nodded to a sheltered spot about twelve feet away. "I'll scare them back and we'll run for that place. Okay?"

Polly nodded and gathered up her skirt.

"You ready?"

"Yes," she whimpered.

"Go!" Aiden jumped up and hurled the rock at the nearest wolf. Polly sprinted away. Aiden yelled and waved his arms. Polly dove into the crevice. The wolf slunk back and then Aiden dashed to the crevice, his feet slipping on the loose gravel. Polly clutched at him. Aiden was shocked by the sudden feel of warm, plump flesh pressed against him. He had never been so close to a girl before. Even with dirt in it, her hair smelled wonderful.

"Someone will be coming after you, won't they?" he asked. "Won't your family know you're missing?"

Polly started sobbing again. "I told them I was going to see Therese Thompson. But that was a lie, for I meant to go walking with Friedrich. Only, when I got to where we should meet, there was Annie talking sweet to him already." Her shoulders shook and dirt crumbled down the front of her dress. "Asking all about his stupid cows—as if she cared about cows! She knew I fancied him! So I was angry and went off here."

The bold alpha wolf crept closer, head low, lips peeled back to show long yellow teeth. He paced back and forth, watching them. Two other wolves skulked just behind him, waiting for their leader to attack. They made almost no noise, just short, low growls. Then there was a rough snort from above. Polly grabbed Aiden so hard he almost dropped the bow.

"Stop it!" he whispered. The luminous eyes in the riverbed grew closer. The wolves knew their prey was trapped and isolated now; all they had to do was close in for the kill.

"Look," Aiden said, trying to sound steady as he eased up to his knees. "They'll soon know in the camp that something's wrong; maybe already. The cattle will smell the wolves and get restless, and the dogs will be barking."

He drew an arrow and fitted it to his bow. Yes, he thought, they might know there were wolves about—Jackson would rouse the men to keep watch and build up the fires—but there was no reason to come looking for a stupid lad wandering in the twilight, or for a sulking girl who missed dances and feather beds.

He heard a snarl, then a dark shadow flew over them, fur bristling so close it almost brushed Aiden's head. Without even thinking, he drew his bow and shot. The twilight was split with a yelp of pain, and the huge wolf tumbled to the ground. Aiden's arrow was buried deep in its back. The wolf thrashed around, whining, scratching desperately with its front paws while its rear legs dragged limply behind it. A chilling chorus of howls pierced the night.

Now everything became strangely slowed down. Polly was screaming, but Aiden could still hear the low growls and the sounds of wolf claws scratching gravel. He could hear the sound of his own heart beating. His hands felt heavy, but he fitted another arrow to the bow, drew, aimed and fired. Another wolf went down, struck cleanly through the chest, instantly dead. Twice more Aiden shot. One wolf yelped, flung itself around and began to lick at the arrow in its rear leg. The next arrow missed entirely, the point striking a spark against a stone.

Aiden had only one arrow left. The pack was hanging back now, panicked by the smell of blood and the howls of distress, but the alpha wolf was undeterred. He crept closer, his yellow eyes fixed and hungry, his haunches tensed to spring. Aiden reached for his last arrow. As he fitted it to the string, he realized with horror that the arrow was bad. The notch was half broken and the shaft was split. He tried to hold the arrow together with his finger and thumb, but when he drew it back, the tension was too much and the string slipped up into the crack. The wolf was less than twenty feet away. Foamy spit glistened around its mouth in the last light of the fading day. Aiden thought he could smell its foul breath.

"Polly, give me your hair ribbon," he whispered. The trembling girl gave him a blank stare. "Polly!" She covered her face and cried silently into her hands. Aiden reached over and snatched the blue ribbon out of her hair. It was silky and slippery, and his hands shook as he tried to wind it around the broken arrow. He couldn't get it to stay just by wrapping it over the end, and if he tied a knot, it would snag on the bowstring when he shot. Two more wolves, emboldened by their leader, had left the damaged pack and were creeping closer.

"I don't want to die!" Polly cried.

"You won't," Aiden said firmly. How was that for a lie? He shoved one end of the ribbon into the split, then wound the rest tightly around the shaft. He held the loose end against the shaft with his thumb and tentatively drew back the bow. The ribbon held the arrow together all right, but he knew it would wreck his aim. He would be lucky to kill a sleeping chicken on its own roost. Aiden carefully drew back the string. His hands were surprisingly steady, though he couldn't feel a thing in the rest of his body.

White light suddenly filled the river bottom. A full moon was rising. It glinted off silver fur and shiny wet noses and the ridiculous blue satin ribbon. The alpha wolf turned its cold gaze toward the moon. Then it turned back toward Aiden. Then it sprang. Aiden didn't even realize he had shot, but he heard the delicate rustle of cloth as the ribbon fluttered free. The wolf froze in midleap, directly over them.

Aiden could see individual hairs on its chest and rough bumps on the pads of its paws. A drip of hot saliva landed on his neck.

The air exploded with gunfire and the wolf flew backward. Dirt crumbled down on Aiden from the top of the bluff, and he threw himself over Polly. At first, time had seemed extra-long; now it felt impossibly short. A dozen men came skidding down the bluff, firing at the wolves. The smell of gunpowder pinched the air. The shooting and noise went on forever, then stopped completely.

"Daddy!" Polly screamed. Mr. Hollingford grabbed his sobbing daughter. Aiden brushed the dirt out of his eyes. He saw Jefferson J. Jackson standing a few yards away, his rifle still smoking. The alpha wolf lay dead, its chest blown open. Aiden's broken arrow stuck out from the wolf's neck, the ribbon end fluttering in the soft breeze.

"Was me killed that bastard!" William Buck, the big braggart, crowed. "Y'all see that? That was my shot killed him dead!"

Jackson glared at Buck, then silently reloaded his rifle. Four wolves lay dead. The rest were running away into the darkness except for one who lay wounded by the river's edge, Aiden's arrow still stuck in its leg. Jackson raised his rifle, pulled the trigger, and shot it clean through the head.

Jackson turned to Aiden. "You all right, boy?"

Aiden nodded. He tried to stand up, but his body was half stone and half jelly.

"Pretty good shooting." Jackson slung his rifle over his shoulder. "Taxing, though, ain't it? Take a minute there; I'll fetch your arrows." His tone was almost gentle. The sky was bright, and men cast long moon shadows as they walked around, looking at the dead wolves. One lifted up a limp paw to admire the huge claws.

"Aiden? Aiden?" Maddy dashed up to him. "Are you all right? Say yes!"

"Yes."

"I told you stay back in camp!" said Jackson, returning with Aiden's arrows in his hand.

"Oh, tell me all you want!" Maddy glared at him. "If my brother gets ate by wolves, no reason for me not to!"

"Well, that'd fix 'em!" Jackson said. "Eating you would be poison for sure, if they didn't choke first!" The arrows in his hand were coated in wet blood and shone like cinnamon candy sticks. Aiden stared at them and felt sick in the stomach. The whole scene felt like a dream, with the moonlight so lovely, shining down on the dead animals. Horrible as they were, the wolves were also beautiful, and wouldn't have had to be shot at all if he and Polly hadn't stupidly put themselves up for feeding.

"I'll clean 'em off for you," Jackson said.

"I'm obliged," Aiden replied softly. Jackson walked over to the river and swished the arrows around in the water, then came back and put them in Aiden's quiver.

"Remember take them out to dry when we get back to camp, else they'll warp," he said.

"Yes, sir." Aiden nodded dumbly.

"How'd you come to shoot a bow so good?" Jackson asked. "Where'd you learn that?"

Aiden shrugged. "Just practiced. Arrows don't cost. Only two guns in the house, and I was the fourth man down."

"Well, ain't that lucky for all concerned." Jackson stuck

two fingers in his mouth and gave a piercing whistle. "Come on, men. Camp still needs guarding." The men began walking back to camp. Aiden could hear Polly's sobs fading in the distance.

"I'll be along shortly," William Buck declared. "I'm gonna skin these bastards! Nice pelts here." Buck pulled his knife out of the sheath.

Aiden stiffened, sudden anger restoring strength to his limbs. He hadn't even thought about the value of the skins but wasn't about to see Buck profit by them now. His hands clenched into fists.

"Two are rightly yours," Jackson said quietly. "Could argue three for the neck shot. But you got a long way to go with that man. And I won't have a fight over a pelt. So figure it out, boy."

He felt Jackson's hand on the back of his belt, half holding him steady, half holding him back. William Buck ran his knife up and down his trouser leg. Aiden hesitated. Should he make Buck an enemy or let him be a bully? Was there some other choice? In a way, wolves were easier to deal with.

Aiden slid the quiver of arrows up to his shoulder and swallowed his anger. "Well, thank you, Mr. Buck," he said steadily. "That's—ah, that's kind of you to offer to help me out. I haven't ever skinned a wolf. And shooting them kind of wore me out. I'd say that fellow is Mr. Jackson's, though"— he nodded at the last wolf shot—"for my arrow never would have killed him. But that other one could make you a nice pelt for sure. If the others who helped shoot it don't object, that is."

Buck scowled and hitched his belt as if he were about to protest. He glanced at Jackson as if the man ought to be on·

his side, but Jackson just gave him a short little smile, like he had no clue in the world what was going on. Finally Buck walked over to "his" wolf.

"I'll skin mine," he said gruffly as he yanked the wolf's head up. "You're free to watch how, but I reckon I done enough for you for one night."

"That's kind of you, Mr. Buck," Aiden said, swallowing hard. "I reckon you have."

"Quick work, then," Jackson said. "I'll send a mule back for the skins."

7

"**M**iss Maddy! Miss Maddy!" Joby came running up to Maddy while she was wiping off the breakfast plates. He stopped abruptly and looked around like a nervous schoolboy used to being frequently scolded but never exactly sure what it was going to be for.

"Calm down, Joby. What's the matter?"

"Miss Maddy, I need a—a—" Joby sliced his hands frantically through the air, then cupped his palms together. "I need—the thing for pouring. I lost the one we had. I'm sorry. I'm always careful."

"Joby, I'm not sure what you mean. You mean a pitcher? Like you pour water from?"

He looked confused.

"Like a jug?"

"Well, no—" Joby's eyes wandered as he struggled for the elusive word. There was nothing about Joby that really made him look different. He had a hesitation in his speech, and a way of gazing off when he talked, but unless you talked to him awhile, you might not even notice. Physically, there was nothing in particular that one could pick out as wrong, but the way he moved seemed awkward and out of place, like a jackrabbit on ice, always scratching for balance. He was neither handsome nor homely, the sort of man a girl might not pick first at a dance, Maddy thought, but wouldn't be too sad about sitting next to either; the sort of man that if he were sweet and kind would get better-looking after time. He was squarely built, with broad, strong hands. He had brown eyes and brown hair that was already getting thin on top, though he probably wasn't more than twenty-two or -three.

"It's like a teacup," he went on. "But with holes in both ends." He cupped his hands together again. "To go from big to small."

"Oh, do you mean a funnel?" Maddy laughed, then caught herself, not wanting him to think she was making fun of him, but Joby seemed only relieved.

"That. Yes. Do you have one?"

"I doubt it. I think I've seen most everything the Reverend and Mrs. True are carrying in the way of kitchen gear. Which wasn't ever much useful." She waved a hand at the pathetic assortment of dented plates and blackened pots.

"Can you pour good, then?" he pressed, looking around nervously. Maddy realized he was trying to whisper, but his voice was loud as ever. She dropped her own voice so maybe he would hear the difference.

"Tell me what you need to do, Joby," she said, trying to make it simple.

"I have to get water from the pail into the poison jug. But my hand shakes too much to pour from the dipper. I need the—the—" Again he gestured.

"The funnel," Maddy reminded him.

"Yes!"

"I can pour from a dipper, Joby. That's no problem. But what are you doing with a jug of poison?"

"Doc Carlos takes it. Every morning I need to put water into the jug. And then he fills up his little bottle out of it."

Maddy remembered seeing Dr. Carlos drinking from a small brown medicine bottle.

"Joby, why does Dr. Carlos drink poison?"

"He got poisoned in the war."

"So shouldn't he take something to cure it? Like medicine?"

"Yes! That's what it is. It's medicine."

"But you said it was poison."

"I don't know, Miss Maddy." Joby shook his hands with frustration. "Sometimes he gives it for medicine. But for his own self, calls it poison. I don't want him mad that I ain't done my job." He began to scratch the back of his head and shift nervously from side to side.

"Yes, Joby, of course."

Joby took her hand and almost dragged her to the doctor's cart, then handed her the dipper. There was a great puddle of water around the jug from where he had been trying to fill it himself. Maddy moved some cloth bundles out of the damp.

"The doctor's gone—to his morning duty," Joby whispered, blushing and nodding toward the latrines. "He'll be back soon."

"Does he hit you, Joby?" Maddy frowned.

"Doc Carlos?"

"If you don't get something right? Does he hit you?" She remembered seeing Carlos kicking the Thompsons' dog.

"Oh no. Doc is my best friend, and I don't want to let him down, is all. He fixed my head. And got us food in the prison. So hurry, please."

"It won't take long," Maddy reassured him. She scooped

up some water from the pail and poured it easily into the jug. By the sound of it, only a pint or so would be needed to fill it. Joby sighed with relief.

"I drive," he declared proudly. "Oxen, mules or horses, don't matter." He held up his calloused hands. "In the war I drove the wagons."

"That's good." Maddy smiled.

"So you could get married to me," Joby went on.

"What?" Maddy sloshed some water. "No, I can't."

"Why not? I'm going to have a job in Seattle, driving heavy loads."

"I, um—I can't marry anyone till I'm sixteen."

"I can drive an eight-mule team."

"But I promised my mother," she declared.

"When is that? When are you sixteen?"

"Two years and one month from now."

"Is that a long time?"

"How long have you been with Doc Carlos?" she asked.

"Since the war began."

"How long is that?"

Joby shrugged.

"How many times did the summer come?" Maddy prompted.

"Well—first summer, we camped in the trees, and it smelled so good. Next summer was a bad time, with fever, and mosquitoes on us all the time. Also, men got exploded. Then the last summer was just chopping off arms and legs too much. And the dogs sneaking around the pile trying to eat them. Then we got captured and put into the prison. And for all the winter. Then springtime came and they said war was over and we could go. So three times summer came."

"Oh." Maddy was trying to find her way around *men got exploded* and *chopping off arms.* "So two years is one less than the time you were in the war." She poured another dipperful of water. The sound told her the jug was full. She put the cork in and punched it down.

"Anyway, I don't want to marry anybody. I'm going to be a doctor."

"Like Carlos?"

"Well, yes, but nicer."

"He used to be nice."

Maddy looked up and saw the tall, thin figure coming toward them, his head down, his shoulders hunched, everything about him coiled and wary.

"I've got to go now, Joby. I got my own chores to do. You keep a lookout for the funnel," she said. "It probably just fell in among the boxes here, okay?"

"Oh yes, Miss Maddy. I didn't mean to lose it."

"No, of course you didn't." She darted off before Doc Carlos saw her.

"Miss Marguerite," Maddy said as they walked along later that afternoon, "do you know much about the war?"

"Mostly from the newspapers," she said vaguely.

"Did they poison people, do you know?"

"Poison? Whatever do you mean?"

"I'm not sure," Maddy went on. "But could someone get poisoned in the war so he needs to keep taking poison after?"

"I don't know."

"Well, have you ever heard about some way poison can also be medicine?"

Marguerite lifted her head, and Maddy thought she saw a keen understanding in the pretty blue eyes. Marguerite's gaze turned toward the wagon train and rested on Doc Carlos.

"I have."

"How can it be like that?"

"There are medicines that take away pain. Pain from the injury, yes?" Marguerite explained. "But sometimes a person may have another kind of pain, pain in the heart or the mind, and the same medicine can feel like it is helping. But if you take it too long, you start to need more and more, and it becomes poison."

"Doesn't it kill you, then?"

"I think if one is careful he can take it for a long time."

Maddy thought about this for a while, listening to the swish of grass against their skirts as they walked.

"What if a person watered down the poison some every day?"

"Ah. Well, that sounds like someone who is trying to quit."

"So why doesn't he just quit?"

"It isn't that easy," Marguerite explained. "A person who needs this medicine will be very sick if he quits suddenly."

Maddy walked on silently. It seemed there was no end to the complexities of hurting.

8

After a month of travel, Aiden could hardly remember that life was ever anything but this: endless miles of unchanging miles. The novelty of the adventure was over. Every day looked the same and felt the same—the constant wind, the creaking wagons, the feel of the hard, lumpy ground beneath boot soles. Dust coated his skin and clung to his eyelashes so that every blink stung. The dull plod of oxen hooves and the constant moaning of the cattle got on everyone's nerves.

"Stupid, stupid cattle!" Marguerite cried. "What do they need to say all the time? Do they talk about how pretty is the hind end of the cow in front of them?"

At the beginning of the journey, women had sung as they walked; children had laughed and chased butterflies. Now they trudged along like battle-weary soldiers. Babies screamed with diaper rash and mosquito bites. The women's skirts were frayed and tattered at the hems. The dogs were matted with burrs. Every day was alike, except when some catastrophe burst through the numbing torpor. Twice, tornados spun dangerously close. Once, on a perfectly sunny day, a single cloud appeared and pelted them with hailstones the size of plums. Another day, lightning struck and killed one of the German brothers' prize cows. But most days were just long and dull. Still, they were making good time, twelve, sometimes fifteen miles a day. Another few weeks and they would see the mountains.

"No better place in all the world than the Rocky Mountains," Jackson said one evening as he scraped the last spoonful of beans off his plate. He was in a good mood, for he liked beans. There was rarely enough fuel or time for the hourlong cooking they needed, but they had been lucky finding buffalo chips that day.

"Going to be a lot of work, hauling all these wagons over," William Buck grumbled.

"Been done plenty of times now," Jackson said. "Won't be easy, but you should have seen it twenty years ago! No real trail then. We were still figuring out ways to get through."

"How long have you been out here anyway, Mr. Jackson?" Aiden asked, taking advantage of the man's rare chatty mood.

"Came out in 1831. Fur trapping. Them was some fine years—beaver everywhere, like mice in a feed bin when the cat's up and died. I brought in near six hundred skins to my first rendezvous, and that was being fresh out of nowhere, not knowing my ass from my elbow."

"What's a rendezvous?" Aiden asked.

"Grandest party ever there was! Once a year, in July, after the spring hunt, all the trappers would meet up in one place for the companies to buy the pelts." Jackson stretched back and got himself comfortable. "Lord—you want to know some fine festivities." He looked at Aiden and smiled big. "Skins went for plenty then—three dollars for the poor ones, six for a good pelt. Trappers came in, got three or four thousand cash money in their hand, then drank and gambled it all away in a week." Jackson tipped his head back and laughed. "Why, a man could go back east and buy himself a castle if he'd a mind to, but instead he'd get stinking drunk and piss it all away."

"How come?" Aiden asked. "How come you didn't, well, piss just half of it away and save you some?"

"Ah—wouldn't that be a smart thing to do." Jackson laughed. "But see, boy—I'll tell you some wisdom. People set up how they want their life to be. Sometimes they don't know that's what they's doing, but it is. The rich folk back east, for example, they pile up accumulations to keep them chained down there. And the mountain man, well, he piles up nothing to keep him chained out there—" Jackson waved a hand toward the western sky.

"Why'd you quit, then?" Buck pressed.

"Quit? I didn't quit. Ran out of beaver. We killed 'em all. I trapped six hundred my first year, not even sixty my last. We killed 'em all. You'll see. Another month we'll be up there and you'll see. Beaver scarce as dinosaurs."

"So what'd you do then?" Aiden asked.

"Oh, various type this 'n' that employs. Went south and shot me some Mexicans in the war, tried out the gold, did some trade." Jackson leaned back and pulled his hat down over his eyes. "Lately I schoolmarmed a bunch of you sorry-ass tenderfoots across the country, which is right now wearin' me the hell out, so enough of the questions."

Aiden had somehow expected to wake up one day and just see the mountains there, tall and snowy and stabbing at the sky like the picture of the Alps in the *Atlas of the World*. But the horizon crept up so slowly that they appeared at first only as a faint rise on the far edge of the earth, like a line of baby teeth. A week later and he could make out some edges and peaks. But they were still at least a hundred miles away.

As the wagon train dragged on across the plains, they began to see the toll the journey had taken on others before them. Broken wagon wheels stuck up from ruts in the ground, their spokes bleached and spiky as fish bones. As the reality of the mountains loomed closer, the group often came upon whole loads of belongings that had been jettisoned as emigrants ahead of them realized the impossibility of hauling heavy loads over the peaks. There were little furniture graveyards full of mahogany chifforobes, oak desks and ornate bedsteads. The wood made for nice campfires.

Jefferson J. Jackson had made it very clear that no one in his wagon train carried more than the absolute necessities. There was barely a blanket chest or a trunk to be found, even among the prosperous families. One day they came across a great load of abandoned furniture. A small piano was set carefully on a smooth bit of ground. Inside was a hopeful note written in elegant script: *Property of Mrs. Richard D. Wainwright, moving to Portland, Oregon. I will pay $100 for safe delivery.*

"Don't nobody even think about it," Jackson said when Maddy read him the note. "I'd sooner tote along a dead elephant. At least you could eat it if you had to."

The piano had ivory keys and intricate pearl inlays that gleamed in the sun. The varnish was starting to crackle from exposure, but the piano was still playable, though a bit out of tune. Even though no one thought to cross Jackson in the matter of transporting the thing, there was a near unanimous rebellion against moving on, despite three or four more hours of good travel time left in the day. People were hungry for music. The furniture would make nice fires too. They would camp right there, they declared, and Mr. Jefferson J. Jackson could very well just accept it. He did. It had been seven weeks since the party in Sweetwater. They were making good distance, and it wasn't a bad idea to store up a few hours of fun against the trials that lay ahead.

While they made camp, everyone who could play took a turn at the piano. Some of the mildest women jostled each other and argued to go next. War nearly erupted among the ten Thompson children. Back home they had fussed through years of piano lessons, sullenly pounding their way through practice, but out here the little instrument was exotic and exciting. Polly and Annie could play all the popular songs: "Beautiful Dreamer," "When Johnny Comes Marching Home" and "Oh Where, Oh Where Has My Little Dog Gone?" Gabriel True gamely thumped out a few marches, but Marguerite didn't play a note.

"A preacher's wife and she doesn't play?" Mrs. Hollingford was scandalized. "Have you ever heard of such a thing? Not a single hymn!" She fluffed her skirts, sat down herself and pounded out a good twenty minutes of dreary church music before someone else managed to take control of the keyboard.

"Isn't it all just too beautiful?" Maddy clutched her arms around her knees and rocked with happiness. She hadn't heard a piano since she was five years old.

"It's not even a real piano," Polly sniped as she sat down beside them. "It's just a little parlor spinet. We had a baby grand piano in Charleston. Stephen Foster himself played it once."

Polly babbled on about all the concerts and recitals she

had been to and the famous singers she had heard. Maddy and Aiden had never heard of any of them, except of course Stephen Foster, who had written every popular song anybody ever sang.

"Look at Doc Carlos," Maddy whispered to her brother. "The way he looks at the piano. Like he's starving for the music. You suppose he plays?"

"I reckon he does. Doctors are smart," Aiden said. "And they come from families with pianos."

"How do you know that?"

"You know what I mean; families with money and schooling and nice things, like those in Virginia. They all played piano. Father and I used to look in the windows for the parties. Our ma served for them, you know. She wore a nice dress and a lace cap."

"Was she beautiful?"

"Like the stars and the springtime," Aiden said. His voice caught in his throat. It was what his father used to say.

"I'm going to ask him to play some," Maddy declared.

"Who?"

"Doc Carlos. He might just be shy. I'm going to ask him to play the piano." The music and the bright campfire, blazing with table legs and dresser drawers, made her feel bold.

"He's gonna say no and go away and leave him alone," Aiden laughed.

"But he won't up and kill me, will he?" Maddy said. She made her way around the circle and crouched down beside the silent doctor.

"Doc Carlos," Maddy said, tapping his shoulder. "Can you play us something?"

He jumped. "What?"

"Will you have a turn at the piano?"

"I don't play."

"Oh, sure you do, Doc," Joby urged. He smiled at Maddy. "He kin play good. Fancy songs. Only no words. And you can't really dance to 'em. But they're nice anyway."

"Play us something, then," Maddy encouraged him.

"I haven't played in a long time."

"Well, I don't think most other folks have either."

"You played that time in the church," Joby urged. "Before it got burned down." He turned to Maddy. "Made all the soldiers cry." He was trying to whisper again, but as usual, this made his voice actually louder.

"You play, Doc?" Reverend True asked. "Go on—otherwise you doom us to eight more rounds of 'Beautiful Dreamer.'"

"It's okay if you make mistakes," Maddy said. "Things don't matter out here the same way. No one's going to laugh at you, especially, for someday they might need doctoring!"

Reverend True laughed. "Go on, Doc! Miss Polly—"

Polly was playing an especially mournful version of "Oh Where, Oh Where Has My Little Dog Gone?"

"Miss Polly, how about we let Doc Carlos have a turn? When you're finished, of course."

Polly played a dramatic flourish, gathered her skirts and slid off the seat in a huff. Doc Carlos unfolded his long legs, got up in one swift, easy motion and strode over to the piano. The sun was just setting then, with a crimson light that turned the pearl inlays a glowing pink. He tried out the feel of the keys, then ran his fingers up and down the keyboard in a sparkling river of notes. All throughout the camp, people stopped to listen. Even the men who had drifted off to pass a

65

whiskey jug came close to hear. The music was strange and complicated and forceful, like the feel in the air when a storm was coming—sharp and heavy and scary and exciting and beautiful all together. Maddy dashed back to sit beside Aiden.

"Have you ever heard anything like that? Do you think that's Hindu music?"

"Hindu?"

"Those pictures in the *Atlas of the World*—the temples and the statues of the idol Buddha and the Taj Mahal, the ladies with those sari gowns of precious silk? Doesn't it sound exotic like that?"

"Carlos isn't a Hindu." Aiden laughed and threw his arm around his sister's shoulders. "He grew up in New York City. His father was from Spain."

"How do you know that?"

"Sometimes he and Joby eat with us. One night, Buck asked him what kind of foreigner he was. Carlos said just that. Born in New York; his father was from Spain."

"Oh," Maddy sighed. "I so want to meet a Hindu."

"The music is called *classical*," Annie said, rolling her eyes. "It comes from Europe."

"I think this piece was written by a fellow called Mozart," Reverend True explained. "German or something."

"Mozart was from Austria, dear." Marguerite leaned her head against her husband's shoulder, a dreamy look in her eyes.

"Well, definitely not a Hindu."

"No, I think not. But Austria is very exotic," Marguerite added, seeing how disappointed Maddy was. "I've heard the

66

whole city of Vienna is painted with real gold! And they drink hot chocolate all day."

"Like the Aztecs!" Maddy was suitably impressed, though she had never tasted or even seen chocolate herself. "They practiced human sacrifice," she added.

"Austrians?" Reverend True exclaimed. Marguerite shoved him and giggled.

"Aztecs," Maddy replied. "To worship their god. They cut people's hearts out alive!"

"Oh my."

"I could play this if I wanted to," Polly said dismissively. "This is all the boring music they make you learn before you can play fun tunes. Beethoven and all of those dull old fellows. You can't dance to it! They aren't even songs! They're called études and—and symphonies. He probably just quit before he ever learned popular songs."

"Ain't it pretty, though?" Joby's whisper rang out loud. "Didn't I say he could play nice? Made the soldiers cry in that church that day. Some not even eating their piece of bread, just listening to the music."

Doc Carlos played for a long time, and no one else ever wanted a turn. The sun set and the full moon rose and a chill mist sent children cuddling close for warmth. More dresser drawers and table legs were tossed onto the fire.

"You know," Maddy said, leaning drowsily on Aiden, "isn't it nice how sometimes the world just turns perfect for a little while?"

Carlos played like he forgot where he was, like the piano was pumping his blood instead of his heart. Sometimes his hands ran out of keys on the small instrument and there were odd spaces in the music. His shirt turned dark with sweat. Joby fell asleep, curled on his side beside Maddy. The sky grew dark. The furniture fire burned down low. Suddenly there was a loud crack like a gunshot. Carlos fell back and flung an arm in front of his face. Some of the men jumped up and reached for guns while women grabbed children.

"Wait, wait!" Marguerite cried. "It is just the piano!"

The back of the piano had split open, and wires sprang out the crack. The jolting of the trail had weakened the joints; the sun and weather had dried the wood. The passionate playing had snapped the wires, and now the music was only memory.

"Looks like the symphony is over," Jackson said gruffly as he got to his feet. "We still move at daybreak, Mozart regardless."

Everyone began to get up and drift off into the quiet darkness. Carlos sat on the piano bench, shivering. Aiden got up, took off his own jacket and put it around the doctor's shoulders.

"Thanks, Doc," Aiden said. "That was real nice."

Carlos felt the coat pockets.

"Where's my medicine?"

Aiden said, "It's not there. It's not your own coat, Doc."

"I need my medicine."

"Hold on, I'll find it for you."

"Joby?" Maddy nudged the sleeping man. "Joby—wake up. The piano's busted and Doc has a chill. I think you need to see to him."

People were gathering their children and blankets and starting toward their wagons. Clouds drifted over the moon and the fire burned low. Joby sat up and swiped his hand sleepily across his face.

"Huh—what's wrong?"

"The piano broke," Maddy said. "And Doc Carlos took a chill."

Joby clambered to his feet.

"Joby? Where's my medicine?"

"Take him home," Maddy said. "There's embers enough for a kettle here; I'll bring you some tea."

"Come on, Doc," Joby said gently. "The medicine's in the cart. Come on, I'll get it for you." He swooped one long arm around Doc Carlos and easily lifted him off the bench.

9

Carlos and Joby had camped away from the others, as they usually did. The little cart looked especially lonely tonight. As Maddy approached, she could see that something was terribly wrong, even in the dim yellow glow of her lantern. Doc Carlos lay on the ground, his whole body twitching like some wounded animal.

"Miss Maddy, please help!" Joby cried.

Maddy heard violent retching sounds and ran over.

"Push him over, Joby, on his side." She knelt down, took Carlos's head in her hands and held it so he wouldn't choke. His shoulders convulsed and his stomach heaved, but nothing came out except some thin spittle.

"It's the poison," Joby said. He looked about to cry. Carlos flung out one arm and tried to push Maddy away.

"Hush, it's all right," Maddy said softly. Carlos's hair was soaked with sweat, his skin cold and clammy.

"Go away," he gasped.

"Miss Maddy brought you some tea, Doc," Joby said, pulling him up.

"I don't want tea," Carlos mumbled. He leaned back against the cart wheel and shut his eyes. Joby clumsily tried to pull a blanket up around his shoulders.

"There's no more medicine," Joby said. "I been putting water in the jug, like Doc said to. But he just took more and

70

more of it. Then he came back just now and finished all of it up. You think he's got poisoned?"

"Doc Carlos—are you poisoned?" Maddy shook his shoulder. "Joby, will you go fetch Mrs. True? The reverend's wife?"

"No," Carlos said weakly. "I'm not poisoned. Don't fetch anybody." He wiped his mouth on the edge of the blanket. "I'm fine. I'm not going to die." He was shaking like a man just pulled from under the ice. Joby looked at Maddy, his eyes wide with fear.

"Do you have any sugar or honey?" she asked.

"Yes, I think—somewhere." Joby looked vaguely at the cart.

"Think, Joby. Which box is it in?"

He seemed panicked and about to cry. "I wasn't always stupid this way."

"I know." Maddy patted his hand. "I mean, you're not stupid."

"Maddy?" Aiden's shadow appeared at the edge of the dim lamplight.

"I'm here." Maddy stood up.

"Is everything all right?"

"Doc Carlos has a fever is all." She came over to his side. "I'm just going to sit with him and Joby awhile."

"Okay," Aiden said. "Can I do something?"

"Can you go ask Mrs. True for some sugar, please?" She dropped her voice to a whisper. "Tell her it's for the doc, who's feeling poorly. Say that his medicine is gone and ask what else she suggests for the way he is." She gave him a look and Aiden thought for a second that she wasn't his little sister anymore, but a grown woman with knowing and secrets.

"And Doc took a chill," she added. "It would be awfully nice to have a little fire over here. There is some wood still, isn't there?"

"I'll clear a place," Joby said eagerly. He got a shovel and quickly chopped away a patch in the grass. Aiden came back a few minutes later with a shovelful of embers and the last bits of broken furniture. Marguerite came with him. She stood in the shadows and beckoned Maddy. They whispered together as Joby and Aiden built a small fire.

"Is he very ill?" Marguerite asked.

"I don't know. He says he won't die."

They could see Carlos gripping a spoke of a cart wheel like a drowning man holding on to a rope.

"Go back to our wagon, Maddy. I can stay with him."

"No, he's mad already that I'm here. Doesn't want anyone near but Joby, only Joby's afraid to be all alone with him. He ran out of the medicine. What should I do?"

"It isn't your charge to tend him."

"He tended Aiden when he was sick," Maddy replied. "And Joby's been a friend to us."

"Very well, then." Marguerite handed her a paper cone of sugar, then took off her cloak and put it around Maddy's shoulders, for the night was getting cool. "The shaking and retching will come and go," she whispered. "But it will be his mind that needs comfort as much as his body. He may see things—like in fever dreams. Talk to him, or read to him. I'll bring you the *Atlas of the World*." She hesitated. "Perhaps you might stay with the happier nations, though," she suggested. "Switzerland, maybe; avoid the Aztecs and headhunters and such."

"I will." Maddy nodded. "Joby, will you walk Mrs. True back to her wagon?"

"Thank you, Joby." Marguerite held out her elbow and Joby took hold of it in a clumsy escort. "Come wake me if you need anything at all."

Maddy went back to the fire. She tapped the lump of hard brown sugar against the side of the enamel mug to break off a bit, poured the hot tea over it and added a little cool water so it wouldn't burn him.

He took a sip, coughed, then drank it thirstily.

"Sweet tea is good after purging so," she said.

His shaking eased a little. He looked around, as if suddenly confused. "Where are we?"

"On our way west; Colorado now."

"Why?"

"Well—for a new life there. You know that."

"Yes. I know." He looked at his clothing as if he didn't quite trust her and there might be clues. Then he stared at the fire. "Is that the piano?" he asked.

Maddy saw one of the carved legs just catching the flame, the varnish bubbling up in little blisters.

"Yes. I'm sorry," she said.

He blinked a few times and seemed to come back to himself. "Where's Joby?"

"He'll be back shortly." Maddy's own hand was shaking as she poured some more tea in the mug. It was awful to see him like this. "Tell me, how did you learn to play the piano so nice?" she asked, hoping to get his mind on a happier subject, as Marguerite had suggested. "Did you have a piano in your parlor?"

"My parlor?" He blinked and stared at the little fire. "No. In the lobby of the hotel where I lived."

"You lived in a hotel? In New York? Tell me all about it," Maddy said eagerly. "Were there chandeliers?"

"Yes." His eyes got a little more normal and he wiped the sweat off his forehead. "In the lobby."

"And velvet draperies with braided cords and silken tassels especially fine?" She blushed. That was from a magazine advertisement that had stuck in her head since she was six years old: *silken tassels especially fine.*

"I don't know. Yes, I suppose, in the guest rooms." Carlos coughed. "We lived in the basement."

"The basement?" Maddy was disappointed but tried not to let it show. "Oh."

"Yes. My father was the hotel doctor."

"Oh, well!" She brightened. "That's—illustrious!"

"What?"

"It means—"

"I know what it means. There was nothing illustrious about it," he said stiffly. He swallowed the last of the tea, then swiped his finger in the mug to scoop up the undissolved sugar at the bottom. "He was there to take care of the whores and tend the drunken businessmen passed out in the hallways. He gave abortions to their mistresses and nursed their wives off laudanum. Do you know what laudanum is?"

"No."

"Opium?"

"What they smoke in China? In opium dens?"

"Yes.

"There's a picture in my book—"

"The *Atlas of the World*. Yes, your bible." Carlos pulled the blanket tighter around his shoulders and wiped his forehead again. The sweet tea had eased his shaking. "Opium is a drug, a soporific. Mixed with alcohol it's called laudanum. Lovely stuff, until you come to need it and can't get it and—well, this is what happens."

"How long will you be sick?"

"The worst should pass by morning."

"Can it be eased somehow?"

"Yes. Go away and leave me alone."

"I'm not tired. And I want to be a doctor; I should learn these things."

Carlos laughed. "You can't be a doctor."

"Why not?"

"You're a girl." His voice was dismissive and sharp, and Maddy bristled.

"Were you always so hateful?" she snapped.

Carlos startled at her response. He looked away and rubbed a hand over his eyes, then finally spoke so softly she could barely hear him. "No. I'm sorry."

"I know it was an awful time you've been through—"

"You don't know anything!" The cruel tone was back.

"No." Maddy stared at him hard. "I don't know war and men getting exploded and all. But I buried my mother and my father, two brothers, one sister and two little babies. I just spent the whole winter freezing and starving to death and thinking of ways to kill myself so my brother wouldn't have to do it, so don't you dare say what I know or don't about awful!"

Carlos stared at her, then scrambled away and vomited again. Maddy heard the crunch of boots approaching and fell silent. Joby had returned. He saw Carlos kneeling off in the dirt and helped him back to the campfire.

"You look much better, Doc," he said unconvincingly. He handed Maddy the *Atlas of the World*.

"Thank you, Joby." Maddy took the book and roughly yanked it open. "We're going to read about Switzerland now." Her eyes were full of tears. She brushed them away. "To ease your sickness."

She pulled the lantern closer and opened the book on her lap. " 'Switzerland abounds in mountains.' " She took a deep breath and steadied her voice. " 'By reason of which she has become known as the playground of the world. Her scenery—great glaciers and deep, wooded valleys, is unsurpassed by that of any similar area on the face of the globe. . . .' "

10

Aiden walked a slow patrol around the sleeping camp and went back to Jackson's wagon. The Kansas boys were playing cards by the flickering light of a nail-punch lantern. Buck and the widower leaned against the wagon tailgate, smoking their pipes. Jackson was sound asleep, snoring like a buffalo. Aiden took his canteen off the hook and had a drink of water. He looked toward Doc Carlos's wagon in the distance, where the tiny campfire flickered. Buck followed his gaze.

"So little sister's taken up with the Spanish doctor, eh?" he said.

"He's sick. She's tending him."

"Tending him," he snorted. "Oh, ain't that nice." Buck winked at the other men. "You know, I believe I feel some fever coming on me!" He put his hand on his crotch. "Oh yeah—it's a fever! A bad one! I believe I need some tending!"

Aiden didn't even think. He just reared back and punched William Buck in the face as hard as he could. Buck stumbled against the tailgate. For a long, slow second, he just stared in disbelief; then he hurled himself at Aiden with a roundhouse punch. Aiden threw up his arm to block the blow, but Buck had a good four inches and sixty pounds on him and knocked him to the ground. Aiden kicked hard at the man's legs. Buck fell. He let out a pained whoosh of breath, but he wasn't winded for long. He threw himself on top of Aiden with an avalanche of blows.

"I'll pound you," Buck snarled. "Then I'll pound your damn sister!"

Aiden slammed his fist into the man's cheek and felt the skin split beneath his knuckles. He saw the Kansas boys trying to pull Buck off him.

"You're shit!" Buck spat at him.

"Cut it the hell out!" Jefferson J. Jackson growled angrily. Aiden rolled over and felt blood pour out his nose. Jackson grabbed Aiden's shirt and hauled him to his feet. "I don't care what this was about!" He glowered at the both of them. "I told you my camp rules, and peacefulness was high up there, was it not?"

"Yes, sir," Aiden mumbled.

"William Buck, you're a goddamn grown man."

"He hit me first!"

"So what? If a kid half your size needs whupping—which I ain't saying he do, necessarily, at this particular nighttime moment, anyway, for God's sake—well, it generally don't take more'n a punch or two. We got a thousand more miles to go. Any more between the two of you and I swear I will leave you both behind and take my own satisfaction out of your sorry-ass hides before I do. Is that clear?"

Buck and Aiden both nodded.

"God damn! And I was dreaming something nice." Jackson stomped back to his bedroll. "All musical and such!" he muttered.

"Maybe y'all ought to shake hands," the widower suggested tentatively, glancing nervously from Buck to Aiden.

"You come see me any time you need to get a hurt on, boy." Buck wiped blood off his chin.

"I catch you near my sister, or think you're even thinking about her, I swear I will cut your heart out," Aiden said.

Joby fell asleep long before Maddy even got to the production of Swiss cheese, but it was a long and terrible night for Carlos. As Marguerite had warned, his mind suffered more than his body. He felt ants crawling all over his flesh. He saw mice darting around in the shadows and flies swarming and packs of black dogs prowling. Joby woke and tried to settle him down.

"No dogs here, Doc. The dogs are gone now," he reassured Carlos.

"He dreams about those dogs all the time," Joby explained sleepily to Maddy. "They used to come around the hospital tents, you see, try and steal from the pile of arms and legs. I'd chase one off and two or three more would sneak in behind. They would be licking at the blood on the ground. You could hear them always licking. . . ."

Maddy shuddered and almost threw up herself.

As the night wore on, the flies and mice went away, but Carlos was still restless. Maddy read more from the *Atlas of the World* and told him about life on the homestead. He knew nothing about farming, had never milked a cow or plowed a field. She tried to tell him only happy things. How nice the hay smelled, how once she had two yellow kittens. She left out the awful bits: how the hay spoiled and the cow died, how coyotes killed the cats. The moon went down and the fire became a small flicker. The camp was silent, even the animals deep asleep by now.

"Now you tell me something." Maddy yawned. She had run out of stories and was too tired to read anymore. "Tell me how you learned to be a doctor. Where did you go to school? Was it hard?"

Carlos looked at her with tired red eyes. One foot moved restlessly back and forth. "Little girl," he laughed softly. "I know you like secrets. So I'll tell you one. I'm not a doctor. I don't have a diploma. I never went to medical school."

"But Joby told me about all the soldiers you fixed in the war."

"Yes, well, there's another thing. I was never in the army either! Not South or North."

"But you came from the army. You were in an army prison."

"They never were too picky about who they threw in prison." He took a sip of water and stared into the dying fire. "I just got caught up. We were in Georgia, the war started, and we just got caught."

"How did you come to be in Georgia from New York?"

"My father was a surgeon. He trained in Cairo—"

"Cairo, Egypt?" Maddy asked excitedly.

"Yes." Carlos smiled and Maddy blushed, embarrassed that he saw how the foreign country impressed her. "My father was Spanish," he went on. "My mother Egyptian. There were great schools of medicine then in Cairo. Doctors there knew about things your surgeons now have never heard of. But still, she died giving birth to me. Three years later, my father brought me to America. He thought there was opportunity here. He was a great surgeon, but he was darker than me." He absently rubbed his cheek. "In New York there were a hundred white doctors for the wealthy. The poor went to barbers or old women with their plants and potions. It was hard for him to practice surgery. He became a hotel doctor. After many years he grew tired of treating syphilis and drunks. A grateful client offered him a position on his plantation in Georgia. It was perfect. There were almost two hundred slaves there, and on the surrounding farms, a thousand or more. They were all valuable property," he added with a bitter note.

"So just as they sent broken plows to the blacksmith, they sent broken slaves to us. It was—there is no way to explain it without sounding horrible, but you already know I'm horrible, so I'll tell you—for a doctor, it was wonderful. The slaves never came to us for ordinary ailments or boring diseases. No gout or indigestion, no headaches or croup. They had their own healers for that. We had complicated, interesting cases and plenty of surgery. We had open fractures and tumors; we had limbs crushed or caught in farm equipment. It was easy to get ether, and we could do surgery for an hour! My father designed new equipment. There was a jeweler in Savannah who made instruments for him. My father saved so many people." Carlos paused. "But we wondered if that was doing more harm than good, fixing them up just to send them back to slavery." He wiped the sweat off his face.

"Then one day a cartful of wounded soldiers came. The war had started. There had been talk of it brewing, but we were in our own world. Suddenly it was on our doorstep. The next day, six more came in, four the day after, then a dozen, and we never even counted anymore. The plantation owners all around began to flee. There was no way for us to get back to New York, and even if we could, every day there were injured men to treat. How could we just leave? When the Union Army got close, the Confederates retreated and took us along with them. There were days my arm hurt from sawing through so many bones. But some days there were only a few injured and we could take our time and operate. God! That was so incredible. . . . I'm sorry, it's no talk for a girl."

"I held the guts down inside an Indian," Maddy said. "While my momma sewed him up."

Carlos almost laughed. "Did he live?"

"He rode away," Maddy said. "Sitting up on his own horse. But after that I can't know."

"Well, then you know how it feels," he said seriously. "When we could save a man's leg—those days were so good."

"What happened to your father?" Maddy asked gently.

"He died of cholera, in the second year. I had nowhere else to go and they had few other surgeons, so I just kept on. I grew out of my coat and they gave me an army coat. My pants wore out and they gave me army pants. So I was in the army."

The eastern sky was starting to turn from black to deep blue. Dawn was only an hour or so away. Maddy felt as if her insides were glass and about to break into bits. She tried to shift the talk to happier subjects.

"How did you and Joby come to be friends?"

"He was the blacksmith's son on the plantation. He taught me how to ride a horse."

"Is that his real name—Joby?"

"Joseph Bradford. We had lots of Joes, so he was Joe B."

"What caused his brain injury? Was he shot?"

"He tripped over a fence rail and was trampled by our own cavalry. It was our first real battle. I cut a hole in his skull to let the brain swell. It saved his life, but there was already damage." Carlos stared at the glowing embers. "He wasn't ever much good for soldiering, even before getting trampled, but he had magic with the animals. He became my driver for the hospital wagons."

"Then what?"

"Then the war just went on. In October of 1864 we were captured by the Yankees and taken to a prison camp. Six months later they opened the gates and told us to leave. So we walked out."

"How did you come to be here?"

"There were hundreds of men walking, all looking for food and a way home. Neither one of us had any family left or home to go to. We came to a train station." Carlos hesitated. "I had the dead money." It was as if he needed to talk now but hated to at the same time, Maddy thought.

"Soldiers sew their valuables into their clothing," he went on quietly. "Coins, rings, watches, whatever they want safe. They sew secret pockets in the lining. Everyone knows it. After a battle, other soldiers slit open the coats of the dead right on the battlefield. But the wounded mostly came to me with their clothes still uncut. If they died in my care, well, I knew as well as the next man how to search out the coins.

"At first I turned everything in to the officers. They said it would go to the families, but I soon learned that that didn't happen. So I started keeping it myself. I wrote everything in a ledger. I thought when the war was over I would get the money to the families somehow. I made a false bottom for my medical case and hid the coins there. It was heavy with the instruments and no one ever found out. But over the years, I began to spend from it, to buy what medicines I could find for the wounded, soap, food, even bandages. The coins came and went. I lost track.

"Then the war was over. I still had money in my case. It was awful, thieving from the dead, but I didn't know what else to do. I bought tickets and we got on the train. I didn't even know where it was going, just that it was heading away from where we were. Three days later it arrived in Independence. Mr. Jackson was there, organizing the wagon train. It seemed like a good idea, to go to the other side of the country. Away from everything." He shivered. "So I gave him money and asked him to buy whatever we needed to provision us. The next day we left. Now I'm here."

Maddy stared at him. "So you mean to say—just two months ago you were in war prison?" Carlos nodded.

"Is that where you got—to needing the laudanum?"

"Yes. I never touched it before. There was precious little to be had during the war, and it would mean some poor soldier going without as I sawed off his arm. But we were in the camp"—his voice broke—"so long." He turned away and steadied himself. "The poppies grew well around there. One of the guards wanted me to brew the laudanum for him, to sell. I took my cut. It's lovely stuff," he sighed. "For a while."

They both fell quiet. Maddy thought over his story, her mind filling in all the things he had left out: the fear, the hunger, the pain and loneliness, the horrible terror and ugliness of death. The first red glow of sunrise crept above the horizon. Carlos closed his eyes. The worst of his illness seemed to be over now. He looked almost calm. He also looked, Maddy suddenly realized, very young. *I grew out of my coat. . . .*

"How old are you, Doc Carlos?"

"How old?" He opened his eyes and blinked at the new light. "Well, yesterday was my birthday," he said quietly. "Now I am twenty-one."

Maddy didn't remember falling asleep, but suddenly there was a hand on her shoulder, gently shaking her awake. She sat up quickly. The sun blasted her eyes and she squinted.

"Maddy—wake up."

She sat up, feeling stiff and cold. She saw Joby sleeping soundly beside the remains of the fire. It felt as though ten years had gone by in one night. Doc Carlos was also asleep, curled tightly on his side, one hand still gripping a spoke of the cart wheel.

"You need to go back now," Aiden whispered.

Maddy blinked and squinted at her brother. His face was bruised, his lip was crusted with dried blood and one eye was swollen shut.

"Aiden—what happened to you?"

"Nothing. I tripped," he said. "Spooked one of the mules and it kicked me."

Maddy didn't believe him for a second. With the way the men had been in her family, she well knew the evidence of a beating.

"Go back to your wagon now," he whispered, pulling her to her feet. "Before everyone is awake and having questions."

Maddy didn't know what kind of questions anyone would

have, but she was too tired to protest, and followed Aiden back to the reverend's wagon.

Marguerite gently took her hand. "Lie down and sleep in the wagon." Maddy curled up on the quilts and slept until the wagon jolted to a start. It was not even a half hour, she thought, feeling grouchy from the lack of sleep. She shifted, trying to find a comfortable position, and felt something hard under her ankle. She sat up crossly but then saw that it was a book: *Comprehensive Anatomy of the Human Body, Including All Circulatory Systems and Muscular Arrangements.* She leaned out the back of the wagon and saw Joby driving the doctor's cart and Doc Carlos walking alone off to the side. He did not look her way. She stroked the soft leather cover and felt as if she had been given the whole world.

"**S**wim! Come on—swim hard."

Aiden couldn't hear the shouts from the distant river-bank. He only felt the force of the current as it dragged him downstream. His leg smacked against a submerged rock, but he was so numb with cold he didn't feel any pain.

"He'll never make it," William Buck said.

"I'll bet he does; he's almost there," the widower said.

"Hell, I'll go one dollar says he drowns altogether!" Buck offered.

Aiden couldn't hear the bets being placed on him either, only the roar of water. He struggled to get his head up for a breath. The rope around his waist was the lightest they'd been able to find, but still dug into him. He was supposed to wave his arms if he wanted hauling back, but if he stopped swimming long enough to wave he'd be sucked right to the bottom. Jackson had said that in twenty years of crossings he had never seen the Arikaree River this high and fast. No ox or mule could make it across. A horse might, but if it got swept away, no number of men could haul it back. Though nobody said it exactly, Aiden knew a horse was far more valu-able than he was. But if he got this first rope across, they could pull more ropes over, then send other men across. Once they had enough men and ropes on both sides, they would take the wheels off the wagons and float them over one by one. Mules, cows and oxen would all be tugged across. It would take two days, but it had to be done. Otherwise, they could be stuck here waiting for the water to go down. "And that could be days," Jackson had explained. "This is the lowest point in Colorado." It was only a few days' delay that had slowed the infamous Donner party in 1846. Even twenty years later, no one journeying west ever forgot. A few slow days and bad detours got the party trapped in the mountains for winter. Half died, and the rest ate the bodies to survive.

But now Aiden was getting close to shore. He could smell the grass! The toes of one foot hit some oozy mud, and Aiden struggled to get his feet under him. The rope was now so heavy it was like having a barn door tied around him. He dragged on for another few steps when the bottom of the river suddenly vanished again and hard, witchy hands grabbed his legs. He tried to kick free but couldn't move. He realized he had been washed into a sunken tree stump and was snared fast in the roots. The rope dug so tightly into his back that he thought he might be cut in two. He fumbled with the knot, but it was too tight to untie. He pushed at the stump with his feet and leveraged his head up to catch another breath. But then, with a sickening, slushy feeling, his foot plunged through the waterlogged roots and the current tugged him deeper. He was trapped fast and completely underwater.

Everything became strangely slow. He saw sky rippling through the water above. It had never seemed so blue. A short burst of bubbles escaped his lungs and twinkled up like little silver bells. Then the world began to dim. He pressed his face toward that distant sky but could not break the surface. He was only inches short, but he might as well have been on the bottom of the ocean.

His lungs burned, but he began to feel peaceful and warm. Then suddenly the sky vanished. A face appeared. It was a dark, rough face with long black hair—an Indian! Aiden saw a huge knife in the man's teeth. A large hand plunged through the water and grabbed his hair. Aiden saw the silver knife blade flash above him as the Indian thrust it down, straight toward his heart. He felt the hard blade press against his chest. He felt the steel sliding down his ribs. The world went dark and soft. Shouldn't he think of God, or something important, as he was about to die? Shouldn't he think of Maddy? But the only thing he could think of was the way a grasshopper smelled when you cooked it, with all the bubbling juice coming out around the neck. Then, in one great gasp, the last of his air bubbled out and the world went black.

Next thing Aiden knew, he was lying facedown on the riverbank. He coughed, and water poured out of his mouth and nose. He rolled over on his back and saw the Indian standing over him. Without thinking, he kicked up hard as he could, right between the man's legs. The Indian howled with pain and crumpled to the ground. Aiden rolled away and tried to stand, but the world spun upside down and he was flat on his back. His head was filled with a buzzing sound, as if the earth itself were humming. When the buzz finally cleared, Aiden realized what the noise was: laughter. Confused, he pulled himself up on his elbow. He saw three Indians. One was curled up on the ground holding his crotch, roaring with pain, but the other two were roaring with laughter. Aiden coughed again and slowly sat up.

One of the Indians, an older man, perhaps sixty, stood knee-deep in the river by the twisting roots of the submerged tree stump that had snared Aiden. He was holding the end of the rope. The loop that had been tied around Aiden was neatly cut. The old man laughed even as he strained to hold the rope against the current, then he shouted to the others in some incomprehensible language. The youngest of the three, who looked about Aiden's own age, jumped up to help. Together they dragged the heavy rope a few yards upstream and wrapped it around the tree Aiden had been trying to reach.

Then the younger Indian sprang back to Aiden's side and squatted down beside him.

"Your eyes are big as the moon!" he said, grinning. "You think we scalp you!" He made slashing motions toward Aiden's head.

"Who are you?"

"My name is Hisemtuksots, but I am called Tupic."

"What—" Aiden coughed out more water. "What are you doing here?"

"What are *you* doing here?"

"Crossing the river."

"Bad place to cross river."

"I think I know that now," he said, feeling more embarrassed than scared.

Tupic pointed downriver. "Ten miles that way you can cross."

"Well, fine." Aiden spat out some dirt and wiped his mouth. "But no little bird came along and told us that, did it?"

"So we come instead," Tupic replied, ignoring the sarcasm. The older Indian squatted beside them and held out a blanket.

"Why you swim river?" he asked.

"To carry the first rope over," Aiden said. "So we could pull the wagons across." The man shook his head, then spoke rapidly to Tupic in their language.

"No—" Tupic interpreted. "Clever Crow asks why *you*? Why not a strong man?"

"I am strong!"

"He says you look like a horse just born—skinny and stick legs." Aiden started to get angry but then realized they were probably right. Even though he had filled out in the past two months, his limbs were still spindly. Tupic was quite a bit shorter than he was, perhaps five foot four, but more muscular. His skin was a smooth coppery brown and his eyes a darker brown. The sides of his hair were braided but the rest was a loose black mane that hung to the middle of his shoulders.

"So why are you the one to swim across?" Tupic asked.

"I know how to swim," Aiden said. "None of the other men do." Tupic translated this. The Indian he had called Clever Crow laughed.

"How you know?" he said.

"How? I learned as a boy."

"No," Tupic explained. "He means how do you know the others can't swim!" Aiden felt his face go hot. As if he weren't already embarrassed enough.

"Here, Wet Pony." Clever Crow's voice was kind as he shook out the blanket. "You cold." Aiden wrapped it around his bare shoulders, as eager to hide his scrawny chest as to get warm.

"What is your name?" Tupic asked.

"Sorry. Aiden Lynch." Aiden held out his hand, then pulled it back a little, unsure whether Indians shook hands.

"Please to meet you," Tupic said with a hint of what might have been mock formality, and shook Aiden's hand. "This man is my uncle. In English he is called Clever Crow, and the one you kicked is his son, my cousin. His name is Silent Wolf."

Clever Crow interrupted with some rapid talk and both he and Tupic laughed.

"Clever Crow says today Silent Wolf has a new name,"

Tupic explained. "Now we call him—well, the translation is 'one whose balls are bruised like soft fruits carried a long time in a saddlebag.' "

Silent Wolf, still lying in a wounded curl, yelled harshly back at them.

"What did he say?"

"He says that we should all go, ah—I'm not sure I know your words for it. It is a rude thing."

"I bet it is." Aiden looked warily at the man, who was now slowly getting to his feet. He was probably in his early twenties, taller than the others, and stockier too. He had a long scar down the side of his face and wide, ropey scars on both arms.

"Tell him I'm sorry I kicked him," Aiden said. "I didn't know he was trying to help me." Tupic shouted a translation at the moaning man. Silent Wolf just scowled.

"How come you speak English?" Aiden asked.

"Missionary school."

"Stand up now," Clever Crow said. "You people worry." He waved toward the opposite riverbank. "Show you— good."

"Yes—of course." Aiden stumbled to his feet, his legs still numb with cold. He saw Jackson and the others standing by the bank. He couldn't make out their expressions, but there was a definite wave of relief as he raised his arm. He cupped his hands around his mouth.

"Can you hear me?" he shouted.

"Yes!" Aiden heard Jackson's faint reply.

"Tell them to walk west," Tupic said to Aiden. "Even with rope, the water is too fast here. We show you a place."

"There is a good crossing west of here!" Aiden shouted.

"You sure?" Jackson yelled back. "You got it right?"

"Yes!" Aiden called. "They speak English."

The three Indians spoke quickly among themselves, then Tupic said, "Your head man knows farther down should not be good. But this year, there is so much water, the river spills over the bank, carves out new place. Once it is fast, deep river, now becomes easy two rivers."

That was an awful lot of explanation to shout across the river. Clever Crow said something more to Tupic and waved toward Jackson. Tupic nodded.

"We are Nimipu," Tupic shouted to Jackson. "Nez Perce."

Jackson was clearly relieved.

"Oh! *Tack mee-wee!*" he shouted. *"Mana wee!"*

Clever Crow shouted what sounded like a similar greeting, then made some signs, sweeping his palms toward his chest, then pointing downriver. That seemed to settle everything, for Jackson tipped his hat in agreement, then turned and began to shoo the travelers back to their wagons.

"You come with us," Tupic said. "We meet them tomorrow at the crossing place."

Aiden hesitated. He had no boots, no shirt, nothing on but his pants. But he wasn't about to swim back, even if they pulled him across on the rope. His arms and legs were still burning from the cold water.

"My horse will carry two," Tupic said. "She is young and strong." The Indians had four ponies: the three they rode and one with packs. They were beautiful animals, smaller than Jackson's two horses but strong and well proportioned, with gleaming coats and spots all over their hind ends. They stamped and whinnied, eager to be off. The only things

Aiden had ever ridden before were farm mules and the family's old mare, who, when she was really motivated, sometimes broke into a slow trot. Tupic grabbed hold of his pony's mane and swung himself easily into the saddle, then leaned down and held out his hand to Aiden.

"Come on."

Aiden grasped Tupic's forearm, stuck a foot in the stirrup and flung one leg up toward the horse. Somehow he managed a clumsy mount and sat behind the saddle. He barely had time to grab hold of Tupic before the horse broke into a wild gallop. Soon the prairie was a blur beneath him.

13

"But how do you know they're friendly Indians?" Maddy pressed Jackson. "How do you know they aren't kidnapping him?"

"They're Nez Perce," he said. "Always been on good terms with whites. It was Nez Perce helped out Lewis and Clark. You heard of them?"

"Lewis and Clark are historical! They came by in ancient times! Before even you were born! Those Indians could have all kinds of grievances by now!"

"But what would they want with your brother?" he scoffed.

"They might want to cut his heart out for their gods, like the Aztecs!"

"They ain't Aztecs."

"Ransom, then!" Maddy said doggedly.

"If that's the case I'll gladly offer up the dollar or two he's sure to be worth. Now we need to get mov—"

"Why did you make him swim out there all alone anyway?" she interrupted.

"I didn't make him!" Jackson said defensively. "He volunteered! Someone had to go." He wiped the sweat off his forehead. "And if you don't want all that work of his to be for nothing, you'll back off with the stink-eye there and let us get rolling. If we get halfway to the crossing before dark and start early tomorrow, we might get over the river by tomorrow night."

"Come on, little miss." Reverend True put a firm hand on Maddy's shoulder. "Aiden's got some wits about him, he'll be all right."

Aiden grabbed hold of Tupic and hung on for dear life. He had never moved so fast. The wind stung his face and whipped his hair. He could feel the horse's hoofbeats thudding deep inside his chest. He bounced hopelessly up and down until he thought his teeth might come loose. It was exhilarating and terrifying.

"Hold with your legs here—" Tupic slapped his own knees. "Make your body easy. Feel balance here." He pressed on his abdomen. "Keep center."

Gradually Aiden began to feel the rhythm of the horse and relaxed his grip on Tupic. After a while, the horse eased down to a trot and finally a walk. Aiden turned and saw the others far behind them.

"This horse is young and likes to run," Tupic explained. Aiden suspected it was Tupic who really liked to run. Tupic reached into a leather saddlebag and passed Aiden a handful of dried berries to eat. They were sweet and sour at the same time, filling his mouth with flavor.

"Thank you," Aiden said. He was suddenly famished.

"Where do you come from?" Tupic asked.

"Kansas," Aiden replied. "Before that, Virginia, where I was born."

"Ah, Virginia—George Washington is born there!"

"Yes. Where is your home?"

"In the land north and west—the places you call Idaho and Oregon and Washington."

"You've come a long way," Aiden said. "What are you doing out here?"

Tupic shrugged. "It is the season to travel. We visit and trade. Do you have peppermint? In your wagon?"

"Someone probably does," Aiden said.

"I learned spelling for peppermint. Ask me any word."

Aiden wasn't sure he would know whether a word was spelled right or not.

"You speak very good English," he said. "Do all your people go to missionary school?"

"No. I was sent to learn your ways."

"What do you mean?"

"Clever Crow says we must find a way how to live with white people. He says I will go to school."

"Is he your chief?"

"He is elder—seer."

"Seer of what? The future?"

Tupic hesitated. "He is what you call godfather to me. One who receives the dreams for a boy and guides him until he has his own vision quest. His spirit power is very strong."

"What's a vision quest?"

"It is—" Tupic shrugged. "It is too much explaining for a short ride!"

"Did you like school?"

"Some. I am glad to learn reading, and to speak English. And I am glad for peppermint candy in the spelling bee. But after that, much is—boring. Mostly they say here—read the Bible, read the agriculture book how to plow and grow food. This we always think silly because there is food everywhere.

98

Then, here, read Christopher Columbus and George Washington. But mostly read the Bible. Too much Bible. I like Jonah and the whale, I like Noah's ark—we have stories of the Flood too. But the Ten Commandments—you know that story?"

"Moses, you mean?"

"Yes. I was excited at first to read it. Your God calls Moses to the mountaintop and sends thunderclouds to bring the commandments. You see, our spirits talk to us this way, through the fire, or the wind, sometimes through coyote or bird, or even mouse. So I think, finally I will understand your God. But all he says is don't kill and don't steal and so on."

"What's wrong with that?"

"Nothing, but that is not what a Spirit comes to tell you! That is what a child learns from his family and the tribe. Why would a god call you up a mountain with thunder just to tell simple rules?"

Aiden wasn't religious, but still felt a twinge of offense. "Well, what would your God tell you?" he said.

"Not tell so much, but to give a vision—signs to find your path. To show each man what he should do with his life besides hunt and eat and dance and make war and have children; about how to find his way—his place—in the world and to complete his journey with honor. About how to live well and how to listen to the spirits."

"Does your religion have a lot of spirits?"

Tupic turned and looked at him with a puzzled expression. "The *world* has a lot of spirits."

They rode on beneath the perfect blue sky, the sun warm and the air sweet with new prairie grass. Months later, in the darkest of dark times that were to come, Aiden would think back on this day and remember it as one of the best of his life. For the first time since he'd been a small child, he had no work or responsibilities. He carried nothing and had no decisions to make. He was entirely at the mercy of these strangers. Whatever was going to happen would happen. Meanwhile, he was riding through the sunshine on a beautiful horse with his mind free to think about God and spirits or nothing at all or everything at once.

The world was an entirely different place from the back of a horse. Walking across the rough prairie, you always had to look down so as not to trip. After a day of walking, Aiden's neck would ache and his eyes saw ripples around everything. But now, on horseback, he could just watch the wind move through the tall grass in shimmering waves. Gone was the cloud of dust that constantly choked the wagons. Tomorrow would bring back the clatter of the group, with their quarrels and burdens and slow, plodding hope, but right now everything was just easy and light. He looked at the three Indians, with their good ponies and small loads. Maybe he could just ride off with them, leave the rest to the dusty trail with their dreary cattle and lumbering wagons. He could live forever on a bag of dried berries and a skin of water, riding lightly across the plains like an Indian.

It was about ten miles to the crossing place, and the afternoon was still young when they got there. The river here had indeed spilled over its banks, quite dramatically. Whole sections of the original riverbank had been crumbled in the force of the water, leaving tall chunks standing like ruined castle walls. The river had originally been thirty feet across and twenty feet deep. Now it was at least a hundred feet across, but shallow enough that Aiden could see grass through the water. Little islands poked up throughout. It would be easy to get all the wagons and cattle across here. The water level had already dropped a few feet since the peak flood, and the bank was littered with sticks and branches. They could make a nice fire tonight.

"Much snow—mountain—winter," Clever Crow explained, waving toward the north. "Now all snow—" He searched for the word. "Gone. With sun?"

"Melted?" Aiden asked.

"Yes. Morning—we look—"

Clever Crow's English stalled, and Tupic explained, "We will ride across on the ponies and make sure there are no holes or trees underwater."

"Yes," Aiden said. "Thank you."

The three Nez Perce took their saddles and bags off the horses, led them to the river to drink, then pulled up handfuls of grass and wiped the sweating animals clean. They talked to the horses in low voices, sweetly, Aiden thought, like a grandmother to a favored child. As Tupic rubbed his pony's coat to gleaming, the horse nuzzled and nipped at his hair.

Once the horses were tended to, the Indians lay down in the grass and promptly fell asleep. Aiden sat by the river, the afternoon sun warm on his bare back. He had met Indians before but had never spent time with them. Whenever Indians had come around the homestead, his family had kept a wary distance. His parents had never called them savages, as many of the other settlers had, but they would certainly never have just invited them in to have tea as they would have white visitors. The Indians brought small game to trade for biscuits or corn bread. Once an Indian woman traded a basket for a knitted baby bonnet, and soon those bonnets became very sought-after items. Aiden's sister Ada was happy to knit them and give them away, but when an Indian woman wanted Ada to teach her how to knit, Ada didn't want to. She was afraid to sit close to her.

"She smells bad," Ada complained. "And her dress is greasy."

How did people get to be so different? Aiden wondered. All the people in the *Atlas of the World*, and all the different ways to live—how did that happen? He lay down in the warm grass to think about it, shifting a little to mash the itchy bits down, but the afternoon was so nice and warm he soon fell asleep himself.

14

Aiden woke to the sound of an arrow whooshing past his ear. It was so close he felt the feathers brush his cheek. He sprang up and whirled around, a sting of panic shooting through his whole body, sharpening his senses so the very air burned his skin. Silent Wolf stood just a few yards away, his bow drawn, another arrow fitted and ready to shoot. They both froze. Aiden could see the Indian's fingers creased red against the bowstring. A rivulet of sweat ran down the scar on his cheek and dripped onto his broad chest. Aiden saw the man's pulse throbbing in his neck. He felt his own heart pounding in his chest, heavy and big as a planet. Aiden did not have his own bow; he did not even have shoes to run away in. He could only hope Silent Wolf's arrow was sharp and his aim good, for he did not want to die slowly.

"Hyah!" Silent Wolf snarled. Then he dropped his bow, loosened the arrow and turned away, muttering something that sounded like curses. Aiden heard a rustling sound behind him and turned to see a small wooden hoop wobble to the ground a few yards behind him.

"Oh—hello!" Tupic called lightly as he snatched up the hoop. "I wondered where you are!" He was oblivious to Aiden's stone-frozen terror. He shouted something to his cousin, then crouched down and rolled the hoop toward him. Silent Wolf raised his bow and shot cleanly through it. Smoothly he pulled another arrow from his quiver and shot again, getting two more arrows through before the fourth one missed and the hoop toppled over. Tupic shouted what sounded like taunts and challenges to his cousin. Silent Wolf ran and picked up the hoop. Tupic fitted an arrow to his bow while Silent Wolf spun the hoop and Tupic took his turn, missing completely.

It was a *game*, Aiden realized, his heart still pounding, as the two men ran and feinted, shot and challenged each other for a few fast rounds. Tupic was a terrible shot, and Silent Wolf teased him mercilessly. Finally they paused, breathless. Aiden's panic had turned to anger now. Silent Wolf had almost killed him and they didn't even care! He saw Clever Crow watching silently, sitting on the bluff nearby. Aiden couldn't tell whether the old man had seen his fear or not.

Maybe they really hadn't noticed him sleeping in the grass. Or maybe they simply enjoyed giving him a scare. But what if they really did mean to kill him? That didn't make a lot of sense, since they had done nothing but help him so far, but all his life he had heard stories of Indian treachery.

Silent Wolf ran up to Aiden and held out the bow.

"You now," he said.

Aiden hesitated. Maybe they wanted him to take the bow so they wouldn't have to kill an unarmed man.

"Go on! It's a child's game!" Tupic urged. "We know you will be a bad shot."

Aiden's hands were still shaking as he took the bow.

"Child's game," Silent Wolf repeated stiffly, twirling the hoop on one finger, still with a decidedly unfriendly glower.

"All right." Aiden took the bow. If they were toying with him, well, he could toy with them as well. "I'll try." He tested the bow. It was a little longer than his own, and stiffer, but not so different. "Go ahead." He nodded to Silent Wolf. The man rolled the hoop, slowly, as if for a child. Aiden made a show of taking careful aim, then let the arrow pop out of the bowstring. The three Indians laughed.

"Try again!" Tupic grabbed up the target. This time Aiden shot the arrow, but deliberately aimed wide of the rolling hoop. Quickly he pulled another arrow out of the quiver and, making a big show of closing his eyes and looking away, got a "lucky" shot clean through. The Indians cheered.

"Good, Wet Pony!" Clever Crow called. "You Indian now!" He smacked his fist against his chest. Aiden knew they were teasing him, but suddenly he didn't mind.

"Can I try again?" he asked. "I bet I can do it faster."

"Oh—you want to bet?" Tupic said. "Nimipu are very fond of bets." He quickly translated to Clever Crow and Silent Wolf, who responded with hoots of encouragement.

"Yes, yes!" Clever Crow shouted. "What you bet?"

"I don't know."

"Horse?"

"A horse? I don't have a horse."

"Sisters?" Clever Crow said. "Soon Tupic need wife!" They all laughed at that.

"I don't have anything, really," Aiden replied, starting to feel awkward.

Silent Wolf said something to Tupic.

"You bet your firstborn child," Tupic translated solemnly. "Against five ponies born from his horse."

Aiden stared at them. They all looked very serious. He swallowed. Clearly, his use of the word "bet" was much more casual than the Nez Perces'.

"Well I—I don't know. . . ."

Then Tupic laughed and smacked him on the shoulder. "You are easy to joke on, Wet Pony!"

Aiden felt the familiar rush of anger at being mocked. He lifted the bow up to his chest.

"Throw it!" he shouted. Tupic spun the hoop as hard as he could. Aiden took aim and shot straight through the target, then quickly shot two more arrows clean through as the hoop rolled along the bumpy ground. The three Indians stared in amazement, then looked at each other, knowing they had been conned.

"You should have bet," Tupic said. "You would be rich in horses!" He ran off to gather the arrows. A cool breeze blew up from the river, and Silent Wolf, his back to Aiden, lifted his hair to cool his neck. I could shoot him easily now, Aiden thought, the bow ready in his hand. But then he felt the last twinges of anger melt away. It was only a game. Why had he never thought about Indians playing games?

Clever Crow watched from the hillside while the three younger men ran and shot some more, until they were sweating and panting. When they were tired of shooting, they wrestled. After proving himself with the bow, Aiden felt confident as he faced off against Silent Wolf. He'd certainly had enough brawls with his brothers. But time after time he found himself flat on his back, without even noticing where the other man had grabbed him. It was like being knocked over by wind.

"Watch here"—Tupic tapped his chest—"not arms and legs. Moving comes from center."

"I'll watch here," Aiden laughed, and sat down, breathing hard. "Let me see your center." Though Silent Wolf was bigger than his cousin, and a far more experienced warrior, Tupic easily held his own. He was faster and more nimble. Mostly he had an uncanny talent for anticipating Silent Wolf's attack and turning it against him. Soon all three were covered in dust and bits of grass, and they ran into the shallow river to cool off. Aiden couldn't remember having played like this since he was five years old.

"Now we have great hunger," Tupic said. "And the time is good to hunt for our dinner."

They walked along the riverbank, searching for signs that indicated where animals came to drink. Aiden didn't see any signs or anything different about the place Silent Wolf chose to wait, but soon after they lay down in the grass, two pronghorn appeared at the top of a nearby rise. They were beautiful animals, with soft white bellies and tawny brown backs. They had short horns, delicate faces and big brown eyes that made them look exotic and wise. Some people said they were a kind of antelope, others a sort of goat; some thought they could be something in between. Aiden only knew they were incredibly fast, easily spooked and very difficult to shoot.

The two creatures sniffed the air and walked gracefully down to the water. Silent Wolf, moving so slowly he did not even stir the grass, knelt and drew his bow. His arrow went so cleanly through that the animal fell with hardly a sound. It was almost two seconds before the other pronghorn noticed them and darted away.

They built a roaring fire with the abundant drift-wood, and the Indians made quick work of the butchering, efficiently slicing every bit of meat from the bone. Tupic carried up some smooth stones from the river and put them in the fire to heat. They skewered strips of the tenderloin on green sticks and grilled those first. The meat cooked quickly, and they sprinkled it with coarse salt and ate it hungrily, the warm juice running down their faces. Next Silent Wolf sliced the liver and laid the pieces out to cook on the hot rocks. They sizzled and sputtered and tasted delicious.

"Do you hunt for all your food?" Aiden asked. "Do you grow anything?"

"We hunt, we fish," Tupic explained, wiping his chin with the back of his hand. "We move with the seasons for the spring berries or the camas root."

"Do you not have a home, then?"

"We have a homeland, and some families by tradition go to some places for the different seasons, but we don't own the land or build houses like you do."

"What do you live in?" Aiden asked. "Tepees?"

"For the camps in summer, we make homes of poles and reed mats, or buffalo skins—what you call tepees. For winter homes, some dig out the hillside, some build a big lodge for many families to share, maybe thirty or sixty people. We live many different ways."

Silent Wolf scraped out a narrow trench in the ground on the downwind side of the fire and raked the coals into it.

"We dry the rest of the meat to carry," Tupic explained. He used a stick to drill a line of holes in the ground along the edges of the trench. Then they cut the remaining meat into thin strips, threaded those onto green sticks and propped the sticks in the holes, angled like fishing poles so that the meat would cook but the sticks wouldn't burn. Then the men all lay around the fire with full bellies, listening to the chirps and twitters and croaks of the prairie as evening fell.

15

"Now you must tell us your stories," Tupic said.

"What kind of stories?" Aiden asked.

"Good ones, I hope!"

Aiden felt nervous. He had read lots of books, but they weren't stories to tell around a campfire. He couldn't very well tell *Romeo and Juliet* or *Pride and Prejudice*.

"I don't think I have any."

"Everyone has stories."

"Tell me one of yours so I will know what you like."

"I like anything I haven't heard a hundred times before!"

"Do you know Aesop's fables?" Aiden asked with sudden inspiration.

"No."

"You didn't read them in your school?"

"No. Only Bible stories."

Aiden felt much more confident now; with Aesop he had a full quiver.

"Here's one," he said. "A magnificent buck goes to a pond to drink. There he sees his reflection in the water and admires himself. He thinks he is great-looking! His chest is strong, and his antlers are enormous and beautiful."

Aiden paused to let Tupic translate, but he only spoke a few sentences before Clever Crow nodded for Aiden to go on. Aiden realized that Clever Crow and Silent Wolf understood a lot more English than they could speak, and Tupic only had to translate bits of the story.

"Well, the buck is disappointed that his legs are so skinny and his feet so small. He thinks he should have grand legs to match the grand antlers. Then a lion jumps out of the brush. The deer runs away and the lion chases him. As he runs across the wide-open meadow, the buck's skinny legs carry him much faster than the lion can run. But then he enters the woods and the big antlers get snagged on the tree limbs. The buck becomes stuck and the lion pounces and kills him."

"Yes!" Tupic said. "That is a good story!"

"Well, it isn't done; there's a moral."

"What is a moral?"

"Like a lesson. What the story teaches you."

"It teaches many things."

"Yes, but at the end of an Aesop fable there is always a moral. It's part of the story."

"All right, tell your moral." Tupic shrugged.

"Well, I don't remember the exact words," Aiden said a bit defensively, sensing that maybe they didn't want the moral. "Usually there are exact words, like *slow and steady wins the race*. In this story the moral is that what the buck thought was his worst part actually was his best part, and the antlers that he thought were so grand caused his death."

The three Indians had a spirited discussion for a few minutes.

"We like the story," Tupic said approvingly. "But there are many other morals."

"Like what?"

"Well, like when you go to the pond to drink, you must

always look out for lions," Tupic said. "Or, why are you going to the pond alone? Where is your mate? If you have no mate to tell you that you are beautiful, maybe you are not so beautiful after all, except in your own thought." They all laughed at this. "Or maybe it just means that your antlers grow bigger and bigger until it is the time meant for you to die." Tupic leaned his head back and smiled up at the stars. "But that is what makes it a good story. I like your Aesop. Tell us some more."

They liked "The Wolf in Sheep's Clothing" but dismissed "The Tortoise and the Hare" as silly, for it was only one stupid hare deciding to take a nap that let the tortoise win.

"Slow and steady doesn't ever win a real race," Tupic protested. "But stupid always loses."

Aiden told about the grasshopper and the ants. How all summer the ants worked hard from morning until night, storing up food for the winter, while the grasshopper just enjoyed the summer sunshine and played his fiddle. The ants warned him that if he didn't work all day he would starve, but the grasshopper was too busy enjoying the lovely summer days and his music.

The Indians debated a long time over "The Grasshopper and the Ants." Yes, they agreed, one had to store up food over the summer to last the winter.

"But the grasshopper was playing music," Tupic pointed out. "The ants should have been grateful for that. It makes their work easier. What good is just living without music and celebrations?"

"Well, what if he wasn't playing music for them?" Aiden said. "What if he was just playing for himself?"

Clever Crow spoke and Tupic translated. "He says—it is

not the job of human being to live long, but to live well. If the spirits give you music, you must live music, and if music becomes your death, it is a good death."

"What about the ants?" Aiden pressed. "Are they bad because they only wanted to work and live through the winter?"

"No," Clever Crow said. "They are just ants."

When they finally lay down to sleep, Aiden's head was spinning. He wondered what Maddy was thinking right now and whether she could sleep. In all his life he had never spent a night away from her. He had watched her grow up, the only baby he'd ever known to grow up and not die. He shifted around on the bed of grass and stared at the stars. Did the Indians miss their families? Did Jefferson J. Jackson miss his? Aiden knew nothing at all about Jackson's family, or whether he even had one. He lay awake a long time with his brain churning, thinking he would never sleep, but suddenly he awoke to blazing sunshine, a rough shake on the shoulder and an urgent whisper in his ear.

16

"**W**ake up!" Tupic knelt beside him. He looked tense and worried. "Get up now, be ready," he said quietly. Aiden squinted at the sun. It was at least two hours after dawn. He never slept this late in the wagon train.

"Ready for what?" he mumbled sleepily.

"Something is coming," Tupic said. "Silent Wolf says it is army. Clever Crow says maybe buffalo."

"What do you mean?" Aiden sat up. "How do you know?"

Tupic looked puzzled. "Don't you feel the ground?"

"No," Aiden said, still groggy.

"Can't you feel it here?" Tupic patted his chest. "Or here?" He put his hand on his jaw.

"I don't think so." Aiden yawned.

"Trust me, then," Tupic said. "Hurry. If it is army, we must hide."

"Why?"

"So they don't shoot us!"

"The army won't just shoot you."

"We will go into the water. The old riverbank will hide us. Hurry."

Aiden pushed aside the blanket and got up. Whatever the threat was, buffalo or army, he felt especially vulnerable half-naked, in nothing but his tattered pants. He saw Silent Wolf packing up the horses and Clever Crow covering up the ashes from their fire, working fast to obliterate any traces of their camp.

"Why are you afraid of the army?" he asked, suddenly suspicious. "Have you done something?"

"Yes, we have done something," Tupic said sharply. "We were born Indians."

"What are you talking about?"

"Soldiers don't need a reason to shoot us! Now come on!" He grabbed Aiden's arm.

"Stop!" Aiden wrenched free, his worry turning quickly to fear. What were these three actually doing out here? "Wait—why were you at the crossing yesterday?" he asked. Was it really just coincidence? What if the Indians had planned to lure them off the trail all along? Aiden thought. What if they had led them down here to rob them? Or worse?

"I told you, we are traveling."

"From where? Your land is hundreds of miles from here." Aiden backed away. "Is this some kind of Indian trick?"

"Yes," Tupic said coldly. "Big Indian trick. We make the river flood so you can't cross in the usual place. Then we bring you here, where a hundred savages hide behind all the trees." He waved his hand toward the empty prairie. "We want to steal your mules because our horses are too fine, and your ugly white women so we can breed stupid children! Like you!"

Clever Crow hissed an admonition. Aiden didn't know what to think now. The Indians had treated him well, but they were still Indians. Maybe they hadn't been planning to ambush the wagon train, but if soldiers were after them, they might get desperate. Still, what could he do? Fighting would certainly be useless, and he could hardly outrun their horses. Maybe he could get to the river—even partway across he might be safe. The river was exposed and the Indians wanted to hide; they wouldn't risk being seen chasing him. Compared to his struggles yesterday, swimming across here would be easy. The low morning sun sparkled on the water. Before he could run a step, Aiden was flat on his back with Tupic's knee on his chest.

"Now, that *is* Indian trick!" Tupic snapped. Out of the corner of his eye, Aiden saw Clever Crow and Silent Wolf leap on their horses and ride toward them with Tupic's pony alongside. There was a quick, angry exchange. Aiden squeezed his eyes shut and held his breath, waiting for the blow that would kill him.

"Leave him!" Clever Crow said. Tupic jumped up. With his back pressed against the ground, even Aiden could feel the vibrations now. Whatever was coming was almost upon them. Tupic threw himself into his saddle and glared at Aiden. In his eyes Aiden saw no anger, only sadness and confusion.

Suddenly a herd of pronghorn, a dozen or more, burst over a rise nearby. They startled at the sight of the horses and darted toward the river, then turned again at the water, scattering along the bank in confusion. The Indians reined in the ponies. Tupic shouted something at his cousin. Aiden did not have to understand their words to feel the wave of relief. *It was only pronghorn!*

Silent Wolf pulled out his bow, expertly turned his pony, galloped alongside one pronghorn and quickly fired an arrow cleanly through its chest. Tupic fumbled for one of his own arrows as he followed. Silent Wolf whipped out another arrow and his nimble pony turned easily toward a second target. Tupic shot but missed. Then Clever Crow gave a short, shrill whistle of alarm. Aiden turned and saw four soldiers galloping over the little hill.

One of the soldiers, caught up in the hunt, chased wildly after the pronghorn, firing shot after shot, but the others quickly reined in their mounts when they saw the Indians. Aiden saw alarm and fear on their faces. Tupic's horse, frightened by the gunshots, began to rear and jump. Tupic struggled to control it. Clever Crow reined his horse to a stop, and Silent Wolf rode to his side. The first soldier shot one pronghorn cleanly through neck. A jet of bright blood shot out of the wound. The soldier gave a great whoop of triumph and fired at another pronghorn. That animal fell with a terrible cry, merely wounded. Only then did the soldier notice the Indians. He yanked his horse around and galloped up to the other soldiers. He was a small, thin man with broad, knobby shoulders and a sharp fringe of greasy black hair stuck to his forehead. There were sergeant's stripes on his filthy uniform jacket. The other soldiers were all privates and looking to him for orders.

"Well, lookee here, boys!" he crowed. "We got us some Injuns."

"We do not fight," Clever Crow said calmly, his hands in the air.

The sergeant looked surprised to hear him speak English. "No? What about you, scar face?" he taunted, riding in close to Silent Wolf. "You wanna fight? You ugly enough I might put a bullet through your head just to save any more looking at you!" One of the other soldiers laughed. Clever Crow spoke to his son, and Silent Wolf reluctantly raised his hands. Tupic's horse shied and he patted its neck. Two soldiers immediately pointed their guns at him.

"Get your hands up, boy!" the greasy-haired sergeant shouted.

"I calm the horse," Tupic said. "We do nothing wrong."

"Yeah, well, I know your Injun tricks!"

Aiden winced to hear the same ugly accusation he had made himself just moments ago.

"Keep your hands up where I can see them!"

As Tupic slowly raised his hands, the sergeant jabbed him hard in the ribs with the muzzle of his rifle. Tupic almost fell off but made no sound and showed no sign of pain. Then a commanding voice thundered from the bluff behind the soldiers.

"Halt!"

Galloping over the rise were a dozen more soldiers, led by a lieutenant atop an enormous and stunning chestnut horse. The lieutenant was a plump little man with a face pink as a boiled ham and shocking orange hair that frizzed wildly from beneath his hat.

"Lower your weapons, boys," he said calmly, his deep, booming voice incongruous with his physique. He looked for all the world like a gnome out of a picture book, Aiden thought. While most men were fat in certain places, in the belly or the face, this man was plump all over. His fingers were sausages, his wrists like bread rolls. His calves oozed over the tops of his shiny boots. There were pads of fat behind his ears, which pushed them out slightly. Despite his odd and somewhat comical appearance, however, he rode very elegantly.

"Looks like we've gone a bit sideways here, boys," he said

calmly. "So let's all catch our breath and live awhile more, what do you say?" No one said anything, but the tension did ease somewhat. He looked very intently at the Indians, like a dressmaker sizing them up for fit and style. The silence was pierced by the terrible cry of the dying pronghorn.

"Sergeant Todd," the lieutenant said, "see to that animal, please."

The black-haired sergeant reluctantly left off tormenting Tupic and rode over to the wounded antelope. Now the lieutenant turned to Aiden, quickly surveying him from head to toe with eyes pale as milk.

"What are you doing here with these Indians, lad?" he asked. "Have you been captured?"

"Captured? No!"

The dying pronghorn gave one last cry; then a shot echoed across the prairie. "Don't be afraid, lad. We're here to help you. Are your people nearby? Have they been hurt?"

Aiden remembered the sound of Silent Wolf's arrow zipping inches from his head the day before. He knew all he had to do was say the word and the soldiers would arrest the Indians, if not outright kill them. More soldiers began trotting over the rise, alerted by the shots. All of them grew visibly tense at the sight of the Indians.

"No," Aiden said. "No one is hurt. These Indians are—" He hesitated. Trust them or not, he had to decide now. The soldiers looked twitchy and eager to shoot at the slightest movement. "They're friendly. They're guides," he said. "For our wagon train."

The lieutenant looked around. "What wagon train?"

Aiden waved his hand toward the river. "They're on the way. They should be here by noon, I expect."

"I'm not sure I understand, boy. If you're with a wagon train, what are you doing out here all alone with these Indians?"

Aiden scrambled to make his explanation work. "We tried to cross at the usual ford yesterday, about ten miles upriver. Only, the water turned out to be too high. I swam across with the rope, then didn't want to swim back. The Indians knew the river had broken out the banks here."

"And how did they know that if they were already with your wagon train?"

The lieutenant had tripped him up already.

"Well, they suspected, I mean. They know the land and how the river is, they suspected it would break out down here. That's why they're our guides."

"Why were you swimming when these men could cross on horseback?"

"They couldn't," he said. "I mean, ah, we didn't believe them at first. We thought we should use the regular crossing place. I—uh, I said I could make the swim, but it turned out the water was too fast. I got stuck on the other side, so they rode down on that side, crossed here, then rode back up to fetch me." Aiden felt woozy with the tension of trying to make his fabricated story fit right.

"And they never thought to bring you a coat? Your shirt or boots?"

"No," he said lamely. "They're Indians." He rolled his eyes and gave an exaggerated shrug, as if to say *What do you expect?*

"Guides, you say?" The lieutenant's piercing gray eyes did not give away what he was thinking.

"Yes, sir. They're Nez Perce, sir. Nez Perce are peaceful," he added.

"No Indians are peaceful out here these days, lad." The lieutenant's mouth made either a slight smile or an involuntary twitch, showing a tiny ridge of very white teeth. "What's your name?"

"Aiden Lynch, sir."

"Irish, eh?"

One could never know if Irish was a good thing to be or not, so Aiden just gave a vague shrug. Maybe if he seemed stupid enough, the damn lieutenant would just leave him alone.

"I'm Lieutenant Caerwyn Gryffud, B Troop, Third Western Cavalry out of Fort Laramie."

It was a Welsh name, a common one in the coal mines of West Virginia, but that still didn't reassure Aiden. The Welsh were as clannish as the Irish, and fights between the two groups were common.

All of the soldiers had arrived now. There were about thirty of them, and most looked mean, hungry and tired. Toward the rear of the group, a few men looked sick and were so weak they slumped in the saddle.

"We'll wait for your wagon train," the lieutenant said. "Franklin, Bailey—"

Two very young-looking soldiers trotted over.

"Take some men and gather wood for fires. Tell Cook we have some antelope to butcher. The men could all use some fresh meat. He's to cook it all and serve it out now. Have him make a broth for the sick."

Now Clever Crow spoke up, his voice as measured and authoritative as Gryffud's.

"My uncle says you may have our antelope as well," Tupic translated. "To feed your men."

"Your antelope?" Gryffud said.

"The two my cousin killed for the wagon train," Tupic said firmly. "We wish to make them a gift to you, in friendship."

Sergeant Todd gave a snort of laughter, but the lieutenant raised a hand to silence him.

"Thank you," he said simply, nodding to Clever Crow.

"I will take the arrow out," Tupic added defiantly. "So it doesn't get broken."

17

The soldiers took the Indians' bows and knives and tied the four ponies up with their own horses but did nothing else to restrain them. They were left alone, and even given portions of the pronghorn once it was cooked. The meat was charred black, tough and unsalted, far different from the tender steaks of the night before.

Lieutenant Gryffud gave Aiden one of his own shirts to wear, for his back was badly sunburned. The sleeves were six inches too short and the tail barely covered his waist, but Aiden was grateful for the protection as the sun climbed higher. The shirt was made of silk, and the strange fabric felt wonderfully cool against his tender skin.

"It's my battle shirt," Gryffud explained. "Better to get shot through silk, you see—leaves a much cleaner wound."

The shirt was clean, unpatched and deeply creased from being folded, so Aiden guessed Gryffud had not had much need for a battle shirt so far in his military career.

"When the wagon train comes, will your Mr. Jackson agree with your story?" Tupic asked when they were alone. "Will he say that we are guides?"

"I don't know," Aiden replied. "Even if he does, there are plenty of others who won't. I'm sorry. And I'm sorry I didn't trust you."

"We have not told you the truth either," Tupic said quietly.

"Not all. You are partly right; we are not just traveling to trade and visit. This is a troubled time."

"Why?"

"Have you heard of Sand Creek?"

"No."

"It was in your newspapers."

"I haven't seen a newspaper for a year or more."

"In your state of Colorado, there was a great chief of the Cheyenne Nation called Black Kettle. One of your soldiers, a Major Wynkoop, talked many months with Black Kettle, to make a peace treaty. Everyone was tired of war. So Black Kettle agreed to a treaty. He brings his people to talk with your chiefs in a place called Sand Creek. Many Indians went, from the Cheyenne and Arapaho. They bring their families, their children and old people, and made their camp. They trusted Major Wynkoop, but over him was an evil man called Colonel Chivington, who did not want peace.

"One morning, Chivington and his men attacked Black Kettle's camp when all were sleeping. Some of the men ran out. They waved an American flag and a white flag of surrender. They did not have guns or any weapons. They think it was a mistake. They put their hands in the air, but the soldiers shot them dead. Then the soldiers killed everyone who could not run away. More than two hundred lives. Babies they stabbed with swords to save the bullets."

Aiden felt a sick twist in his stomach. It couldn't be true. No soldiers would do such things. But then he thought about how ready Sergeant Todd had been for violence. Tupic reached into a saddlebag and took out a rolled-up piece of leather. He lifted the flaps on a sort of envelope, took out a page from a newspaper and handed it to Aiden. It was yellow

124

and stained, but the photograph was still clear. It was the inside of a grand theater with a chandelier over the stage, on which smiling soldiers and men in suits stood proudly in a row. *Colorado soldiers have again covered themselves with glory!* read the caption under the photo. *Colonel Chivington triumphs over the savages. Not one soldier perishes!* To one side of the stage was a line of people dressed up in their Sunday best: men, women and children waiting to view an exhibit, a long string of what looked like small animal pelts.

"Those are Indian scalps," Tupic explained in a flat voice. "Also, the parts of Indian men." He looked away, embarrassed, and pointed to his own crotch. "Also their ears. Also the hair from the women, the hair from their woman place. Your soldiers cut them." Tupic looked out over the calm river.

"All is different now," he said. "Sand Creek changes the way the heart beats in a man. It changes the way stars move in the sky. Your Constitution, your books of law, your Bible, all are now waste to us."

"I'm sorry," Aiden said lamely. Tupic folded the clipping and put it away.

"After the massacre, there were months of revenge attacks," he went on. "Indians burned white houses and knocked down the telegraph. Your army sent out many soldiers, like these." He nodded at the regiment nearby. "But since winter, Cheyenne and Arapahos, Teton Sioux, Nimipu, many others, ride to councils with the other tribes."

"That's why you're out here? For councils?"

"Yes. For many years Clever Crow talks peace with other tribes."

"So what did your councils decide?"

"Most agree to stop the revenge, to take time and think. After that, I don't know."

"What do you think will happen?" Aiden asked.

"Some say white men will kill all Indians and take our land and we will be gone from the earth, so we must be ready to return to the spirit world. Others say we should fight; that even if you kill all of us, from every drop of our blood will grow ten new warriors." Tupic looked at the soldiers lounging in the grass.

"What do you say?"

"I say it is wrong to die today, on a beautiful day when peppermint candy is coming to me." Tupic stared at the white clouds drifting across the clear blue sky. "That lieutenant does not believe your story."

"I know."

"Your head man Jackson knew our greetings," Tupic said. "Do you think he knows more of Indian ways?"

"He's been out west a long time. He was a fur trapper," Aiden said. "I'd say yes."

"We will try to use sign, then."

18

Shortly before noon, a dust cloud across the river heralded the approach of the wagon train. Aiden climbed the bluff and saw Polly and Annie Hollingford and Therese Thompson and some other girls walking together as if they were on a holiday outing. In a way they were, with an easy march of only five miles along a riverbank on a nice summer morning. As the wagon train neared the crossing, people began to notice the soldiers. Aiden saw the girls giggling with excitement. He searched the column for Maddy, and soon saw her running ahead and looking for him. He whistled and waved and she waved back. Then Aiden saw Jackson halt the wagon train and ride out alone into the river. Aiden ran down the bluff.

"Come on," he said, nodding to the Indians.

"Mr. Jackson, Reverend True, William Buck." Tupic quietly reviewed all the names Aiden had taught him as they walked toward the river. Lieutenant Gryffud rode up beside them on his chestnut horse, and Aiden slowed down to let him pass. They couldn't very well do any secret signing with the officer right next to them. Gryffud reined his horse to a stop near the water's edge and waited for Jackson to come across. The other soldiers all watched from their camp on the bluff. As Aiden had hoped, midway across the river, Jackson looked at him and tipped his head slightly in query. Aiden nodded at Clever Crow, and the older Indian quickly made some signs. Aiden couldn't tell whether Jackson saw them or not, or understood them if he did.

"What did he say?" Aiden whispered to Tupic.

"That one moon is passed, one month, and that we feast together. It is a way to say we are friends," Tupic explained. "Also the sign for 'look' or 'seek the way.' Sorry—sign is a very simple way of talking."

Simple or not, the message seemed to get through to Jackson, or he guessed the situation on his own. Cavalry and Indians could never be an easy combination. As Jackson approached the riverbank, Aiden waded out to meet him and took the horse's bridle.

"*Tupic* and *old Clever Crow* picked out a good place to cross, didn't they, sir!" Aiden said, stressing the Indians' names. "But I guess that's what you've been paying them for all this time, right? And *Silent Wolf* saved you a chunk of meat from our dinner last night. He shot a pronghorn."

Jackson paused, then frowned. "Well, I hope it ain't old and tough like the last one."

Lieutenant Gryffud clicked at his horse and rode a few steps forward, until the two men were only a few yards apart.

"Good morning," Jackson said cautiously, like one who never quite trusted authority of any kind, and soldiers especially.

"Good morning, sir," Gryffud said in his most authoritative voice. "I am Lieutenant Gryffud, B Troop, Third Western Cavalry out of Fort Laramie."

"Jefferson J. Jackson." Jackson touched the brim of his hat.

"The boy tells me these Indians are in your employment."

"That's right."

"So you will vouch for them?"

128

"I will."

"They've given you no trouble?"

"Not so far."

Gryffud seemed to be looking for a little more information, but Jackson remained taciturn.

"Where's their horses?" Jackson asked.

"I secured them with our own," Gryffud said. The day was warm, but he wore his uniform coat fully buttoned, so his pink face was turning bright crimson.

"Well, I'd appreciate it if you unsecured them now," Jackson said firmly. "I need all my hands."

The lieutenant looked for a moment like he might question things further, but then ordered two soldiers to retrieve the Indians' horses.

"I'll ride back over and start things moving," Jackson said by way of ending the conversation. He pulled one foot out of his stirrup and held out his hand to Aiden so he could mount. "Get on behind, boy. You're no use to me idling here." Aiden climbed on the back and Jackson wheeled the horse around. "Don't dawdle," he called to the Indians.

"Aiden, I thought you were drowned!" Maddy threw her arms around Aiden's neck as soon as he slid off Jackson's horse. Aiden, glad to see her but embarrassed, pried her off.

"You saw I was fine," he said. "You know I can swim." He took her hand and pulled her close. "Now I need you to do something for me quick. Help me tell as many as you can that these Indians are our guides and have been with us one month. Will you do that? Quick as you can? Otherwise, they may get killed, and they did save my life."

"Killed? Why?"

"Don't ask me now; please just trust me."

"Shouldn't I know their names, then?"

Will she always be one step smarter than me? Aiden thought. He told her the three Indians' names, and Maddy darted off. Aiden saw Mr. Hollingford and some of the other men in a tense discussion with Jackson, but somehow Jackson convinced them all to go along with the ruse.

"We'd still be sitting around waiting for the river to drop if not for them," he pointed out.

By the time all the wagons and cattle were across, it was late afternoon, and there was no sense in trying to move another few miles when they could camp near the water. The settlers and soldiers alike, tired of their own company, were glad to mingle with new people. The men joined the army officers to sit in the shade of some wagons, smoke their pipes and talk. The Thompson boys and some of the other young men got up a game of baseball with the soldiers, who had a real bat and ball. The soldiers even knew the latest scores of the club games, which came over the telegraph to Fort Laramie.

Some of the women did washing, but there was no privacy for bathing with forty soldiers camped nearby. Babies and the smallest of the children did get a scrubbing, and the prairie afternoon erupted with howls of protest. Older children were sent scrambling back and forth to the riverbank with armloads of driftwood, and the women began to prepare the special meals that could only be made when there were generous fires and plenty of cooking time.

Meanwhile, Aiden was on a quest for peppermint candy. He knew Marguerite had lemon drops, and there was horehound and rock candy to be had from the Thompsons, but it was peppermint that Tupic had learned to spell for, and Aiden suspected the Hollingfords would have that.

Despite his having saved Polly from the wolves, Aiden had never received more than grudging thanks from Mr. Hollingford. But Mrs. Hollingford was eternally grateful, so sometimes she slipped Maddy a jar of jam, a tin of sardines or some other treat from their abundant supplies. Once she even snuck out a pair of new socks for Aiden. They came from a store, had been knitted by a machine and were amazingly smooth. So when Aiden came asking her for peppermint, she was so glad to be able to do something for him that he was afraid she might cry. She looked around to be sure her husband wasn't watching, then climbed into the back of their stores wagon and carefully pried the lid off a tin box. A wave of sweet peppermint smell smacked Aiden in the face so hard he thought he would fall over.

"For the Indian boy," she said as she quickly wrapped two sticks in paper. "And for you too!" She added two more.

"Thank you, Mrs. Hollingford."

"Break them up!" she whispered. "Don't take out a whole stick! Tell him that so he understands! Just little pieces, all right? So no one sees!" She pinched her fingers quickly to show him; then her hands fluttered back into a fretful clench. "Those are from a nice shop, you see. If anyone saw, they would guess where they came from!"

"We'll be careful," he reassured her. He felt sad and a little angry to see her so frightened. They were clearly the richest family in the group, and she should have been able to give away candy without worrying what her husband

131

would do. What would he do, anyway? In the coal town lots of men had hit their wives, but Mr. Hollingford was no coal miner. Even Aiden's own father, who would beat his sons at a hint of sass, had never laid a hand on his wife or the girls.

"Aiden?" Mrs. Hollingford whispered urgently as he turned to leave.

"Yes?"

"Those Indians—they won't hurt my girls, will they?"

"No, ma'am."

"Well, if they get—you know, if they get the way Indians get—promise me you'll keep them away from Polly and Annie. Will you?"

Aiden felt a sourness rising in his throat but just nodded. "Yes, ma'am."

"Promise?"

"I promise." He started to leave but stopped. "You know, Mrs. Hollingford, they have families too," he said. "With daughters and all. You don't have to worry, ma'am."

He tucked the peppermint sticks in his pocket. The thought of tasting one himself made his mouth water, and he considered saving one for Maddy, but Tupic would certainly go much longer than either of them without another chance at such a treat. Once Aiden started work in the logging camp, he could buy candy for Maddy. Even with a year of debt to work off, he would have to get a little pocket money, wouldn't he?

He saw Maddy sitting next to Doc Carlos in the small rectangle of shade from his cart, a heavy medical book opened on a blanket on the ground between them. Aiden had been surprised when Maddy told him that Carlos was only twenty-one, but lately the doctor had begun to look more like his age. He had put on some weight and, while still terribly thin, did not look like a corpse anymore. He still startled easily and mostly kept to himself, but he was not nearly so twitchy and nervous. Since Maddy had nursed him through the night of his strange sickness, he had been generous with lending her his books, and now Maddy spent every free minute studying.

Aiden fingered the candy sticks in his pocket. He could break off a little piece for her. She had done a good job of convincing people to back up his story. Tupic would want her to have a bit of his treat. As Aiden veered over, stealthily cracking off a piece of candy, Jefferson J. Jackson appeared from behind the cart.

"Doc Carlos? Sorry to interrupt your study there," Jackson said. "I'm coming to ask would you check on a couple of the soldiers. They've got some flat-out sick and another few doing poorly. Would you mind looking them over?"

Carlos stared hard at his book. He had not mingled with the soldiers so far and seemed reluctant to have anything to do with them now.

"I haven't any medicines," he replied quietly. "Whatever they have, there isn't anything I can do for them."

"Yeah." Jackson scratched the back of his neck. "I figured as much, but see, the lieutenant would be obliged, though. And sometimes, with soldiers, it's a good idea to oblige. If we got a doctor with us and they got sick men, well, it'd be kinda unfriendly if you wouldn't take a look, you know?"

"Yes, of course." Carlos got to his feet. Maddy shut the book and jumped up as well.

"You stay here," he said.

"Why?"

"It might be contagious."

"How do I learn, then?"

"I'll tell you all about it later."

Carlos started walking toward the army encampment.

"Wait!" Maddy said. "Don't you want your bag?"

"There's nothing in there for sickness," Carlos said, almost rudely. "There's precious little in the world for sickness, and what there is I don't have."

"Well, you look more like a doctor with it," Maddy said gently. She pulled the leather bag out of the cart. "And that might be comforting to sick people, don't you think?"

Carlos stared at her as if she were speaking a foreign language but took the bag.

"Aiden," he said, still looking hard at Maddy, "would you mind bringing me a bucket of water? Just bring it close; you needn't come near the sick." He turned and strode away.

Four soldiers lay on blankets on the ground in the scant shade from the supply wagon. Three of them were very still, with glassy eyes and the sweaty pallor of fever. The fourth was curled on his side, agitated and moving restlessly, clutching a coat to his face and moaning.

"The light hurts his eyes," a young, blond-haired soldier explained listlessly. He sat nearby with another six men. These seven were also ill, but not so bad as the four on the ground.

"When did you start feeling sick?" Carlos asked the blond soldier.

"Two days ago," he replied. "Those others a couple days before that. Are we gonna get that bad?"

"I don't know." Carlos knelt beside one of the sick men and felt around his neck. "You have a fever—what else hurts?"

"I hurt all over: my head, my back, my belly. My eyes hurt—and just all over."

Carlos helped the man off with his jacket. Aiden arrived with the bucket of water and stood awkwardly nearby, waiting for direction.

"It feels worse than just regular sick somehow," the soldier groaned. "I had the influenza bad last winter; ague too—twice in my life. This is different." The soldier was trembling. "It's like bugs are inside me and scratching up on the bottom of my skin."

"Lie still, let me examine you." Carlos felt under his arms, lifted his shirt and pressed on his groin. The man groaned.

"Sit up now. Turn your face to the sun, there, so I can examine your throat."

Carlos put a flat metal stick in the man's mouth and pressed his tongue down. Aiden saw Carlos tense, but his hands remained steady.

"All right, you can lie back down."

Aiden didn't need to know anything about sickness or medicine; the air just felt heavy with doom. He watched Carlos move along the line of men, looking in their mouths and up their noses, examining their hands and the soles of their feet. Then he went back to the moaning man and pulled the jacket away from his head. This time he did not look in the man's mouth, just quickly draped the jacket back over his face and stood up. He wiped the sweat off his

135

forehead with his sleeve, walked over and sat down beside Aiden.

"I need you to stay quiet," he whispered. "It isn't good."

"All right."

"The soldiers have smallpox."

19

"Have you been vaccinated?" Carlos asked Aiden. "Do you know?"

"Yes," Aiden said.

"Maddy too?"

"Yes, when we were small in Virginia, we worked on a plantation. Everyone was vaccinated."

"Good," Carlos said. He opened his bag and took out a piece of soap wrapped in cloth.

"So we won't get it, right?" Aiden asked.

"The vaccine is never a hundred percent reliable," Carlos said as he washed his hands in the bucket. "But it's usually pretty good in the East."

Aiden didn't find that answer particularly comforting.

"I've been around those soldiers since yesterday. What if I did catch it?"

"Even if you did, which you probably didn't, it takes at least a week from the time of infection until you can pass it on to someone else." Carlos offered no other words of reassurance, though Aiden dearly would have liked to hear some. He knew about smallpox; it was the worst disease there was. Epidemics killed hundreds of people—and many said you were lucky to die. Carlos stood up, rubbing his damp hands against the sides of his legs. Once again he looked like an old man. He poured out the bucket and watched the foamy water sink into the ground. A few small, shimmering bubbles clung to blades of grass.

"What've we got, Doc?" the blond soldier called. "Is it something bad?"

Another of the sick soldiers got unsteadily to his feet. "It is bad! You know it is! When it ain't bad, they say so directly!"

"Just sit down there, Private," Carlos said calmly. "I'm going to give you all something for the fever.

"Go get me Jackson," he whispered to Aiden. "Get me the lieutenant and—and Reverend True. I don't want a panic. Then get your Indians together. Don't let them ride off."

Aiden, too shocked by the news to talk, just nodded.

"Smallpox is worse for Indians. Much worse. Do you understand?"

"Yes."

"Can you explain to them? Are you on terms for that?"

What kind of terms would that be, Aiden thought, to tell someone they had just been exposed to the most horrible disease on the planet.

"Yes, I guess."

"It can't be the pox," Gryffud insisted. "They don't have spots!"

"The first sores appear in the mouth and throat," Carlos explained. "Seven of these men have those, and one is just starting to break out on his face. He'll be covered by evening. When was your last contact with other people?"

"Ah—we—ah, we saw a wagon train four days ago," the lieutenant stammered. "And some scouts two days before that, but just in passing."

138

"No—no, it wouldn't be that recent," Carlos told him. "It takes at least a week after exposure for you to show any symptoms."

"We left Fort Laramie just two weeks ago."

"Was there sickness there?"

Lieutenant Gryffud's round face turned even pinker with anxiety. "Well—of course, there are always soldiers sick, but no one said anything about smallpox! You must believe me! I wouldn't have gone in! This isn't my fault!"

More soldiers were gathering around now, suspicious at the furtive conversation.

"I'm not blaming you," Carlos whispered sharply, glancing at the uneasy soldiers. "I'm trying to stop an epidemic."

"Of course." Gryffud's face turned even redder. "Yes, of course."

"All we can do right now is prevent it from spreading any further, and that means a quarantine on all your men."

Jefferson J. Jackson walked up just then, with the Reverend True beside him.

"The soldiers have smallpox," Carlos told them simply.

"Are you sure?" Jackson asked. "Could it be measles?"

"No. We need to separate our people from the soldiers immediately," he said to Jackson, then turned back to Gryffud. "Your soldiers will need to be quarantined; even those with no symptoms. They can't have contact with anyone else for three weeks."

"I can't sit this wagon train out for three weeks!" Jackson protested.

"You don't have to. . . ." Carlos hesitated, grasping for a way to explain the complicated business of disease. "The soldiers were exposed two weeks ago. They already have pustules, so they're contagious. But if any of our group has been infected today, they won't feel sick, and won't be contagious for at least a week, more like two."

"So at least one week before we could pass it on to anyone else?" Jackson rubbed his sleeve across his sweating forehead. "You're sure?"

"We don't know everything about smallpox," Carlos admitted. "But we do know that."

"It's just—I can't have any epidemics on my page," Jackson said, almost whispering. "I got enough marks in the bad column already." Aiden hadn't thought of Jefferson J. Jackson as one to be keeping a spiritual tally sheet and found it touching. "We won't join the main trail until the South Pass in Wyoming territory," Jackson went on. "That's nearly three weeks. Will you know for sure by then if we're clear?"

"Yes." Carlos nodded.

"All right, then." Jackson put his hat back on. "Reverend True, can I press upon you the job to help me tell our people? How you preachers do—for bad-news telling. Doc will explain the particulars."

"And my men—will you explain to them, too?" Gryffud asked Carlos, almost pleading.

"I've nothing to do with soldiers," Carlos said tersely. "You're their commanding officer."

"I'm a *painter*," Gryffud said desperately.

"What?"

"I only came out here to paint! I've never commanded anyone to do anything but sit still so I could *draw* them!"

"Paint? Like pictures?" Jackson said.

"Yes, pictures—landscapes, Indians."

"But you been in the war?" Jackson persisted.

"As an artist! I drew pictures of soldiers and camps and battles and such, for the newspapers. I never did any fighting!" His sausage fingers made nervous sketches in the air. "Then I asked for a western posting so I could see the mountains and draw the Indians."

For a moment everyone was silent. Even Jackson didn't know what to say. It would have been funny except that the stakes were so high.

"Well, you've *seen* officers before, haven't you?" Jackson asked in a sharp tone.

"Yes. Of course."

"For painting them, you observed how they acted and so on?"

"Well, yes."

"So, goddammit! Just act like you observed! However you wound up with those stripes, you're still in charge!"

Carlos closed his bag. "Some of the men will want to run," he said. His voice was flat. "You need to be prepared to stop them."

"Stop them?" The little lieutenant was completely flustered. "Yes, of course, I'll tell them."

"No," Carlos said. "Some will want to get away. You can't let them. You need to get your mind ready for that."

Carlos picked up his bag and strode off toward the wagon train.

"What did he mean, Mr. Jackson? Do you know what he meant?"

"I guess he meant shoot 'em," Jackson spat. "They try to run, you shoot 'em."

20

"Ah!" Tupic sucked noisily on a piece of peppermint, pursed his lips and drew a breath in. "If a man could eat the stars and breathe the snow, they would taste like this!"

Aiden smiled. "You're very poetic."

"You will come to one of our festivals someday," Tupic said. "You will hear poetries that will put your heart in the sky. Silent Wolf is a very beautiful poet."

"Silent Wolf?" Aiden looked over at the tough, scarred man wading in the river nearby. His disbelief must have shown on his face, for Tupic laughed.

"A man can be a great warrior and still make poetry."

They sat by the river's edge. The three Indians had passed the afternoon by building a fish trap. It was not as elaborate as a real fish weir, Tupic explained, but an easy effort for an easy afternoon. They had cut willow branches and staked them out in a line into the river so they formed a little fence that directed any passing fish toward the shore, where they would wind up trapped in the shallows. Silent Wolf swept a basket through the shallow water, plucked out a fish and flung it up onto the bank, where it flopped at Tupic's feet. It was so peaceful here now that Aiden could almost forget what was going on in the camp just a short distance away.

"Tupic," Aiden said, trying to find a way into the difficult subject. "When you were at the missionary school, did they ever give you a vaccination? Do you know what that is? A scratch on your arm, so you don't get sick?"

Tupic looked at him long and hard.

"For the smallpox?"

"Yes."

"I have the scratch."

Tupic stabbed his knife through the fish's spine to kill it, then slit the silver belly and scooped the guts out. "Is that what your powwow is about?" He tipped his chin toward the soldiers' camp, obviously aware of the tense consultations that had been going on.

"Yes. Some of the soldiers have smallpox. They didn't know," he added quickly. "They didn't have spots until today." Aiden looked away, embarrassed to remember how the soldiers had taunted the Indians. "We weren't really near the sick men," he went on. "Doc Carlos says it isn't very likely any of you have caught it. But if you have, about a week from now, you will be contagious." Tupic began to scrape scales from the fish. Aiden wished he would say something. "Doc asked for you not to ride off, because you could give it to others."

"I know about the smallpox. All Indians do."

"He says it's worse for Indians."

"Yes." Tupic tossed the cleaned fish into a basket. "You people." He spat out the last bit of peppermint candy. "All you bring with you are bad things."

As evening fell, driftwood campfires began to flicker throughout the camps, but there was no music or laughter. The mood was somber. Even the cattle and horses were still, as if they could sense the dread in the air. Aiden sat with Tupic, Silent Wolf and Clever Crow around their own little fire apart from the others. Many people just wouldn't believe that Aiden and the Indians were not immediately contagious.

"You absolutely can't catch it from any of them right now," Carlos explained over and over. "It takes at least a week. . . ."

But what if? *What if?* Smallpox was just too big a risk. Mothers gathered their children up and dosed them with castor oil and ipecac to make them purge, rubbed them with ointments to ward off the poisonous vapors. There were arguments and prayers, accusations and threats. The Hollingfords, though they had all been vaccinated, separated their wagons entirely from the rest of the group. They would not even let their hired girl draw water from the river until no one else had been near it for at least ten minutes.

Aiden was glad to be banished. Even from a hundred yards away he could feel the tension in the camp like the front edge of a storm, a dense wall of pressure promising worse on the way. But the Indian camp was like a little island of peace.

"It is gone out from our hands," Clever Crow said simply. "Eat fish."

They baked the fish on stones heated in the fire, seasoning them with sorrel, sage and wild onion. With part of his mind, Aiden knew the fish was delicious, but at the same time, he could have been eating old socks.

"Even when you can't change a thing," he asked, "don't you worry? Or pray?"

The three Indians had a prolonged conversation before Tupic translated for Aiden. "Your missionaries teach that suffering on earth means a better place in heaven. We believe that suffering on earth tells us that we should make better things on earth. The white man who made the vaccination did not worry or pray, he worked and used his mind."

Clever Crow tapped a finger to his head. "Mind"—he tapped his chest—"and strong spirit—make no more—" He said a Nimipu word.

"Suffering," Tupic translated. "No more suffering for all people."

The first spots appeared on the sickest soldier by sundown, tiny red pustules blooming across his face like a thousand ant bites. The plague had started. It would take a full month to finish. A month of pain and pus and burning, rotting skin that stuck to blankets and ripped off in great bloody strips. The soldiers with no symptoms kept far away from those already diagnosed. The battalion had no medic. The best Lieutenant Gryffud could come up with was an apprentice carpenter who had built coffins for an undertaker and so was not uncomfortable with death.

"Surviving is mostly about food, water and keeping clean," Doc Carlos explained. "And luck." He showed the carpenter how to roll a patient and prop bolsters under him so the sores didn't stick at any one place. He showed him how to drip water into the side of a sick man's mouth so he didn't choke.

"With healthy young men like this," Carlos said, "you might have two out of three live if you take good care of them."

It was dark when Aiden saw Carlos appear like a specter at the edge of their campfire, carrying a kettle, waiting silently to be invited in.

"I've brought some kind of tea," he said. "Your sister collects all sorts of flowers and plants," he said to Aiden. "I thought it better to bring it myself. Might as well keep her away from your little quarantine here—even though it's ridiculous." He sighed. "People will come to their senses soon."

"Please come sit," Tupic invited politely, getting to his feet and waving Carlos to a place on the upwind side of the fire. Carlos folded himself cross-legged on the ground.

"Oh—do you have cups? Sorry, I didn't think about that." His voice was hoarse and he looked very tired. Aiden realized he had probably talked more that day than he had during the whole trip so far.

"Yes," Tupic said. He took out three enamel mugs and Carlos filled them. Tupic then handed one to Aiden and one to Carlos. "We will share," he explained as he passed the last mug to his uncle.

"It's supposed to strengthen the blood," Carlos said. "I don't know much of plant medicine." The Indians passed the mug around, sniffing the brew and discussing what might be in it. Whatever it was, they seemed to approve of its medicinal value, though Tupic didn't know any of the English names for the plants they identified.

"Have you actually seen it?" Aiden asked Carlos. "The smallpox?"

"Yes. Twice during the war."

"Is it bad as they say?"

"No." Carlos gazed into the fire and sipped the tea. "It's worse. Whatever anyone says, it's worse." He leaned back on his elbows and stared at the fire. His dark eyes were glassy and blank. "I've seen death in a hundred disguises," he said.

"Sometimes she dresses in lace and waltzes in on a summer night, sometimes she hides beneath a hood and scratches through the frost of winter. Sometimes she wears brass and braid, sometimes velvet slippers." He tipped his head and looked up at the stars. Aiden had never heard Carlos talk this way.

"But this death is the worst," he went on quietly. "This death is a devil child playing with a paintbox, just spattering all over. You reach out to grab its hand and make it stop, but you find this devil child is made of smoke."

Tupic softly translated the doctor's words. He must have captured the harsh poetry as well, for Silent Wolf nodded.

"But here's the irony." Carlos pulled his jacket tighter, as if he were suddenly embarrassed. "Smallpox probably saved my life." He shifted back to his usual, more distant manner. "Without it, I would probably be just another beggar in the gutters of Madrid right now."

"What do you mean?" Aiden asked.

"These days we grow the vaccine in cows," Carlos explained. "But long ago the only way to vaccinate was from person to person. The king of Spain wanted to bring the vaccine to the colonies in the New World. So he collected some orphan boys and put them on a ship where doctors kept the vaccine alive across the ocean by passing it from boy to boy."

"They gave smallpox to the boys?" Tupic asked, clearly horrified.

"It was cowpox—a milder disease, but yes," Carlos explained. "When one boy got sick, they scratched the sores on his arm with a quill, then took the same quill and scratched the arm of the next boy. This was 1803, only a few years after Edward Jenner discovered vaccination. It was a crude method, but it worked. The vaccination was brought to the Caribbean and South America. None of the boys died. In reward for their service, they were brought back to Spain and given educations."

He pushed a stick farther into the fire and an explosion of sparks lit up his troubled face.

"My grandfather was one of those orphan boys." He curled his long fingers around the warm mug, as if the thought of the ocean voyage had given him a chill.

"With his education, he studied and became a doctor, as did my father after him. Without that education—well, an orphan had little chance in the world."

Tupic translated the story to his uncle and cousin, hesitating over parts. There were no Nimipu words for *ocean voyage, colonies* or *vaccination;* but more difficult for all of the Indians was understanding the idea of an orphan. Tupic translated it as a child with no one to take care of it, but Clever Crow frowned in puzzlement. They discussed it for some time.

"We still don't understand," Tupic said finally. "How can a child have no one to care for it? If the parents are dead, it is the duty of the grandparents, aunts and uncles."

"Sometimes there aren't any."

"If all the family is dead, it is the duty of the tribe. Even the enemy child taken as slave after battle is protected. Why should anyone be an orphan?"

Aiden stared at the fire. What possible answer was there to that? He looked at Carlos, but if the doctor had any answers, they were not on offer that night. All five fell silent. The night grew cool against their backs as the generous fire sent sparks into the vast, indifferent sky.

Aiden saw the sparks in his dreams, a whirling tornado of red flickers that spun through the camp singeing everyone it touched. He saw Maddy lying on the ground, screaming with pain as angry red blisters covered her skin. Aiden woke in a panic, his heart pounding. It was just a dream, he told himself. But then he sensed that something really was wrong. He leaned up on one elbow and stared into the darkness. Carlos had awakened too. Then, out of the corner of his eye, Aiden saw Silent Wolf roll out of his buffalo skin and throw it over the fire.

"Man and horse," the Indian whispered. He grabbed the knife from his belt and crouched low. Clever Crow was also alert. He put his hand over Tupic's mouth and gently shook him awake. The moon was waning but was still bright enough to show the shape of a man leading a horse, walking toward them from the bluff. As the man got closer, Aiden saw he was carrying a saddle and bridle, leading the horse with a halter rope. The man hadn't seen them.

"It's Sergeant Todd!" Aiden whispered to Carlos. Even in the starlight he recognized the man's knobbed shoulders and wiry frame. Todd stopped about thirty feet away, glanced back toward the camp, then slipped the bridle over the horse's head. The horse gave a nervous sidestep. Todd threw the saddle on, reached under the horse's belly, grabbed the girth strap and began to fumble it into place.

"That's one of the German brothers' horses!" Aiden whispered. He recognized the distinctive white sock on the horse's left forefoot. "He's stolen it—he's escaping!"

"Shhh!" Carlos pulled him down. "He's also armed."

Aiden saw the bulge of a pistol on Todd's hip and the long barrel of a rifle slung across his back.

"We can't let him go!"

Carlos squeezed Aiden's arm. "Wait! Can you throw a rock that far? Hit the horse?" Aiden nodded. He wriggled over to the fire, where they had made a ring of stones, and reached his hand under the buffalo skin. The rocks were still hot and his fingers jerked reflexively as he touched them, feeling for one small enough to throw.

Todd got the girth strap through the buckle. Half a minute more and the man would be riding away. Aiden and Carlos watched and waited until Todd started to tighten the strap; then Carlos tapped Aiden's back. Aiden jumped to his feet and pitched the rock at the horse, smacking it square in the middle of the rump, then dropped back down in the grass. The horse reared and whinnied. Up in the camp, a dog began to bark, then another and another. That was all the alarm they needed. Soon shouts rang out and a bugle sounded from the army camp. Aiden saw Sergeant Todd frantically trying to mount as the frightened horse wheeled away from him. He got one foot in the stirrup, swung into the saddle and kicked the horse. Now he was galloping straight toward the five hiding men. Carlos flung himself on top of Aiden, smashing his nose into the rough grass. Aiden felt the hoofbeats in his chest, but when the horse was just a few feet away, it balked and reared. The saddle slipped and Todd fell to the ground. He was on his feet in seconds, his gun drawn.

"Goddammit!" he gasped. "God damn! Who's there? Stand up, all of you, where I can see!" He waved the pistol back and forth, unsure which of the shapes to aim at. Shouts rang out from the bluff and lanterns began to flicker.

"I'm about to start shooting!" Todd's voice was pitched high with nerves.

"All right," Carlos said calmly. "Don't shoot. We're getting up." Slowly they all got to their feet.

"Go back to your unit," Carlos said. "Leave the horse, we won't identify you."

"Like hell!"

"We'll say the horse just ran off."

"With a saddle and bridle on?"

"We'll hide the saddle," Aiden suggested.

"Just go back," Carlos urged.

"And die of smallpox? I don't think so!"

"If you have it and run away, you'll die anyway."

"But I'll be drunk and whoring when I do," Todd spat. "You're the doc, ain't you?" He glanced nervously back at the bluff. The soldiers couldn't see them yet, but they certainly knew the general direction the noise had come from, and the fire was still smoldering beneath the leather, sending out a drift of smoke that anyone could smell. The soldiers' camp was only a hundred yards away; it wouldn't take them but a minute or two to find Todd.

"Get your ass over here, Doc." Todd waved the pistol at him. "And don't you try nothing, smart boy! I got plenty bullets for all of you! And I don't mind shooting Injuns especially. You fix that saddle!" Todd pointed the gun at Carlos. "Know how to do that, Mr. Doctor?"

"Yes." Carlos walked toward the horse. It was a well-trained

151

animal and, despite its fright, stood quietly as Carlos took the reins. He patted its neck and made soothing sounds to calm it.

"Hurry up!"

Carlos slid the saddle back into place and lifted the flap to tighten the girth. Aiden saw a dozen soldiers trotting toward them, a line of shadows in the moonlight.

"Now get on!" Todd ordered. "I'll ride behind you. No tricks—I will shoot you dead."

"There!" A cry rang out. The soldiers had seen them. The line quickly converged and galloped toward them.

"God damn!" Todd knew there wasn't time to escape now. He grabbed Carlos's arm, pulled him back from the horse, twisted his arm up behind him and stuck the pistol against the side of his head, using him as a shield.

"Stop there!" Todd shouted at the soldiers. "Stop now or I swear I'll kill the doctor!"

"Whoa!" Lieutenant Gryffud held up his hand and the soldiers halted.

"I got the doc here!" Todd said. "I got a gun right to his brain, can you see that?"

"I can see," Gryffud said.

Jackson, the German brothers and several other men were approaching on foot with lanterns, throwing ghostly shadows over the ground.

"Surrender now, Sergeant," Gryffud said. "And I promise you won't be hanged."

Todd laughed. "Oh yes, I do prefer the firing squad!" He jabbed the gun hard against Carlos's head.

"I give you my word—you won't be executed."

"So what? So I can go back and catch the pox? Or just rot in jail my whole life? That don't sound so good either!"

Aiden felt Tupic nudge him and turned. Silent Wolf caught his eye, looked down at his bow, then nodded at Aiden.

"I'm riding out now!" Todd shouted. "And Doc here is coming with me."

"I can't let you do that, Sergeant," Gryffud said. One of the soldiers slowly began to ease out to one side, trying to flank the man.

"You halt, goddammit!" Todd drove his knee into the back of Carlos's, knocking him to the ground. Aiden heard the cold metal click of the hammer being cocked.

"You tell them put those guns down!"

"I can't do that," Gryffud said.

"You know I'll kill this man! And shoot two or three more of you before you kill me—you do know that!"

Gryffud hesitated. The soldiers evidently knew it was true, for most lowered their guns even without the lieutenant's order. Aiden looked down at his bow. Silent Wolf was a better shot, but no Indian would dare shoot a soldier, even a deserter with a hostage. If anyone was going to shoot Todd, it would have to be Aiden.

"Let the doctor go and I'll let you go," Gryffud offered. "Go on and ride out."

"You think I'm an idiot?"

"Then take me instead. These people have nothing to do with us," Gryffud said. His booming voice was shaky, but he seemed to have found some sense of command since his dithering that afternoon, Aiden thought. Todd rocked back and forth a little, considering.

"No, no, no, I don't think so." He jabbed the gun harder into Carlos's head and pulled on his twisted arm. Carlos grunted. "Get up!" Todd took a step backward, pulling Carlos with him. Aiden slowly squatted down, keeping his eyes fixed on Todd. Could he do it? Could he actually kill a man? For his shot would have to kill. A wounded Todd would certainly empty his pistol in rage.

Carlos had talked about death in different guises, but to Aiden, death had always been invisible. His father was plowing, and then lay dead in the furrow. His mother blinked, then did not. Ada had breath, then none. But this death would have weight and time. He looked up at the stars, but there were no celestial answers beaming down for him. Someone was going to die, Carlos or Todd, and his not choosing would still be a choice.

So.

Aiden pushed away the questions and brought his mind around to the work of it. An arrow to the chest would have to slip between the ribs to pierce the lung. There was a fifty-fifty chance of hitting a rib and bouncing off. A strike in the flank would be easy but might not even knock the man down right away. The only certain killing shot was to the neck. Aiden had hit plenty of bull's-eyes from greater distances. He had also missed. And he had never tried it when a miss could have such dire consequences. If the arrow went two inches one way it would miss entirely. Two inches the other way and it would hit Carlos. Part of his brain was oddly surprised to find the other part doing these cold calculations. But if Todd got on the horse with Carlos as hostage, Aiden knew Carlos would be dead. And Maddy was in love with him.

He didn't know why that occurred to him just then, but it did. It was like a blindfold lifting off his eyes. He had seen the looks between them, the way they kept a careful distance, but the way that distance always felt charged, like the air before a thunderstorm. She was too young, he was too damaged; Aiden didn't like it, but it was there regardless, and he would not have it ended this way. Carefully he reached down, drew an arrow out of the quiver and shifted it to his right hand.

Keeping his eyes on Todd, he felt for the bow. Todd seemed to have forgotten about them, but Aiden knew the smallest sound would panic him. He fitted the arrow, stood and drew the bow. Blood pounded at the sides of his head, but when his fingers curled around the string, he felt suddenly calm and steady. A good shot came from stillness. Time stopped. He slowly let out his breath and focused on the small target. He let the arrow go. He could see it move slowly through the air. He could hear the sharp point punch through the tough neck muscles and the soft whooshing pop as it pierced the throat. He saw Todd's head slowly snap to his left, as if giving an exaggerated shrug. He didn't hear the man hit the ground. He didn't even hear the shouts and gunshots that followed.

Things happened and people moved around and sounds were made, but Aiden couldn't hear them. Todd lay motionless on the ground. Gryffud dismounted, walked slowly over and fired one shot into Todd's head. Friedrich caught his horse. Carlos walked off alone into the darkness. A shooting star blazed across the sky. But all Aiden heard was the river and the wind and Sergeant Todd's blood bubbling softly out of his wound.

"You all right?" Jackson stood in front of him.

"Yeah." Aiden blinked and things got more normal. "Is Carlos all right?"

"Yes."

"You sure?"

"He's walking, ain't he? He went off. The way he does. Joby will catch him up."

Silent Wolf pulled his buffalo skin off the fire. The leather was singed and smoking. He threw it on the ground to cool. The breeze spun through the coals and made them glow anew, casting yellow flares of light on the men nearby. Aiden put the bow down and turned his face away from the fire.

"Is there something I should do now?"

"Like what?"

"I don't know. You ever killed a man?"

"Yeah."

"What did you do after?"

"Buried him. Took his boots and buried him." Jackson spat a stream of tobacco juice. "Soldiers will tend to that."

One of the soldiers led a horse over. Two men lifted the limp body onto the saddle. Gradually the army began to vanish into the darkness beyond. Tupic threw some more driftwood onto the fire. Silent Wolf sat down in the shadows and began a soft chant. Clever Crow came up to Aiden and rested both his hands on Aiden's shoulders and murmured some words.

"It is prayers," Tupic explained. "For the warrior who has killed in battle. Silent Wolf chants to send the bad spirit away."

"Well, that's welcome." Jackson nodded. Aiden didn't know what to think. Prayers hadn't ever done any good before; he wasn't sure what they were supposed to do now.

"Come sleep back with the wagons," Jackson said. "Never can know if a dead man had friends, though I'm not thinking that likely with that son of a bitch."

"They don't want me there."

"You ain't catching. Doc said so."

"I don't think I want to be among people right now."

"You did no wrong here," Jackson said. "That man needed killing." He slung his rifle up on his shoulder and picked up his lantern. "Still, it ain't like shooting wolves, is it?"

"No," Aiden replied. "Nothing like that."

The wagon camp was surprisingly quiet. People had been wakened by the commotion, but once the men all returned and word went around that the stolen horse had been recovered, most went back to sleep. The whole thing had happened so quickly. It wasn't fifteen minutes, Aiden realized, from bugle call to blood on the ground. Jackson ordered the men who had been there to shut up until morning. The gunshots were explained as a soldier matter. Gossip would be thick tomorrow, Aiden knew, but for now only a handful of men knew what he had done. Even Maddy, who knew he was camped out there and waited to hear he was safe, didn't know the drama had involved him so directly. It was easy for Marguerite to coax her back to the bed of fragrant quilts.

Back at Jackson's wagon, William Buck and the widower, who had been left behind to guard the camp, were awake and eager to hear the story, but Jackson stopped their questions cold with a glare. He pulled a key out of his pocket, unlocked a wooden box and pulled a stoneware jar out of its bed of straw. He uncorked the bottle, took a long drink, gave a sigh of satisfaction and wiped his mouth on his sleeve. He turned to Aiden.

"You ever drink whiskey before?"

"No."

"Then use a cup, else you'll choke."

Aiden obediently pulled his tin cup out of his kit bag and held it while Jackson poured out a generous amount. Cup or not, the whiskey still made him choke and burned all the way down, but soon a warm, peaceful feeling flowed through his whole body. All the jitters and awfulness melted away. He felt his mind go soft and easy.

22

Aiden woke with a chill. When he groped for his blanket, a sharp pain stabbed through his right hand. He looked at it and saw red spots on his fingers. He sat up with a gasp. His first thought was smallpox, but then he remembered picking up the hot rock from the fire. It was only little blisters. He felt a flood of relief. He gingerly pushed back the blanket and got unsteadily to his feet. It took a few minutes for the world to sort itself out. It was barely light but people were already breaking camp, eager to get miles between them and the soldiers' pestilence.

He saw Doc Carlos walking toward him.

"The Indians want to talk with us," the doctor said without overture. His voice was hoarse and he had deep circles under his eyes.

"What? Why?" Aiden's head felt foggy and thick.

"We have to hurry, the wagons are moving soon."

"Yes, sure." A breeze brought the scent of carbolic soap, and Aiden noticed that Carlos's hands were raw and pink from scrubbing and his hair was slightly damp.

"Did you take some kinda whole bath or something?" Aiden asked.

"Yes."

"In the middle of the night?"

"I was covered in blood," he said flatly, clearly not eager to discuss it any further. "Come on."

Clever Crow, Silent Wolf and Tupic were waiting for them down on the river plain, near where they had camped the night before. Clever Crow wore a beaded band across his forehead, with three eagle feathers on each side. Silent Wolf and Tupic both wore beaded belts. They had painted designs with charcoal on the necks of their horses. It was clearly a more formal meeting than Aiden had expected. Clever Crow greeted them in English but then nodded to Tupic and began to speak in his own language.

"Our hearts are heavy today," Tupic translated. "But at the same time they fly—are free, I mean—ah, like the heart of a bird—" He faltered and tried again. "When men go through a—trial, a challenge—it brings the, ah—the touch—of our spirits—closer."

Tupic paused and turned to Clever Crow. They had a quick exchange, then Tupic relaxed a little. "My uncle speaks in a way that is difficult for me to translate. It is for cere-monies or important talks," he explained. "It is a way of speaking that I don't know how to put in English. It is both formal and like close family will speak, or friends when they have traveled long together. There are many more—colors—to the words. Do you see?"

He paused again and Carlos and Aiden nodded.

"We come to ask what you call a favor, but in our lan-guage, it isn't a favor. It is something we need, but that we expect you will do because it is right and necessary; so not a favor in your sense exactly. Can you understand that?"

"I think so," Aiden said.

"All right. Dr. Carlos." Tupic's tone became very formal. "We believe you are wise in the way of white man's medicine. We ask you to make vaccine for our people."

"What?" Carlos said, obviously blindsided by the request.

"We will pay you with many horses."

"I can't." He looked directly at Clever Crow. "It isn't the payment; I'm sorry, I just can't."

"You said last night the vaccine is made in cows," Tupic said, dropping the more formal speech. "There are many cows here. We will pay for cows as well. My people are rich in horses."

"It isn't that," Carlos said. "I would do it if I could, of course. I just don't know how."

"But other doctors before you figured how to do it, didn't they?"

"Yes—yes," Carlos said. "And I know generally how it's done, but even then, it takes time—several weeks, I think—to make a vaccine in a cow. I could experiment, but it still wouldn't help you in time."

"Then do as your king did with the ship of orphans," Tupic said, tapping the vaccination scar on his own arm. "Take my vaccine and give it to my cousin and my uncle."

Carlos pressed his fingers hard against his eyes. "It doesn't work that way. I am sorry. You were vaccinated too long ago. If there was anything I could do for you, believe me I would."

Clever Crow, Silent Wolf and Tupic spoke together in their language.

"We understand that there is no vaccine," Tupic translated. "But there is time, yes? Seven days—before we make others sick, this is right?"

"Yes," Carlos said cautiously.

"My uncle fears that other soldiers travel like these and

161

might be sick. These soldiers might take the smallpox to other Indians. We will ride to Indian places and bring the warning. After one week, we will make a camp alone away from all people. We will not bring the sickness to our people."

"No," Carlos protested. "If you do get sick you will need care. Stay with us. I will take care of you."

Clever Crow spoke and Tupic translated. "Our guardian spirits will care for us."

"Smallpox doesn't mean you have to die," Carlos said. "Many people recover. But you will need someone to take care of you—to bring you food and water."

Clever Crow shook his head and spoke again while Tupic translated.

"He says if we keep our people from the smallpox it doesn't matter if we die. He says this is a selfish act for us. If it is our time to die, we will live very well in—the spirit world. If we keep others away it will not be so crowded. We will have the best cuts of buffalo. We will have the fat from the hump and the tongue and the marrow all to ourselves. We will eat great baskets of berries. All this because we keep other of our people from crowding in. This is his decision. This is what his spirit has told him to do."

"Goodbye, Wet Pony." Clever Crow smiled at Aiden. "Many more river for you. Every river make you more—strong." He gathered up his reins and turned his horse around. Silent Wolf followed.

"Goodbye, Aiden," Tupic said. "In a different world, I would keep you as my friend."

"Yes." Aiden nodded and held out his hand. "I would like that different world."

"Gentlemen." Gryffud nodded as Aiden and Carlos returned to the camp. "I want to apologize for the events of last night," he said with a stiff formality. "Sergeant Todd was under my command, and as such I am responsible for his actions, which I deeply regret."

He looked as if he expected one of them to say something, but the awkward silence was broken only by the clink of harnesses as the first wagons started to move out.

"Thank you, Doctor, for tending to my men. And thank you . . ." He looked at Aiden and faltered. Aiden almost laughed. What was he going to say? *Thank you for an arrow in the throat; thank you for a geyser of blood in the starlit sky?*

"Here." Gryffud took out two rolls of paper. "It's nothing really, just some drawings. Your sister," he said as he handed one to Aiden, then gave one to Carlos. "Mr. Jackson said you didn't have anyone, so I drew a general scene for you." Gryffud turned bright red with embarrassment as he realized what he had just said to Carlos. "I mean—ah, I drew daily life in the wagon train."

Aiden unrolled his picture and saw sketches of Maddy. She was laughing in one, running in another. There was a sketch of her carrying water, and it looked as if she might walk off the page. There was a profile of just her face, and she looked serious and beautiful.

"They're brilliant," Aiden said. "They could be from a book."

"Thank you." Gryffud relaxed and turned a lighter shade of pink. Jackson rode up.

"Lieutenant." He tipped his hat. "We're moving out."

"There's a small fort, an outpost really, about three days'

ride from here, on the Laramie River, just between the two ranges," Gryffud said. "It doesn't even have a name, though most call it Fort Nowhere."

"I reckon I know the place," Jackson said. "Used to be a fur depot."

"If you want to avoid Fort Laramie, I believe you'll pass by there instead. I'd be grateful if you would carry some letters."

Jackson nodded and took the packet, eager to be off.

"I trust you will personally convey the urgency of our situation," Gryffud added. "I have provisions for four or five days at best. I can't enforce a quarantine with starving men."

"I will convey." Jackson tucked the letters into the leather pouch. "I'm sure they'll send back supplies, and there seems to be game about, so you'll be just fine."

"I believe so," Gryffud said stoically. "Good luck to you, then." He turned and walked back to his camp, his short legs working hard to climb the slight bluff.

"We kept some coffee hot," Jackson said to Aiden and Carlos. "If you hurry."

"I need to talk to Maddy," Aiden said. "Tell her myself what happened before she hears it elsewhere."

Maddy didn't say much when he told her, but she went so pale that Aiden thought she was going to faint. He took hold of her hand and told it all as plainly as he could.

"I think I had to shoot him," he said. "I think he was a crazy man, and desperate."

Maddy stared beyond him to where Carlos was helping Joby hitch up the mules. Her eyes shone with tears. She brushed them away and took her brother's hand gently in her own.

"Come let me put some salve on your burns." She took him back to the Reverend True's wagon and found a jar of salve and a bit of cotton rag for a bandage.

"Do you feel bad for the killing?"

She studied his face, and Aiden found himself unnerved. He had lots of practice keeping himself unreadable to her. All through the terrible starving winter he had fooled her childish eyes with feigned confidence. But now that little girl seemed to have vanished entirely, and in her place was—who?

"I don't know," he said.

"You could do the Act of Contrition," she said. "I remember how it goes."

"What for?"

"Getting forgiven, I guess."

"By who?"

"Well—by God."

"God could have stepped in any time and he didn't, so I don't need him forgiving me anything now." He felt as if he might start crying himself and turned the feeling into anger. "Are you sorry Carlos isn't dead instead?"

"No. You know that."

"Then shut up about God." Aiden pulled his bandaged hand away. "God could have done a lot of things a whole lot better in this world. He could've left out smallpox, for one! So I ain't looking to him now for any damn Act of Contrition."

Aiden turned away.

"Stop—" Maddy grabbed his arm. Her blue eyes searched his face. "We're all right now," she said quietly. "We're going to be all right."

Aiden bit his lip and just nodded, not trusting his voice or words. Maddy ran her hand gently down his arm and patted the bandaged hand.

"Don't itch at it."

Once the wagon train was on the move, Aiden walked even farther out than he usually did. As the news of his killing Todd trickled through the group, people kept glancing at him and whispering. He didn't care. He just wished the sergeant's death would get out of his head. He kept seeing it over and over in his mind like a bad dream.

When the army camp was finally out of sight, people began to relax. In the bright light of day, reason prevailed again. Almost everyone in the wagon train had been vaccinated after all, and no one had really been in close contact with the sick men. At any rate, there was nothing anyone could do about it now one way or another. The usual work of a day on the trail was occupation enough for most people. No one had come on this journey expecting it to be easy. The Oregon Trail had some hard facts and figures.

"It's said there's a grave a mile," Jackson had told them bluntly at the start. "I've known some wagon trains to lose half their people to the cholera. But even without disease, there's starvation or thirst, storms, Indians, stampedes, rock slides, drowning—or pure awful accident. Any way you can think up to die is out there waiting. One out of ten is the average."

The reality was dire, but those committed to the journey were unmoved. Epidemics of measles or influenza regularly swept through cities, killing hundreds at a time. Mines caved in and farm animals trampled children. Childbirth killed one out of ten women. The only thing you could really count on anywhere was death, so the wagons rumbled on.

23

Aiden landed flat on his back and gave an exaggerated groan of pain. "Enough—I give up!" He looked up at the triumphant face of his opponent standing over him, shaggy blond hair bright against the blue sky. He was a ferocious wrestler—all thirty pounds of him. Aiden jumped to his feet, then swung the child up over his shoulder. "You beat me!" Cheers and laughter filled the air. The little boy howled and grabbed at Aiden's neck. Matthew Thompson was four years old, still young enough (and indulged enough by his older brothers) to believe he had really beaten Aiden in wrestling. A dozen other small boys jumped and shouted, tackled each other and rolled in the grass like puppies. It was late June, and the long summer evenings gave plenty of time to play. Only two days had passed since they'd left the soldiers behind in their plague camp, but there was a light-hearted air that evening.

"I think everyone is just tired of fretting," Jackson said as he sat on the back of his wagon watching the wrestling with the Reverend True. Since Aiden had shown the other boys the techniques Tupic had taught him, Indian wrestling had become the center of activity for the boys in the wagon train.

"I'll have a go now!" Peter Thompson jumped up to face Aiden. While the little boys were content with play, the older boys were actually interested in learning the technique. Peter was a good two inches taller than Aiden and had a long reach, but every time he lunged, Aiden stepped nimbly away.

"Watch here." Aiden tapped his chest. "Not my face. The face will lie." He darted his head to the right and Peter instinctively followed, but Aiden moved the other way. "Movement comes from the center." He could almost hear Tupic's voice in his ear telling him the same thing. There was so much more he wished he could have learned from the Indians. Aiden's moment of distraction was all Peter needed to lunge for his feet and take him down. Once they were on the ground, the larger boy had no trouble pinning Aiden. Like Matthew, Peter was good-natured, but he didn't share his little brother's need to crow. He gave Aiden a hand up, at which time John and Joe, the next-down brothers, promptly jumped on the both of them. The rough play went on until all were tired and dusty and parents came to herd their children home.

They were in the foothills of the Rocky Mountains now, and travel was more demanding. The next day they came to a place so steep they had to hitch two teams to each wagon to pull them up and slip blocks under the wheels as they went to prevent them from rolling backward. Despite the new challenges, they made good time and arrived at Fort Nowhere that afternoon.

The fort was a small collection of rough log buildings behind a wall of narrow tree trunks set upright in the ground. Aiden suspected the average Indian could get over this wall in a minute or so, and even the oldest and feeblest could breach it with a leg up. It was a lonely little outpost with only about thirty soldiers. Few wagon trains ever came here—most stopped at Fort Laramie, which was on the main part of the Oregon Trail about seventy miles north—so the soldiers were always eager for visitors.

"I'm going to ride up ahead," Jackson said to Aiden. "Explain our situation." But he hadn't gone even a hundred yards up the trail when a corporal came riding out to meet him. The soldiers in the fort had seen the dust cloud of the approaching wagon train.

"We're glad to see you," the corporal said, "but you can't enter. There's smallpox in Fort Laramie." He halted his horse some twenty feet from Jackson. "None of our soldiers are sick, but some have been up there lately, so we're under quarantine for the time being. You're welcome to camp in the clearing nearby, but the orders are to have no physical association." His eyes landed briefly on Polly and Annie, and his shoulders slumped with disappointment.

Jackson explained about Lieutenant Gryffud's detachment being in similar circumstances.

"We have a doctor with us, says we ain't catching," Jackson added. "But I do agree, might be a good thing for us to socialize from a distance."

The wagon train camped at the edge of the clearing, and it was agreed that the two groups would maintain a distance of twenty feet. Boundary lines were scratched out in the dirt. Jackson placed Lieutenant Gryffud's papers on a stump between the two camps, then walked back while the corporal came up to retrieve them. There was some debate over whether smallpox could be passed on through objects. Carlos said not likely, but some feared anyway. Desire finally won out, however. The soldiers had newspapers

170

and magazines and even some books to pass along. People were bored and hungry for new things. Therese Thompson wanted a birthday present for her brother John, who was turning fourteen. She pleaded with Aiden to take him hunting to get him away from camp. Aiden knew that with so many soldiers around there would be little chance of finding game, but he figured they could at least shoot for practice. He went off with John and Peter and even let little Matthew tag along. Once they were gone, Therese, assisted by all the girls in the wagon train, carried on negotiations with the soldiers all afternoon.

"First she had to trade with our folks to get anything the soldiers might want," Maddy explained to Aiden later. "Then we had to negotiate across the stump for something John would actually like."

The girls had said no thanks to a belt, a pipe and a badly stuffed squirrel in a miniature Indian war bonnet. They weren't sure what "French postcards" were, but Marguerite had advised against them. "I'm sure she was right," Maddy said. "Those Thompson boys never have been much interested in the *Atlas of the World*." Aiden said nothing. He didn't know what "French postcards" were either, but somehow didn't think the pictures would be of the French countryside. Aiden was glad to see Maddy engaged in some foolery. She had become so serious with her studies and spent far too much time lately with Doc Carlos and his books.

"So finally, Therese made the deal!" Maddy told him with some triumph. "She traded one jar of strawberry jam, which she got from her own mother for a promise to do all the baby's washing for the next week; six pencils, a gift from Marguerite; a peppermint stick—from Polly, but she made her give three hair ribbons! Also a perfumed handkerchief. That was my idea! Rose offered the handkerchief and Marguerite put some of her perfume on it," Maddy explained excitedly.

"So what did Therese trade all that for?" Aiden was already lost in the intricacies of the girlish dealings.

"Oh, a beautiful folding pocketknife with a polished bone handle. It was easily worth twice the jam and all the pencils at the very least."

"Shoot," Jackson laughed when Aiden told him later. "I reckon those soldiers would have swapped out their own teeth just to watch those girls scamper back and forth to the stump all afternoon."

Everyone cheered when John opened his present and was truly amazed at the splendid knife. There was little left in any wagon to make even the poorest sort of cake, but Mrs. Thompson opened another whole jar of jam and gave every child in the camp a half teaspoonful. They lined up, spoons in hand, then scampered off with their glistening treats, some to lick it slowly, others to pop in the whole sweet gob at once. As evening fell, one soldier played the fiddle and the emigrants and soldiers all danced. It was a queer way of dancing, with a twenty-foot gap between the two groups to keep the plague at bay, but out here it did not seem so odd. This was a new time in a new land, and so there had to be new dances.

24

A week later, as the fateful days of quarantine passed, people eyed each other suspiciously. They were afraid to cough, even when it was clearly from the dust. Carlos checked throats but saw no sores and felt no fevers. After the next week passed without symptoms, people grew more hopeful. Finally, three weeks after leaving the infected soldiers, with not a single person showing any trace of spot or sore, Doc Carlos declared the danger officially past. It felt like Christmas and Fourth of July rolled into one.

That evening Matthew Thompson was bitten by a rattlesnake while gathering wood. He died before morning and was buried at dawn. The grave was small but deep, for there were lots of brothers to dig him safely down where animals would never disturb his little body. He was the first of their group to die, but not the last.

Jackson led them deeper into the Rocky Mountains. With ropes and sweat and strain, they made their miles. Sometimes they traveled precariously along a trail so narrow that the wagon beds scraped the sides of cliffs. In the high passes, cold winds cut through their clothes. Down in the valleys, they lived in shadow with no horizons, the sun only dappled light through the trees. No one but Jackson had ever experienced anything like it. In the settled world of the East, trees had been cleared for hundreds of years, and even the thickest old stands were broken by farms and fields. Many felt claustrophobic and uneasy, but Aiden liked the dark forests. Out here the earth felt new and untouched. Even the rain felt different, sweeter and more nourishing. Above the tree line, the landscape was even more beautiful, so jagged and fierce it did not even seem to be the same world. It was late July, but some of the peaks were still covered with snow. For all the savageness of the place, there were also touches of gentle beauty. Tiny wildflowers covered the high meadows and sprang from between the rocks. Hawks and eagles soared overhead with harsh, lonely cries. Blue jays were unusually bold and curious up here. They would perch on the toe of your boot and take food from your hand.

Every morning Aiden woke feeling new. Even on days of backbreaking work, with double-teaming up steep trails, he felt a happiness he had never known before. He was excited, he was strong, he was walking into a brand-new world where anything seemed possible.

"I think I want to see more of the world for myself," he said to Maddy one night. "After I work off our passage, I'll work some more and save. Then we'll go off on a ship and see every country in the atlas. Maybe we can write a new atlas. This one is twelve years old now; I think a lot has changed."

"All right."

He looked at her, puzzled by the lack of enthusiasm.

"Do you not want to see the world now?"

"Yes." She looked away. "But maybe I have other things to do first."

"Other things? Like what?"

"I could go to school."

"Of course you'll go to school. I'll see to that."

"Not just regular school. I want to go to medical college."

"You can't. Girls can't do that."

"Maybe they can now. Marguerite says women can flourish in the West."

"Well, that's a ways off still. You're barely fourteen."

"There's a medical college in San Francisco."

"Fine, but we're going to Seattle. Don't worry; I won't let you be a housemaid. I'll find something better for you. Maybe a shopgirl—you're so good with numbers."

She twisted a stem of grass between her fingers and looked up at the distant peaks.

"Maybe I can work with Doc Carlos when he sets up his clinic. I can be his assistant. I can learn a lot from him, and we'll save money, and in a couple of years we'll both go to San Francisco for medical school. He needs a school degree too. Though he knows plenty more than the college people already, I think."

Aiden felt blindsided. "What are you talking about? You're not going to marry Carlos."

"I didn't say I was. I only said I could work with him."

There were a thousand arguments to be made against this. Aiden chose the simplest.

"No."

"Don't say no right now—"

"I will say. You're my charge."

"I am not your charge!"

"Carlos is not right in his own head, and I won't have him putting ideas into yours." He jumped to his feet.

"Stop, Aiden, don't go fight now!" Maddy grabbed his

arm. "It wasn't his idea! I haven't even talked to him, and if I did he would probably start a fight with you himself to keep me from it. It's just my own thoughts. I don't want to marry him or anybody. I just want my own chance. We aren't coming all this way to have ordinary lives! Let me work on my chance."

25

The wagon train crossed into Idaho Territory, and by the middle of August, as they neared Fort Boise, they were forced to join the main portion of the Oregon Trail. At first it was exciting to see so many other people. During the last three and a half months they had seen only six other wagon trains; now there were that many in a day. Sometimes the trail was so crowded that they moved in a cloud of dust from morning to night. Often there was no room to pass, and they were stuck behind another group for days. Thousands of wagon wheels had carved ruts two or three feet deep in places, and the numerous animals fouled the streams. They still had at least six weeks of travel ahead of them.

Food was still adequate but dull and tasteless. There were no wild greens to be found, and even dried vegetables were mostly gone by now. There was no game, not even a bird or rabbit anywhere near the trail.

"You'd have to go miles off to find anything wild alive," Jackson said. Lard was going rancid in the summer heat, so the corn bread tasted foul, and most people switched to corn-meal mush. But it was nothing they couldn't bear. Nothing ten thousand others weren't bearing with them in this long march west. So the thousands of them simply walked on.

In the Salmon River Mountains it rained for three days straight, a steady, determined rain, neither heavy nor dramatic but relentless and unchanging as multiplication tables.

Everything was damp and smelly, and even if they found wood for a fire (again, no easy task with so many people on the same trail), nothing ever really dried out. The trail turned to mud, sloggy and slippery, sucking at wagon wheels. One day Mr. Handeveld slipped and fell, startling his mule, which kicked him in the head. He was dead before word even got back to fetch Carlos. Two more died when their wagon overturned on a slippery pass and plummeted a hundred feet down the mountainside. The dead oxen provided welcome meat, though hauling the bloody chunks up the ravine was a tiresome business. The mood in the wagon train was silent and grim.

But finally one morning the rain stopped. By noon the sky was cloudless blue and the sun pounded a welcome warmth. Jackson called for an early camp so everyone could dry out. Soon clotheslines were strung wagon to wagon with sheets and shirts flapping in the breeze. Sodden canvas wagon covers actually steamed in the heat of the sun. Soaked shoes were set out on branches stuck in the ground until the camp looked like a bewitched village of stick-legged people buried upside down.

Aiden, having few possessions to dry out, took some fishing lines and the old tablecloth net down to the river to try his luck. The warm grass felt good on his bare feet, which were white and puckered after days in wet boots. He had only managed to catch a few small fish when he suddenly heard a noise in the bushes.

"Who's there?" He turned, expecting to see one of the children playing some game. But there was no reply. He felt the hairs on the back of his neck prickle. "Go on, say something or I'll shoot!" he called. Was it a bear? A mountain lion? He kept his eyes on the bushes where the noise had come from and edged up the bank to where he had left his bow. Then he heard a crack and a thump behind him, followed by a shriek loud enough to wake the dead. Something leaped on Aiden and knocked him to the ground, then nimbly rolled away before he had a chance to swing.

"Tupic!"

"My friend!" Tupic held out his hand and Aiden grasped it. But instead of shaking, Aiden pulled Tupic toward him and stuck out his leg to trip him. Tupic fell to the ground.

"Nice Indian trick!" Tupic laughed. Aiden pulled him up and the two embraced.

"You're well!" Aiden exclaimed.

"I am."

"And the others? Clever Crow and Silent Wolf?"

"My uncle was spared." Tupic frowned. "But Silent Wolf was very sick. We hear now he is getting better. He stays in a camp of the sick Indians. There are some missionaries and old women that care for them."

"Are there many sick?"

"No—maybe twenty in that camp."

"Tell me what happened." They sat down on the riverbank.

"After we left you, as we rode to make council, we hear the smallpox is already in many places," Tupic said. "Indian camps far away already have sickness."

"How many?"

"No one knows." Tupic threw a pebble into the water.

"How did you find us here?"

"My people are nearby now." Tupic seemed relieved to change the subject. "One day walk from here is our summer camp to fish for the salmon. It is a good season, and we come here to the trail every few days with fish to trade. I think this will be the right time for you to pass, so I ask for news of your wagon train. I ask about the group with the pretty cows and the leader called Jackson and the two blue wagons with all the yellow-haired children. And now I have found you." He looked at the two small fish on Aiden's string. "And I see you are a very bad fisherman."

"No, I am a good fisherman. These are very bad fish!"

"Clearly!" Tupic got up. "Come on, I will show you how to catch the bad fish."

They spent a quiet afternoon fishing, talking of small things. Tupic looked different, Aiden thought. He was not the rangy traveler Aiden had first met. His face could not be called plump, but the flesh now had a certain generous glow that only came from abundant food and a mother's solicitous care. But the light in his eyes had dulled and the playful energy was more subdued.

Tupic knew how to find dry branches in the wet woods, and he built a small fire to cook some of the salmon. Aiden had never tasted anything like it. The flesh was red, the skin crackled and crispy, with a juicy layer of fat just beneath it. It had been weeks since Aiden had eaten any fat and he craved it. Then Tupic took some roots out of his bag. They were about the size of a baseball and looked a bit like turnips.

"What are those?" Aiden asked.

"Camas," Tupic said. "It is our bread." He dug holes in the hot coals and popped the camas in to roast.

"Where do you grow it?"

"We do not grow it. The earth gives it to us. But this summer is very bad. So many wagons and cattle pass through and tear up the fields. The creeks are bad from your cattle. The elk are shot, everything is shot. You spoil all the land," Tupic said with a bitter tone that Aiden had not heard before.

Aiden stared into the glowing fire. In the distance, he could hear the noises of the hundreds of wagons camped nearby. It was true what Tupic was saying, he knew. He felt bad, but also angry. Where were they supposed to live? What were they supposed to eat? Who decided who got to live by the rivers full of fat fish and who had to scratch at the harsh Kansas prairie for barely enough food to survive?

"My people—white people—" Aiden said tentatively. "Where do you think we came from?"

Tupic nudged some of the coals up around the roasting camas. "We believe all peoples came from a great beast that lived in the Kamiah Valley long ago," he said. His tone was softer now, as if he was embarrassed to have spoken that way to a friend, especially a friend who had no more power to change things than he did to realign the planets. "The people were trapped inside the belly of this beast. But Coyote tricked the beast and went inside his belly. There he took five stone knives and cut out the heart," he went on. "Then Coyote cut the beast up, and from the pieces made the tribes. The Flatheads were made from the head of the beast; the Blackfeet came from the feet, and so on. As we tell the story now"—Tupic smiled—"white people were made from the asshole."

"Well, that may be true." Aiden couldn't help laughing. "But did you know that my people—white people—all once lived just like Indians do now? They probably don't teach you that in missionary school—hell, I think most white people would never admit it, but it's true. We weren't just born into cities and farms. In ancient times, we lived just like you do now, hunting animals and finding food. But the land can't support many that way."

"It has always taken care of our people."

"Have you never had bad years when there wasn't enough food?"

"Of course. But then we pray and fix our hearts to be right again with the spirits."

"How many children do your families have? Ones that live, I mean."

"Three, four, some more."

"All right, say that you have ten women in your village and each one has two girls that live." Aiden picked up a stick and scratched out the figures in the dirt.

"Each of these girls has two girls. Now there are forty new girls. Then each of them grows up and has two girls and so on. After eighty years, you have three hundred twenty girls. After a hundred years—ten women become six hundred and forty." He scratched out the numbers three times because he couldn't really believe them himself. But it was simple multiplication, even for him. "And that's not counting boys and men, or adding in the people who are still alive through all those years. I don't even know how to figure all that in. Still . . ." He tapped the stick on the calculations. "In five generations, it is more than a thousand people from just two."

Tupic looked at the numbers in the dirt.

Aiden picked up one of the little roots. "Will the earth give you a thousand camas every day of the year? How many salmon do you need to feed a thousand people? How many buffalo each day—twenty? Can your best hunters kill twenty buffalo every day?" He was annoyed with himself, for he felt as if he was scolding. But he knew starvation too well. And he knew the stories from Ireland, how a million or more people had died in the Great Famine only 20 years before. "And what about the Flatheads and the Paiute?" he went on. He felt oddly angry now, angry that he had to feel guilty. It was only numbers. Only the limited earth. "The Crow, the Cayuse, the Shoshone? All of the tribes you already fight with for land? Their numbers will grow the same way." Aiden spread his hand toward the mountains. "Even if we never came you would become too many."

"Indians have always taken land from other tribes," Tupic said. "But we take it as warriors. You don't come as warriors and kill us in battle. You sign papers, you make promises, then you shoot us all in our camps with our hands raised. You bring your Bible and your Constitution, then say, here—eat the pages when you are hungry. Here, melt the ink from the words and feed that to your babies."

"But we don't want to kill you for your land," Aiden said. "Most of us don't, anyway."

"Still you will take it."

"Yes," Aiden sighed. "We are more than you. So many more. You could kill us forever and there will still be more coming behind those, because we have nowhere else to go. More people, more guns, and trains coming soon. Until we can plow the sky and eat the stars, we will take your land." The sun fell behind a mountain peak and cast them into sudden gloom. "I don't know how to make it right," he said. "I don't know how to make it fair. But I don't want to meet you as a warrior in battle and kill you either. I would rather be your friend. I would rather fish."

Tupic stood up and rubbed out Aiden's multiplication with the toe of his moccasin. "I must go back now."

"I'm sorry, I didn't want to have such a dismal conversation with you. Come back with me to the camp; Carlos will be glad to see you. Stay the night. No more big talk—I promise."

"I must travel while there is light," Tupic said.

"I can get some peppermint."

"No. Thank you."

"I missed you," Aiden said. "I missed the way we were—friends."

"Yes." Tupic stared back at the camp, where smoke from cooking fires was starting to drift up. "Please give my respect to your sister and take the fish to your people. I wish you a safe journey."

26

In early September, they crossed out of the Blue Mountains, and the group that had come so far together now began to break apart. Near Fort Walla Walla about half would turn west and follow the Columbia River to the Willamette Valley. Jackson and the rest of them would cross the river and continue on north along the Cascade Trail to Seattle.

Hans and Friedrich (now calling themselves Hank and Fred) left at the split, apparently without breaking the hearts of Annie and Polly Hollingford, who were going on to Seattle. Eleven out of fifteen of their prize herd had made it across alive, including the two valuable bulls; a stunningly successful number. News of the fabulous stock had traveled before them with other wagon trains, so miles before they reached the cutoff, farmers began to appear on the trail, eager to bargain for a chance at the bulls. Some actually brought their cows to be bred right there, and the brothers soon had two bags stuffed with coins.

"We will name the first bullock after you, Mr. Jefferson J. Jackson!" Hank said.

The ferry landing at the Columbia River was like a carnival. Most wagon trains camped at least one night as groups broke up or formed anew according to their final destinations. There were tents and shacks offering everything from fresh vegetables (at exorbitant prices) to barbering. There was a tinker to mend pots and a cobbler for shoes. There were fortune-tellers, patent medicine salesmen and half a dozen land agents promising the best acreage in Oregon. But most of the commerce was small barter between emigrants. Children walked through the camp with outgrown shoes dangling from sticks, looking to trade for a bigger pair. Women met in little groups, their bonnets huddled together like ships in a harbor, trading baby clothes and books, tonics and salves.

It was a gorgeous September day, with a cloudless sky of brilliant blue. The world felt generous and easy. The only touch of gloom came from a blind fiddle player who sat by the ferry landing all day. He played poorly and only knew about a dozen tunes, but people tossed him pennies anyway, for it seemed bad luck not to.

"He is so dreary," Marguerite said. "What would it cost to have him not play for a while?"

There was one major ferry operator at this part of the river, plus two men who ran small rafts that could carry one wagon at a time. The big ferry could carry up to four wagons, depending on the river conditions. There was a turnstile on each shore where oxen plodded around and around, winding the heavy ropes that pulled the boat across. Two men on each side helped load and unload, then worked the guide ropes and handled the oxen. They were brusque, short-tempered men who had no tolerance for delay. They wanted three crossings an hour, and that meant having everyone lined up and ready to go exactly where and when they were told. It cost ten dollars a wagon, but there were plenty of wagons in line even at that price. Livestock were swum across, guided by Indians on horseback for ten cents a head. With so many wagons arriving at the same time, the wait this time of year could be two days, but Jackson had made arrangements to pay eleven dollars a wagon for priority crossing. The price, of course, had been collected with the general fee in the beginning. Those in other trains, unaware of the steep fare, either had to risk the cheaper small rafts or dig deep into emergency money. Some sold their jewelry. The Columbia, even at its mildest, was not a river to cross in bullboats or makeshift rafts.

Jackson had sixteen wagons to cross here. Aiden, the widower and the Kansas boys worked nonstop, helping to guide them onto the boats, while Jackson saw to the cattle. William Buck spent a lot of time directing and advising. The teams didn't like being harnessed but going nowhere and so had to be hitched up at the last possible minute. Most animals did not want to board. They balked at the first strange feel of being afloat and had to be dragged and whipped aboard. The deck was wet and slippery, and there was always danger from a shifting wagon or crazed animals. Aiden's arms were just about yanked out of their sockets and his legs were bruised from hoof kicks. When they were on the third trip, Aiden realized his sister was nowhere in sight.

"Where's Maddy?" he asked Reverend True.

"One of the ferrymen broke his arm last night," he said. "They asked Carlos to fix it properly. Don't worry, I just sent Joby to fetch them."

Aiden watched a flock of young Thompson children scamper past, with the older ones herding them diligently out of trouble. The little ones were never good with idleness. The family was still mourning the death of Matthew, but young children could switch more easily from grief to play, and a day this exciting could push away sadness for a while. Aiden saw the Kansas boys struggling to load the Hollingfords' stubborn mule and ran to help them.

Once that load was under way, he turned to the final four wagons to be sure they were ready to go. Finally it was an easy group, Aiden thought. Mr. Thompson had his two wagons all set, with Peter, John and Joe helping to hold the mules. Gabriel and Marguerite's oxen were calm animals by now, thanks to Joby's tending. The ferry captain had actually tried to hire the man away, after seeing how well he handled the animals, but Joby turned him down to stay with Carlos.

"I'm going to drive big teams in Seattle," he explained. "And see the Pacific Ocean waves." He wasn't actually sure what waves were, but was excited about seeing them.

Carlos and Maddy came running back just in time. They looked so happy and excited that for a few seconds Aiden felt cross. He was tired, bruised, wet and covered in crap. They looked as if they had come from a picnic.

"Oh, Aiden, you should have seen it!" Maddy's eyes were bright with excitement. "Doc nailed the man's elbow down to a board and twisted it right into place!"

"It wasn't the elbow itself I nailed," Carlos laughed. Aiden was startled. It was the first time he had heard the man really laugh. "You wrap a cloth around the elbow and nail that down, then put another nail in the board—"

"Then you tie a loop of cloth around the wrist and over

the nail," Maddy broke in. "Put a little stick through and twist it for traction. They gave him lots of whiskey first."

"You have to loosen the muscles," Carlos explained.

"He still screamed terribly," Maddy added. "Worse than Ma ever screamed for the babies, and it didn't take but a minute! But we pulled the bone exactly back into place! It was perfectly smooth—you could feel it!"

Carlos looked like a different man, Aiden thought. He looked content, confident—even happy.

"Well, I'm glad for you," Aiden said. "But the ferry is coming now—go on up," he said to Maddy, nodding toward the reverend's wagon. "Stay in the wagons for the crossing. Some of the mules may get spooked."

"Come sit on the cart," Carlos said. "I'll show you the arm muscles in the anatomy book so you see what we've done."

Aiden saw the look between them and bristled.

"Wait, Maddy." He caught her arm as Carlos walked off. "You should ride with Marguerite," he said.

"Why?"

"Well, um—she might be nervous."

"Of what?" Maddy asked. "We're crossing a river, not rounding Cape Horn!" She turned around with a twirl of her skirt and ran after Carlos without another glance.

"Stand by to load!" the boatmen shouted. Aiden ran to help guide the wagons on. Joby took the mules under his firm hand while Carlos and Maddy climbed up onto the cart and pulled out the anatomy book.

They loaded quickly. The Thompsons' two wagons were on the downriver side, with the reverend's wagon first on the upriver side, then Carlos's cart just behind them. As they pulled away from shore, Aiden felt a deep sense of relief. He could see the rest of their train already forming up on the other side, ready to move on. Jackson was eager to get away from the crowds and congestion and mud. Despite his soaked and stinking pants, Aiden felt good. Another three weeks or so and the long journey would be over. He would begin a new life in a new land where anything seemed possible.

"All on!" shouted the boatman as he lifted the rear gate and latched it into place.

"All away!" He waved to the men on the opposite side. The drover flicked his switch and the animals began to walk their slow circle, winding the rope to haul the heavy ferry across. Aiden stood at the front, leaning on the railing. He looked back and saw Marguerite sitting beside Gabriel on their wagon seat, her head on his shoulder, his arm around her. At the back of the ferry, he saw Carlos and Maddy. They sat a few feet apart, not touching at all, but in a way that was conscious and aching. The ferry lurched a little as it caught the current, then settled into the laborious trip. The river was all pale green and foaming white. Halfway across he heard Catherine, the Thompsons' three-year-old, scream with delight.

"Look! The cow is swimming! Cow is swimming!"

Aiden saw little Catherine's bright face, framed in golden curls, peeking out of the Thompsons' wagon. She squealed and pointed to the river. He turned to follow her gaze. There was indeed a cow in the water, just upstream of their ferry. It shouldn't have been there—the cattle were swum across downstream—but Aiden wasn't worried at first, for there were hundreds of cattle here and any number of mishaps that could cast one in at the wrong place. Aiden saw a flash of its terrified white eyes and the desperate twitch of its black nose. Then he heard shouts and screams and saw the real danger.

One of the makeshift rafts upriver had snapped its lines and was now loose in the swift current, rushing straight toward them. There were people in the water, two tiny faces and a desperate flailing hand. He saw the ferrymen on the opposite bank whipping the oxen to tow their own ferry out of danger, but Aiden knew there was no way they would avoid collision.

"Hold on!" he shouted. "Everyone hold on!" But who could be strong enough to hold against this? And what should they hold on to? He grabbed the railing and braced himself.

The cow hit first, then the raft, squashing the animal so hard between the two boats that its belly split open and green stomach muck shot up and spattered over the deck. Then Aiden heard wood crack. He could even smell it splintering. He was thrown up into the air and landed hard on his back. All around was crashing and breaking, a fractured chaos of wheels and hooves, sliding, slamming; then, finally, a terrible pause. He felt weight on his legs and water rushing over him, but when he pushed himself up he found with relief that it was only inches deep. The two ferries were smashed together, the force of the crash tipping them both up in the middle like a mountain range. In the tumbled, twisted wreckage, it took Aiden long seconds to sort things out. The wagon on the other ferry had skidded into Gabriel's wagon, knocking it like a domino into the Thompsons' wagon. The reverend's front axle had broken and the wagon wheel now pinned Aiden to the deck. He wriggled and pulled but could not get himself free.

"Help! Aiden, help!" He saw Mrs. Thompson, clutching Catherine and hanging on to the seat. Her wagon had been knocked half off the ferry. The front wheels and most of the box balanced on the edge of the deck, with the rear wheels in the river. The two front mules were in the river, already half sucked beneath the ferry, while the rear two were on their sides on the deck, kicking wildly at the sky. The heavy canvas cover had been washed back and was caught in the current behind like a great sail, threatening to drag the wagon off at any moment.

He saw Catherine's face pressed up against her mother. Water rushed into the wagon box, swirling around their skirts. Therese had managed to brace herself against the side and held her sister Rose by one arm, while Rose clung to baby Andrew.

"Help us!" Mrs. Thompson screamed.

"I'm stuck!" He turned and pressed both hands against the wagon wheel but still could not pull himself free or even gain an inch. He looked around for a piece of rope, anything to throw, but there was nothing.

"Therese!" he shouted. She looked terrified but resolute. "Look—there—see the brake stick? Grab that and pull yourself up. Hand me Rose and Andrew."

"Hold him!" Therese shouted to her sister. Rose, a skinny girl of eleven, shook with fear, but wrapped her arms around her baby brother as tightly as she could. Therese, still keeping a grip on the girl's narrow wrist, reached up and got one hand around the wagon brake handle.

"Good!" Aiden shouted. "Pull yourself up!" Therese felt for footing on the submerged boxes, pulled with all her might and managed to wrench the three of them out of the water and up to the front. She pushed Rose and the baby toward Aiden. Aiden grabbed Andrew first. He was plump and slippery, but Aiden managed to get a good hold on the hem of his dress and yanked as hard as he could. The baby looked very surprised, but when Aiden finally reeled him in, he did not even cry.

"Here, up here!" Reverend True shouted. Aiden craned his neck and saw True lying on top of the wrecked wagon above, reaching down. Aiden flung baby Andrew up like a sack of flour, and True caught him. Then Therese pushed Rose up and Aiden grabbed Rose's arm and pulled, her bony knees knocking his ribs as she scrambled over him to safety. Therese kept hold of the brake with one hand and stretched back to take Catherine from her mother. She dragged the child through the water and handed her up to Aiden, who passed her on to True. The big blue wagon gave a terrible lurch, and Mrs. Thompson slipped and tumbled back into the wagon box.

"Come on, Ma!" Therese cried, still clinging to the brake stick. "Crawl on the boxes! Come on!" Aiden craned his neck, looking for Maddy. He saw that the Thompsons' other wagon had been knocked on its side. It was still on the ferry but the heavy canvas cover was in the river, trapping the rest of the family beneath it. Aiden could see hands and heads desperately pressing against the canvas as they all struggled to get out before they drowned. Peter had been on the front seat and so had jumped free and was now struggling to get the mules up, hoping, Aiden guessed, to haul the wagon up or at least hold it in place.

"Ma! Come on!" Therese shouted. Slowly Mrs. Thompson made her way up through the floating boxes and blankets, struggled through the rushing water and caught her daughter's hand. Together, they clutched at the sides, scrambling over shifting crates, and made their way forward. Aiden reached as far as he could and caught Therese's hand. He felt the metal wheel rim cut into his back. But he caught her hand and pulled as hard as he could. Her wet skirts made her heavy as a log. But finally Therese grabbed hold of the wheel rim and reached back to help pull her mother. They clambered up to safety. Aiden saw Marguerite still on top of their wagon, holding Andrew and Catherine, while Rose clung to the seat.

"Ed! Ed!" Mrs. Thompson screamed for her husband.

"Where's Maddy!" Aiden shouted to Gabriel. "Where's Maddy?" The river was loud as a hurricane.

"Oh God, there's Paul!" Mrs. Thompson screamed. The boy suddenly popped out from under the canvas. Aiden saw Peter stumble down the steeply pitched deck and grab him. Paul was choking and gasping for breath.

"Help—they're all drowning!" Mrs. Thompson wailed.

"Peter! Here!" True threw him a rope. The first toss was wild so he had to pull it in and try again. The second time Peter caught the end and quickly tied it around Paul. True hauled the child up to safety. Then Aiden saw a flicker of sun on a knife blade and suddenly the canvas split open. John's head poked out. He had sliced them all free. Three more heads popped out, gasping for breath. Joe, a gangly boy of twelve, clutched his little sister Monica. Ed, their father, shoved them all forward. Quickly they slithered up through the cut, clawing their way over the sinking canvas to the edge of the ferry, where Peter pulled them to safety.

"Where's—Maddy?" Aiden gasped. The bright sun hammered down on them all, cheerful and golden as a picnic.

"Doc's got her." Reverend True's voice was faint above. He climbed down from his teetering wagon. "Help me lift this!" he yelled at the Thompson men.

The Thompson brothers and their father all heaved on the buckled wheel that had pinned Aiden. The first attempt did nothing. A small, twinkling bottle of perfume crashed out of the wagon, rolled past Aiden and broke open, flooding the air with heavy scent. Then Mrs. Thompson and the rest of the children squeezed in to help, and this time they managed to shift the wheel just enough for Aiden to drag himself free. His body was numb and he struggled to get his feet working. He could see the shoreline getting closer. A dozen men were pulling on the ropes. All around him the chaos and noise continued. The foundered animals were the worst of it, with their desperate bellowing and their legs flailing everywhere. But finally Aiden crawled a few feet through the debris, pulled himself up on a crate and saw Maddy.

The doctor's cart was on its side, and she and Carlos both sat up against it. They might have been a courting couple leaning against a rock. But their expressions were hardly tranquil. Carlos had one arm wrapped in a rope on the cart and the other in a desperate grip around Maddy. He had one leg on top of her and the other braced against the gate at the back of the ferry. It was a precarious hold against the tilted deck.

"Maddy!" Aiden shouted. He knew she could not hear him over the current, so he willed her to look at him. Aiden saw pain on Carlos's face, and the stark sinew of his arm straining to hold. Then Maddy turned and her eyes met his. She smiled. It was a childlike smile of relief. She saw her brother and knew she would be all right.

They were near the shore now. Aiden could smell the stomped muddy grass, could even feel the heat coming off the land. A few more minutes and they would all be safe. She would smile that way forever. She would love and grow up; she would dance and have a warm fire always, plenty of food, a wooden house and china plates, kittens safe from coyotes and babies that lived.

Then some twist of current surged beneath them. It jostled both ferries, and the smaller boat slipped under their own, thrusting it up. Aiden saw the cart shift and jerk to one side. Carlos and Maddy slid down the steeply pitched deck. An ox slid past Aiden, its horns carving a groove in the deck. Its leg caught in the spokes of the wheel and was ripped clean off as the rest of it was dragged into the fast water. Aiden saw Carlos jerk violently to a stop, his arm still twisted in the rope. Maddy slipped from his arm.

"Maddy!"

She was in the river now, the foaming water rushing around her. Somehow Carlos still had a hold on her wrist, but he could not pull her up. His feet scrambled against the deck, trying for a foothold. He strained to pull himself up by his lashed hand, but the arm looked grotesquely stretched and unstrung. Aiden crawled toward them, pulling himself through the broken crates and shattered wheels, between the kicking hooves and splintered boards.

Her head was barely above the water. The current was too strong for her to even raise her other arm. Carlos's fingers tore through the fabric of her sleeve and dug into the flesh of her arm. He strained and pulled and Aiden saw her shoulder appear. Carlos heaved and suddenly she was halfway out. He saw her free arm swing up and grasp the deck. A rope flung from shore landed across her back. Aiden's heart surged with relief. Then the ferry heaved again and in an instant, she was gone. The last thing Aiden saw was her small white hand, frail and fluttering like a bird in a storm. Aiden scrambled after her, but Carlos grabbed him by the shirt and held him back.

"Let me go!" Aiden tried to wrench free. Carlos flung a leg over his back and pinned him down. Then someone else grabbed him and pulled him back. There was a sudden bump as the ferry slammed into shore. A dozen men swarmed onto the ferry with ropes, and then Aiden was being dragged across the deck. Then Jackson was there, and too many men holding on to him; then things went all soft and quiet for a while.

When Aiden came to a few minutes later, he was sitting on the muddy bank, propped against a gatepost. He saw Carlos lying on the ground nearby, Jackson standing over him with a boot on his shoulder, pulling up on his arm. Carlos gave a brief, thin cry, then rolled over and pressed his face into the ground.

Things happened in little bits.

A mule stumbled with a broken foreleg, the bone ends sticking out and horribly white.

Carlos lay terribly still, holding his damaged arm tight to his body.

Marguerite cried.

Someone shot the mule in the head.

The Thompson children were a great pile of each other, hugging and crying.

Strong men, urgent and all the same, pulled ropes and heaved parcels and dragged damage up on the shore.

The Reverend Gabriel True lay propped against a crate, his face ghostly white. Marguerite held his head in trembling hands and talked to him in French. Jackson bent over Carlos, then lifted him under the good arm and brought him to the ailing man.

Aiden tried to get up and discovered he was tied to a gatepost.

"Hey!" he shouted. "Cut me loose!" He thrashed from side to side and jerked his wrists against the rope.

"Quiet." Jackson came over and squatted beside Aiden.

"Where's Maddy?"

"They're still looking."

"Let me go. Why am I tied?"

"Don't need any more bodies in the river today."

"I need to find her."

Jackson said nothing, just stared at him grimly. "Plenty of men out looking."

"She could be washed up in any bend!"

"We're searching all the bends."

"Her dress is brown. She could be missed. Let me go!" Aiden kicked at Jackson, wild with fury. Jackson backhanded him hard across the face.

"Settle down, boy! You don't own all the grief today! Joby's gone. Three others gone. The reverend's had a heart pain, and Carlos nearly got his arm pulled off trying to save your own sister and you both." Jackson wiped the sweat from his forehead. "Took four men to drag you back already. I have to keep you tied. No good you doing something crazy. You understand."

"Yes, I've a debt to pay," he said bitterly.

"You've a life to live," Jackson said as he got up. "Besides the debt."

All afternoon, men rode down both sides of the river. After them, women walked, examining the bends and crevices, while older children searched on the banks, calling the names of the missing. Six people had wound up in the river. One was pulled out alive. A man from the other ferry was found dead close by, and the top half of another man was discovered a mile away, torn apart on the rocks. That man's wife had also been thrown in and was still missing, along with Joby and Maddy.

Boxes and crates, dead animals and bits of broken wagons were brought in. There was no rhyme or reason. An iron skillet was found folded like a badly flipped pancake, while a china statue of a dancing lady washed up on a sandbar without so much as a chip. The Thompsons' dog was found two miles down the river, scared and shivering but alive and unbroken. An ironclad wagon wheel was twisted into a pretzel, but Carlos's anatomy book was found between some rocks, wedged so tightly the inside pages were dry.

It was dusk when they brought Joby in. His face was gray but unbattered, and in the soft evening light, he almost appeared to be sleeping. But as they laid him on the ground, Aiden saw how his head dangled, as if his neck were made of rope. Carlos didn't say anything. Someone had tied his injured arm up in a sling. In his good hand, he held a small piece of Maddy's sleeve, which he rubbed constantly. Aiden would not speak to or even look at him.

Three graves were dug on a hillside nearby. There was no preacher for a service, for Reverend True was still sick, but people came up with enough Bible verses to satisfy the occasion. The two dead oxen were butchered for food, and the dead mule went for the dogs. They were the only ones resting easy that night, lying about nearly comatose, bellies swollen with unexpected plenty, tongues lazing out, paws twitching in fat, contented dreams.

Aiden was left tied. Marguerite, Mrs. Thompson and some others came over and tried to comfort him, but he would not have anyone near. He gouged his wrists bloody struggling to get free. Finally, Jackson and the Kansas boys all held him still while the widower forced a dose of laudanum down his throat.

As the queer, peaceful feeling overtook his body, Aiden watched night fall. Cookfires appeared. Torches twinkled on both banks, and the light sparkled on the rushing water so it looked like the river was full of stars. It could have been a beautiful parade, the welcoming for an ancient king. And it was, Aiden thought, for death was the most ancient king, and his entourage too fond of sparkle.

He felt himself floating up and looking down on the river. He did not want Maddy's body found. He could stand her being dead if he didn't have to see her body. He could not bear to hear the dirt fall on another coffin. He thought of the babies; sad, vague little bundles, swaddled in a mere apron or strip of worn-out sheet. He remembered their exquisite little fingernails and the tiny delicate ears, monstrous for their awful perfection. Every time, though they measured well, the coffin turned out to be too big. There hadn't even been a good coffin since Ada. His father's was barely a platform of broken boards, and his mother had none at all, for the fire had burned everything of wood. They had wrapped her in only a sheet. Maddy had wanted to use the quilt, for softening, but Aiden wouldn't let her. Winter was coming. She fought him for it. He hit her then. The only time ever. After that he went out on the burned ground and cried so hard it was like his insides had turned liquid and poured from him, from his eyes and nose and mouth. No ordinary tears, but something foul and thick, and disgustingly sweet. But he won in the end. They laid her down wrapped in only a sheet and came through the winter because of that quilt.

Why? Why had he even bothered? He felt the drugged calm overtake him. Better Maddy be torn apart on the rocks. Better to have her swept to the sea, to someplace else in the *Atlas of the World*.

Someone brought him a drink of water. Campfires and torches swirled through the darkness. He waited for more visions. He waited for his whole lost family to show up, happy now, for a picnic in the green fields of heaven. But the only field he saw was full of dying potatoes swelling like corpses and collapsing into their wet black skins. Finally the drug overwhelmed him and he fell into dense, boggy sleep.

People searched all night, but by morning, the awful tally could not be denied: one alive, three dead, two unrecovered. Aiden woke groggy and numb, though he was untied and wrapped in blankets. His wrists were swathed in thick bandages. His feet were bare. This angered him. Did Jackson think he would not go after Maddy just because his boots were gone?

The morning sun was warm and indecently bright. People moved about with a jittery purposefulness, fidgeting with harnesses and fussing with knots, for there was nothing else really to be done. Everyone wanted to leave but felt wrong to suggest it. Finally, just after noon, Jackson gave the order to move on. They could not camp forever here on the muddy bank. The ferry was repaired and had to resume traffic. The season was too short and the trail too long to delay others from crossing. And the river was too fierce and cold to allow any hope by now.

"I'm known in these parts," Jackson told Aiden. "Word will get to me if her body is found."

And so they moved on, in a silent, numb march, grim and guilty in their fortunes.

CHAPTER
28

It was another sixteen days to Seattle. Aiden spoke to no one. He walked and did his work. Food came to him and he walked west and that was all. The Cascade Mountains were beautiful, but it was like a picture seen through a window in someone else's parlor as you passed in the street outside. The Reverend True recovered and Aiden was glad, but it was a flat, distant gladness, like hearing the crops were good that year in Australia.

Sometimes as he walked, Aiden thought up ways that Maddy might have survived. If she rolled up in a ball, the current could have carried her miles and miles through the rocks and rapids and let her off gently on the bank of some distant village. She could be miraculously unbroken. Perhaps not the smallest bones, the delicate seashell bones of wrist and ankle, where she would have grasped at rocks, but she could climb the bank with these small bones broken—in pain, yes—but she could climb and be found. A letter would come soon. But he knew too well the power of the river and the deep cold there.

It was only the walking that gave him solace, the steps taken over and over each day with incalculable rhythm and dull aching. At the end of each day he went off into the woods by himself and built things—huge piles of rocks or stacks of branches. He did not know why he did it, except that it occupied his mind and his strength. He could not sit around the fire at night, or lie in his blanket and look at the stars. He could not bear to talk to people or hear them talk, because it meant that they were all alive when Maddy was not. Not a word or a glance passed between him and Carlos.

As the days wore on, Aiden's constructions became more elaborate. He laid the stones in spirals or twisting paths through the trees. If there was a creek, he would make dams, diverting the water into trenches he carved in the dirt, as if compelled by some strange ancient force, maybe the force that had spurred Stonehenge and Easter Island and the Great Sphinx of Egypt. Maybe he was going insane. But maybe, maybe Maddy would see from heaven and know it was for her. He had missed the work of digging her grave, so he would carry rocks instead. The only thing he was sure of was that by the time he wore himself out with stones and the sweat began to chill his skin, he would have peace enough to sleep for a few hours before dawn.

They camped the final night ten miles outside Seattle. Jackson had arranged for a man to take his two wagons on to Seattle, then ship the trade goods by boat up the coast to a trading post he owned north of the city. In the morning, the group would continue on alone to Seattle while Jackson went north to the logging camp to deliver his "strays" and collect his bounty.

That night, Aiden did not go back to the camp at all. He could not bear farewells. All these people had become part of his life, but that life was over now, and he wanted no reminders: no thoughts for the future, no wishes for luck or Godspeed. God had stepped out of his journey long ago. Aiden sat out the night, watching the moonlight cast stick-stripes on the ground as it moved across the sky. In the morning he waited until he heard the wagons roll out, then went down from the hillside.

The camp area looked forlorn, nothing but flattened grass and wheel scars, charred remnants of cookfires and a maze of footprints in the damp ground. He recognized Marguerite's, from the tiny triangle of her instep and the way the toes pressed down as if she were always dancing. For a bizarre few seconds, he found himself automatically looking for Maddy's nearby. He jumped when Jackson walked up beside him.

"I sent your books along in my wagon," Jackson said simply. "I'll keep them for you. I would have asked was there any you wanted to take with you, but—"

"Thanks," Aiden interrupted. "I'm grateful."

"Well, guess we're ready, then," Jackson said. Aiden looked around at the other "bound" men. He hadn't spent much time with them during the journey, and they seemed even more foreign to him now. The gloomy widower seemed not to have changed a bit in two thousand miles. The Kansas boys, who of course did have real names but were so inseparable and nearly identical that everyone in the wagon train eventually just called them the Kansas boys, had lost a lot of weight but none of their enthusiasm. They had proven to be good workers, though Aiden knew Jackson found them suspiciously happy. William Buck was just meaner than ever, acting all the time as though the hardships of the trail were his own private tribulation.

"There's a river landing about a mile from here," Jackson went on. "We're supposed to meet up with a drover there. Help him bring fresh mules and oxen upriver to the camp."

"How far we gotta go?" Buck asked.

"Till we get there." Jackson spat and mounted his horse.

It was a slow journey along a rough and rutted track, but finally, late on the afternoon of the next day, in a cold, steady drizzle, they arrived in East Royal St. Petersburg. The name would have been pompous for the biggest city in the region, but it was especially absurd attached as it was to the small collection of shacks and outbuildings that made up Napoleon Gilivrey's logging empire.

"Well, here you go, boys," Jackson said. "You can wait there under cover." Jackson pointed them to a woodpile in a three-sided shack. Even with the shelter the pile had sprouted a light carpet of moss. Buck stretched himself out over the stacked wood, took out his pipe and filled it with tobacco. Aiden leaned against a pole and looked around the camp. A couple of men eyed them from the barn, but no one came over. It was not a chummy sort of place.

In the center of the clearing there was a log cabin with a rough front porch. On one side, separated by a sheltered walkway and boardwalk, was a smaller cabin. There was a Chinese man outside, vigorously scrubbing shirts on a washboard in a tub. There was a clothesline nearby, empty right now, as Aiden expected it was most of the time in this damp place.

Fifty yards away was a bunkhouse, and farther down from that, a stable big enough for maybe a dozen animals. Chickens scratched at the grass in a small pen, while a dog dozed on some planks nearby. A toolshed, a cookhouse, a tack shop and a blacksmith's forge made up the rest of the "town." Three outhouses were sheltered by some spindly saplings. A great haphazard pile of logs lay by the riverbank, but the only live trees within a hundred yards of the river were no thicker around than a man's leg. It was a sad, dreary place. The gray drizzle made the world seem two-dimensional and especially grim.

Jackson went into the office and came out again in less than five minutes. He turned his collar up against the damp. Aiden could see the bulge of gold in his pocket. So the deal was done: five hundred dollars' bounty for the men, and another five hundred for their passage—no, six hundred, Aiden corrected himself. There had been six passages. He did not begrudge the man a cent. Jackson had been fair all the way. Still, it was a painful lump of money to think about. The whole next year or more of his life was in that little bag.

Jackson walked over to the woodpile where the men waited.

"You'll stay in the bunkhouse here tonight." He nodded toward the low building. "Head for your camps in the morning."

"We don't work here?" Buck said.

"Hell no. Look around. What the hell you gonna cut here? Gilivrey works small camps up the streams from here. Floats the logs out whenever the water is high enough."

"Wait a minute." Buck got up. "That ain't what you promised! I ain't living up some godforsaken backwoods stream! Logging camps I heard about got saloons and whores nearby!"

"I imagine he ships in the whores now and then," Jackson said in a steely tone. "But there was nothing to that regard in my promise, if you recall. It's a year. One year of your sorry-ass life. Ain't nothing so bad for only a year's time."

The Kansas boys looked like startled pups. Jackson softened his tone. "Mr. Gilivrey, well, he's a hard man. Ain't downright evil, see; ain't even cruel exactly, but—well, he operates on the rough side of things. If he had the plush sort of camp, he wouldn't be buying his hands this way, now, would he? Do your jobs, keep out of trouble, you'll be all right.

"Good luck, then. I'll be on my way. If you're ever down by Brightfish Bend, at the mouth of Toolkia Sound, come by the trading post. If you need boots or such, fishhooks, skillets, blankets, come see me there."

One of the Kansas boys—Michael and Gerry they were, Aiden remembered; or Gary—held out his hand. "It's been good traveling with you, Mr. Jackson," he said. Despite the momentary nervousness, the two of them were once again upbeat and ready for the next stage of their big adventure. "We'll be sure to come see you, sir!"

"You do that." Jackson touched his hat and nodded to Aiden. "Walk along, will you, lad?" he said. Aiden walked the short distance to where Jackson's horse was tethered. She tossed her head and twitched her nose in the damp piney air, as if she knew the long journey was over and she was nearly home.

"I told you at the beginning how I'd figure things out to the day," Jackson said awkwardly as he fished in his pocket. "In the event of . . . well, of you not both making it all the way." He pulled out some coins. "So, it ain't much, but here's for the days extra."

"Extra?"

"For your sister—for the days she didn't cost me for her keep."

Aiden stepped back, staring at the coins as if they were hot coals.

"Go on, take it."

He'd forgotten all about that part of the deal.

"No."

"Don't be stupid." Jackson grabbed his arm and pressed the coins into his hand. "Being poor won't make her alive again."

"I don't want it."

"Then don't take it against that, but for earnings. You done more work for me than I expected, so it's only what's fair to you."

Aiden felt all the blood draining out of his brain; like everything inside him was small and breakable and spinning. The coins felt extraordinarily heavy in his hand, the awful weight of missing days.

Jackson squeezed his arm hard, which brought his brain back around. "Stand up now," Jackson said. "You'll do all right. Stay out of trouble. Watch your temper. Don't rile William Buck." The worn saddle creaked as he mounted. The horse whinnied and nosed Aiden's arm as if to say farewell. Jackson touched his hat. "She was a good girl," he said. "I got to like her some." He clucked at the horse and rode off without a backward glance.

The door of the little office creaked open and Napoleon Gilivrey stepped out onto the narrow porch. The first thing Aiden noticed was that he was cleaner than any man he had seen since Virginia, and certainly cleaner than anyone out here had any right or need to be. While most men had dirt crusted in their skin all the time, his face glowed a pearly white. His black mustache was perfectly trimmed, as if chopped straight across with a cleaver. His black hair was thinning, but what locks remained were smoothed with pomade and grown long, so that the ends curled extravagantly on his shoulders. He was an average height but had a curious build, his body very square both front to back and side to side, like a stone gatepost. His posture was perfectly erect. He had a broad forehead, wide-set gray eyes and a nose that might have been elegant on a kinder face but that on him just looked sharp.

"Gentlemen." Gilivrey stepped to the edge of the porch and eyed the muddy street disdainfully. "Please listen carefully, as I've neither the fortitude nor the forbearance to repeat myself." He folded his hands lightly, so as not to crush the elegant cuffs of his starched white shirt.

"You are now in my employ and subject to my rules and whims, which may or may not conform to your ideas of justice and fairness. For this I do not care. You are bound to me for a debt. I will see that debt fulfilled."

He had a slight accent that Aiden couldn't place. It was a bit like Hans and Friedrich's, but smoother.

"There is a gold rush in British Columbia at the moment, so there are only two ways to keep loggers working right now," he said. "One must be nice, or one must buy them. I'm afraid, gentlemen, I'm not very nice." Gilivrey flicked a handkerchief at the mosquitoes that hummed above his oiled hair. "You may not be slaves, technically, but until you pay off your debt, you belong to me as surely as any of those chained beasts. You will start at one dollar a day. Those are standard wages, the same as you would get in any camp. If you develop skills, your pay will rise accordingly. Buckers and fallers make a dollar fifty. Your room and board are two dollars and fifty cents a week, also standard. You will receive fifty cents in cash each week for personal money. We work seven days a week, half day on Saturday, noon start on Sunday. There are some minimum standards of clothing I require for safety and health. I will not have my operations hampered by illness or injury. If you do not have them, they will be provided to you from company stores and the cost put on your account. Most of you will make up your debt in a year, at which time you will be free to stay or go as you wish."

Gilivrey looked at Aiden and lifted his long pointy nose. "You're the lad in for two, aren't you?"

"Yes, sir," Aiden said.

"I do hope she's worth it."

Aiden felt his face burn with anger but would not give this man the satisfaction of a reaction. "Yes, sir," he said.

The door of the other little house opened and a man came out, stooping to get beneath the doorframe.

Gilivrey pivoted neatly and nodded toward the man. "This is Mr. Powhee," he said. "My boss-logger. He will handle you from here on. Do what he says, do not give him trouble."

Aiden doubted that anyone anywhere was likely to give Mr. Powhee any trouble. He was the biggest man Aiden had ever seen. He was six foot two at least, and his chest was broad as a wagon. His legs were bigger around than most of the nearby tree trunks. His skin was tawny brown and his black hair was wiry, almost as curly as a Negro's. He had a round face, exceptionally white teeth and fierce, dark brown eyes. The most remarkable thing, however, was that his face was covered in tattoos. Lines and scrolls were inked on his chin, and wavy patterns curled around the sides of his eyes. At his neck, a curled, polished pig tusk the size of a saucer dangled from a leather thong. Aiden guessed, from so many readings of the *Atlas of the World*, that he was from Polynesia.

"I care nothing about you, or your hopes or dreams or sufferings." Gilivrey turned back to his new loggers and glared at them. "I want trees cut and money made. It isn't that hard to do here. Succeed and I will be satisfied. Fail and I will make your lives miserable. Run away and I will have you killed. Do you understand?"

"Yes, sir," one of the Kansas boys said brightly. Gilivrey glared at him and he shuffled back a little.

"Mr. Powhee will acquaint you with your accommodations. My clerk will arrange your kit. Supper is in an hour. No lamps after dark. You leave at sunrise." He spun around and disappeared into his house.

29

"Ide govis, ana boos. Ye 'ave udda troosa?" Gilivrey's clerk looked Aiden up and down over his spectacles, the lenses of which were so smeary Aiden didn't know what good they were to the man: everything must have looked as if it were underwater. He was a small, wiry, one-armed Scot with an extravagantly brushy mustache. He had been a logger once himself until a rigging chain snapped and whipped his arm off just below the shoulder. The tail end of the chain had also crushed part of his upper jaw, so half his face was caved in. What with the injury, the mustache and his naturally thick accent, his speech was barely intelligible.

"He says you need horsehide gloves, hobnail boots and do you have other trousers?" Mr. Powhee translated.

"An wooo sock, free air."

"Wool socks, three pair."

"I have two pair," Aiden said. "I don't need three."

"You do," Powhee said. "Nothing dries in a day here, and foot rot costs the company. One pair wool socks," he said to the clerk, who wrote in careful script in the account book.

"You all are required to have three pair of wool socks, two pair of wool long johns," he said to all the gathered men. "A wool hat, two pair of canvas pants, oiled is best. One sweater, one jacket, horsehide gloves, nailed boots." Powhee's voice was surprisingly soft, and his accent had a gentle, lilting rhythm.

"Don't complain for the cost," he went on. "The price here is twice any town price. But as you've seen, we're two days' walk to any town. And if I find your kit short in the far camp, it will be five times that."

Aiden watched the pen scratch out numbers on his account page. Each dollar meant days, but for once the debt didn't bother him. Days had no value anymore.

The bunkhouse was packed to overflowing, with at least thirty men in a room built for twenty. They slept all over the floor, some squeezing under the lower bunks to avoid getting stepped on. Some had been there for three days, waiting for the full group to assemble for the trek upstream to the far camps. The only comfortable place was one corner by the stove, where a group of eight men played cards in a haze of pipe smoke and chased away anyone else who dared to come close looking for a scrap of space. They were seasoned loggers, big hard men who had found themselves with big hard gambling debts to pay off and a choice between Napoleon Gilivrey and the sea. Between the gold rush and the building boom in San Francisco, merchant ships were as desperate for men as the logging camps. Gilivrey had covered their debts and now owned them until they earned the money back.

The rest of the group, as far as Aiden could make out, seemed to be a mix of all possible failures in the known world. There were other busted homesteaders, failed gold miners and leftover soldiers, one nearly blind. There were two Negroes, a Mexican and a big gloomy Russian, impoverished and alone since the death of his dancing bear and the loss of his acrobat wife, who had run off with the ringmaster of their little circus, married a shopkeeper in Portland or fallen from a tightrope. He was pretty drunk and the story

215

kept changing. There were petty criminals directly from the Seattle jails and one man, it was rumored, fresh from the lunatic asylum. There were sailors who had abandoned their ships and men who had abandoned the world. It seemed as if anyone with nowhere else to go and no way to get there wound up here, bound to Napoleon Gilivrey by debt, failure or desperation.

Aiden lay on the floor listening to the grunts and arguments, farts and snores and complaints of all the other men. William Buck, who had bullied his way into an actual bunk, cursed Jackson continually under his breath.

"Damn his eyes. Damn his ass and the horse it sits upon! He tricked us here. Goddamn tricked us!"

Arguments erupted over nothing, and if Mr. Powhee hadn't confiscated all knives and guns, Aiden was sure there would have been blood on the floor by now. As it was, a violent fistfight broke out over floor space and was only contained when the lunatic began flapping his hands and shrieking loud whooping noises that startled everyone into peace.

But in the midst of this chaos Aiden felt a strange sort of calm. It was almost like the feeling he'd had with the Indians that one grand day, when everything was simply out of his hands. Every bit of the world had become so strange, from the intense landscape to this insane room, that he felt any last bits of normal life had been sucked out into space and all feeling swept from his soul. He was disconnected from the world and all things in it. He would live or die and it didn't matter. He would work to dying and it didn't matter. He could be crushed dead by a falling tree and it didn't matter. He had a brief thought of Gilivrey's maimed clerk and felt a flicker of horror at the possibility of dismemberment, but even that didn't really bother him for long. As long as he had one arm left, he could always kill himself. There was no one else he had to think about anymore.

He woke the next morning to the sound of a gong so loud it made his ribs vibrate. He had slept in all his clothes, so there was no need to dress. The men quickly shuffled into the dining room and dropped onto the long benches around the rough-hewn tables. Mugs of coffee and bowls of oatmeal steamed at every place, with enamel pots and iron kettles sitting in the middle of each table, ready for refills. There were plates of sliced bread and bowls of butter to spread on it. It was so crowded that the men ate with elbows pressed against their sides, but they still managed to devour great piles of food in fifteen minutes.

The gong sounded again and Mr. Powhee stood in the doorway. The cook came through the room with platters of sandwiches for dinner on the trail.

"Take two," Powhee directed. "Saw men meet me by the toolshed, the rest of you by the stores hut. We leave in five minutes."

Mules loaded with supplies were already moving up the muddy trail by the time the men joined the march. All the supplies came by river from Seattle to East Royal St. Petersburg but then had to be packed up to the far camps on foot trails. The river was only high enough a few times a year to float anything heavy, and then it was full of logs. No one traveled lightly. Along with their own packs of personal gear, each man carried various awkward items that would not easily be strapped on a mule. Aiden was given a large can of kerosene. The experienced saw men carried new cross-cut saws, nine feet long, thin as paper and shiny as ice. They flexed and vibrated to a dangerous degree as the men walked, despite the men's experience in handling them.

The trail wound along beside the river and made the first of its splits just about a half mile north of East Royal St. Petersburg to follow one of the smaller tributaries. Napoleon Gilivrey had the logging rights to land around all five of the streams in the area. The land was rich in timber, but it was so difficult to get the trees out that no one else had been very interested in it. Gilivrey's system required expert management and exquisite patience, with logs piled on the riverbank for months, waiting for enough water to float down.

The forest they were walking through had already been logged, so only the most enormous trees were left, those with trunks twelve feet or more across—simply too big to cut and too heavy to haul. Gilivrey's camps moved farther and farther upstream each year to cut the smaller, more manageable trees. This land was different from anything Aiden had ever seen or imagined. Over every surface, on every rock and limb and fallen tree, grew a hundred shades of moss. The ground beneath the trees was not the tangle of brush and shrub as in the East, but a bare, flat land covered in brown pine needles and punctuated with stumps. Everything was green and damp and soft, carpeted and quiet. There were old fallen trees so rotted you could see through them like lace, yet still so huge they blocked out the sun. They could be a thousand years old, Aiden thought, or older. They could be from the time of Rome.

The mule handler was a rough and impatient man, and Aiden found himself wishing for Joby, who could coax the most stubborn animal along with little more than a click of his tongue and a gentle switch. At each split of the river, Mr. Powhee read out a list of names and directed men and mules to continue on a new path to the various camps upstream. The Kansas boys broke off first, the widower in the third group. Aiden and William Buck walked on with the last group. It was late afternoon by the time they came to their camp, which Aiden guessed was about five miles from East Royal St. Petersburg. He was well used to walking by now, but his arms ached from carrying the kerosene and his legs were bruised from the knocking of the can. The camp was nothing but a few forlorn wooden buildings. There were two small bunkhouses with a third building between that served as cookhouse, dining hall and the only other place to be if you didn't want to be in your bunk. Mr. Powhee had his own lodging, a pole-and-canvas tent-house with its own little stove. A row of outhouses was set back in the trees. There was a stable for the oxen and mules, and a small toolshed with a blacksmith's forge and grinding wheels. Everything was roughly built, for it would only be used for a year or so, then knocked down and moved upriver after all the suitable trees nearby had been cut.

Each of the two bunkhouses held twelve men, in bunks stacked three high against each wall. There were ten men already in the camp, and they had taken the top bunks, which were most desired for the winter, as the rising heat kept them warmer. Aiden hung back, waiting to see which house William Buck chose, then took the other for himself. The bunk frames were strung with rope and covered with thin mattresses stuffed with pine needles. There were hooks on the wall for coats and on the bedposts for each man's kit bag.

The walls were chinked with moss and lined in places with salvaged canvas or sailcloth. There was a small iron stove in the middle of the room with a few rough-hewn chairs around it. Clotheslines hung above, crisscrossing the room like a giant spiderweb. Aiden chose a bottom bunk, uninterested in fighting for a better space. The other three bottom bunks were already taken by the two Negroes and the Mexican. Ranks were clear in a place like this, Aiden knew. He wondered where the lunatic fit in.

Supper was a dismal mush of boiled corned beef, onions and rice. Some of the new arrivals grumbled. Food was generally very good in the big camps, and the experienced men knew it.

"No talking at the table!" the cook snarled at the newcomers. He was bald as a stone, and his arms were massive from lifting heavy pots.

"Cook don't bear complaints well," one of the men whispered to Aiden. "But don't worry, it's usually better. This is the last of the stores, you see." He nodded at the unpleasant stew. "Food came up with you today, and the mules generally come each week, and sometimes we get fresh fish or game from the Indians," he added.

Aiden didn't care. Everything tasted the same to him. After supper Mr. Powhee distributed fresh apples and rations of whiskey, the usual treat when a pack train arrived. There was some vigorous trading, with the few nondrinkers walking off with six or eight apples, and a couple of men dead drunk by nightfall.

30

"**Y**ou!" Powhee glared at Aiden and held up an axe. "You know which end to hold?" The other new men laughed, though none too boldly. They knew they were just as likely to be picked on. "Your job is to clear a path, build the skid road, same as there." Powhee pointed at the ground nearby, where smaller trees, a foot or less in diameter, had been cut so they fell like railroad ties over the soft ground. The oxen teams could then drag the heavy logs along this skid road to the river.

"The way is already marked." He tapped his huge palm on a tree that was painted with a red X. "Cut the ones with an *X* so they fall that way." He pointed toward the east. "The trees with an *O* fall the other way. Here—chop."

Aiden had never chopped down a tree in his life. He hadn't even cut firewood since he was a boy in Virginia. There was nothing to cut in Kansas. He swung the axe into the tree trunk as hard as he could. A steely jolt shot up his arms and a tiny chip of wood peeled off the tree. Powhee said nothing as Aiden went on with awkward strokes. Sometimes the blade would get stuck, or he would hit at the wrong angle and it would bounce back.

"See there," Powhee announced after Aiden's first dozen strokes. "Everything wrong you can do!" He took the axe back.

"So watch!" He swung with an easy motion that used his

whole body and snapped the blade into the trunk as if it were a loaf of bread. He showed the men how to angle the cuts and when to start the back-cut. A spiral tattoo on his forearm pulsated over the bulging muscle. In his skillful hands, the little tree fell in a couple of minutes.

"That's all there is to it!" He handed the axe back to Aiden. His dazzling grin took the sting out of the criticism. "Once it's down, you cut off all the branches. Try not to cut your foot off as you do!" He pointed the other four men toward the waiting trees. "Ten a day will make you full wage."

Ten a day; it seemed impossible. Even with the horsehide gloves, Aiden's palms were bleeding by noon. A constant river of sweat trickled down his back and his muscles began to ache, but still he kept on. Trimming the branches off was even harder. The green wood refused to be cut clean through, and sometimes there was a tough knot where a branch joined the trunk.

By the end of the day Aiden had cut and trimmed only seven trees, and two of them had fallen in the wrong direction. Even though no one else had made the quota, and two of the men had only managed four, he felt embarrassed.

"Hey, girls!" the other men taunted the novices as they dragged back to the bunkhouse. "Let's see your pretty hands now!"

"You cryin' for your mommy yet?"

"Cry a little louder—I hear she's coming on the next Bandy ride!"

Aiden didn't know what a Bandy ride was, but the rude laughter gave him some clue. He ignored the teasing and plunged his hands into the creek until the icy water numbed them and turned the blisters white. He could barely carry his axe back to the sharpening shed. He didn't even know what supper was that night, only that it was hot and plentiful and stopped one part of the overwhelming hurt that throbbed in every bit of his body. He had pains in muscles that he didn't even know he had. Even his hair hurt. But the pain was also welcome. It was simple and complete and left no room for any other feeling.

He woke the next morning actually craving more of it. By noon that day, he had cut down five trees. His limbs were trembling and his hands bleeding when he sat down to lunch, and his hands shook as he shoveled food into his mouth, but he was proud to think he was halfway to quota. As they were heading back out for the afternoon, Mr. Powhee nodded his tattooed chin at Aiden.

"Hey, you—Prairie Boy." Powhee knew few actual names and didn't use them even when he did, but Aiden wondered where he had picked up that particularly annoying one. He didn't have to wonder long. "Take this one along." Powhee tipped his head toward William Buck. Buck glowered at Aiden. "Teach him to cut down little trees," Powhee said.

Buck had gone off the first day with the fallers and buckers, claiming he had experience. He was certainly convincing with his great size, but evidently he hadn't quite measured up. Aiden said nothing. When they reached their work site, Buck swung his axe angrily into the side of a tree.

"Crap operation this is!" he grumbled to the other men. "They don't know squat up here and the saws are bad and don't half these men know how to hold their end up."

No one said anything. Finally Aiden spoke up. "Trees with an *X* fall that way, *Os* go the other."

He ducked his head and got back to work. He'd cut a total of nine by the end of the shift, though he got only eight fully trimmed. After a few more days, though, cutting trees felt like the most natural thing in the world. He liked the feel of the axe on the wood. He liked the sweet hurt the first stroke made each day, the stab at his palm and jangle up his arm. After that, it was just a good long burn in his muscles. He liked the noises a tree made just before it was about to fall, all the creaks and groans and the slow, fragrant splintering of the heartwood.

For the first few days everything hurt, but then his blisters turned to calluses, his back stopped aching and the little trees began to fall like cornstalks under his blade. He woke eager to chop and stopped only when the gong surprised him and food had to be packed into his body. It was true what the men had said about the food being good. Except for the last day or two before the supply mules came in, there was always plenty, and often a good variety, with vegetables and apple pie not uncommon. Aiden never really noticed what it was, though, only the feel of it going down, hot and filling. He had never known food that came along so easily, so much and so often. Sometimes he thought he could even feel it flowing into his muscles, the way a wilted plant plumped up with water.

Days passed in routine, and for the first time in Aiden's life, everything was reliable. He swung the axe, the tree fell; again and again, always the same. He didn't have to think about rain or drought or taking care of anyone else. Out here among the grand trees, he was gratefully and vastly alone. Out here he was simply arms and back and swing and balance. Life was nothing but the damp wood and the piney quiet, the ache of morning and the soft balm of night. For the first time since Maddy had died, the crushing terrible panic was gone. It was cold kindness, but Aiden had learned to take kindness in the smallest dose that came his way. Best of all, he did not have to be himself anymore. Out here he could be no one at all. He swung the axe, the tree fell.

"Hey, Prairie Boy, you—Eeden." The tall Negro Ezekiel squatted beside him at the stream one day as they washed for supper.

"My name is Aiden, not Eeden."

Ezekiel slept in Aiden's bunkhouse, but Aiden had never spoken to him before. Aiden didn't really speak to anyone except for the most necessary communication. They were both on the skid road crew, but their paths didn't cross since Ezekiel worked the oxen, dragging the trees into place. His accent wasn't Southern, and he didn't look like the slaves Aiden remembered from Virginia. He was tall and thin, with fine features and skin so black it was almost purple.

"Howeva you name—I just pass you news. Warn you stop cutting so much tree," he whispered.

"What?"

Ezekiel glanced around to be sure no one saw them talking. "Powhee say ten a day. You cut twelve—fifteen now sometime—dis is no good. I hear dee other men complain. No good fa' you show off so."

"I'm not showing off. I just like cutting down trees," Aiden protested.

"Ah, well." Ezekiel stood up and shook the water from his hands. "Just tell you is all fa' me."

"I'm not asking for more pay." Aiden splashed the cold water on his face. "I'm not asking for anything. Just to be left alone."

But they weren't about to leave him alone. Two nights later Aiden woke suddenly from the dead of sleep with a hand slapped hard across his mouth. Other hands quickly grabbed his feet and arms and dragged him out of the bunk. A burlap sack was pulled over his head. A rag was tied around his mouth before he had a chance to cry out. The men bumped him roughly across the bunkhouse floor, out into the damp night. The gag pressed the hairy burlap between his teeth and against his tongue and made him choke. He kicked hard at someone; then a fist slammed into his stomach and knocked the wind out of him.

"Don't wear us out, boy," a voice hissed. Aiden smelled boots and sweat, tobacco stench and sour clothes. He felt a piece of rope cinch around his hands and a knot tied tight. He steeled himself for a beating. He was pretty sure they wouldn't actually kill him; no sane man would do that. But then again, few sane men wound up in the lost corners of Napoleon Gilivrey's empire.

Then he heard the soft flick of a wooden latch, the squeak of hinges and the creak of a door. An unmistakable stench smacked him in the face. He knew where he was now. Hands grabbed the waist of his pants; other hands grabbed his ankles. Aiden felt himself turned upside down.

"Here's for showing us up."

They dunked his head into the foul outhouse hole. He choked on the stench. His shoulders banged against the wooden seat; his head was enveloped in the overpowering stink. Someone tried to force his shoulders together to shove him all the way through, but Aiden struggled and kept himself braced against the seat.

"Come on!" someone whispered. "Be done before you wake the whole camp!"

Aiden couldn't place the voices to any man, but he was certain William Buck had to be in on this. He worked hard not to vomit, but the smell and fear were overpowering. Thick bile rose in the back of his throat and burned through his nose. Next thing he heard was hammering, then laughter. He heard the door slam and the men running off into the darkness.

Aiden gagged again. Flies buzzed around his head. He was stuck upside down, his head in the hole, his hands tied together and his pants nailed to the wall. He crunched his abdomen, wriggled his shoulders and pulled his head out. They had tied his hands in front, so it wasn't too hard to pull himself up and tear his pants free. He crashed back down on the wooden seat, knocking his head hard. Desperately he tore at the gag, pulled the sack off his head, fumbled for the latch and tumbled out into the cool misty night.

31

Aiden said nothing the next morning. If any of the men knew anything, they were also silent. He finished his breakfast, got his axe from the sharpening shed and started walking down to the end of the skid road.

"Hey." Aiden heard Powhee's distinctive whistle. "Prairie Boy!" Aiden turned. "I got enough men there now. Come to the big trees."

Powhee handed him a can of kerosene and a maul, which was like a sledgehammer with a shorter handle. "You do the dog work again, but better kind of dog work now, eh? Learn to cut the big trees, you're a rich man!" Powhee laughed. "Go with the old guys."

The "old guys" were an established team, both in their early forties. One was a tall Finn with ice blue eyes and thick gray hair that he wore in a long braid down his back. He had an unpronounceable name and so was simply call Old Finn. He was generally a quiet man, but Aiden had seen him dance on tables when drunk.

"Your job is to clean the blade, knock the wedges in, stay out of our way and run like hell when I call timber," Old Finn instructed him. Aiden looked at his new tools with skepticism: a can of kerosene for cleaning the blades, a bucket of iron wedges and the heavy maul for pounding them in. He didn't like the idea of sawing; it looked like dull and numbing work. Sawing with the crosscut also required working with another man, timing your rhythm and pitch. He did not like having to pay attention so closely to another person. But it would mean fifty cents more a day to start.

"It's keeping the saw blade level that's the trick!" Roger Charbonex said. He was the same height as Old Finn—buckers pretty much had to be—but he had a stockier build and dark features. He was French Canadian and probably had some Indian blood in him, as most French out here did, and was called Bony. Bony had come up from East Royal St. Petersburg with Aiden's group, but something about him made Aiden think it was not his first time working for Gilivrey, nor would it be his last. Aiden remembered Jefferson J. Jackson telling him about the fur traders who made and spent a fortune every year, and figured Bony might be of similar habit.

Old Finn and Bony took up their axes and swung in a quick alternating rhythm to make the first cut. Then they picked up the long saw and slipped the blade into the cut. Their back muscles strained against their shirts as the metal whizzed through the soft outer bark.

"See how the sap and sawdust gum up the blade?" Bony explained, breathing hard. "Pour the kerosene on."

"And ready the wedge," Old Finn added.

Aiden cleaned the saw blade, then shoved the pointed piece of iron into the cut and drove it in with the maul. This would keep the massive weight of the trunk from squeezing the saw blade.

"Blade!" Bony called. Aiden put down his maul and scrambled back for the can of kerosene. The gummy mess had to be cleaned off frequently, and soon the mixture of sap, sawdust and kerosene stung the back of Aiden's throat.

It was always exciting to see a huge tree fall, but the

process of getting it there was slow. The men worked for hours, stopping frequently for short rests, for the job required endurance.

"Here—have a practice," Bony finally offered when they were halfway through. He stepped back and let Aiden take his end of the saw. Aiden squared his feet the way Bony showed him. The sawing was much harder to do than it looked. It was difficult to keep the long blade level. He got stuck several times, but Old Finn was patient and Aiden finally found a workable rhythm. They showed him how to make the back-cut and how to direct which way the tree would fall.

"Though there's still no guarantee," Old Finn said grimly. "Sometime they jump."

"Jump?"

"Whole tree jumps up off the stump like a jig dancer," Bony explained.

When the tree came close to the fall point, Old Finn blew a whistle. Other whistles answered from all over, warning everyone throughout the woods. The tree fell with a crash that shook the ground. There was a burned smell in the air from the friction of tearing wood. Aiden looked at the raw new stump. Sap was still welling up, forming shiny little amber beads, as if the grand old tree were actually bleeding.

They heard other men coming. A larger crew would now spend the rest of the day cutting off all the branches and sawing the giant trunk into manageable lengths. It took many men several days to finish a tree like this. Then it would be hauled out along the skid road with chains and teams of eight or ten oxen. One man, usually the lunatic, walked in front of the team with a bucket of foul-smelling dogfish oil, which he spread on the tracks with a dipper. Without the oil, the friction of the logs rubbing over each other could easily start a fire.

"Bandy girls are two days overdue," Old Finn sighed as he sipped his nightly whiskey. "Must be some fine-looking young men over in camp four."

"Those Kansas boys were pretty, I recall," Bony laughed, and nudged Aiden. "And I hear the Bandy girls do like prairie boys."

Aiden said nothing. The nickname seemed to have stuck to him, but most of the men made it feel friendly enough. By now he had heard plenty about the Bandy girls. They were prostitutes who rode a circuit, servicing all five of Gilivrey's camps as well as East Royal St. Petersburg. Spending two nights in each camp brought them around about every two weeks, just as the men were aching to throw their meager pocket money away.

"They ain't the prettiest of whores," Bony said. "Some all fat or crippled or the like. One of 'em's got half her face all droopy so her lip hangs funny."

"She drools out that side some," the cook said.

"That ain't necessarily a bad thing!" someone else added. A nasty laugh erupted around the circle.

"And she is a nice girl."

"She is that. Will talk with you some."

"And deals her cards fair." The Bandy girls also brought with them gambling games and musical performances.

There was a murmur of agreement and some discussion about the other girls. Bony leaned toward Aiden.

"They aren't all so bad-looking," he said. "And you know, out here, you take what you can get!"

"God, yes," the cook laughed. "Well, Bandy herself's all pocky, you know. But if you put out the lamp, you don't have to see her face anyway," he added.

"Oh, as if you would know," Bony scoffed. "Bandy don't do the likes of him," he explained to Aiden. "Or me. She's the boss."

"I heard they got a couple of China girls," Buck said, "who can do Oriental things on a man."

Aiden got up to leave. He had no idea what that meant, but the whole subject gave him a twist of disgust.

"What'sa matter, boy?" Buck said with a sneer. "We offending your sensibilities?"

"I'm just tired," Aiden said. "Good night, all."

"There's a preacher rides through every couple of months," the cook said. "You can wait for him instead!" The men erupted in laughter.

"Thanks all the same," Aiden said.

"Good Lord—you know what! I bet we got a virgin boy here among us!" Bony said. The laughter grew louder, but Aiden just ignored it and went on toward the bunkhouse.

"You know he is," Buck shouted. "Plucked right off the prairie. Fifteen years old, living out there all alone since a little boy, with not even a sheep for miles around. Unless, of course, he was doing his own little sister, as I hear is the common practice among his kind. . . ."

Aiden stopped. A piercing tone started up in his ears, like a saw blade being sharpened. He did not feel the usual white explosion of temper. Instead he felt a cold, hard anger. He slowly turned.

"I'll take your apology for that now," Aiden said quietly.

This anger was factual as iron and passionless as stone. The other men all saw the change come over him and fell silent.

"I don't recall offering you one," Buck scoffed. "Or saying anything in need of one," he spat. "Prairie Boy."

"Then I'll kill you," Aiden said calmly. Bony and the others backed away as Buck got to his feet.

"Now wait a minute, son," Bony said nervously. "Fighting's costly, now. Mr. Powhee will dock your pay. So maybe you should just calm down."

"I am calm," Aiden said, walking slowly toward Buck. "Watch me be calm."

"How about you take it back, Buck," Bony encouraged. "What you said. Sure—sure, you don't talk about a man's sister that way, especially a dead one. And you don't want to be all bruised and sore when the Bandy girls show up, do you?" There was some nervous laughter. "They got to be here tomorrow or the next day."

Aiden saw a flicker of fear cross Buck's big dumb face as he realized they now stood almost eye to eye and Aiden's shoulders were nearly as broad and strong as his own.

"I'll count to three." Aiden smiled. "Can you count that high?"

As Aiden had expected, Buck swung at him immediately. Aiden ducked the punch, slammed his shoulder into the man's chest and took him down. He still didn't have enough weight to really hold him, but Buck's surprise at the takedown gave Aiden an extra few seconds to land some punches.

Buck punched back, but Aiden felt no pain. There was

233

nothing left in the world that could hurt him now. They rolled across the damp ground and slammed into a stump. Buck tossed him off and scrambled to his feet, but Aiden was much quicker, with a fist ready before the man got his balance. Aiden threw a hard punch and felt Buck's nose crack under his knuckles. But the momentum of the blow pitched him forward and Buck drove his own fist into Aiden's stomach. Aiden gagged and fell to one knee.

A bunkhouse door opened, casting a rectangle of lamplight over the ground as men came out to watch. Buck wobbled back a step, then kicked at him, but Aiden grabbed the man's foot, twisted and pulled him off balance the way he had learned from Tupic. Buck fell to the ground like a tree. Aiden straddled his chest and began pounding his face with his fists.

There were shouts and whistles now and occasional hands grabbing at him, trying to pull him off, but all Aiden knew was the swing. Swing an axe, swing a fist—it didn't matter—something would fall tonight. He did mean to kill William Buck. His mind was clear on that. It was different from the way he'd meant to kill Sergeant Todd. Shooting Todd had been like a math lesson: where to aim, when to shoot, how many bushels of wheat. . . . This was like Shakespeare. He never understood half of Shakespeare, but what he did made him feel like this, urgent and all-in. Blood streaked down his face and burned his eyes and it felt good. There was mud in his mouth and it tasted fine. Buck threw Aiden off, but the man was so worn that he could hardly get to his feet. Then they all heard the crack of the bullwhip and fell silent. Through the smear of blood in his eyes, Aiden saw the towering shadow of Mr. Powhee slice across the ground.

"Stop it now!" The boss strode toward them. The tip of the whip snapped in the dirt.

Powhee glowered at Aiden, his eyes opened wide so the whites glistened. The firelight shone on his face and Aiden suddenly understood the purpose of the "Strange and Fearsome Tattoos of the Warriors of the South Pacific." Powhee's face was the scariest thing he had ever seen.

"Get up!"

Aiden slowly got to his feet. The earth tilted and he leaned over, resting his hands on his knees for support.

"Your bodies are my machinery!" Powhee thundered. "You will not break my machinery! Two-dollar charge for both of you! Anyone else want to fight? Give me your dollars now!" He folded up the whip. There was a moment of silence. Powhee turned and stalked back to his tent.

"Damn—don't want to mess with the Prairie Boy, now, do you?" someone chuckled.

"Come on." Bony took Aiden's arm. Aiden shrugged him off.

"You're hurt, boy."

"I'm fine," Aiden said.

"You aren't the first to be carried home around here."

Aiden wiped some blood off his mouth with his sleeve. The anger had faded and now he just felt pain and stupidness. The other men went to retrieve their mugs and bottles and began to shuffle back to the bunkhouse. Suddenly a chorus of cries burst out. Aiden turned, and from the corner of his eye he saw an arc of gold shoot across the black sky. For a half second he thought it was a shooting star. It was not. William Buck had grabbed a burning log out of the fire and swung it toward his head.

32

Aiden woke to hurdy-gurdy music and the sounds of laughter and stomping feet. He was in his bunk. It was dark outside, but the bunkhouse was empty. He started to sit up, but there seemed to be an axe stuck in the side of his skull. He lay back and felt his head. It was wrapped in bandages, but there was no actual axe to be found, so he cautiously sat up again. In a little while more, he managed to get his pants on and fit his feet into his boots. He tried to stand and found it possible. He stumbled to the water pail and pulled up a dipperful, for he felt a frantic thirst. Then he crept slowly toward the door, holding on to the bunks for support. He was confused. It had been night when he and William Buck had fought, but this couldn't be the same night because outside, the camp had become a carnival. A small stage had been put up with oil lamps set all across the front, tin reflectors casting the light onto the platform.

There were women dancing on the stage. Aiden had rarely seen a woman's leg above her ankle, and never above the knee. These women were all knee and above. They weren't exactly modest on top either. These were the Bandy girls, he realized. The men sat on crates or logs, hooting and hollering as they watched the women dance. Aiden remembered the men talking about how ugly the Bandy girls were, but he hadn't seen a woman of any kind for almost three weeks now, and they all looked marvelous to him. Of course, the world was still spinning and nothing was very clear. But he did see brightly colored dresses with sparkles and fringe, satin and silk and layers of ruffles. And there were breasts. He had seen breasts, of course, but there had always been a baby stuck to them. These breasts were all tidy and pushed up, and plump like fancy yeast dinner rolls. They jiggled over the stiff corsets, like—like nothing he knew of in nature. The women had ribbons in their hair and very red spots on their cheeks. So red that he worried for a moment they might be ill.

"The show's five cents." A tall man in a top hat appeared beside him. Aiden blinked with confusion, for the man looked like Mr. Powhee but wasn't. He had the same eyes, the same skin and teeth, though fewer tattoos. He was leaner all the way through but just as tall.

"I'm just walking around," Aiden said feebly. "I just woke up."

"And now your eyes are pointed at my dancers," the man said, holding his palm out. "Five cents."

"I haven't any money on me now."

"Find some, then, or go sit in your bunkhouse and whack yourself off dreaming of what you might have seen for real."

"Hey—lookie there, the lad's alive!" Bony jumped up from his stool and came over to Aiden. "Good to see you! How's your head?" The lady onstage flung her leg up into the air, gave a little jump and came down with both legs split in front and back in a way he would never have thought even possible.

"I don't know," he said, dumbfounded.

Bony laughed and grabbed his arm. He reeked of liquor and grinned like Christmas morning. "Come an' sit, then." He fished in his pocket, pulled out some linty pennies and counted out five. "Here's for the lad." He pressed the coins into the man's palm. "And bring us two good drams, will you, please, Mr. Hi-yow? Tally it to me, Mr. Roger Charbonex." Bony steered Aiden to a seat beside a now very cheerful Old Finn.

"When did the ladies come?" Aiden asked.

"No ladies here!" Old Finn whooped. "Oh, Jesus, wouldn't that spoil things! It's the Bandy girls! You've been out since last night. You talked some this morning, but only head-smack talk."

The man in the top hat returned with two tin cups of liquor. "Here—drink up," Bony said. "May do you better and can't do you any worse."

The liquor was harsh, and one sip made him feel like throwing up. He poured the rest of his into Old Finn's cup.

"Where's Buck?"

"Still moaning in his bunk, I suppose," Bony said. "Besides your damage, Mr. Powhee gave him a few lashes himself. But forget him now and watch the show! It tends to be brief. Bandy girls aren't here to dance for pennies, after all!"

There were two more short song-and-dance numbers, and one girl did some rope-twirling tricks that ended with her lassoing someone in the audience, to much applause. Then all the girls came out in a line and did a few kicks and twirls and the music stopped. The men surged toward the stage. Aiden saw Mr. Powhee and the top-hat man standing guard to keep some order.

"Here's how it works," Bony explained. "Those little tents there are for the high-price girls." He nodded at a row of tents set up under the trees. "Two dollars they are, some up to five." He looked at them longingly. "For special treatment and so on. The regular girls are one dollar and work in the bunkhouse, in the toolshed, the barn there, wherever. So—" Bony got up. "I got some scheduling to keep here myself. You talk to Bandy—she'll take good care of you."

"Okay, thanks."

Aiden leaned against a tree and watched the lanterns move through the trees. People turned into shadows and vanished into the night. A waning moon and high thin clouds cast soft light that seemed more suited for a fairy story. Outside each tent a little red glass lantern glowed.

He was aching by now and longing to lie down but suspected the bunkhouse would not be a place for resting just at the moment. He buttoned his jacket, wincing at the pain in his ribs. They didn't seem sore enough to be actually broken, but work was going to hurt for a while. He hadn't thought to bring his cap, but the bandage around his head helped a little against the cold. He wondered if the cook had sewn him up and hoped not, for he hadn't seen much tidy work out of the man.

Aiden sat down and leaned against a giant fir. Thinking of stitches made him think of Maddy. All the Lynch men had quick tempers and ready fists, so there were wounds to be stitched at least once a month. Maddy would sing to them while she sewed. Aiden traced his finger along one of the scars above his eyebrow, so pretty and neat. He squeezed his eyes shut. He wasn't sure he could push her out of his head right now in his weak state. So he pressed his hand against his bruised ribs to make them hurt instead.

"Hello?"

Aiden startled.

"Shush," a gentle voice whispered. "It's only me, Bandy." Skirts rustled and sweet perfume drifted over on the misty air.

"May I sit?" she asked.

"Um—yes." Aiden desperately wiped his eyes and nose on the rough jacket sleeve.

"Things are quiet now," she said. "All my girls are settled and I can have a bit of a rest." He heard the cork pulled from a bottle.

"It was a nice dancing show," he said awkwardly.

"Thank you. Did you see the contortionist?"

"I—I'm not sure I know what that is."

"Someone who can bend her body into remarkable postures."

Every posture he had seen from those women seemed pretty remarkable, and he didn't want to seem ignorant, so he just nodded. Confident that his tears had stopped, and that the dim light would hide any lingering evidence on his face, Aiden glanced at her. He was surprised to see she was wearing a veil. It was a fine net of dark silky material with tiny amber beads at the hem. It was very odd, for he thought women didn't wear veils except for mourning, but then he remembered the conversation from the campfire the night before. *Bandy herself's all pocky, you know.* Embarrassed, he turned his gaze away and stared straight ahead at the flickering red lanterns.

"Those tents are unusual," he said, trying to hide his discomfort. "I've never seen the like."

The tents were of very light canvas with no poles. A rope thrown over a tree limb held the peak and a wooden hoop near the top gave it some shape. There were pockets sewn along the bottom edge into which stones had been put to hold the sides down.

"They're my own design," she said. "I needed something easy to carry." She waved at the tangle of tree limbs above. "A bit of rope, a branch, some rocks and a candle and we have a sultan's tent."

"Do—ah, do they keep the rain out?"

"Not a downpour. They're more for privacy. And atmosphere. One needn't succumb to barbarism at every level. Would you like a drink?" Bandy handed him a bottle of whiskey.

"No thank you."

"Go on, I'm not going to charge you—poor boy wounded for his dead sister's honor!" She laughed at the expression on his face. "Well, don't tell me you think there's one of us who hasn't heard the story and sobbed her eyes out! Good Lord, my best five-dollar girl would love you up for two bits if we weren't afraid it might kill you, the state you're in. So drink!"

He laughed at that, though it hurt his bruised face, and took the bottle. It was much smoother than the other stuff, and his stomach didn't rebel. She took another big drink from the bottle and put it down between them.

"Are you hungry?" She crinkled some paper open in her lap. "The cook in camp four is from England and makes lovely meat pies." She offered him one.

"No thank you." He was ravenous but could hardly take her supper.

"Please? I hate to eat alone. And they're far too rich for me anyway. I've nothing but a figure to offer and have to keep it neat."

"All right, thank you." Aiden took one of the little pies.

He ate half of it in one bite. It was rich with beef and potatoes, onions and gravy, the crust crispy and light. He had never tasted anything so good.

"Did you teach them all how to dance like that?"

"Oh no. But it isn't very hard to do, just a lot of kicking and spinning around. No, I only know waltzes and quadrilles, all the proper dances for a Philadelphia girl."

"Is that where you're from?"

"Yes."

"Did you come across in a wagon train?"

"No, by ship, and never again!" She shuddered at the memory.

"Why?"

"Why? It was awful! I was seasick the whole way."

"I meant, why did you come? What compelled you?"

"Compelled me?" She laughed. "A new life, adventure, independence." She took out a little ivory pipe and a pouch of tobacco. "My father was a grocer. I was the fifth daughter and never a beauty, even before this." She waved a delicate gloved hand toward the veil. "My looks could have stood me being third, maybe even fourth, if we had a little more money or position. But a grocer's ugly number five! Well, I might have landed a nearsighted clerk, or a fat cobbler. A great hairy butcher, perhaps—at least a dull preacher, but I couldn't bear it. I'd seen sisters and cousins and friends, pretty ones too, all marry and have such dreary lives. Then there was an advertisement in the newspaper with an offer to teach school in San Francisco. They would sail us there in exchange for three years of teaching. After that I could make my own contract as I wished and marry if I wished." She opened a tin, took out a match and a folded bit of sandpaper, then snapped a flame. The pipe stem was long enough that she did not have to lift her veil to smoke, but the glowing tip made the amber beads sparkle.

"In Philadelphia everyone is stuck," she went on. "Everyone has a rank in society, and you dare not think to change it. You live in a house all crowded with rugs and carved settees and needlepoint footstools and pouchy chairs and fringed lampshades and heavy draperies and yappy little dogs and stupid novels about love in England, and I wanted more from life. The offer seemed perfect to me, and it was a relief for my family, I suspect. A respectable way to be rid of me." She took another swallow from the bottle, then handed it to Aiden, who did the same. His head was feeling much better.

"How long did you teach?" he asked.

"Not at all. I caught the smallpox on the ship, from a port in South America, most likely. My father did not believe in vaccination. He thought it went against God's divine will. So . . ." She shrugged. "That was how the will of God turned out for me. They said that I would frighten the children. They didn't hold me to the cost of my passage, but they gave me no employment either. So there I was, stranded across the world with no means or friends or home. I found an honest job, cutting fish in the market. Ten hours a day standing over a table of stink and your hands cold and aching. And after a week, I found out you're raped no matter what. Though, scarred as I was, it was twelve days for me." The beads on her veil clicked softly as she blew out the smoke. "It was a gallant lad who did it. He didn't hurt me too much, did it quick and even brought me some sweets the next day. I threw them in the guts pile. But I'm a smart girl. It didn't take me long to figure the ways of the world. Men would take what they wanted anyway, so why not make them pay for it?"

"Pay for what?" Aiden asked awkwardly.

"Oh goodness—" Bandy said, after a pause. "Oh, dear boy, do you know what rape is?"

"Some kind of a beating?" he guessed, for clearly it had hurt her.

"Well, partly, I suppose," she said. "You do know what sex is?"

"Of course. The act of marriage." He blushed. "And— well, what your girls do here."

"Yes. Well, if a man forces a woman to do the marriage act when she doesn't want to, that's called a rape."

"Why would a man force her?"

"Oh dear." She handed him the bottle. "Why is there any evil in the world?" Aiden took a drink. He certainly had no answer to that.

"But when men pay—it's all right?"

"Yes. Well, it can also happen without paying. With love, of course; so I've heard. But whether for money or love, if a girl agrees, it's all right. And with pay, then it's a business. Most say a bad business. Well, I say, fine, don't do it, then. But it's my business, and fairer than most. My girls—well, we take care of the needs of those who aren't married. We're like doctors," she laughed. "But without the nasty medicine and bloodletting and such."

Aiden paused a moment to let his brain sort all this out. He knew the mechanics and results of sex; any farm child did. He knew the swoony lovey bits from Jane Austen books and the wagon train girls with their flouncy tilts and candy smiles. He knew the physical urgency from his own body, and how to satisfy that for a while. He also knew there was something more—deeper, sharper, awful and grand, that some married people had. He just wasn't exactly sure how all these bits fit together.

"Is it . . . ?" He faltered. "I mean—you don't—mind?"

"I minded starving. I minded a lifetime trapped on the docks and men taking—" Bandy caught herself with ladylike restraint. "Well, men *taking*," she finished simply. "I met H'aiu soon after. He was working passage north on a ship, on his way to join Pu'heea, his cousin, up here." It was the first time Aiden had heard the exotic names pronounced correctly.

"So it was he who brought you up here, then?"

"No." She lifted her veil. "It was this that brought me here!" In the faint lamplight, Aiden could see how horribly scarred she was. Her whole face was pitted and blotched. Her eyes, pulled tight by the scar tissue, looked almost Chinese. He looked away. He could see shadows moving in the Arabian Nights tents, and it was as if an avalanche of understanding came down on him.

"No normal man will have me like this," Bandy said. "Not even in Seattle, where there are fifty men for every woman. Not to look at day after day. But out here, well—" She inhaled deeply. "Out here the light is dim and the men are desperate. Out here I can run my own show. And it's quite the show! Don't you think?"

"Yes!" Aiden agreed.

"Did you see anyone you particularly liked?"

"They all looked nice—" He stopped and felt a flush of embarrassment, realizing what she was really asking him.

"Here." Bandy offered him her pipe.

"No thanks, I don't smoke."

"You may have too many virtues to survive out here, young man."

"It's not virtue, it's cost," Aiden protested. "Tobacco costs, liquor costs. . . ."

"Whores cost. . . ."

"I didn't mean any disrespect."

"You're a sweet boy, Aiden Lynch." She gently laid her hand on the side of his face. "Does everyone pour out their life story to you upon first meeting?"

"I don't know."

Bandy laughed and swept gracefully to her feet. "I'd do you for free, only it shouldn't be something like me your first time."

"No—you're nice." He got up staggering and nearly fell over. Bandy caught his arm and steadied him.

"And you're clearly too battered to live through it anyway, so go on to bed. You look like death on a platter. The bunkhouse will be quieting down soon. Go on now." Bandy kissed him gently on the forehead. Her lips through the veil were both soft and scratchy.

33

"**Y**ou broke his nose," Mr. Powhee said solemnly. "And some ribs. His lost days are on your page now."

"A man can do some work with broken ribs. Could grease the skids," Aiden said.

"Some could." Powhee gave a rare smile. "But if William Buck had a splinter in his little finger he couldn't wipe his own ass. You are lucky you broke just his nose and not your own hand. Broken hand and you're out of work. All the bones matter here, you see? Arm? Elbow?" He wrapped his huge hand around Aiden's arm and bent it up. "Little finger bone here?" He grasped Aiden's finger and squeezed it until Aiden thought he might really snap it.

"But there are ways to fight without breaking the bones." Powhee dropped Aiden's hand and sat back. "I can teach you."

"How about you just send me to a different camp?" Aiden proposed, thinking about the delicious meat pie from camp four.

"I'm not talking about Buck. Buck can go to hell," he spat. "Bandy girls aren't the only entertainment out here. Men like fighting, and there's money in fighting."

"I learned that for my two dollars already."

"I don't mean that. I mean real fights." Powhee laughed. "My fights. There are rules, but the fights are real enough."

"I'm listening," Aiden said.

"They're held every other Saturday in camp three. You have to fight without damage. One dollar is guaranteed each fighter; the rest is wagers. After payout, thirty percent of the bets goes to me, ten to each of the other camp bosses, twenty-five percent to the winner, five to the loser."

"Meaning what? For a loser?"

"Any man can fight," Powhee explained. "But no one bets much on the bad fighters. For a bad fight, the loser might earn just fifty cents. But for the best matches, even if you lose, you get two, maybe three dollars."

"On top of the one guaranteed?"

"Yes."

This math was easy enough; if a loser was getting two dollars, the winner made ten.

"What are my chances?"

"You are tall, agile and fairly strong. You are good at sensing a person; that will help. You are too quick to anger; that will hurt. You learn fast, but you think you have learned more than you really know." Powhee tapped his fist on his chest. "You have no center, so you slip. You have a quick mind, so you recover. You don't care if you live or die. That could work either way." Aiden blushed under the cool assessment of his character.

"But we don't want men to die," Powhee went on. "Or even lose a day of work, so if it goes bad, we usually can stop it in time."

"How often have you failed at that?"

"Once."

Aiden nodded. Those odds were the best in his life so far. "All right, then. I'll fight."

Powhee trained him every night for a week. They slipped away to a different place in the woods every time, for there were always spies to fear. The fights, Aiden soon discovered, were good business. A few tips on a man's style, strength or tactics could greatly influence the wagers. It wasn't just Napoleon Gilivrey's camps involved either. The fights drew Indians, prospectors and traders. It seemed there was any number of shadowy people living up here in the distant forest eager for entertainment and the chance at riches.

There were few rules; essentially, no punching to the head with a closed fist and no head butts, eye gouging or biting. Kicking was legal to take a man down but not to break a knee and not at all once he was on the ground. If you wounded a man so he couldn't work, you were docked twice his pay for each missed day and banned from the next fight. But as Aiden soon found out, there was still plenty of hurt to go around. The fights were mostly a sort of wrestling. There were points for taking a man down and more points for lifting him whole off the ground while doing it, the higher the better. You won by pinning a man, by throwing him entirely out of the circle or by having more points. The awarding of points, however, was generally thought too complicated; the winner was more often chosen simply by the more raucous approval from the crowd.

Powhee taught Aiden useful skills: how to hunch against an avalanche of body blows or use leverage to escape a pin. He also taught him some show moves: how to dart in and slap his opponent silly, fake a dramatic fall and then spring up and slam the man down.

"They're stuck out here," Powhee explained. "So give them some show."

Aiden fought three times his first night. He was pinned within a minute his first time but won his second, though with little pride, for his opponent was slow and drunk and hardly worth the effort. But the third was a good match, long and difficult, exciting enough that betting was vigorous. Even though Aiden lost, and with a black eye and hurt upon him everywhere, the spectators cheered him off, and he pocketed three dollars from bets, plus the one guaranteed.

"Well done, lad." Bony slapped his back and handed him a bottle of whiskey. "You made me a tenner there—though I was fearful a few times you might turn it around!"

"You bet against me?" Aiden took a deep swallow.

"Of course! Jesus, I've seen the other fellow spin a man over his head like a baby. What do you think? It ain't a charity, lad."

34

Winter settled in, with a strange and disconcerting mildness and the same bleak dishrag sky day after day. Aiden did not miss the bone-scraping winds and terrifying blizzards of Kansas, but he did long for the clear winter sky, the deep, sharp blue that made his teeth sting. Here the occasional snowfall dusted the trees, but it was a desultory effort, like an ancient auntie applying powder for a dance where she knew she would just sit in the corner, saved from solitude only by young nephews charged with her attendance, dutifully arriving with cups of punch. Still, overall it was better than Kansas, who was just an old witch, purely out to kill. Once there was a real snowstorm and the men worked quickly to move fallen trees, for snow made the easiest road of all. Soon the banks of the creek were crowded with timber awaiting the spring floods.

Aiden was getting better with the crosscut saw, but didn't like it as much as the axe. Still, it was exciting to see a huge tree come down. Felling was a dangerous business, with many ways to go deadly wrong, but that just made it more interesting. A falling tree sheared limbs off other trees as it broke through the canopy. These branches, justly called widowmakers, could fly anywhere and crush a man before he saw them coming.

"I saw a fellow impaled once," Bony told him grimly. "A branch as thick as my arm went right through him here to here." He touched his chest just below the collarbone, then the back of the opposite hip. "Pinned him to the ground like a spear. We had to saw the branch through to get him free. The boss went ahead and shot him in the head first. He was lucky. Some won't do that."

Aiden said nothing. Mr. Powhee usually wore a pistol, but Aiden had figured it was for show.

His new life settled into a comfortable routine: cut down trees, eat, sleep, fight. With days of work, nights of liquor and the constant bruising of the fights, time passed in acceptable numbness. There were only two or three miles between each of the five camps, but since they were located in stream valleys, there were steep hills to cross in between. Aiden didn't mind the walks; in fact, he liked them. The trails were good, and climbing the hills strengthened his legs for the wrestling. He usually left as soon as the Saturday noon whistle halted their work, grabbing some sandwiches to eat on the way while the others ate their full meal and took a nap before departing.

He liked walking alone. He liked the mossy solitude of these strange, dense woods. He liked the silent cushion of pine needles beneath his feet and the way shafts of sunlight sometimes broke through and lit up the mist between the massive tree trunks. Along the trails, moss grew in thick emerald green carpets, punctuated by little clusters of mushrooms. He did not even mind the rain. There was no slant to it here; it fell straight and steady with a gentle percussion. Aiden liked these walks mostly because, for a little while, time and the world did not exist.

The fights generally started around four, as darkness fell early in the North Woods in winter. He would fight two or three men a night and sleep there after, for the trail was too dark and his body too thumped for the journey home. Increasingly, he was too drunk as well. Whiskey was a welcome friend after the brutal nights, and those who won money on him were always generous.

On Sunday morning at first light, after mugs of strong coffee and plates of bacon and eggs, the men would all walk back to their own camps, pick up their tools and start work again.

Aiden came to know men in all the camps but still generally kept to himself. The Kansas boys lived in camp three and so were always at the fights. They had both become fallers and were gaining a reputation as the fastest team in any of the camps, able to zip the long saw through the biggest tree trunk as smoothly as a hot knife through butter. They loved to bet and always put something on Aiden, even when he was clearly outmatched. Somehow they generally broke even and never seemed to lose their high spirits.

William Buck was usually at the fights as well, though he kept a careful distance. Powhee had transferred him to camp two, which was populated by the roughest down-and-outs, scary, evil-eyed men, sneaky and grim.

"It's the worst timber there," Old Finn explained. "Steepest hills and weakest stream. Hardly worth the effort to run a camp, but they need someplace to put the bad ones, and Gilivrey will always manage to squeeze out a profit."

Buck liked to bet but would not fight himself.

"It's a stupid kind of fighting," he declared frequently. "Ain't really even fighting when you got all kinds of rules and can't even punch a man in the face!"

Aiden never spoke to him but was secretly pleased to

notice the permanent squashed mess of his nose. The widower showed up now and then but never bet, for he was intent on saving every penny.

"They say the railroad will be across in another three or four years," he told Aiden one night. "I can bring my children out then." It was his only goal.

A few of the Bandy girls usually arrived in camp three for fight night, but rarely the whole group, and they never bothered with the musical show. It wasn't a good night for them; half the men would have lost all their money, and the winners were generally too drunk and raucous to spend much on the girls. But Bandy usually came along to mind her few charges, while sending Mr. Hi-yow to guard the rest of the girls in another camp. She and Aiden would sit up late talking and drinking together like old friends. She was the only person he felt comfortable with. She was twenty-three, he had learned, and her real name was Amanda. She had a nice singing voice, could shoot his bow amazingly well and owned two full sets of long underwear made of China silk. (She hated the feel of wool against her skin.) She could make any dog, anywhere, do anything she asked with just a soft word and a wave of her hand. Talking with her was easy. He even let her sit beside him one night while the cook sewed up a cut on his head. When the clumsy needle jabbed him painfully deeply and he yelped despite himself, she grasped his hand, and he did not pull away. Her palm was soft, but he could feel the scarred skin stretched tight. She had not shown him her face again since the first night they had met.

"You actually like the fighting, don't you?" she asked. "It isn't just money or pride for you."

"Yeah." He winced at the tug of thread against his scalp. Maddy had been so gentle, he'd never felt her knots.

"Why?"

"I don't know. Makes you feel something."

"Makes you feel hurt."

"Yeah, but hurt is something." The cook finished and clipped the thread. Aiden gave him a quarter and took a deep drink of whiskey. The cut was on the back of his head, so it didn't matter how it looked.

"My girls can make you feel something."

"So I hear."

"You're a rich man now, and sixteen years old. Aren't you feeling some . . . longing?"

"I'm done with all longings."

Bandy burst out laughing. Aiden pulled away. "I'm sorry." She caught his arm tenderly, then giggled again. "It's just the way you said that—it's like a line from a melo-drama!"

Aiden hunched up and looked into the fire.

"Oh, dear boy, don't become all . . . all grim, and moody and—starey at the coals! All you big strong men and not one of you can take a little ribbing. 'I'm done with all longings,' " she mimicked.

"I wouldn't think you had to drum up business," he snapped in a flash of anger. "Fights get everyone riled up and ready to rut; I would have thought that would be enough on my part."

"Now you're being mean."

He could hear the hurt in her voice. He blushed, for it was true.

"It's all right to have longings," she went on. "After all, you're not dead!"

"Well, I should be! Better me than—than—" He stopped. "Sorry. My head aches and I'm tired. I have to go." He picked up his jacket and started to walk away. "I didn't mean any insult to you."

"Aiden." Bandy caught his arm. "Wait. Is that what you're thinking? Is that what you don't want to feel? Why you would rather have your head bashed open?"

A group of men walked by and she fell silent until they had passed.

"You couldn't have saved your sister," Bandy whispered. "You know that."

"No, but—" His voice was shaking. He hadn't talked about Maddy with anyone since she'd died.

"But nothing!" Bandy pressed. "The river is like a tornado—you can't hold against it!"

"I should have taken her out," he said, the words tumbling out before he could hold them back. "I should have got her back east somehow right after the fire. I should have thought up some way. Instead I thought up reasons not to. I told myself it was outlaws and blizzards, but really it was just me being afraid. Any way I pictured it, either she would die or someone would take her from me. I didn't want to be the only one left. I was ready for us both dying, but not her being gone and me the only one left. I was selfish."

"Love is always selfish," Bandy said softly.

"Love is supposed to be the opposite of selfish," Aiden protested. "Like you would run into a pack of wolves to save someone you love."

"Exactly. Because feeding yourself to the wolves is easier than to go on living without the one you love. Listen to me now, Aiden Lynch." She squeezed his hand. "I don't know what I know about love. But I do know you did not fail your sister for lack of it."

Christmas came, and some of the men received letters and packages. There was roast beef for dinner and extra whiskey. It snowed on New Year's Day, only a few inches, but the scheduled fight was postponed a few days so the men could slide trees closer to the stream banks. When they finally gathered, everyone was in extra-high spirits.

"Well, Prairie Boy." Powhee's white smile gleamed. "I hope your pockets are strong, for we're going home rich tomorrow!"

"All right with me." Aiden watched the men stamping and shivering around the circle. He had won two fights already, though one opponent had been an old alcoholic miner so staggering and frail that Aiden had had to work hard not to hurt him.

"Who do I fight for these riches, then?" he asked. "The Chief?" He looked at the stocky man laughing with some other men across the ring. He was a big-money fighter, a half-Indian French Canadian who lived in the backwoods upstream somewhere. It was rumored that he had two or three wives and showed up for fights whenever he had a falling-out with one and needed cash for a peace present. He was a strong and challenging opponent, but he lacked imagination, and after losing to him twice, Aiden had figured him out and defeated him dramatically in their last bout, the upset earning him a fortune of twenty-five dollars.

"No, you're ruined with the Chief now. Everyone knows you'll beat him. I have much better for you—there!" Powhee nodded toward the bunkhouse, where the door flung open.

"Damn, no!" Aiden's heart sank. Framed in the doorway was the Bull, a pure monster of a man. His head barely missed the lintel, and his arms would have scraped the door-frame had he not turned a little as he walked through.

"Bull! Bull!" the men started cheering. The nickname was fitting, for besides being as big and strong as a bull, the man had all the explosive power of the animal. The first time he'd fought the Bull, Aiden had been on his back before the echo of the starting gong had stopped.

"Christ almighty, Powhee!" Aiden protested. "The ground is frozen! It'll be a damn hard landing!"

"You're a good fighter now, Prairie Boy. You might stand a full round."

"Sure—if you nail my boots to the ground."

"I have a strategy."

"What? Give him a hammer and saw and have him build my coffin?"

"Ha—it's good to joke in the face of disaster." Powhee clapped his broad hand on Aiden's back. "Feint to the left," he whispered, glancing around to be sure they were alone.

"I feinted last time."

"He'll remember that. But you tried to take him down last time. This time you're just going to hold on."

"To what?"

"To him! Like a slug, you know?" Powhee made a wet sucking sound and slapped his palms together. "That's the strategy! One round and we're both rich."

"How about two rounds—we could be millionaires!"

"Feint left."

"My left or his left?"

Powhee waved impatiently. "That way."

"Right."

"No, left! I have learned that his left eye is almost blind."

"Why didn't you tell me earlier? I could have been pre-pared."

Powhee shrugged. "The only preparation you could have done was make a will, and I know you have nothing to leave, so why ruin your whole day? Go on now. If you hang on, he can't throw you out of the ring. All we need is one round!"

Aiden walked grimly into the ring. *Be the slug,* he said to himself. As a totemic animal, it wasn't exactly inspiring.

"All bets in!" The tote men hurried to get their money. Betting for a Bull fight was especially complicated, as no one made a simple win-lose wager. The winner was a given; the money was on timing and style. A loser was a winner if he simply stayed a full minute in the ring; a whole round was unheard of.

"Jesus, lad, there's bets for if you just don't wet your pants!" Bony laughed. "Or how long until you cry!"

"Some cry before the gong!" Old Finn added.

"Gentlemen!" Mr. Powhee waved the two men into the ring and the crowd cheered. Aiden actually liked the Bull. Outside the ring he was good-natured and mild. He had been a mer-chant sailor before misfortune brought him to the camps, and after their first fight he'd gotten Aiden generously drunk and told him stories about China. He was four inches taller than Aiden and had forty more pounds of solid muscle and the strongest legs anyone had ever seen. His arms were like roof beams, bigger around than some men's thighs. Nice as he might be in real life, in the ring he would turn a man inside out without a second thought.

Aiden braced. The gong sounded. The Bull charged. Aiden feinted. The Bull was indeed slowed—for half a second. Instead of a full-on body slam, he merely threw one mighty arm out and crashed it across Aiden's chest. Aiden was knocked back but flung both his arms over the Bull's arm and held on. The Bull whirled around so fast Aiden's feet dragged a circle in the dirt, as if he were a child being spun in a game.

Aiden used the momentum of the man's blow to swing his legs up. He wrapped them around the Bull's waist and clung with everything he had. He couldn't have been more sluglike unless he'd sucked on the man's face. The Bull smacked him hard between the shoulder blades. It was an open-handed smack, completely legal, but so hard Aiden wondered if his heart could actually burst.

"Don't make me hurt you!" the Bull growled.

I am the slug. Aiden focused. A round was two minutes long. They were about thirty seconds into it now. The Bull had never needed to pin a man, so Aiden had no idea how he would go about it. He could just drop down and flatten Aiden beneath his body. Or he could kneel down and pin him with the one arm to which Aiden still clung like some wretched baby monkey. Aiden closed his eyes, hoped against hope and let go of the Bull's arm. Then he arched his back, still hanging on with his legs, reached back and grabbed the Bull's knee. He yanked hard and the man stumbled forward.

The crowd went crazy. There were thirty more seconds of frantic, muddy thrashing, but miraculously, the first-round gong sounded with both men still inside the ring and Aiden not yet pinned. Aiden's every muscle trembled from the effort it had taken just to hold on. He loosened his grip and slipped off like a gob of mud. The Bull grinned, grabbed his hand and pulled him up. Aiden felt as if he had just flown around the world: exhausted but exhilarated.

"Nice job, Prairie Boy," the Bull growled. "How do you want it now—down or out?"

Aiden spat out a mouthful of dirt and wiped his face on his sleeve.

"I don't fancy being crushed, thanks," Aiden panted.

"Out it is, then."

Aiden was not about to yield, but the choice was never his to make. The gong sounded the second round, and this time the Bull simply grabbed him by the arm, flipped him over, caught hold of his leg and yanked him into the air. Aiden thrashed, but the Bull didn't even flinch.

"You want to slap me some?" The Bull leaned over close enough for Aiden to smack him in the face, which Aiden did, with real anger and hard as he could, open-handed for the rules, but with the heel of his hand driving at the man's jaw. The Bull actually flinched, frowned and did not have to make a show of pain, for his eyes watered and blood dripped from the corner of his mouth.

"Damn little bastard, aren't you?" the Bull laughed. Then he tightened his grip, dangled Aiden like a lamb, walked over to the edge of the circle and dropped him gently out of the ring.

"**Y**ou fight like an Indian."

Aiden was startled by the voice in the darkness and strained to see beyond the shadows.

"Who's there?" His head was buzzing, and the noise of the crowd still swirled around the clearing. "Is someone there?"

"Just a friend, Wet Pony."

Aiden's heart jolted and he took a step deeper into the darkness. Behind him, a log tumbled the fire into a flare of brightness, and he caught a glimpse of a ragged figure.

"Tupic? Is that you?"

Aiden went to him, surprised and glad, but stopped in shock as he saw him up close. The man in the shadows was indeed Tupic, but Aiden wasn't sure he would even have recognized him in passing. The once-muscular body was now thin. Where Tupic always stood boldly, this wraith seemed skittish, like a kicked dog. Tupic's hair was long and glossy; this man's was dull and crudely cut. He wore filthy clothes and boots too big for him.

"I am glad to see you. You look well," Tupic said.

"You look terrible," Aiden said without thinking. "What happened? What are you doing here?" The noise of celebration roared up and startled Tupic. "Here, come with me," Aiden said, taking Tupic's arm. He almost recoiled at the smell of him.

"Hey, you," Aiden called to the whistlepunk, a boy of twelve who did scut work in the camp. "Bring us food and coffee to the stable. And my blanket," he instructed. "And whiskey. Go, hurry now." He steered Tupic toward the stable. Most of the visiting loggers slept there, but it was empty right now, as everyone was still out waiting for the next fight. They went inside and found an empty stall. Tupic sank back into a pile of hay.

"Where did you come from?" Aiden asked. "How did you find me?"

"I came from Seattle, from the jail there."

"Jail?"

Tupic coughed and shivered.

"Are you ill?"

"No. Just tired. I have had a long journey."

Aiden took off his jacket and draped it over Tupic's shoulders.

"Tell me what happened. Why were you in jail?"

"Clever Crow is dead," Tupic said. "Of the Devil's Paint."

"Smallpox? But you said he was all right!" Aiden protested. "That he didn't get it."

"Not from the soldiers, not that time, but after." He pulled the jacket tightly around his shoulders. "Your people have found gold in the land you call British Columbia, and many travel there. They bring the sickness with them everywhere now."

"But—why were you in jail?"

Tupic rubbed his eyes and settled back in the straw. "After I saw you the last time, at the river, I was angry from our talk. I was also sad, for we parted in argument. My spirit was uneasy. I went away into the woods to seek answers. I prayed and fasted as we do, but the visions that came were confusing. I wanted to talk to Clever Crow, for he has knowledge of visions. He was in a fishing camp farther north, with the people of his wife, so I rode to meet with him. But on the way I learned that he was dead of the sickness."

"I'm sorry," Aiden said. "He was a good man."

"He was close to the spirits. So we have only the sadness of missing his company. We do not fear for the journey of his soul. Do you understand?"

"Yes." Aiden shivered. He thought of Maddy and wished he could believe in the journey of the soul.

"Clever Crow is—was—to me what you call godfather. He is the one who guided my path and gave my name."

The whistlepunk arrived just then. He had a tray with two steaming mugs of coffee, half a loaf of bread, a chunk of cheese, a quarter of an apple pie, some boiled onions and a whole roasted chicken leg on a tin plate.

"Cook says special for you," the boy said as he set the tray down. "He won twenty dollars! For you lasting the round—that was how he bet his one dollar."

"Tell him thanks." He gave the boy a few pennies for a tip.

"And this is from the Bull!" The whistlepunk pulled a pint bottle of good whiskey out of his pocket. His eyes shone with admiration as he handed it to Aiden. "That was great, Mr. Aiden! Weren't you afraid?"

"He was never going to kill me," Aiden said tersely. He had never been called "mister" and it felt very strange. "Go on now," he told the whistlepunk. "Give my thanks to the Bull." He pulled the cork from the bottle and took a deep drink. His whole body was shaking and he didn't want the boy to notice. The whistlepunk ran out. Aiden offered the bottle to Tupic, who shook his head.

"Whiskey is not good for Indians."

"Glad I'm not Indian, then," he said. "Eat." He waved at the food. "I'm not hungry." Actually, he hadn't eaten since a sandwich during his walk, and his stomach was growling. Tupic picked up the chicken leg and took a ravenous bite. Aiden took another big drink of the whiskey and felt the quivers beginning to fade.

"Tell me all that's happened," he said.

"In my visions I saw soldiers coming to kill all my people," Tupic said. "I saw them running away into the mountains. The path was covered with blood, like a river washing over their feet. So this was my question for Clever Crow: Do I see the future of my people? And if so, is there power to change it? But my uncle was dead and I did not know who to ask. Please—" Tupic paused and held out a chunk of bread and cheese to Aiden. "I see that you are hungry."

Aiden took it and tried not to devour it too obviously.

"I learned that in a camp nearby was my good friend," Tupic went on. "His name is Hinmaton-yalatkit. He is also called Joseph, after his father, who the missionaries named Joseph. He is maybe thirty years old, and we are of different bands, but I know him since I am a small boy, when all come together at the festivals. To the little boys, he is like a hero. He would shoot with us, and wrestled and played our games. He never chased us away. To be near him, you feel—our word for it means lightness in the heart; also, peaceful feeling at home after a journey. I had not seen him in almost two years, but he remembered my name. He is Thunder Coming Out of the Water, I am Sunlight Shining Deep into the Water. So he always makes jokes, you see? But now I saw Joseph with the—pose?—of a chief." Tupic frowned. "I don't know the word."

"The bearing," Aiden suggested. "The presence of a chief."

"Yes. I saw the touch of spirit on him. I talked to him late into the night. I told him my dream and he says he will pray to see the meaning. That night I dreamed again of my people on the blood road. This time, I saw Joseph lead them to safety. But when he turned I saw his face is covered with spots and he is only a ghost. Then all our people disappeared in the forest like smoke."

Tupic's dark eyes searched Aiden's face.

"I woke that day with understanding," Tupic went on, his voice fading slightly with fatigue. "I saw that our people face bad times and need great chiefs. What if these chiefs all die from the Devil's Paint? I decided I will go to Seattle and buy the vaccine. I thought this was the call of my dream. I talked with the elders and with Joseph. They all agreed. We had money from the salmon. I thought it would be simple."

Tupic took a drink of the coffee and winced at the bitter taste. Aiden felt bad that he hadn't thought to ask for sugar.

"Silent Wolf was now strong, and so he came with me to Seattle," Tupic went on. "I never saw such a place, so many people and buildings and ships. I thought I knew about your people, from the missionary school, but I was very stupid. We saw a building that looked like the most important building. I thought it should be for the doctor. It was made of brick, not wood, and the sign was FIRST SECURITY over the door." Tupic shrugged. "*First* means the best, right? And *security* is to be safe. So was I really so stupid to think this?"

"No," Aiden said. His heart sank, for he knew disaster was coming. "I would have thought the same."

"As soon as I went in, I knew it was not a hospital, but I did not know what it was. It was not a store. A man said to leave, that it is a bank and we have no business there. I know a bank is for money, and that money is dangerous with your people, so we went. The man had buttons on his jacket like the army. Down the street, we saw a church—that is easy with the cross. So we went in there. We asked for a doctor. The preacher showed us where to go. We asked the doctor to sell us the vaccine. He said no. He cannot give the vaccine to Indians. I told him not give; we have money to buy. He said no vaccine for the Indians. Then police came. They put us in the jail."

Tupic seemed exhausted from telling so much.

"Why did they put you in jail?" Aiden asked.

"They said Indians plan raids. I told that we only want to buy the vaccine. But they keep us prisoner. Every day they asked us questions about Indian plan. We do not know the tribes near Seattle, I told them. They are Salish and Yakima, we are Nez Perce. But they tied us up and beat us. They said all the Indians will join together to raid and kill.

"Days passed, and Silent Wolf was very angry. He said we cannot trust white men, to remember Sand Creek. I thought of Sand Creek, but also of the missionaries at my school. I know the bad soldiers and bad people in your wagon train, the man named Buck, the ones who looked evil at us, but also, I know many are good: you and your sister and Mr. Jackson." Tupic paused. "Excuse me, for I do not ask of them. They are all well?"

Aiden hesitated. "Yes," he lied.

"I am glad for that." Tupic went on, "I told Silent Wolf the jail men will not kill us. I know the Constitution of Thomas Jefferson and the Bible of Jesus. We have done nothing wrong. I asked to send a letter to Mr. Jackson. But weeks passed and we were still in the jail. When they talked to us we were always tied on the chair. Then one day the man put a rope on my neck. He said Indians attacked a farm and killed the family. They said to Silent Wolf they will hang me if he does not tell of the Indian plan. But we don't know any plan. When the guard comes near, Silent Wolf kicked him hard so he fell. Then Silent Wolf smashed him with his head and with the chair still tied on him. The chair crushed the guard's throat. Then more men came in and killed Silent Wolf with sticks."

Tupic looked up at the barn rafters. Outside, there was a roar of noise from the fights. "I tried to think of something to tell them—but no plan made sense. Why would we come so far from our homeland—ask to buy vaccine—if we wanted to hurt the white people? What plan do we have?"

Aiden felt his heart beating so hard he wondered if the Bull really had smashed it.

"I am sorry," Aiden said. Tupic only nodded. Aiden saw him trembling and thought he might be about to cry. He gave his friend some time to recover. Tupic took another drink of the coffee and Aiden saw that two teeth had been knocked out from one side of his mouth.

"At the time of your New Year," Tupic finally continued, "four days ago, many people were in the jail. They were drunk and fighting. I took the belt from one. He was drunk asleep. I rubbed the buckle on the stones to make it sharp and I cut off my hair. Then I changed his clothes with mine. The jail police also drink all night. When they let all the New Year men out, I went out with them."

Aiden heard the gong sound for a new fight. His mind was spinning in a dozen different directions. "How did you find me?"

"Everyone in the jail knows the camps of Napoleon Gilivrey. He pays the jailers to send him men to work. So I think this is also the place where Mr. Jackson should bring you."

Aiden rubbed his cold hands over the bruises on his face.

"I'm glad you came to me," he said. "I can find a place for you to stay for now and then help you get home. I have some money saved, from the fights. . . ."

"I do not go home," Tupic said. He sat up straight and looked at Aiden with a steady dark gaze. "I came for the vaccine. This is my . . . journey. You can buy the vaccine for me. I still have the money. We buried it."

"What do you mean? I can't buy vaccine around here."

"In Seattle. You are white. They will sell it to you."

"I can't." Aiden recoiled. "I can't leave. I have to work."

"It is a small journey."

"They won't let me go." Aiden looked away. It was true that Powhee would not easily let him go, but it was more true that he did not want to leave. He didn't want to go back out into the world. He didn't want to talk to anyone or figure anything out or have to make anything come out right. Hard as this life was, the hurt was clear and predictable. This pain had rules and ends. Bad was really just fine when you knew the size and shape of it.

"I can't," he said. "I'm sorry."

"We are friends."

"No."

"Is our friendship only smoke?"

"No, but it was between different people in a different life."

Tupic stiffened and Aiden suddenly saw the same chiefly dignity of Clever Crow. "It is not our way to make something important the same as trade of fish or blankets; to make it *this for that*," Tupic said coldly. "But I am tired now, and my cousin and my uncle are dead, and all my people are in danger, so I will make it that way. We saved your life in the river. It is your duty now to repay. I must ask you this for that."

"**I** need a week off work," Aiden said. The fights were over, the camp quiet. Powhee was sitting alone in the cook-house by the stove, having a last smoke before bed. He had a cot set up for his use in a corner of the room.

Powhee just laughed. "Me too, Prairie Boy."

"I have business in Seattle."

"Seattle? What possible business could you have there?"

"I will pay you for my days. A week for me now, after board, is ten dollars. You know I have the money."

"One week is not ten dollars." Powhee's tone turned sharp as he realized Aiden was serious. "For one week we pay you ten dollars, but the trees you cut bring Mr. Gilivrey much more."

Aiden felt stupid for not thinking of this.

"How much more?"

"More than you have, or will ever have." Powhee smiled. "So forget it."

"Count it up," Aiden said coldly. "Write it down. I'll work it off."

"It will take you months."

"Well, I'll do my best to live that long."

"No one leaves the camps until their debt is finished."

"I don't intend to skip out."

"Of course not. Mr. Gilivrey would pay twice your debt to anyone who brought in your head. Your real head." Powhee sliced a finger across his own throat. "He'd take no other proof. Rotting in a sack, pickled in a crock, even skinned, just the face, peeled off the skull, wouldn't matter as long as he could see it was you."

"I don't intend to skip."

"San Francisco, China, Japan, it wouldn't matter how far you went. Hawaii? I have fifty-seven cousins there."

"I will come back in one week."

"You are not going anywhere."

Now Aiden chose his words carefully. "Mr. Gilivrey must be a little bit pleased with me, for I've won so much in the fights." He took a deep breath and proceeded very cautiously. "He must enjoy his cut of the betting, after all."

Powhee clenched his jaw and his spiral tattoos swirled in the shadowy light.

"Like everyone else in the camps," Aiden went on. "Like the camp bosses, the men who handle the bets, the cook who sews us up, even the Chinamen who wash the blood out of our clothes. And of course, you, Mr. Powhee; how much of your percentage goes to Mr. Gilivrey anyway?"

"Do you think you are the first piss-pant to threaten me this way?" Powhee said angrily.

"No," Aiden said. "But I think I'm the first to make you enough money to have it work."

"Who is that Indian?"

Tupic's presence in the camp had of course been noticed, but Aiden was surprised that Powhee had connected them so quickly.

"An old friend," Aiden replied.

"He is trouble for you."

"I know."

273

"What does he want you to do?"

"A favor."

"And how am I supposed to explain your absence?"

Aiden hadn't thought of this. "I don't know. You are a smart man. And fearsome."

Now Powhee's tattoos relaxed and he looked resigned, almost sullen. "If I let you go, it would be logical for me to help you accomplish your task."

"I guess it would," Aiden said simply. "But I'm not all that logical. We'll leave before first light. We won't be seen. I'll need some of my cash winnings for the trip, though. Twenty dollars should do."

Powhee stared at him, then reached into his moneybag.

"You can't go through East Royal St. Petersburg," he said. "So from camp five, go west over the Saddle ridge and follow the first creek down. It will put you on the river about a mile south of there. You can follow the river all the way to Seattle, but don't be seen, for I won't say I allowed you to leave."

"All right."

"Don't trust anyone for anything in Seattle," he said. "Go to Ruby's on the docks for a room; she's clean enough, mostly fair and she pays guards to look out for the Shanghai crews. Anywhere else you go, watch your back, watch your drink—they'll slip you a knockout potion and you'll wake up on a ship to China."

"I'll be careful."

"Everyone knows Napoleon Gilivrey. And almost everyone owes Napoleon Gilivrey. Remember that."

"I will." Aiden nodded and pocketed his money. "Thank you."

Aiden felt restless when he lay down in the straw, but the long day soon caught up with him and he fell asleep quickly. He still woke well before dawn, just as the darkest black began to seep from the sky. Tupic was already awake, or perhaps he had never slept. He sat up in the corner of the stall, the blanket wrapped around his shoulders, rocking slightly as he chanted softly under his breath.

Aiden got unsteadily to his feet and found his kit bag. The two crept quietly out of the stable and into the thick mist. They covered the trail in good time, and it was still before sunrise when they reached camp four, but Aiden knew the cook would already be awake. He had Tupic stay in the woods while he slipped closer and waited until he saw the cook go outside to smoke his pipe. Then he snuck in and took a loaf of bread and a chunk of ham. He looked around hopefully for some of the famous meat pies, but there were none lying about.

Men were starting to rouse by the time they reached camp five, so they crept around the outskirts. The vast trunks of the trees too big to cut stood like solitary giants among the hundreds of stumps. Tree limbs, twisted and crushed by the fall of the timber, littered the ground like monster bones. But as Aiden and Tupic moved toward the ridge, the normal forest returned. The sun broke as they crested and was strong enough to warm them as they made their way down the other side. They reached the main river by midafternoon.

"Wait here," Tupic said. It was the first either had spoken all day. "I have a canoe hidden in the brush just downriver. I borrowed it from a Salish village outside of Seattle."

He was gone less than an hour, but to Aiden it felt like a

lifetime. Every scratch and twitch in the forest set his spine tingling. His ears strained to hear voices. There shouldn't be any loggers around here, for every right-sized tree was already cut, but he still feared discovery. Finally Tupic returned, sliding the dugout silently up to the muddy bank. Aiden stepped in and the little boat rocked drastically.

"Can this thing really carry us?"

"If you don't lunge around like an elk."

Aiden lowered himself cautiously and Tupic pushed them out into the slow current. Aiden had never been in a canoe of any sort, but the dugout felt especially tippy. Every time he paddled, the wretched boat would tilt and wrench sideways.

"Don't lean so much," Tupic said. He sat in the back, trying hard to compensate for such a clumsy partner. "And don't stab the water."

"I haven't paddled a lot of damn canoes!" Aiden said.

"You paddle like you're chopping down a tree."

"Well, how should I paddle?"

"Smooth, like you are brushing your horse's neck."

"I haven't brushed a lot of horse necks either."

Suddenly the heaviness between them began to lighten. The afternoon was sunny and mild, the current light, and after a while Aiden did get the hang of paddling, though Tupic still had to work to keep them near a straight line. For a little while it began to feel like just a pleasant outing, two old friends off to fish and camp in the woods.

39

Although he had walked alongside this same river when Jackson had first brought them to East Royal St. Petersburg, Aiden didn't remember anything of the landscape. It seemed like an eternity ago, though it was just over four months. They stopped to camp when Aiden guessed they were several miles from Seattle. Aiden knew the camp supplies had come up the river two days earlier, so there would't be another of Gilivrey's boats for three days. Still, he preferred to remain hidden from the world.

They had no hooks or line for fishing, no leather or twine to make a snare and no bow and arrows for any birds or small game, so they had to be content with the last bits of bread and ham for a poor supper. It barely stopped their stomachs from growling. They did not risk a fire but made a simple lean-to for shelter, carpeting the ground with pine needles. It was a rare clear night, cold, but not unbearably so. If they kept their heads covered and huddled close beneath the one blanket, they might even sleep some. With so little to do, they lay down long before they were sleepy, poking their heads out of the lean-to so they could look at the stars through the branches overhead.

"That's the one thing I miss from the prairie," Aiden said. "On a moonless night, the sky is just dripping with stars. It feels like you could just reach up and scoop up a handful. Toss them around, eat them, feed them to the chickens if you like."

"What would they taste like?" Tupic laughed.

"Cold, I always thought, and a little sour."

"I always thought sweet. Like rock candy."

"You just like candy."

"Yes."

"Maybe if you floated up there and ate them directly, they'd be sweet," Aiden agreed. "But I think everything turns sour that comes to earth."

"In our stories, the night sky is a very busy place," Tupic said. "There are always people being turned into stars; usually lovers who can't marry each other. Powerful shamans may become stars, and certain animals who bring gifts to the people. And warriors, of course," he laughed. "Especially if they also have the love problem! I think anyone can be a star with a good story."

"When I was a child," Aiden said, "I thought the sky was a blanket, separating earth from heaven, and the stars were holes in the blanket, letting the light shine through. Whenever someone good died they poked a hole in the blanket, so finally, there would be enough holes made in the blanket that it would just crumble away, and then we would all be in heaven."

"Is that the Bible or Aesop?"

"No," Aiden said. "Just childish thoughts."

"It is a long time since we were children."

"Yes," Aiden said. Wispy clouds filmed across the sky, blurring the stars. "I have to tell you something. When you asked about Maddy, I lied. I didn't want to talk of it then. But the truth is, she died, drowned." He told the story in the barest of words. Tupic listened silently, then turned on his side, rustling the pine needles.

"So now there is one more hole in your blanket."

"Yes."

"And the Great Spirit is learning about all the countries in the *Atlas of the World*."

Aiden laughed and quickly brushed the tears off his face, pretending to scratch his forehead.

"What do you think happened to Dr. Carlos?" Tupic finally asked. "It must have been terrible for him."

"I don't know," Aiden said coldly. "I don't care."

He felt the chill start to creep through his clothes.

40

Breakfast was a drink of water from the river. Then they dragged out the canoe and were paddling downriver before the morning mist had lifted.

"How far until the Salish camp?" Aiden asked.

"Maybe another mile."

"Can I walk in by myself?"

"They are used to white men, but I will be with you."

"No. The police in Seattle will be looking for you in every Indian village nearby."

"They would not betray me."

"Not one?" Aiden pressed. "What if there's a bounty on your head? You escaping out of jail is bad enough, but they're sure to put the guard's death on you too, and that's hanging. Even if no one betrayed you, if they all protected you, what if the police found out later that the Salish helped you—what would happen to them?"

Tupic was quiet, but Aiden felt him paddling extra hard.

"I will go in alone," Aiden went on. "I'll say I found the canoe abandoned on the riverbank. I'll get food for you; then you will go to Mr. Jackson's trading post. It's on the sound, a place called Brightfish Bend, north of Seattle. You'll have to make your own way to the coast, but then there should be a trail."

"But I have to go with you to get the money," Tupic protested. "I can't describe where we buried it."

"I don't need your money."

"How will you buy the vaccine?"

"I'm not going to buy it," Aiden said.

"What do you mean?"

"Why would someone like me need to buy smallpox vaccine? Did you think about that? Do I just walk into the general store and ask for it?"

Tupic looked surprised, then embarrassed. "You get it from a doctor."

"Just like that?" Aiden sighed. "Do you even know what it looks like? I mean—how it comes? Is it liquid in a jug? Or in little medicine bottles? Or is it a powder?"

"I don't know," Tupic said. Aiden knew it wasn't Tupic's fault, but he still had to fight the urge to grab him by the throat and throw him out of the canoe. Aiden was about to walk into a strange city to somehow obtain something, he didn't know what, from someone, he didn't know who, and transport it out again, he didn't know how.

"Just get yourself to Mr. Jackson's trading post and wait there."

"What will you do?"

"Figure something out."

They paddled in silence for a while. "Allow two days for me in Seattle," Aiden went on, thinking aloud. "Then a day to Jackson's place." He counted up the days and felt sick at the lack of them. "I have to get back to the logging camp by Sunday. If I can't make it to Jackson's, I'll send word." It was a rickety little plan, but it was the only one he could come up with.

The city of Seattle was nothing like Aiden had imagined. He felt guilty for how nice he had made it sound to poor Polly so long ago, on the night of the wolves. There were no ice cream parlors or music halls. Aside from a few brick buildings, most were rough clapboard, weathered gray and all the same. Some of the downtown area along the shops had boardwalks, but to cross the street he waded through ankle-sucking mud thickly studded with horse droppings. The breeze smelled of tidal ooze, and the sky was thick with sooty smoke from the piles of burning sawdust slag at the sawmill. He ran a finger down the side of his face and found it black with grit.

It wasn't even four o'clock, but the winter twilight combined with the smoke in the air had lanterns flickering in windows. As he walked down the main street, voices called to him from every doorway, offering jobs, berths on ships, clean rooms, the cheapest whiskey, fair gambling, good laundry, the salvation of his soul and the best women.

"You hungry?" A Chinese boy grabbed his hand and tugged him toward a saloon. "Need best room? Golden Palace for you. Good stew here, real beef! No mule, no dog, no rat!"

"No thanks," Aiden said. "I'm looking for Ruby's place. Can you show me?"

"Ruby no good! Bugs in bed, water in whiskey! Come stay Grand Palace! Very nice here," the boy said loudly. Then he winked, tilted his head and cupped his fingers in an unmistakable way of asking for a tip. Aiden walked on, and when they were out of sight of the Grand Palace, he stopped.

"Well?" he said, casually tumbling a penny between his fingers.

"You need wash? Pretty girl? Good job? I know!"

"No thanks, just Ruby's."

"Down there." The boy pointed at one of the shabby buildings at the bottom of the hill.

Ruby was unimpressed with Aiden's mention of Mr. Powhee's name, but she seemed like a woman who would be unimpressed by anything short of Christ himself sitting on a unicorn, and even then she would bite his coin.

"Fifty cents for a bunk. Twenty-five more to guard your kit," she said. "I have a locked room, and this is the only key." She pulled a sturdy metal key out from the bosom of her dress. She was a tiny woman with streaky red hair and just enough of a mustache that it showed in a certain slant of light. It was difficult to place her age; she could have been fifty or a hard-living thirty. She wore ropes of beads and silver necklaces, long sparkling earrings and rings on every finger, though Aiden suspected more glass than jewels.

"I'm looking to meet some old friends," he said. "Perhaps you have heard of them. They arrived in a wagon train in late October."

"People come and go."

"One is a preacher—the Reverend Gabriel True. Also a doctor . . ." He hesitated, finding it hard to even say the name. "Carlos Perez."

Ruby laughed. "I have little need for preachers or doctors unless there's a dead body around, and when there is, names are not handed about." She looked at him over a pair of gold-rimmed half-glasses that she wore on a beaded chain. "But my cook is a Bible fellow, you can ask him if you like."

"How about any old doctor, then?" Aiden asked. Ruby narrowed her eyes and looked him up and down suspiciously.

"You can't stay here if you're sick."

"Sorry, ma'am, I'm not sick at all. It's just that I'll be going north for the gold mining come springtime, and I hear there's smallpox up there. I mean to get myself vaccinated while I'm here."

She sniffed, and pushed her grimy sleeves back, displaying rows of bracelets on each arm: thin gold and silver bands, Indian beads and Chinese ivory.

"Dr. Abradale can do that, I suppose. He's a queer one, and English, but he's the only one there is." She pulled a heavy gold pocket watch out of her skirt. She must be wearing twenty pounds of jewelry and baubles, Aiden thought. "It's just after five, and he leaves his office at six o'clock promptly to take his supper at the Golden Palace, so you'll find him easily enough. Will you be dining here?"

"I don't know," Aiden said. "I will have a bed, though, thanks." He put fifty cents on the counter.

"And your kit?"

"I don't really have any," he said, nodding to the small bag he carried over one shoulder. She examined his coins carefully and pointed out the room where he would have a bunk.

"I have three clear lanterns out," she said. "Two yellow is Sally's next door. Before that, two red for Little Joe's; his whores are all diseased, so talk to Sally if you have that need. That marks your path from the high road. We have our guards, but be mindful nevertheless."

41

D r. Abradale's office was easy to find, a low narrow building squeezed between a hardware store and a burned-out church. There was no bell, but the front door was open, and so Aiden walked into a vestibule with two benches.

"Hello?" he called. "Dr. Abradale?" He entered the examining room and saw a battered wooden cabinet against one wall, two chairs against another and in the center a table with an enamel top. Aiden had never seen a doctor's office before, but it seemed as if there should be more to it. There was another entry at the rear of this room, and he had just raised his hand to knock when the door suddenly flew open.

"Someone there?"

Aiden saw a plump little man with thick spectacles, wiry, uncombed gray hair like a clump of lichen clinging to his head, a soiled smock and a scalpel in one hand.

"Yes? Hello? What's the problem?" the man asked brusquely.

Aiden looked warily at the raised scalpel.

"Oh, sorry." Abradale lowered the knife. "Just trimming some specimens. Come, come."

Aiden entered the second room, not sure exactly what sort of specimens were being trimmed. He was relieved to see the table covered with plants.

"Good lot of new ferns today, you see," he said in a

clipped English accent. "Fascinating phylum. Pteridophytes; most primitive of the vascular plants."

"You're the doctor?" Aiden looked doubtfully at all the plants.

"Yes." The man stared at him impatiently, his eyes big as chestnuts through the thick glasses. "Botany is a hobby. Though I am published in the field. Orchids were my original subject. Named three in Surinam. But there's a lady botanist down there now, you see. Paints pretty watercolors. Weak on taxonomy, in my opinion, but she's popular. So I came up here. Not a glamorous field, ferns, but fascinating. And no ladies up here doing watercolors, eh?

"So what's wrong?" He peeled off the thick glasses and gave Aiden a quick glance up and down. "You look fine."

Aiden explained that he wanted a smallpox vaccination.

"Good idea, very smart," Abradale grunted. "Surprising how many don't take the vaccine, in this day and age. There's some religions against it, do you know? And some just bloody stupid. But I cannot give it to you."

"Why not?"

"Well, I don't keep any here. Especially not now."

"Why not?"

"There's Indians on the hunt for it. Came right here to my own door. Bad business. Police caught them, though. A whole band of them ready to murder. Killed a police guard. Crushed his throat. I did the postmortem. Brutal."

Aiden didn't know what a postmortem was but felt it best not to ask about anything brutal. He had to work to push away the image of Silent Wolf being beaten to death.

"Come back in two weeks." Abradale took off his

stained smock, then tenderly draped a sheet over the table of ferns.

"I won't be here in two weeks," Aiden protested. "Is there someone else who has the vaccine? Another doctor?"

"There's none to be had right now. No. Sorry. Good evening." Abradale waved a hand toward the door. "Now do excuse me. I've a table kept for me at six at the Golden Palace. Latecomers eat standing, and the meat is largely gristle by then." He put on his jacket and picked up his hat.

"Might I impose upon you for company, then?" Aiden jumped at the tiny opportunity, racking his brain for polite words. "I—I would like to hear more about the ferns. I've often admired them, as—ah, I'm a logger, and there's ferns all over." He couldn't tell one fern from another but figured the man for one who liked to talk much more than listen, so he should be all right.

"Awfully young for a logger, aren't you?"

"No," Aiden said lamely.

"Well, come along, then; you might as well fill the other seat. But step lively."

Aiden's plate was clean and his brain was numb with long Latin words about ferns before he managed to get Dr. Abradale back around to the subject of smallpox vaccine.

"That must be a fascinating process too," he offered. "Making vaccine for people out of cows. How do they do it, anyway?"

"Nothing to it, really." Abradale shrugged. "Scratch a pustule on an infected cow and put the pus to another cow. On the udder, I think, tender skin there. The new cow develops pustules and you pass it on. Goes on forever." He spoke with the careful overenunciation of too much wine. Aiden had insisted on treating for a jug of it. It was thick and terribly sweet, and he could hardly drink it himself.

"So is there a farm of cows just for that?"

"Um-hummmm." Abradale nodded as he chewed.

"Where?"

"I've no idea. Cow country, eh! Down the valley, I suppose."

Aiden poured him more wine.

"Thanks, lad." He took a deep drink. Aiden choked some down too. The Golden Palace was indeed full, with men standing around the walls eating quickly off tin plates. A piano player pounded out lively music. There were no women except for one serving the tables.

"How do you actually get the vaccine from the cows to people?" Aiden asked.

"What? Oh, well, threads, generally." Abradale sopped up the last smears of gravy with a piece of bread. "Bits of cotton string soaked in the cow pus, you see? Prick the arm, then lay on the string. They used to just take the cow around door-to-door and scrape it right from the cow into your arm! But this is the modern age, eh?" He plowed the last bit of bread around the bare plate in vain hope. "There's a team going about now, I believe—something about it in the *Gazette*."

"Going around where?" Aiden asked hopefully.

"Oh—logging camps, trading posts, forts and the like, I think. It's January, eh? Vaccine doesn't travel in summer, goes bad in the heat, so winter is the time to take it around. Get to everyone while they're gathered up."

"Will they bring it to the Indian villages too?" Aiden proceeded cautiously now.

"Oh no. Can't do that!"

"Why not?"

"Ah, well. Complicated," Abradale said. "Different species. Well, not species, exactly—not like ferns and orchids. But different enough for disease. Influenza, whooping cough, measles—our diseases are much harder on the red man. Kills them four to one."

"So—shouldn't that be more reason to vaccinate them?"

Abradale leaned forward, peering at him closely. "You're a Christian lad, eh—" Aiden wasn't sure if that was a question or not, but Abradale quickly went on. "Of course you are—you don't look a bit like a Jew—so you must believe God knows what he's doing, eh?"

"I'm not sure what you mean, sir."

Abradale stirred three spoonfuls of sugar into his coffee and took a delicate sip. "Let God's will be done. You see? The good Lord can save the Indians if he wants!" Abradale patted his hand on the table like a judge. "Perhaps he doesn't want to. We shouldn't be interfering with vaccinations."

The argument seemed so ridiculous that Aiden didn't even know where to start. Hadn't millions of good Christian white people died before the smallpox vaccine was invented? Had that been God's will?

"Will you have some pudding, Dr. Abradale?" The waitress, a plump young woman with shiny apple cheeks, leaned down over their table, showing a generous bosom and a tray of desserts. "Ah!" Abradale beamed with happiness. "Have the pudding, lad—it's lovely."

"I—ah, I'm full, thanks," Aiden lied. He felt slightly nauseated and dizzy. Not from the rich food or syrupy wine but from the calm cruelty of Abradale's twisted logic.

"It's cherry!" The waitress tilted the tray toward Aiden and pointed to a little china dish with a piece of cake studded with purple cherries, swimming in custard and syrup.

She was not especially pretty, but her round face was smooth and the skin clear. Aiden thought of Bandy and what a different life she would have had if she weren't all scarred. She would be in San Francisco, teaching school and living in a cozy little room with gaslights and rugs. She could go to musical recitals and plays and have nice men courting her.

"No thank you," Aiden said. He watched Dr. Abradale spoon up a glistening purple bite. "What about Christian Indians?" he asked. "Shouldn't they be vaccinated?"

"Ah, well, difficult that—" Abradale looked unhappy to have the conversation steered from cherry pudding back to smallpox. "You must understand, the vaccine isn't perfect for our own. It sometimes fails. Imagine the trouble if we start pricking the red devils! Remember the Whitman Massacre? Oh, it's nearly twenty years ago, and measles, not even smallpox, but no one forgets it around here." He spoke quickly between spoonfuls. "The Indians got the measles and thought the whites were working evil magic on them. They slaughtered thirteen or fourteen people at the mission. So you see the problem, eh?"

"But couldn't you explain the risks to them and let them decide?"

"Explain? They have witch doctors!"

Abradale scooped out the last drop of syrup, patted his lips, surrendered his napkin and pushed away from the table. "Fine evening!" He stood and shook Aiden's hand vigorously. "Call on me in two weeks, eh? I'll get some vaccine for you. Awful thing, the smallpox."

42

Aiden walked back to Ruby's in a gloomy frustration. The rutted mud road had stiffened in the cold of night, and he stumbled over the lumpy ground. He turned his jacket collar up against the chill wind. He felt stupid. He should have thought this through before he left the camp. It had been a fool's errand from the start. Stupid Tupic coming here in the first place. Stupid Indians dying so easily. Stupid white men thinking everyone else was stupid. Stupid everyone in the world.

He had not slept much in three days now and was unimaginably tired. He tried to remember the lights. Two red, one white—three clear? As he skidded down the steep path to the waterfront road, he suddenly heard scuffling in the shadows. Aiden stopped, his skin prickling. He should probably be afraid, he thought, but was actually more annoyed. He was no longer a stick-legged pony. He had learned to fight and learned to hurt, was tired of both and didn't want to do either right now.

"Who's there?" he called out. "I've a damn grim attitude, so come on if you want! But you'll need four to take me down and I'll cut at least two of yours balls off as we go!"

The night fell silent. He thought he heard a woman giggling from one of the houses. The clink of a metal chain gave him a moment's warning, then it was all grunts and boots, clubs, chains, sticks and planks. Aiden ducked and swung a hard punch at the nearest figure. He felt his fist connect with ribs, hard enough to wrench out a grunt of surprise. But then a hard whack knocked the back of his legs and his knees hit the ground. He dropped, rolled and kicked, and heard someone fall with a gasp of pain. Not a second for satisfaction, though, as a chain slammed into the mud inches from his head. He crabbed away, grabbed a chunk of dirt and flung it up toward the voices. A boot kicked hard against his side. He waited for the next kick, then grabbed the man's foot, twisted and flipped him to the ground.

Aiden scrambled to his feet and punched his fist into the man's stomach. The man groaned, but then a bat slammed across Aiden's back, knocking him facedown into the hard rutted road. He struggled to get up. It was so dark he couldn't tell if there were two or twenty men, but even the Bull couldn't fight off two men with clubs. He steeled himself for the next blow, but then there were shouts and gunshots, and as quickly as it had all started, it ended.

The attackers ran off. Someone took his arm and helped him to his feet. There were two big men with clubs of their own, and another with a pistol and a lantern.

"Well, there's one less for the bilge business!" One of them laughed. "Anything broken?"

"No." Aiden bent over, waiting for the world to stop spinning. He wiped blood from his face with the back of his hand. Someone held the lantern up close to his face and Aiden squinted.

"Lookit there, Mack—he's a young one! Boy don't even shave yet!"

"They'd like him for a sailor, eh?" They all laughed.

"I do shave," Aiden said defensively, stupidly, as if that

were all at stake in the world right now. It wasn't often, and only his chin, but he did shave.

"A few bruises, but still pretty enough," the man said. They laughed some more and Aiden heard a bottle being uncorked.

"You fight like a man, anyway." The man with the club took a drink and handed him the bottle. "Where are you staying? Ruby's or Little Joe's?"

"Ruby's."

"Come on, then; we'll see you safe home."

They walked him there, bid him good night and returned to their patrol. Aiden found a pitcher of water and some tin cups on a stand by the desk. He took a cupful outside, where he did his best to wash the dirt and blood off his face. He went back inside, felt his way down the dim hallway to his room, stumbled quietly to his bunk, pulled the rough blanket over his head and shivered. Seattle was notorious for Shanghai crews. It was the only way most ships got a crew these days. Knock a man on the head in a bar and he would wake up at sea the next day with no way off. Powhee had warned him; Ruby's guards took it as routine. So why did he feel there was something more to this attack?

Cold morning. What now? In the dining room, Aiden poured himself a cup of coffee and eyed what looked like the worst corn bread in the history of the world: flat doughy squares, shiny raw in the middle, where leavening had clearly failed. They looked worse than "corn jelly meat," if such a thing were even possible. Still, he choked a couple down. They weighed in the bottom of his stomach like lumps of clay.

He was tired, for he had wakened often throughout the

night with storms in his mind. *Save the Indians. Get back in time. Stay alive.* How to do all that? He thought about going to the vaccine farm itself, but even if he found out where it was, what was he supposed to do—sneak into the barnyard and grope around the undersides of cows soaking bits of string in their pustules?

The door swung open and a boy came in.

"*Gazette!*" he called. "Latest news! Two bodies in the harbor! Chinaman cannibal in jail! Dined on the flesh of those he lured with opium! Indian rampage! Cruelest, most vile slayings! Nine Christian souls sent home to Jesus! New invention called dynamite blasts away mountainsides!"

Aiden nodded at the boy and he scurried over with a paper. Aiden gave him a penny and took the paper.

"Do you have past copies?" he asked with a sudden idea.

"Why? Ain't news when it's past."

"I like history."

Dr. Abradale had mentioned stories in the newspaper about the "Indian attack," as well as something about the vaccine.

"You might find some around," the boy said. "In the fish market, or underneath the bums in the square."

"Thanks." Aiden ignored the boy's cocky attitude and fished some more pennies out of his pocket. "Or maybe the newspaper office keeps some?"

ow can I get to a place called Brightfish Bend?"

Ruby looked at him skeptically. "Jefferson J. Jackson's place?"

"You know him?"

"Everybody knows Jackson." Aiden couldn't tell by her tone whether this was a good or a bad thing. "What do you want with him?"

"I came out here in his wagon train. He kept some things for me. Books."

Ruby looked at him skeptically. "It's a long day on horseback," she said. "Twelve or fifteen miles. Best way is by boat. I might be able to find someone or other headed up that way." She jangled her baubled wrists in a clear demonstration of the emptiness of her palm. Aiden fished out some more coins. His twenty dollars was quickly running out in this place.

Aiden wasn't sure what he had expected Jefferson J. Jackson's trading post to look like, but it certainly wasn't this. It looked more like a small village, he thought as he walked up the boardwalk from the little dock. The main house was a big, sturdy L-shaped log building with a wide front porch facing the sound. Every pillar was beautifully carved with Indian designs. Between the pillars dangled strings of shells that clicked in the wind with gentle music. The wing at one end of the building was clearly the store, while the rest looked like a home, though far bigger than any one family's home.

There were at least six other buildings that he could see, scattered back among the trees but all connected with boardwalks. As he walked toward the main building, he heard giggling from above and looked up to see a dozen small Indian children waving to him from a little tree house. They climbed nimbly down and swarmed around him, laughing and chattering in a combination of English and some Indian language.

The door to the main house opened and Jackson came out. Aiden was surprised to see him. Jackson's gaunt face had filled out, and his once sinewy limbs now seemed more suited to armchairs than to a saddle. He wasn't fat like a banker or any other rich man, but a different person entirely from the stringy old trapper Aiden had known on the trail.

"I didn't really expect you till tomorrow," he said.

"Tupic got here all right, then?"

"He did. Yesterday evening." Jackson looked him up and down, but said nothing about the fresh bruises and scrapes on his face. "He's out with the men hunting seal." Jackson looked around the quiet compound. "Everyone else has gone down to the beach for the butchering. Tide will have them coming in soon."

The children continued to dance around Aiden.

"Go on, all of you!" Jackson waved the children off. They scampered around but didn't leave.

"Go on, git!"

"Go on, git!" one little boy mimicked him, timing it perfectly so they shouted in unison. The children shrieked with laughter.

"You little savages!" Jackson growled and stomped in their direction. The children didn't seem particularly scared of him but scampered off toward the water. Jackson motioned Aiden toward one of the porch chairs. "Come sit while we have the sun, and the quiet."

Aiden sank gratefully into the chair. Last night's beating was starting to ache on him, and though the water in the sound was calm today, the voyage from Seattle in the small boat had made him seasick. The chair was made of bent willow branches and was amazingly comfortable. It creaked gently as he sat down and seemed to bend around his body. The afternoon sun was low and beamed in under the roof. Jackson went inside and came out a few minutes later with mugs of coffee, a bottle of whiskey and two glasses.

"Thanks," Aiden said. They raised their glasses and drank. "Nice place. Who are all those children? Who lives here?"

"My family."

Aiden's astonishment must have shown on his face.

"Don't be surprised," Jackson laughed. "I been around a while, boy. Family happens." He put his feet up on a stool, using his hands to help lift the stiff limbs. "My first wife was Shoshone, from Idaho. Back in the thirties, when I was trapping, I wintered with her people for nine years. We had six children, five that lived. Three of them live here now—with their children, twelve or thirteen, I think."

"So those are your grandchildren?"

"Some. But the smart-mouth one—well . . ." Jackson gave him a proud smile. "He's direct. Bit of a surprise there. He just turned five. I have six by my third wife, Salawee. She's Yakima, from north of here. Married her in '51."

"Six?"

"Four sons, two girls. The oldest one's fourteen, teaching English up north on the reservation. In between was a Mexican wife. Died birthing a son—Francis. I hardly even knew her. Pretty girl, though. Her folks died too, and Mexico all tore up on account of that war, so I brought the boy back with me and the Shoshones took him in with the rest."

"But how did all this"—Aiden looked around the compound—"come about?"

"Remember I told you of the rendezvous, how trappers would squander a year's fortune, and you asked why didn't they just squander half and save the rest?"

"You saved the rest?"

"I did." Jackson gave him a sly smile and poured them both another drink. "And with the wagon train money, and the logger bounties, I did all right. About ten years ago I found this place and saw some possibility. Didn't know what would come of Seattle then—it's only been a city since '51— but I figured this land here, with the harbor, timber, might do all right. If nothing else, it was pretty, and you could live well enough off the land, if you like fish. Salawee's people owned it, such as owning is with them, but with Indians getting put on reservations, we worked it out for me to buy it. Then a few years ago when things got bad on the plains, I brought my Shoshones, those who wanted, out here from Idaho."

"How do you all live?"

"Some fish, hunt seal, raise chickens and goats. Some work as loggers. The girls do weaving, make baskets, and the men build these chairs." He slapped the arms proudly. "Sell for twenty dollars in San Francisco. Francis, the Mexican one, turned out smart with trade and such. He married a Yakima girl and they have two babies."

Aiden gave up trying to count up Jackson's progeny.

"So you see, I got a good life here now." Jackson gave him a long, hard look. "I don't need any trouble," he said with clear meaning. The sun was dropping and the sky turning the plummy blue of winter dusk. Aiden saw four small boats approaching and heard the welcoming shouts of the women and children drifting up through the trees.

"What did Tupic tell you?"

"I told him tell me nothing. But I got a message a couple weeks back that some Indians were in the jail saying they knew me—that's trouble enough."

"You know they killed Silent Wolf?"

"I get the newspaper. Didn't figure it all out as to who it was until after Tupic showed up here, though."

A door opened in one of the other buildings and two young women, eighteen or twenty years old, came out carrying infants. They waved to Jackson and hurried down the hill toward the shore to join the others.

"So you know why they came," Aiden pressed. "For the vaccine?"

"Stupid idea."

"Clever Crow died of the smallpox."

Jackson rubbed his gnarled hand over his face. "That's a damn shame."

"Your family, have they all been vaccinated?" Aiden asked quietly.

"That ain't gonna work on me." Jackson shook his head. "Wherever you think you're going with that—guilty feeling or moral right, or what have you—ain't no use. I have sympathetic feelings for others' plights, I do." He looked out over the village. "But I know the clear fact is—Indians are doomed one way or another." He took another drink. "There was warfare here ten years ago. Puget Sound War, they call it now. Indians lost. Result was they all got bound to reservations. But this is my private-owned land, and with my Indians being half-breeds and family as they are, it works in the law all right. These ones here I can see to. But there's plenty folks around still don't like it."

Aiden nodded. "I understand."

Jackson got up, pushing hard on the arms of his chair.

"I ain't done much in the world but make this place and look out for my own." He coughed and spat. "I never looked for fixing all the world."

A butter-colored cat leaped up out of nowhere and butted imperiously at Jackson's hand. "You and Tupic are welcome to stay the night," he said, scratching the cat's ears. "There'll be a feasting supper, I imagine, with the seal. I don't like seal meat myself, but it's healthful in the mid-winter."

"Thank you," Aiden said. "But I was planning to travel on tonight; the moon is bright enough if the clouds stay off. I was hoping to buy a horse from you."

"With what?"

"I have cash, a hundred seventy dollars. Mr. Powhee holds it for me and will see that you get it."

"A hundred seventy dollars—Ah—you're fighting, then?" Jackson nodded. "You must be all right if you won that much." He grinned. "I can't imagine the no-damage part would be easy for you, though."

"You know about the fights?"

"Of course."

"Well, Napoleon Gilivrey doesn't, so I'd be grateful if you didn't mention it to him the next time you see him. That's the only way I got Mr. Powhee to let me go for a week. I threatened to tell Mr. Gilivrey about the fights."

Jackson let out a big laugh and picked up the languid cat.

"Boy, for as smart as you are sometimes, you also astound. God almighty, ain't nothing Napoleon Gilivrey don't know about what goes on in his camps. He knows every man's shoe size and which tree he pisses on! If Powhee thinks Gilivrey don't know about the fights, it's because Gilivrey wants him to think it."

"Why?"

"Well, first of all, if the fights weren't a secret, the men could pay off their debts with the winnings. Gilivrey would rather have the loggers bound to him and cutting trees. You know how far he goes to get men these days—dragging some skinny-ass boy halfway across the continent." Jackson raised his glass to Aiden and tipped up the last sip of whiskey.

"Second, it keeps Powhee and the other bosses happy with extra bonus money that don't come from Gilivrey's own pocket, plus it gives him leverage over them if he should ever need it. Hell, I wouldn't be surprised if Gilivrey got the fights started in the first place!" Jackson added. "Loggers borrow against their wages to bet and dig their debt bigger. Gilivrey is happy to just keep adding days to their tally."

Aiden looked away. This feeling stupid was getting too familiar. Then he had another thought, even more chilling. He touched the bruises on the side of his face. Now he knew what was bothering him about last night's attack. Just like the camp fights, real Shanghai crews probably weren't out to injure a man. They wanted someone who could work on a ship. Bashing a man's skull in wasn't likely to get that.

"Papa! Papa!"

The shouts startled Aiden. A wave of children burst out of the trees into the clearing. All but the smallest toddlers carried baskets or bags of seal meat. Bright red droplets of blood left a wobbly trail behind them as they ran.

"I have three horses I could sell," Jackson said, dropping the butter cat gently to the porch.

"Tupic knows horses," Aiden said. "Let him choose."

The sun was setting and the sky turned a deep red, as if God had just scratched a gash in the horizon and made it bleed. Behind the children came the women, carrying the rolled-up bundles of sealskins. The silvery brown fur glistened in the sun. The men, their work done now, carried nothing but their harpoons. Everyone was laughing and talking, and a group of young boys, nine or ten years old, were leaping about, arms waving, clearly telling some wild tales from their day's adventure. Aiden could see some physical differences between the Shoshone and the Yakima, but the Indians did not seem to be separated by tribe as much as age. The young boys were together, the mothers, babies and older women in another group. The scampering toddlers ran like a flock of ducklings. Young Indian girls walked close the same way white girls did, heads together in hushed confidence and unconscious beauty, like small important butterflies. The subject of their glances and giggles today seemed to be Tupic, who walked on obliviously with the young men.

"Papa!"

Jackson walked down the stairs into the middle of them all and was swallowed up in touch. He took a fat baby from a woman's arms and kissed it on the cheek. The little boys tugged at his hands. Aiden watched from the porch. He did not want to know these smiling women and triumphant young men, these pretty girls and giggling children with their chasing games and songs. He wanted only to be back in the dark woods, with the muscled days and thick black nights, with the anonymous fill of food and the coffin-shaped space of his bunk. He wanted the foggy chill of morning, the prick of sweat on his back and the soft sink of drink at the end of the day. He wanted to fight and work and sleep. It made a manageable life.

He realized he hadn't eaten since the morning's lumpy corn bread, and the whiskey was spinning his brain. Then Tupic saw him and ran up onto the porch. He looked like a new person, his hair neatly cut, his eyes bright again.

"Aiden!" he called. Aiden saw the brightness fade when Tupic read his face. "You didn't get it."

"Not yet," Aiden said. "But I have a plan."

"What do you mean? What happened?"

Children began racing up the steps and into the house as the swarm of people filled the clearing.

"I'll tell you everything later," Aiden said. "Trust me. We need to leave after supper and travel tonight. Jackson will sell me a horse, and you need to choose it."

Tupic gave him a long, searching look but finally nodded. "I will go look at the horses," he said.

Jackson came back up on the porch just then, his hand on the arm of an Indian woman, escorting her as if she were the queen of the world. Aiden jumped to his feet.

"This is my wife, Salawee," Jackson said. He sounded oddly shy.

"I'm pleased to meet you, ma'am." Aiden wasn't sure how to greet her, but Salawee eased the awkwardness by stepping forward and kissing him on both cheeks.

"Welcome, Aiden. I am happy to meet you. I hear much of your help to Mr. Jackson on the journey."

She was a small woman with large brown eyes framed by thick black lashes. There were threads of gray in her hair, and

Aiden figured she was in her early forties, but she was still quite beautiful.

"Please, you will honor us and join the meal?"

"Yes, ma'am, thank you."

"I must go, then." She looked sharply at two of the other women. "Or some will cook the seal too much." She smiled and disappeared into the house.

"They do snipe some," Jackson sighed. "Oh well, go on inside, make yourself comfortable. I'll show Tupic the horses, and Francis will open the store if there's anything else you need. I'll put it on your account."

45

The main house was a single large room with a fireplace against one wall and a wood-burning stove at either end. One side of the room was full of cushioned chairs, tables and lots of good reading lamps. There were bearskins on the floor and colorful weavings and baskets and drawings hanging on the walls. Aiden recognized a pencil sketch by Lieutenant Gryffud, scenes from the wagon train.

Around the great room, bookshelves were built into the walls. On the lower shelves were stacks of grade-school primers for reading and arithmetic. On the higher shelves were dozens of leather-bound books. Aiden saw his own books there, all together in a row: Shakespeare, the mouse-eaten remains of *Aesop's Fables* and, of course, the *Atlas of the World*. Sitting there on the raw wooden shelf, it looked tattered and ordinary, with a battered spine inches thick that would repel any sensible child from ever taking it up. He reached out his hand to lift it but found himself frozen, unable to even stroke the worn leather cover with a finger. He could not bear the rustle of the pages or their rich smell. He did not want to remember all the dark nights he and Maddy had read together, those awful lost nights when fear had been blunted by stories of the Congo, Iceland and Rome. He shuddered and turned away.

The children dragged tables and benches into the center of the room and carried in piles of enamel plates and cups.

When the dinner was ready, Aiden and Tupic were seated across from Jackson and Salawee, in the place of honored guests. Everyone spoke some English, or at least understood it, but conversations still often got tangled in translation, with much debate and laughter around the table. The seal meat did taste strange, but not so strange that he would pass it up in his hunger. There were roasted carrots and some kind of pickled cabbage. There were baskets of flatbread and sourdough bread, even dishes of fresh butter.

"It is not a proper feast," Salawee explained apologetically. "That would have many special foods. A feast must have many days to prepare. But when the seals come and the sea is good, the men hunt."

"Seal don't keep well," Jackson added. For one who didn't much like it, he had put away quite a plateful. After dinner, the women put out bowls of dried berries and roasted nuts and some of the men smoked pipes. Aiden felt dozy and warm and wanted nothing more than to just stay here forever in this peaceful and abundant place. Instead, he got up and looked around for Francis.

"Could you open the store for me?" Aiden asked. Francis looked nothing like his father upon first glance, but when he walked, Aiden could see an uncanny similarity in their posture and gestures. "There are a few things I need to buy for the trip home."

"Yes, please come." Francis led him outside and around the corner of the porch, then unlocked the door. "What do you need?"

"Well, some light rope might be useful. A new blanket, two pair of socks and a pistol. A box of cartridges too, I guess. Oh, and a couple of those kerchiefs."

The moon was just starting to rise when Aiden met Tupic outside, holding the reins of two horses instead of one.

"This one is only to borrow," Tupic said, nodding at a desultory brown mare. "Jackson knows even desperate Nimipu would never buy a horse this poor. He says you can send it back to him with someone from your camp whenever they travel this way. But this one is not too bad." He patted the neck of a sturdy black horse with two white stockings and an eager gleam in his eye. "Not as good as our poorest horse, but I will not have shame to ride it."

"Well, good." Aiden smiled. "That was a top concern of mine." He was glad both animals were dark and wondered how much Jackson had guessed of his plans. They walked the horses out of the clearing onto the forest trail.

"Where are we going?" Tupic asked.

"North, along the coast."

"Why at night?"

"Because now we are bandits," Aiden said. He handed Tupic one of the kerchiefs and kicked his horse into a trot. Soon the lights of Jackson's compound disappeared and the night closed in around them with a soft chill. When the trail broadened, Tupic rode up beside him.

"Talk to me now," he said firmly. "You are not my chief. What do you plan?"

"There's a party of men out now, traveling with a large supply of the vaccine," Aiden explained. "They're bringing it to towns and settlements all over the region. That's why the police were so suspicious of you and Silent Wolf. They thought there was an Indian plan to steal the vaccine."

The brown mare shied as some branches smacked her

nose. Aiden worked to pull her back. "The team only carries a few hundred doses of the vaccine at a time, so they cover one area, then return to Seattle for more," Aiden went on. "They left again just two days ago, going inland to logging camps."

"How do you know all this?"

"There were stories in the newspaper over the past month. I went to the newspaper office and read them there."

"But how do you know where they are going now?"

"Seattle isn't really such a big city. Comings and goings are high interest. Yesterday's paper said they were headed north by boat to Everett, then inland to some logging camps. I know that the first big logging camp near Everett is Alvin Tesler's." Some wispy clouds drifted over the moon and a cold wind blew. "The boatman who brought me up to Jackson's says it only takes one day with good wind and sea from Seattle to Everett," Aiden went on. "So if they take one day, which would be today, to vaccinate people in Everett, that puts them riding east tomorrow morning toward Tesler's camp. If we ride all night and get ahead of them, we can find a place to intercept them."

"Intercept?" Tupic fingered the kerchief. "You mean we steal it?"

"They'll just go back to Seattle and get some more. They have a whole farm of cows to make it. All they lose are a few days."

"Will this work?"

"God's own toss," Aiden replied. "But if you have a better plan, I'm eager to hear it."

"How many men in the party?"

"Three or four," Aiden said.

"Why don't we wait until night? Follow them and sneak into their camp at night while they're sleeping?"

"I don't reckon they'll be sleeping out," Aiden said. "After Tesler's camp, there's only about five miles to Grandview camp. Besides, there's at least a hundred men in Tesler's camp and another fifty or sixty at Grandview. That might use up all the vaccine they have."

They rode on for a while, the only sound the soft thud of horse hooves on the pine-needle path.

"I will agree to this plan," Tupic said.

46

They rode on through the night. The trail was narrow but clear, and the horses walked steadily. Aiden fell into a sort of trance with the motion. The moon misted in and out of clouds and the air turned uncommonly cold. The sky was starting to lighten when they came to the river just south of Everett, and Tupic found the eastward trail easily. It was a well-traveled path, which made Aiden even more nervous.

A low ceiling of gray clouds muted the sunrise. They rode silently for about an hour, then came to a rocky outcrop near the top of a ridge. From there they had a good view of a bend in the trail below, about fifty yards away.

"What do you think?" Aiden asked. "We can hide behind these boulders here and still see them coming from far off."

"How will we make them stop?"

Aiden pulled the pistol out of his bag.

"You can't shoot them," Tupic said.

"Believe me, I don't plan on shooting anything but the sky, and I'm hoping for not even that," Aiden said. "But as long as they don't know that, we might pull it off. It isn't as if they're getting robbed of their own money. Be stupid to risk their own lives over something they can get more of easy from a cow."

"All right." Tupic nodded. "I will tie the horses back in the woods."

Aiden settled into a place among the boulders and leaned

against the cold stone. Wisps of fog rose up from the river and melted into the trees. What was he doing here? This wasn't his fight, wasn't his cause, wasn't even his people. He had done plenty enough already to satisfy any debt to Tupic. This could go bad in so many ways. He should just leave now, go back to camp and the bearable life he had found there.

He suddenly had no more time to contemplate his decision, for the first horse came into view on the trail below. Aiden turned and was relieved to see Tupic creeping silently toward him. They watched a second horse appear, then a third. Aiden squeezed his eyes shut and tried to steady himself. He had thought they would have a little time to figure out a plan.

"You sneak around and come up behind them," Aiden whispered. "I'll jump out, tell them to stop. Then you shout to them don't turn around—so they won't see that you don't have a gun." His heart was pounding so loud he feared the three men could actually hear it. "Keep your hat on and your face covered." Aiden pulled his kerchief over his face. "They can't know you're an Indian."

Tupic nodded, then darted off silently into the woods. Aiden heard the sound of hooves and the snort of a horse. *I don't have to do this. I can just let them ride on past.* He pressed his back against the stone, took some deep breaths and tried to steady his shaking hand. *This isn't my cause.* He heard the horses approaching, heard the men's voices. *There must be some other way.* The horses were so close he could smell them now.

It's got to be someone's cause.

"Stop right where you are!" He sprang up and pointed the pistol at the three men. "Put your hands up!"

Two of the men shot their hands into the air, but the third just stared at him, then slowly raised one hand.

"Don't move!" Aiden shouted. "We've got you surrounded."

"Don't turn around." Tupic shouted his line like a nervous actor in a bad play.

"Hands up!" Aiden repeated, waving the pistol at the man in the back. "Both hands!"

"Sorry," the man said calmly. "That hand doesn't go up."

Aiden felt as if he'd just been stabbed through with cold steel. He knew that voice! It was the last voice he had ever expected to hear and the last in the world he wanted to. The man's face was gaunt; he had a beard and long ragged hair, but there was no mistaking his eyes. It was Doc Carlos.

"We have nothing to steal," the man in front said. "All we're carrying is medicine."

"I know what you're carrying," Aiden said. His knees were quivering so hard he thought they might buckle. He didn't know whether Carlos recognized him. "Get off your horses," he said. "Slow, now. I can see where your guns are and you can see my finger on this trigger." He almost laughed, for it sounded like a silly line from a dime novel. He wrenched his mind around and tried to focus.

"Kneel down on the ground. Do what I say and you won't get hurt."

"It ain't any value to you," one of the men said. "It's just vaccine."

"And men will pay for it," Aiden said, trying desperately to keep a clear head. "They'll pay plenty up north at the gold mines. Tommy!" he shouted. He hadn't thought to make up a white man's name for Tupic before this. "Tommy! Get over here." Tupic appeared, bandana pulled high, hat pulled low, head ducked. "Take those two and tie them up to some trees," Aiden directed. Tupic got the rope and quickly secured the men. "The other one comes with us." Aiden waved the gun at Carlos. "He's our hostage."

"You can't just leave us!" one of the men shouted.

"Someone will come along and find you before long," Aiden said. "The trail looks busy enough." His kerchief was slipping and he could hardly breathe through it. "Don't try to follow us, don't send any law. If we smell a posse, we kill your friend dead, you understand?"

Tupic finished tying the first two men up and tucked their blankets around them.

"Get this one on his horse, Tommy. Tie his hands, then go fetch our horses," Aiden said, his voice breaking. "Hurry." Tupic helped the third man to his feet but stopped in surprise when he saw who it was.

"Doc? Is that—?"

"Go on now!" Aiden snapped. "Move!"

47

They rode hard through the trees for ten minutes; then Aiden reined in his horse, slid out of the saddle, stumbled off behind a tree and vomited his guts out. He waited to catch his breath, staring down at the dewy ferns. *Not glamorous, pteridophytes, but very interesting.* He wiped his mouth, then strode back, grabbed Carlos's jacket, yanked him off the horse and smashed a fist into his face. Carlos fell to the ground, a gush of blood pouring from his nose. Tupic jumped off his horse, grabbed Aiden and pulled him back.

"What are you doing!"

Aiden lunged again, but Tupic held him. Carlos flinched in anticipation of another blow but made no move to fight back.

"Stop!" Tupic shouted. "Are you crazy?"

He flung Aiden to the ground, but Aiden, well practiced by now in fighting, easily dragged Tupic down with him. They rolled together, grappling and kicking in the slippery pine needles, until Aiden abruptly stopped himself and shoved Tupic away.

"You are not my fight!"

He got to his feet. Tupic sprang up after him.

"Carlos is not your fight either!"

"He let Maddy die!"

The accusation hung in the air like the burned smell of

torn wood, the awful words finally out. The world was silent except for their hard breathing and the restless clink of a horse's bridle. Carlos slowly sat up, blood dripping from the corner of his mouth.

"What are you talking about?" Tupic wiped his mouth on his sleeve. "You said she drowned."

"Because he let go of her!" Aiden flung Tupic's restraining arm away and turned back to Carlos. "It was you who should have drowned!" he said bitterly.

"Yes," Carlos said. His voice was flat. If he was as shocked to see Aiden as Aiden was to see him, it did not show on his face. If anything, he seemed inordinately calm. He looked almost as bad as the first time Aiden had seen him, just weeks after release from the prison camp. He pulled his damaged arm into his lap but made no move to get up. Thin morning sun streamed through the clouds in steamy stripes of soft gray light.

"That is how you hurt your arm," Tupic said quietly.

Carlos did not answer. Aiden went back to his horse and grabbed the rest of the rope. "We'll leave him here."

"He did not cause your sister's death!"

"You weren't there. You don't know!" Aiden could feel the awful panic rising.

"I know that no man can hold against fast water," Tupic said gently. "Were you about to pull yourself free from the river when we found you?"

Aiden knew this was true, had always known it was true. But he would not let it be true. If there was no fault, there could be no anger, and without anger the space inside him would fill up with pain that he could not bear. The pain of

317

every death and the waiting on death, the raven's claw around his heart, the terrible burn on his palms from a shovel handle worn silky smooth.

"You are wrong to blame him," Tupic went on.

"He's alive. Maddy's dead."

"And the river still does not care."

Aiden clutched the coiled rope.

"We do not leave a broken man tied in the woods far from the trail. We let him go free or we take him with us."

"Fine." Aiden held up his hands in surrender. "You do whatever the hell you want! I've done my part. I'm through." He stumbled toward the brown mare and fumbled for the stirrup. "You have the vaccine. You're on your own now." He mounted, yanked the animal's head around and kicked hard.

48

Tupic and Carlos caught up to him less than a half mile away near a small stream. Aiden was sitting against a tree, sharpening his knife on a stone while the brown mare stood nearby, feet firmly planted, eyes closed, velvet lips pulling hungrily at the small tufts of grass. No one said anything at first. The mare lifted her head slightly to glance at the new-comers, then turned away and seemed to plant herself even more solidly.

"A horse will not walk all night and then all day," Tupic said simply. "It must rest and eat. There is no way to make it go."

He and Carlos were riding two of the vaccine party's horses, leading the third, with Jackson's black horse plod-ding along behind.

"These other horses are fresh," Tupic said. "Take one of them if you must go."

"I have two days left," Aiden said. "I can walk it in two days. Just give me some of the food."

"The weather is changing," Tupic said. "Snow is coming. We should ride east over this ridge, then make shelter in the valley before the storm."

Aiden got up. His anger had ebbed; now all he felt was overwhelming emptiness. "I just want to get back to camp." He picked up his bag and slung it over his shoulder. Suddenly a loud crack shattered the quiet morning and splinters of wood rained down on them. Aiden, used to logging, immediately looked up, expecting a falling branch to come crashing down. Carlos, used to war, slid off his horse and pushed Aiden to the ground. Tupic flattened himself beside them. Suddenly the woods were crackling with shots. The horses shrieked and stamped with fear. Chips of wood flew all around and the forest floor erupted with little bursts of pine needles.

"Damn!" Aiden cursed. "How could they be after us so soon?"

"Not them, others," Tupic said.

Of course, Aiden realized. Even if the two men from the vaccine team had gotten themselves free, they didn't have their horses. Others must have come along, found them and decided to give chase.

"Five horses—we are easy to track," Tupic said.

Aiden groped for a new plan, but he was wrung out by now. His mind and heart were ash.

"Take the vaccine and go," Carlos whispered. "It's in the black saddlebag. I'll stay here."

"We will not leave you," Tupic said.

"They don't want me, I'm your hostage." The sudden clear danger had brought out the quick-thinking and decisive side of him that Aiden had glimpsed in other times of crisis. Carlos, in his damaged heart, was still a surgeon and a soldier.

"Those are rifle shots," Carlos said. "They're still a way off." The gunshots stopped, but they all knew it was just so the pursuers could listen. "Shoot your pistol," he said to Aiden. "Then hit me."

"No—" Aiden's brain felt slow. He looked at Tupic, who nodded.

"It is good," Tupic said.

"Where's the gun?" Carlos reached impatiently for Aiden's bag.

"That will let them know just where we are," Aiden protested, starting to summon his wits.

"I think they know that already," Carlos said. "But your shots will make them think twice before they ride right in."

Aiden fumbled in his bag and pulled out the gun, rolled on his back and fired up into the trees.

"Thank you." Tupic squeezed Carlos's shoulder.

"Hurry!"

Tupic crawled over to the vaccine party's three horses, mounted the one with the black saddlebag, and held the reins of another for Aiden. Jackson's two tired horses ignored everything as they browsed for grass.

"Now knock me out," Carlos said urgently.

Aiden's hand shook and the blow barely left a mark.

"Harder!"

"I'm sorry," Aiden whispered.

"Just do it."

"I mean for blaming you."

"Go." Carlos's face was tense but determined.

"You loved her," Aiden said quietly.

"Yes." Carlos smiled. "And it wasn't easy."

Aiden blinked back tears and took a deep breath.

"Now hit me hard." Carlos squeezed his eyes shut and Aiden brought the butt of the pistol down as hard as he could. It landed with a sickening thud and a small gash opened above Carlos's ear. He fell, not unconscious, but definitely dazed. Aiden ran to the horse, grabbed the saddle horn and swung himself up. He fired a couple more times, wildly into the sky.

They rode hard, the horses snorting great steamy blasts in the cold air, but there were no more gunshots, no galloping pursuits. The wounded "hostage" apparently was a good delay. There was a rock outcropping at the top of the ridge, and they lost precious time picking a way through it before they could start the descent. The sky grew thicker and more ominous. The wind howled and the temperature dropped even as they descended into the sheltering valley. Around noon they came to a stream and stopped to water the horses and fill their canteens.

"How far do you think we've come?" Aiden asked.

"Four, maybe five miles," Tupic said. "We should make a shelter now; snow will come soon."

"No," Aiden said. "They could catch up."

"The men will also fear the storm," Tupic pointed out. "They will go back to the town or the logging camp for shelter."

"It could be a light snow."

"This does not feel like light snow," Tupic said.

"Just a little farther," Aiden pressed. "If we go down this valley a little more, we'll at least narrow their approach routes and see them coming."

The horses suddenly lifted their heads together, gracefully, like dancers, and sniffed the air. Tupic and Aiden both tensed, but it was only snow beginning to fall. Blizzards were rare here, but when they came they could be furious.

"Just a little more," Tupic agreed.

At first the snow fell in large wet flakes that melted in damp blotches on their clothes, but soon it was swirling hard. They followed the stream for another half mile, until they came to a small waterfall.

"We will find a place here!" Tupic shouted, waving toward the rocky ground on either side. They tied the horses near the waterfall. The noise would help them find their way back in the increasing roar of the storm. Aiden had a few yards of rope left in his bag, and they tied themselves together. In a strong blizzard, they could be lost a mere six feet apart. The world was now nothing but heavy steps, smacking branches and stinging snow. They groped almost blindly, searching among the rocks for any kind of shelter. Finally they found a narrow strip of dry ground beneath an overhang. A cluster of dense pine trees beside it broke some of the wind. It wasn't much, but they might be able to build a fire at least. Then, as they started back to retrieve the horses, Tupic saw a dark shadow among the rocks.

"Here. Look!" It wasn't exactly a cave, but it was palatial compared to the first spot. Two slabs of rock had fallen from a large outcropping, leaving a crevice between them that offered enough room to lie down and four feet of headroom in the middle, like a small rock tent. Carefully stamping out a trail to find their way back, they retraced their route to the waterfall and retrieved the horses. They tied them in the shelter of the original overhang and wiped them as dry as they could with pine branches.

49

They had been awake and traveling for more than thirty hours by now, but there was still much work to be done before rest. They carried the saddles and bags over to their shelter, then went back to the stream and cut willow branches for the horses to eat. It was poor fodder but better than nothing. The world became a timeless blur of relentless howling, stinging cold and the urgency of survival. They laid branches over the gaps in the rocks, then piled snow on top to make a snug roof. Once the roof was tight, they swept out all the snow from inside and laid down more pine boughs for insulation against the cold ground. All along they piled up whatever dry wood or pinecones they found to use for a fire.

Finally they crawled into the little shelter. Tupic reached out and dragged the saddles close to the entry hole for a makeshift door. He stuck a branch upright between them like a flagpole to keep a smoke hole open.

They were wet through from the sweating, and shivering hard. Aiden found a tin of matches in the pack and they soon got a little fire burning. When the tentative flickering finally settled into a reliable blaze, they felt triumphant.

"Food." Aiden handed one of the stolen saddlebags to Tupic and opened the other himself.

"Bread." Tupic plopped a heavy chunk down. "Cheese. Fish." They were both so exhausted it was an effort to speak even in single words.

"Cup—" Aiden pulled out an enamel mug and held it while Tupic filled it from the canteen. Aiden set it in the fire to warm. Tupic turned the rest of the bag out and found a pair of very smelly socks, some candle stubs in a nail-punched tin can, a small bag of tobacco, a pipe and a woolen shirt. He unrolled the shirt and out tumbled a little package, wrapped in newspaper and stained with shiny blotches of grease. He lifted a corner of the paper and found two golden brown meat pies.

"Ooh—what is this? It smells good," Tupic said.

"Meat pies." Aiden stared in disbelief. There was no mistaking them, from the aroma to the distinctive crimped pattern on the crust. These were camp four meat pies. And they were fresh. A new fear stabbed him now.

"Why do you wait?" Tupic said. "They look very good."

"Yes," Aiden said. "They are." Tupic took a bite of one and his eyes grew wide with delight. Aiden couldn't taste his; his mouth had gone too dry. His mind was churning. The men who had shot at them that morning were not just accidental travelers between Everett and Tesler's logging camp who happened to come across the tied-up men and then gave chase. It had to be a two-day journey overland from Gilivrey's camp four to Tesler's on horseback, and there was no real reason for anyone to make it, especially in winter. The two camps had little business with each other, and any they did have would be done in Seattle. Even if someone did want to travel between the two camps, it was easier to go downriver to Seattle than up the coast, and it would still take two days. Tesler's men never came to Powhee's fights. Bandy's girls never went there; Tesler had his own resident girls. Meat pies did not fly. Someone had sent the men specifically to find him! *Ain't nothing Napoleon Gilivrey don't know about what goes on in his camps . . .* , Jackson had said. But why?

"Tupic, how did you find our way today?" Aiden asked. "Once we left the trail."

"What do you mean?" Tupic popped the last bite of his meat pie into his mouth with satisfaction and licked his fingers. "We just went east."

"We could never see very far ahead in the woods and you don't know these mountains, yet you knew when to climb a ridge and when to follow a valley."

"I don't know these mountains," Tupic said. "But I know mountains and the way they make paths."

"So trying for due east like we are, how many places would you expect to find to cross?"

"Two or three places would be easy. None would be impossible, I think. These are not real mountains. But some ways would be difficult." Tupic's dark eyes searched Aiden's face. "You are troubled."

"I think the men who shot at us this morning came from Napoleon Gilivrey's camp. I think they were looking for us."

"Us? Or me?" Tupic asked. "Because of the dead jail man in Seattle?"

"I don't know why else."

They lay quietly for a long time. Aiden put another stick on the little fire.

"If the men find you alone, they will take you back?" Tupic asked. "They will not hurt you?"

"No. I don't think so. Gilivrey won't want that."

"Then you will go alone on the good path and I will go alone on a bad path."

"No—"

"I will soon go alone anyway," Tupic interrupted. "Before we near your camp. This is only one day before."

Of course they would have to split up. Aiden hadn't had time to think this far ahead.

"But how were you planning to travel? You can't go near Seattle."

"I will find a way. Put the shirt on," Tupic said, handing Aiden the woolen shirt. "You shiver too much."

The blizzard grew stronger. Their shelter held, though occasional blasts of wind roared in through the smoke hole, stirring the fire into sparks and dusting Aiden and Tupic with snow. Somewhere in the sky, beyond the storm, day turned to night. They rationed the firewood carefully, keeping a dollhouse fire so the heat would not melt their roof. They wore every scrap of clothing they had and huddled together under the two blankets, hoping to fall asleep before the cold overtook them. But despite their exhaustion, sleep did not come. Tupic turned on his side, leaned up on one elbow and gazed into the red glow of the fire.

"Why do you think human beings are not better?" he said. "With all the time of history and all the books, the Bible and Aesop, the wisdom of your people and mine and the *Atlas of the World*, shouldn't we all just be—better?"

"Yes."

"Can I see the vaccine?" Tupic said.

"Sure." Aiden rolled onto his back and reached for the black saddlebag, which was tucked in a niche out of the way. He handed it to Tupic. Tupic unbuckled the straps and lifted the flap. The pouch was stuffed with straw. Carefully cushioned in this nest were six brown glass medicine bottles, each individually wrapped in a bit of flannel. Tupic gently drew one bottle out and held it up to the light. The cork was sealed with melted wax. Inside were many bits of string, each about an inch long.

"This is the vaccine? It is string?"

"Yes." Aiden took the bottle and examined it. There was a label with dates and numbers on the outside. Each bottle had originally held one hundred strings, but one was empty and the seals on two others had been broken for the vaccinations in Everett. "That's how they transport it." He told Tupic all he had learned from Dr. Abradale.

"So each string is one life," Tupic said as he wrapped the bottle back up.

"Yeah." Aiden lay back down.

"We carry many lives."

Aiden said nothing. He could not summon much hope to hang upon these strings. He pressed his hands hard against his eyes. He saw everyone from the wagon train, Polly and Annie, Reverend Gabriel True and Marguerite; everyone from the coal mine towns before that and the plantation before that and Ireland before that. He saw soldiers missing arms and legs. He saw Bandy with a smooth, beautiful face, dancing at a ball. Each string became a person, then a spark, then gone. What did any of them matter?

50

Aiden woke disoriented. The air was stuffy. He sat up and looked around. It was completely dark. He heard nothing but the blood pulsing in his ears. He took a deep breath, hoping to clear his head, but the breath felt empty. With sudden fear, he realized what was wrong.

"Tupic." He nudged him. "Tupic, wake up!" Aiden groped for the candle and matches. Tupic woke with a start, sitting up so quickly he hit his head on the low rock ceiling.

"What?"

"I think we're snowed in," Aiden gasped. His hands shook as he snapped a match and lit the candle. The flame was weak. Tupic grabbed the stick that had once poked out their airhole and shook it, but it was wedged tight and broke in his hand. He pushed and pulled on the saddles, but neither moved.

"Hold this." Aiden handed the candle lantern to Tupic and scrunched around so his feet were toward the front. He lay on his back and kicked the saddles. Nothing. Tupic scraped at the snow around them with his knife, but they still didn't even wiggle. He and Aiden lay gasping and silent for a few long seconds. There was no denying the awful truth. They were buried alive, sealed in a space a little bigger than a coffin. In a frantic burst of energy, Aiden turned back around, grabbed the enamel cup and began to dig.

"Wait." Tupic put the candle lantern down.

"No—we have to work fast!"

"But let us work well." Tupic pressed a hand on Aiden's arm. "We must move the snow back."

Aiden saw that his mad digging had already made a pile of loose snow around his knees. Of course, they had to move the snow back out of the way.

"Here." Tupic grabbed one of the empty saddlebags. Aiden scooped the loose snow into it with the cup while Tupic began to dig more out with his knife. When a saddle-bag was filled, they swung it to the back of the cave, tipped it out and kicked the snow down to compact it. After a short time they were both sweating heavily and had dug extensively around both saddles but still had not broken through.

"It can't have snowed this much in one night," Aiden said, panting.

"No." Tupic took the sock off his hand and wiped his forehead. "But wind blows snow to—little hills?"

"Drifts."

"Yes."

Suddenly Tupic's knife hit a pine branch, flicking bits of needles over them both. They dug around it, thinking it was just a fallen branch that had been swept up in a drift. But as they dug deeper, they hit a larger branch, then another.

"Wait." Aiden got the candle and held it close. The flame melted tiny rivulets of snow off the branches and glistened on the sides. Neither said a word. This was far worse than a snowdrift.

"It's a whole tree," Aiden said. "Came down in the storm." He knew by the thickness of the branches that this was the top part of a huge spruce tree. No amount of digging could get them through the dense branches, nor would it likely even yield an airhole. Aiden felt light-headed and saw golden tadpoles swimming around inside his eyelids. "We'll dig there." He waved toward the back of their cave.

"We can't squeeze through the rocks back there," Tupic said weakly.

"No, but—air," Aiden gasped. "Maybe not so many branches." Their shelter was close to the rock face; the tree would have fallen at a steep angle from above, so there was a good chance that the trunk would be high enough to leave some space. But that was too complicated to explain. "Maybe air," he said.

Tupic nodded, pulled his knees up to his chest and shifted around. He grabbed Aiden's jacket and helped him turn; then they lay on their backs and began to dig again. Snow fell into their eyes and down their necks. Their arms grew numb and the skin on their hands began to crack. Blood trickled down Aiden's wrist, making lacy stains on his shirt cuff. Meanwhile, their body heat was melting the snow from the roof, so cold water dripped on them and the floor had become a puddle. They dug only six inches before they both dropped in exhaustion, gasping for breath.

"I can shoot a hole," Aiden said. His voice sounded far-off, tinny and small. "But I don't know what time it is. If the men are anywhere near, it will give us away."

Tupic didn't say anything. "Tupic—come on." Aiden shook him, but Tupic didn't respond. If Tupic was losing consciousness, Aiden knew he didn't have much longer himself. He had to take the chance. Anything was better than suffocation. He dragged his bag over and took out the pistol, aimed it up, turned his face away and pulled the trigger. The noise was deafening, but the tiny patch of blue sky was the pretti-est thing Aiden had ever seen. Even through the acrid sting of gun smoke he could feel a trickle of good air drifting in. Aiden shot again to enlarge the hole, then took some deep breaths.

"Come on." He slapped Tupic's cheek and shook him hard. "Move, I can't drag you!" Tupic roused enough to flop himself over. They lay like hungry puppies, drinking in the sweet fresh air. Aiden closed his eyes. They were still in a hundred kinds of trouble, but none felt so terrible now that he could breathe. After a while, Tupic wriggled back around, got the stick from their original airhole and used it to widen the opening a few more inches, giving them a small disk of blue sky.

They must have dozed off then, for the next thing Aiden knew, a shower of snow fell down on his face and the sun blazed brightly above. A stick came thrashing down through the hole, grazing the side of his face just inches from his eye. He threw up his hands and rolled away. The air was suddenly plentiful.

"There they are! Rats in a hole!"

Aiden brushed the snow out of his eyes and stared up at the grinning face of William Buck.

51

Buck and his men had a camp shovel and a small axe and got to work digging and chopping a passage through the branches of the fallen tree. As the blockage was being cleared, Aiden could see three men besides Buck. Two were loggers from his own camp: Sam and Eight-John, so called because he was missing two fingers on his left hand. Aiden knew Eight-John was part of the group that had nailed him in the outhouse, because of the strange grip of that hand. The third man was an Indian who sometimes came to the fights and often sold game and fish to the camps. Aiden didn't know anything about him but suspected that he was probably the one who'd tracked them and wouldn't be doing it for free. So Napoleon Gilivrey must be behind this.

"Come on out!" Buck shouted as soon as the hole was big enough. "Don't waste our time." The men were in evil moods after the hard work.

Aiden crawled out first, expecting to be hit immediately, and he was not disappointed. As soon as he was halfway out, Buck kicked him in the ribs so hard Aiden flew backward, crashing into the limbs of the fallen tree. Then Eight-John grabbed his jacket, dragged him to his feet and held him while Buck backhanded him across the face and slammed a punch to his stomach. It knocked the wind out of him, but Aiden was hardened to punches by now and didn't collapse. This infuriated the men even more. Eight-John kicked the back of Aiden's legs so he fell to his knees, and Buck punched him a few more times, then shoved him back into the snow. As he heaved for breath, Aiden looked up and saw Doc Carlos sitting against a rock. His hands were tied. One eye was bruised and swollen shut, his lip was cracked and there was dried blood above his ear, clear signs of a beating.

"Doc?" Aiden gasped. "What's he doing tied up? He wasn't any part of this!"

"Shut up!" Buck shouted. "Now you, Injun!" he yelled into the hole as he picked up a broken tree limb.

"Don't kill him!" Aiden spat blood into the clean snow.

"There's a bounty on his head in Seattle, Prairie Boy. One hundred dollars dead or alive."

"I can match it. You know I have fight money. You can have it all."

"I can have it all anyway," Buck laughed. "Besides what I get for bringing in the vaccine! Probably a bounty on your doctor friend too, for aiding the Injuns in an illegal way."

"He wasn't aiding us," Aiden said. "We came on him by chance and took him for a hostage because he's cripple-armed. You know he's no friend of mine."

"Shut the hell up! Come on out, Injun—you got no escape. Make it easy and we'll kill you quick."

"Shoot them, Tupic!" Aiden yelled. "They're going to kill you anyway!"

"Oh, goddammit, don't make complications." Buck went to a horse and pulled a rifle out of its sheath. He came back and pressed the muzzle against the back of Aiden's head, pushing his head down.

"Now you see what's going to happen?" Buck shouted to Tupic. "You throw the pistol here or I shoot his brains out."

Aiden stared at the snow crystals twinkling in the sun. Time became very slow.

"All right." Tupic's voice drifted out of the cave and barely sounded above the roar in Aiden's ears. "Here it comes." He tossed the pistol out. Eight-John snatched it up and aimed it at the entry hole.

"Now the vaccine. Hurry up!" Buck shoved the rifle harder against Aiden's head. The metal barrel burned cold on his scalp. He heard the rustle of branches as Tupic handed the black saddlebag up through the hole. Aiden tensed, every nerve coiled. He knew what was going to happen next. He squeezed his eyes shut and focused only on the feel of the rifle barrel on his skull. It was as if he could hear Buck's heartbeat through the metal. The instant Buck swung the rifle toward Tupic, Aiden sprang.

He smacked the barrel aside just as Buck pulled the trigger. The bullet ricocheted off the rock and zinged harmlessly away, but the rifle spun out of reach before Aiden could grab it. He smashed his fist against the side of Buck's knee, grabbed his leg and wrenched him down. They tumbled together through the top of the fallen tree, branches smacking and snapping beneath them. There would be no "play wrestling" now. Rules didn't matter; hurt didn't matter. Aiden was set on damage. He drove two quick punches into Buck's nose. He felt the skin on his knuckles burst open but did not register the pain. Buck howled and threw him off. They were clear of the treetop now, and Aiden plunged through the crust into a drift up to his waist. He struggled to get out, but it was almost noon. The day had grown warm and the snow was sticky. Buck staggered forward a few steps, then bent over, resting his hands on his knees, breathing heavily.

"Pull him out, boys!" Buck yelled to Sam and Eight-John. Buck picked up a tree limb from the litter of broken branches. It was two inches thick and a yard long—ripped down the middle with jagged ends, the wood inside almost white as the snow. Aiden tried to kick and pull himself out of the drift, but his arms broke helplessly through the frail crust.

"I been waiting a long time to knock you into place!" Buck laughed. It was the oddest thing, but for a moment all Aiden could think about was what a pretty day it was. The snow glistened on the dark trees and glittered in blue ripples over the ground like hair ribbons. The two men flailed clumsily through the branches to get to him. Aiden waited until they reached for him, then grabbed one sleeve in each hand and pulled them forward. He jabbed the heels of his hands up, one into each man's face. He punched Eight-John squarely on the chin so hard he could feel the reverberation of teeth crashing together. Aiden's hand slipped off Sam's beard, but the blow was still strong enough to jar him. As they fell, Aiden pushed his palms against their backs, using the leverage to pull himself out of the drift.

Before Aiden could get his footing, Buck swung the stick like a baseball bat. Aiden darted back, avoiding it by inches. He saw Tupic climbing over the fallen tree, scrambling to help him. But the Indian tracker had recovered Buck's rifle and pointed it at Tupic. Buck swung again, and Aiden slipped in the snow. His wet clothing slowed him down, and before he could get back on his feet, the club caught him hard against his leg. He scooped up a handful of snow and threw it in Buck's face, then rolled out of the way and sprang up. Buck cursed, swiped an arm across his eyes and swung again.

Aiden threw up his left arm to block the blow, then

caught hold of the stick with his right hand, yanked it as hard as he could and purposefully fell backward, pulling Buck toward him. Aiden felt the end of the limb hit his shoulder, glance off, then plunge through the snow crust and hit the ground below. He felt splinters gouging his palm as the wood slid through his hand. Then he felt Buck's body, heavy as a sandbag, landing on the jagged point. The tree limb pierced his flesh with a dainty pop, like tearing silk. The torn wood slid neatly between his ribs and ripped through his flesh; then Buck lay motionless, half on top of Aiden, his face in the snow. A thick stream of bright red blood poured out of his neck. Buck made a strange gurgling sound. One hand clawed at the snow, then began to quiver. The stake had gone through at an angle, from stomach to throat, skewering every organ in its path. William Buck's blood steamed and melted a little hole in the snow.

52

Aiden let his hands be tied, let Sam and Eight-John drag him to his feet. They weren't bent on killing anyone. They were glad now just to be done with this hunt and on their way home. They slung Buck's body over his horse and roped it into place. Then captors and prisoners all mounted and set off in a silent walk through the snowy woods.

The storm had largely stopped at the next ridge, and what snow there was melted quickly in the afternoon sun, so the going was easy. Time passed and miles passed. The sun drifted across the sky. The trees marched on, all the same. The dead hands of William Buck swung rhythmically and turned dark blue.

It was twilight and Aiden was dozing in the saddle when he found himself pulled off the horse in East Royal St. Petersburg. His legs were cramped and he could barely stand up. He looked around for Tupic and Carlos but did not see them. The door of Napoleon Gilivrey's small house opened and the man stood there, quickly taking in the scene. His hard glance paused only briefly on the dead body of William Buck.

"Did you get it?" Gilivrey asked in his clipped voice.

"Yes, sir." Sam untied the black saddlebag of vaccine.

"Bring it. Bring him." Gilivrey turned and walked back into his house.

"Come on." Eight-John grabbed Aiden's arm, then dragged him over to the house and up onto the small front porch.

"No boot, sir." Gilivrey's Chinese servant pointed to the bootjack. "No boot."

Aiden jammed the heel of his wet boot into the notch on the board and pried one foot out, then the other. Though he'd only removed his boots, he felt naked as a raw chick. Aiden stood at the threshold and blinked. He had never seen a house like this anywhere, let alone in the godforsaken middle of the forest. The floor was crowded with so many carpets their edges overlapped. The windows dripped with red and gold brocade drapes. Gilivrey sat down at an ornate gilded desk beneath a gold chandelier.

"Untie him, please," he said to Eight-John.

"He's dangerous, sir."

"I am well guarded, thank you," Gilivrey said.

"William Buck is dead." Eight-John shifted uneasily on the porch.

"I did presume that, yes." Gilivrey's face twitched slightly. "By the position of his body dangling across the horse, which I observed as you made your arrival."

"He killed him." Eight-John nodded at Aiden.

"That will be all."

Eight-John pulled out his knife and cut the ropes around Aiden's wrists.

"My clerk will see to you," Gilivrey said to Eight-John. The man looked as if he might say something more, then thought better. He handed the black saddlebag to the Chinese servant, glared at Aiden and left. The servant brushed past Aiden and shut the door behind him. He walked silently across the room and placed the bag on Gilivrey's desk. Gilivrey nodded dismissal and the man vanished through a side door.

"Please, Mr. Lynch, come in. Have a seat." He waved toward a settee, which had already been draped with a quilt to protect the sumptuous fabric from Aiden's filthy self.

"Where are the others?" Aiden said.

"In the stable."

"Alive?"

"Had I wanted any of you dead, you would be dead by now." Gilivrey flashed his thin, reptilian smile. "Death is always an . . . inelegant solution. Also, I've found that anyone really worth murdering is generally interesting enough to keep alive."

"Then why did you send William Buck to kill us?"

"I sent Mr. Buck precisely because he was too stupid to kill you. Please, sit."

Aiden had never walked on carpet, and it felt creepy. The settee was unimaginably soft, and he floundered to keep from sinking. The room was overheated and crammed with furniture. Gilivrey opened the black saddlebag and parted the straw carefully so as not to let a stray bit loose to fall on the carpet. He drew out each bottle and held it up to the light to examine the contents. When he was satisfied, he got up and went to a small table in the corner of the room, where there was a silver tray with a cut-crystal bottle and some strange glasses, huge and round as a ball.

"Will you have some cognac?"

Aiden didn't know what cognac was but was glad to smell something like whiskey in the queer glass. It was awkward to drink from, but he managed a deep, burning swallow. Warmth began to spread to his freezing limbs. Gilivrey settled back in his chair.

"Why did you send Buck after me?" Aiden said.

"Mr. Buck originated the plan, you see; it seemed only fair." Gilivrey settled into a plush brocade chair opposite the settee. "He was eavesdropping on you and your Indian friend in the barn that night after your fight with the Bull. He heard about your plans to get the vaccine and thought that I would be happy to have your effort foiled and to receive the supply of stolen vaccine myself. He thought it would win him favor with me."

Gilivrey rolled the glass in his hand and sniffed the aroma with satisfaction. "He had become friendly with one of the boatmen on my supply team who was in camp that night. They hatched a plot to foil you in Seattle. Buck couldn't go, of course, but the boatman beat you there easily, for he did not have to scurry roundabout through the forest as you did. Once you arrived in Seattle, you were easy enough to find. After you visited Dr. Abradale, he assumed you had obtained the vaccine and determined to take it from you."

"He got men to jump me that night?"

"Yes. Focused on a task, you see, but sadly lacking the intelligence to investigate the situation fully. To learn, as you did rather easily, that the vaccine was already gone and where it was going. I, of course, knew this. All the logging camps were notified, weeks ago, to expect a vaccination team sometime in late January, weather conditions permitting, et cetera. Buck, you see, failed to consider that smallpox vaccine would hardly have the same value to me as it would to your Indians, being as it is a commodity I can readily obtain." Gilivrey turned the lamp wick up a bit. "You're not hurting too badly?" He peered at Aiden's bruised face.

"I'm fine," Aiden said, though a slow trickle of blood from a gash on his forehead was carrying grit into the corner of his eye. He brushed it with his sleeve, a gesture that caused the fastidious Gilivrey to shudder slightly with disgust.

"I knew you wouldn't obtain the vaccine in Seattle," he went on. "But I was fairly sure that, being of persistent temperament, you would pursue other means to secure it for your Indian. That gave me exactly the opportunity I was looking for."

"I don't understand. It was coming to you anyway—why go to all this trouble to steal it?"

Gilivrey put his crystal glass down soundlessly on a glossy table beside his chair. "Do you play chess?"

"I know how the pieces move."

"You do have a certain honesty that one might admire were one more . . . sentimental." Gilivrey's lip twitched in what might have been something like a smile. "So you know what a pawn is?"

Aiden recognized that as a clear insult but kept his temper.

"I needed to obtain a supply of the vaccine in secret, and I needed everyone else to think it was gone—stolen for your Nez Perce, sunk in the river, lost over a cliff, it didn't matter, so long as the vaccine was presumed lost and yet came to me. I had been considering options for several months; Mr. Buck just presented me with the ideal one."

"Why?"

Gilivrey picked up a leather folder, took out a stack of papers and handed them to Aiden. The pages were covered with complicated drawings and notes, some with mathematical equations in the margins.

"This business is changing," Gilivrey said. "This is a system of levers, ropes and pulleys that will enable us to cut and carry logs from the steepest hills. With these rigs, I can get logs out of impossible places. I can go back into a worked-over forest and pull out trees that no one could cut before. Besides that, the steam engine will be here in another year or two. An engine that can drag ten times the logs of an ox team, maybe even power a mill to cut the trees where they fall. It isn't secret, everyone knows change is coming."

Gilivrey took back the papers, tapped them neatly together and put them safely away.

"Just north of here is an Indian reservation. No one has cared about that land before now. The hills are far too steep to log efficiently and the river too feeble to carry much out. It was useless land, which is why it was given to the Indians in the first place. But with this kind of engineering, everything changes. Now, soon there will be a million dollars of harvestable timber up there."

Gilivrey pulled an immaculate white handkerchief from his pocket and dabbed his temples. "Now everyone is looking with hunger at that land. But those Indians are my neighbors, and I am concerned for their continued good health."

"You mean you have deals with them?" Aiden said, suddenly understanding. "Deals to cut trees on their land?"

"Ah, good boy."

"But if they all die of smallpox, their land is up for grabs."

"And I would stand no chance in the grabbing," Gilivrey said. "I am a foreigner. I came from Russia with nothing and have made my fortune as an outcast, squeezing profit from hostile acres with bound men. I am both admired and resented because of it. I have no connections in the government, nor expectations of fair play. If the Indians all die of the pox, the timber rights will be given to Alvin Tesler or Aloysius Grand. So it serves me that the Indians not die."

"So vaccinate them," Aiden said bitterly. He could see how this twisted story was unraveling now. "It isn't against the law."

"No," Gilivrey calmly agreed. "But it is understood. Supplies of the vaccine are carefully controlled and monitored."

It is understood. The words gave Aiden a sickening chill. He remember Dr. Abradale's cool, insidious words. *The good Lord can save the Indians if he wants.*

"But what about the Nez Perce? If you take the vaccine, what happens to them?"

"Find me some value to their lives and I'll gladly help them out too." Gilivrey shrugged. Aiden strained to keep his composure.

"What happens now?"

"Your Nez Perce are too far away to be any threat to me. As for you, despite all the torment and such of your unfortunate life full of dead sisters, et cetera—I do not believe you actually wish to die just yet. So you will leave tonight and never speak of this." Gilivrey got up and went to the gilded desk. "Mr. Powhee has packed up your belongings. A boatman will carry you down the river tonight to Seattle." Gilivrey walked over to the desk and took out a small leather purse. He handed it to Aiden. "This is all your fight

344

money; one hundred and seventy-nine dollars, plus fifty for your excellent—service." He made the word sound foul. "In addition, your debt to me is forgiven. Your indenture is completed, you are free."

Aiden's brain was spinning in so many directions he didn't know what to think.

Gilivrey sat down and leaned back in the chair with a regal air.

"If you speak of this to no one, I give you my word, I will not send anyone to hunt you. However, my reputation does exist. So I suggest you pursue your new life at a considerable distance. Everyone for a hundred miles around will assume there is a bounty on your head. The law may be loose up here, but you did kill a man."

"Did you mean for me to kill Buck?"

"I knew there was bad blood between you. I knew he was a violent man, and stupid. I knew you were Mr. Powhee's new champion fighter. I hoped for the best. He would have been troublesome for me." Gilivrey swallowed the last of his cognac and put the crystal glass down on the table. It caught the light and flashed a brief startling rainbow across the man's smooth white hand. "Do we have an agreement?"

"Yes," Aiden said. He held up the purse. "I owe money to Mr. Jackson for the horses and some supplies. Will you take it from here and see that he gets it?"

"I can send the horses back to him."

"My friend will need one of them."

"The Indian?"

"He goes free. He had nothing to do with killing that prison guard, and stealing the vaccine was my own plan. He meant all along to buy it."

345

Gilivrey frowned, obviously annoyed that Aiden had declared and not asked.

"I have no interest in all that. I will neither pursue nor protect him. I cannot speak for others."

"And the other man that was brought in with us—" Aiden went on. "He was purely our hostage. He's a doctor. He was the one doing the vaccinating, so you need to let him go too."

"Is there anything else you'd like?" Gilivrey said sarcastically.

"One bottle of the vaccine," Aiden replied coolly.

"No."

"You'll still have at least three hundred doses. There can't be three hundred Indians living up there."

Gilivrey said nothing. He rang a little bell and the Chinese servant reappeared as if by magic. "Have the cook pack food for a journey. This man leaves as soon as the boatman is ready." The servant bowed and left.

"We're done, then?" Aiden stood and took a step toward the door. He was glad to see his wet feet had left damp dented prints on the plush carpet.

"Why did you risk your life for this fool's errand?" Gilivrey asked.

Aiden turned and looked directly at Gilivrey, this odd, pale, fastidious man sitting at his golden desk in his plummy house tucked among the grand trees, living a pinched and suspicious life, scratching at profit and waiting, always waiting, for the river to rise.

Aiden shrugged. "Not much of a life to risk."

53

Aiden stumbled out into the cold night. The little "town" of East Royal St. Petersburg was almost empty, and quiet; very different from the last time he had been here. Lamplight from the bunkhouse spilled a soft arc on the muddy ground. He heard the sounds of men talking and smelled meat cooking. Was it just now suppertime? Time had lost all meaning for him. He looked up at the sky, but there were no stars to be seen. Everywhere in the world, he thought, people were going on with their ordinary lives; Hindus and pygmies, soldiers, settlers, Indians and artists, and some were good and some were horrible and no one knew why.

"Aiden?"

He looked around, startled. The veiled figure came out of the shadows.

"Bandy?"

The rustle of her skirts hit him with shocking happiness. Out of nowhere, tears flooded his eyes and he reached for her. They hugged, for they couldn't not, then quickly stepped apart, for they never had before. "Are you all right?" she asked anxiously.

"I'm fine." He couldn't see her eyes through the veil but knew she was examining his face. He took her hands. "What are you doing here?"

"Is everything—settled?"

"What—what do you mean? What do you know?"

"Dear lad. I know you are wonderful and brave and I will never see you again."

"Was it you that kept Gilivrey from killing me?"

"Mr. Gilivrey talks with me, that is all. But I—" Her voice broke. "I know you must go now." She pulled a thin chain off her neck. "Take this." On it was a small ring, a thin gold band with a tiny ruby in the center, flanked by two pearls small as a baby's tears.

"It is a child's ring," she explained. "Though I wore it until I was nineteen. It doesn't fit anymore." She paused. "The scars, you see. But it is a token of happier times." She handed it to Aiden. "So you won't forget me."

"I couldn't ever forget you. Bandy, you're—"

"Don't." She touched his cheek. Aiden pushed her hand away, lifted her veil and kissed her on the lips. She tensed at first, then went soft in his arms and kissed him back. It was like fresh cream and summer night. When she pulled away, Aiden stumbled into a swoop of cold.

"Go now," Bandy whispered.

"Where do I go?"

"I don't know." The musical voice faltered. "Somewhere in the world. Somewhere better."

"Where is better?"

"Wherever you are."

She pulled her coat tighter, turned and walked away into the darkness.

A lantern hung on a post by the stable, and Aiden took it with him as he pushed open the heavy door. Carlos and Tupic were asleep in the hay but sat up quickly as the light flickered across them. Aiden hung the lantern on a nail and knelt to untie them. The three of them, with their damp, dirty clothes, sweat and crusty wounds, smelled more pungent than the whole rest of the stable.

"Listen to me, for I don't have much time," Aiden said. "I'm leaving soon. You will also be let go." The knots were difficult to undo, tightened by movement during the long day's ride. Touching Carlos's limp arm made him feel oddly embarrassed. "But I think it would be best for you to leave before daylight," he said to Tupic.

"Where do we go?" Tupic asked.

"Not we. I'm going alone." The rope finally came free, and Tupic rubbed his wrists where deep red marks carved his skin. "You can keep Jackson's good horse," Aiden said. "I bought it. Gilivrey promises he won't chase you, but there is a price on your head in Seattle."

"Why is Gilivrey letting you go?" Carlos asked warily.

"He got what he wanted." Aiden looked back toward the door, listened for the sound of anyone coming, then turned back. "But so did we," he said softly.

"Yes?" Tupic's eyes shone with hope. Aiden reached into his little bag and pulled out the old socks they had found in the stolen saddlebag. Even among the animal smells and their own stink, the socks were still noticeably pungent. Tupic took the bundle as if it were a sacred object and stared at it. The lantern light softened all the desperate edges and filled the stable air with golden dust.

"They did not find it!"

"No."

Tupic carefully unpeeled the socks over his lap. Out tumbled the little match tin. He twisted off the cap and his shoulders dropped with relief as he saw the strings tucked inside. He tipped the tin to show Carlos the contents.

"We took a few strings from each bottle," Aiden explained. "While Buck and the men were digging us out." He couldn't read the expression on Carlos's face. "Just a few from each, so they wouldn't be missed. It isn't much, maybe fifty or sixty strings, but—"

Carlos turned his head and held up his hand as if trying to stop the words in the air.

"—you could make it into more."

"I can't." Carlos's split lip cracked open as he talked. A slow drop of fresh blood beaded out. "I only vaccinate people; I haven't even seen the production farm. And there is no way I could smuggle any more out for you, if that's what you're thinking. Be glad for your fifty doses."

"We think, not modern vaccine," Tupic said. "But the old way. Like on the orphan ship."

"No." Carlos wiped his mouth.

"Arm to arm."

"You could vaccinate all the Indians in the country that way!" Aiden said. "You just have to get it started," he rushed on, as if a second's delay would give too much time for sense to crumble the plan. They had come up with the idea while trapped in the rock shelter, in those few frantic minutes while shovels stabbed at the snow above them and Buck's axe chopped through the fallen tree. "You can teach the Indians how to do it themselves!"

"No!" Carlos stood up angrily, but there was no place he could go. He sank into the corner of the stall just a few feet away. "It's crazy. Forget it." A mule in the next stall stamped and tossed its head, annoyed by the disturbance.

"I know of the problems," Tupic said. "I will tell the problems to my people. Let each one decide if they will take this chance."

"It isn't that simple!"

"But it is!" Aiden said. A strange feeling was rising within him; something like panic and anger but at the same time, the opposite; something like hope. It was unreasonable and stupid and put splinters in his throat. "You saw more horror than any of us." Aiden felt crazy beyond any drunk. His lips burned from Bandy's kiss. "But you had hope again when you fell in love with Maddy."

"Stop."

"She would do this. You know she would."

Carlos pressed a hand to his eyes. "The Indians are doomed," he said sharply. He stared at the lantern flame, his eyes dark as a swallow's wings. "Smallpox, massacre, starvation—why this lost cause and not another?"

"This one came along," Aiden said simply. The barn door opened and a stream of light knifed across the straw between them.

"Boat's ready," a voice called.

"Yes—I'm coming," Aiden said. He turned back to Carlos. "I'm tired." He struggled for words to fit. "I'm tired of there being nothing good. I'm tired of hopeless. Maddy was good. And Clever Crow, and your father—" Aiden took the little match tin and carefully pushed the lid back on. "If we don't have some kind of hope, it's like—like we cancel out their lives."

Aiden took the heavy purse from his pocket. "Just get it started. Please. This will pay for your journey."

"I don't need your money," Carlos said. He brushed his

good hand across the sides of his face, smoothed his hair and tugged his jacket into place. "I will have to go back to Seattle for a while or I'll look suspicious. I'll show you how to vaccinate with the strings," he said to Tupic. "We will figure the rest out."

"Thank you," Tupic said. Silently they all stood up, the matter settled, the future fixed, for a little while, maybe; for a few people, maybe. It was a forlorn hope, but it was hope.

"Where will you go?" Carlos asked Aiden.

"I don't know. Somewhere in the world." Aiden picked up his canvas bag and slung it over his shoulder. He did not want to leave. After the cold, lost horrors of the past few days, the warm stable felt like Christmas. He would likely never see these men again. He had spent little time with them, but they felt closer to him than brothers.

"Goodbye, then," he said.

"Wait—please, take this," said Tupic, and lifted a leather thong with a small beaded bag off his neck. "We call this *ipetes*," he said. "It holds the sacred objects from the teaching spirit." He opened the bag and tipped its contents into his hand. It looked like bits of rubbish: a small stone, a carved bit of wood, two tiny shells, a piece of bone, a feather, some beads.

"This belonged to Clever Crow before me. I cannot give you his sacred objects, but I can give you a place to put your own as they come to you." He put the thong around Aiden's neck. The leather was warm from Tupic's body.

"Thank you." Aiden pressed his hand on the token. "I have to go."

"Wait—" Carlos reached into a pocket inside his jacket. "Take this. For your pouch." He pulled out a scrap of cloth. It was brown, with a faded flower print, and worn almost through, stained with three small spots, tiny half-moons of blood in the shape of fingernails. It was the scrap of Maddy's dress that had torn off in Carlos's hand. Aiden felt his knees go wobbly. He quickly balled the scrap up and tucked it into the pouch; then he walked out into the night.

The boatman waited in the darkness. Beside him on the ground were a canvas pack, a bedroll, a canteen and—Aiden noted with surprise—his bow and quiver of arrows.

The river was high and the boat sailed easily on the current. The journey was startlingly easy. Aiden sat watching constellations and clouds, empty night and the black feather-sweep of ancient trees across the midnight sky. Sometimes he dozed, lulled by the steady shush of moving water. Sometimes the boatman sang.

It was just midnight when they bumped against the dock.

"We've a hut here," the boatman said. "You may sleep on through the night."

"Thank you," Aiden said. "But I think I'll walk awhile." He had slipped past exhaustion into a restless exhilaration that demanded motion. He had no idea where he was going, but his body needed to move and so he went along with it. The path was clear and would lead eventually to the sea. He couldn't get lost, so he walked. The forest rustled around him. The moon broke through the clouds and spilled silver on the tips of branches. Aiden walked until he came to a little clearing on a hillside. He could see the flat square shapes of Seattle and the shimmering water just beyond. Here was a path to the world.

He was sixteen years old. He had killed two men. One

he'd had to, one he hadn't meant to, but regardless, it was done. He had lost eight members of his family and buried six of them with his own hands. It was the middle of night, the middle of winter; he was alone in the world, and a fugitive. But there was a path, at least for the next little while. He laid his hand over the leather bag and pressed it against his chest and walked on.

Whites, Indians and smallpox: What's the real story?

I got the idea for *The Devil's Paintbox* several years ago while visiting the Royal British Columbia Museum in Victoria, British Columbia, Canada. There was a copy of a newspaper article (*The British Colonist,* July 11, 1862) that reported a controversy going on at the time over whether or not Indians should be vaccinated against smallpox. I knew, of course, that racial discrimination has always been a sad part of our human story, but I was still surprised. How could anyone even consider withholding a lifesaving medical procedure from one ethnic group? Imagine if we had an AIDS vaccine today but some people insisted that no Chinese, or African Americans, or whatever race would be allowed to have it.

Today most Americans accept that the history of white dealings with the native populations of North America is generally not something to be proud of. Some government policies were sincere but misguided attempts to "civilize" the Indians, such as forcing native children into white-run boarding schools and forbidding them their language and culture. A few, such as forced relocation to unsuitable lands (the 1864 Navajo internment at Basque Redondo; the 1838 Cherokee "Trail of Tears"), are, quite arguably, examples of what we would today call ethnic cleansing.

One of the greatest atrocities, the 1864 Sand Creek Massacre (depicted in *The Devil's Paintbox*), was committed under the direction of an individual officer and not sanctioned by the government. Several of the other officers under his command refused to participate. At dawn on November 29, 1864, in Sand Creek, Colorado, Colonel John Chivington and 800

U.S. soldiers attacked Black Kettle's sleeping camp and killed between 150 and 200 Cheyenne Indians, nearly all women, children and elderly men. Some of the soldiers mutilated the Indians' bodies, cutting off scalps, ears and genitals, which were later displayed to the public in a theater in Denver.

While the U.S. government subsequently denounced the action, the response of the many local white citizens who lined up to see the sickening trophies, like some kind of carnival attraction, demonstrates a level of racial intolerance that we don't like to face.

But did white people purposefully try to infect Native Americans with smallpox?

When I told people that my new book involved Indians and smallpox, almost everyone mentioned a belief that the U.S. government had tried to exterminate Indians by giving them smallpox-infected blankets. I don't address that allegation in this book, but it has become so prevalent in popular culture, cited in movies and television shows and dozens of Web sites, that I wanted to say something about it here. Is it true?

I believe—basically—no.

There *is* one reliable account from 1763, during the French and Indian War, in which a British commander, Jeffrey Amherst, gave an order that blankets taken from smallpox victims be sent to "hostile" tribes. (He also referred to the Indians as "vermin" and "this execrable race" and lamented that he didn't have dogs available to simply hunt them down.)

We don't know whether the blankets were actually sent in that instance. But after lots of research for this book, I found no evidence that this was ever a common practice, if it happened at all. And it was certainly not a U.S. government policy.

This was probably due less to any great virtue than to fear.

Though the smallpox vaccine was widely available by the mid-1800s, it was never completely reliable, and everyone knew it. Unless someone had actually had smallpox, they could never be 100 percent sure they were safe. Even where Indians and whites lived apart, there was still enough contact through trade that a smallpox outbreak in an Indian camp could easily spread back to white towns and cities.

There is also the simple fact that transmitting smallpox on blankets isn't effective. The smallpox virus is primarily transmitted through the air, like the flu. While it may well be possible to infect someone with a blanket, it is unlikely. People back then would not have known this, of course, but even if they had wanted to infect Indians with blankets, it just wouldn't have worked.

Certainly many whites were happy to see the Indians die by whatever means possible. There were those who believed that smallpox was God's way of clearing out the country for white settlement. And there really was controversy over whether or not to vaccinate Indians. But I don't believe that the smallpox-blanket stories are true, not in any widespread or officially sanctioned program.

Why is this a big deal? Just as it is important to identify human atrocities, both historically and in our own times, so it is important to avoid exaggeration, for exaggeration gives doubters a foothold toward dismissal.

❧ FURTHER READING ❧

On the smallpox-blanket question:

Adams, Cecil. "Did Whites Ever Give Native Americans Blankets Infected with Smallpox?" *The Straight Dope*, www.straightdope.com/classics/a5_066.html

On the history of vaccinations:

Allen, Arthur. *Vaccine: The Controversial Story of Medicine's Greatest Lifesaver*. New York: W. W. Norton & Company, 2007.

On smallpox in general:

Fenn, Elizabeth A. *Pox Americana: The Great Smallpox Epidemic of 1775–82*. New York: Hill and Wang, 2001.

Tucker, Jonathan B. *Scourge: The Once and Future Threat of Smallpox*. New York: Atlantic Monthly Press, 2001.

On the history of Native Americans:

Kehoe, Alice B. *North American Indians: A Comprehensive Account*, second ed. Upper Saddle River, N.J.: Prentice-Hall, Inc., 1992.

Utley, Robert M. *The Indian Frontier of the American West, 1846–1890*. Albuquerque: University of New Mexico Press, 1984.

On American frontier life:

Stratton, Joanna L. *Pioneer Women: Voices from the Kansas Frontier*. New York: Simon and Schuster, 1981.

Individual stories from the Oregon Trail:

www.over-land.com/diaries.html

Victoria McKernan is the author of the acclaimed *Shackleton's Stowaway*, a historical novel for young adults about the eighteen-year-old stowaway on Ernest Shackleton's ill-fated 1914 expedition to the South Pole. She has also written four novels for adults.

Victoria McKernan lives in Washington, D.C., with a dog, two cats, and one boa constrictor.

Read an excerpt from

SON OF FORTUNE,

the sequel to

THE DEVIL'S PAINTBOX

Aiden Lynch walked off alone into the night forest. He had no real idea where he was going, but his body needed to move so he went along with it. He had slipped past exhaustion into a restless exhilaration that demanded motion. The path was faint, but as long as he walked west he would come soon enough to the sea. The sea offered escape, and he needed escape, for he had just killed a man. The stain was still on him. The blood had soaked through his coat and through his sweater and the shirt beneath that and onto his skin where it had dried and itched for hours; a rude smear, crisp and foul like a smashed bug. He had washed at the river, rubbing the place with cold handfuls of water until his skin felt raw, but even now, many hours later, it seemed he could still feel it, the poisonous crackle of another man's blood drying slowly on his own flesh.

William Buck was no loss to the world, but Aiden could have easily gone his whole life without killing him. That the death was in fact mostly accidental changed little. Buck was not a virtuous man, nor really even liked by anyone, but the raw truth was, at the time of his death, he was pursuing a thief, a highway robber who had ambushed a medical team and stolen precious smallpox vaccine. In another day or two, Aiden knew, the name of that thief would reach Seattle, and that name was his own. So Aiden Lynch, sixteen years old and alone in the world, was on the run.

The fight wasn't even a whole day ago. His left leg throbbed where Buck had clubbed him, and there were splinters still buried deep in his palm where he had grabbed the stick. There was a deep pain across his lower ribs, a tender, swollen eye and raw cuts on his face where little shreds of broken skin were beginning to curl. He had a deep, pulpy bruise just below his collarbone, where one end of that stick had landed while the other end, accidentally sharper and more fatefully positioned, had pierced the neck of William Buck. The blood had poured out amazingly fast, awful red and dense as mercury, steaming a hole in the fresh snow.

Aiden's legs felt shaky and he stopped, light-headed. He bent over and rested his hands on his knees. The sharp tang of urgency that had carried his muscles along so far was starting to evaporate. He felt frail and drenched with mortality. The sweet scent of pine needles drifted up from the ground like incense. He slumped into the fragrance, resting his head on his arms. In the few months that he had worked as a logger, he had come to love this land and was sad to be leaving it. These northwest woods with their enormous, ancient trees were insane and delicious, strange as Mars yet calmly beautiful.

He yearned just to lie down and sleep, but he struggled to his feet again. It was January and even on a mild night like this, with no wind and the temperature in the forties he knew that he could freeze to death lying on the bare ground. The moon broke through the clouds and spilled silver on the tips of branches. In a far part of his brain, Aiden recognized it was lovely, but he was numb to beauty right now, numb to everything but the rhythmic solace of his footsteps. Tree roots braided the path before him. He didn't know what came next, and he wasn't sure he had the strength to find out, but there were, as always, only two choices. He could go on or he could die. There had been grander chances to die so far, so it didn't seem justice to do it now.

The sky was beginning to lighten behind him as Aiden stood on the last hill overlooking the Seattle harbor. It would still be a while before the sun actually rose above the trees, but he could see the flat, square shapes of the city streets and the shimmering water of Puget Sound just beyond. He saw fourteen ships anchored. Nine were lumber ships, in various stages of loading. The rest he didn't know. Aiden had never seen the open ocean and knew little about ships, but he did know the ones in Seattle always needed men. There was a gold rush in British Columbia and it was common for whole crews to desert in Seattle to chase their fortunes. He also knew he had to be careful. Seattle and Portland had long been notorious for shanghaiing—men were fed knockout potions in saloons and dropped through trapdoors only to wake with throbbing heads, far out to sea with the roll of the ocean beneath them, forced into service as deckhands on their way to China. Aiden was determined not to fall prey to anyone. If he did decide on the sea, it would be on his own terms, and those terms, he knew, would be best made in San Francisco. He made his way down to the harbor as the sun rose behind him.

"You have never been to sea." The captain squinted at him suspiciously and twitched like a fly had landed on his ear. "And so I should hire you as sailor for why?"

"I'm not asking for pay," Aiden replied. "Just to work my passage."

"The fare to San Francisco is ten dollars. The pay to a sailor is two dollars a day. It is four, maybe five days to San Francisco. Can you think the numbers?" The captain tapped one finger on the side of his head. He had a thick Swedish accent, so the question sounded almost like a child's rhyme. *Caan you tink da nuumbers?* So many of these lumber boats that ran along the coast were run by Scandinavians that they were sometimes called the "Swedish Navy."

"I can sleep on deck."

"Go away," the man said. "You are no use to me."

"I've worked lumber," Aiden said.

"The lumber is already loaded." The captain shrugged.

"I just meant—I know hard work," Aiden pressed.

"I have no hard work. I have a steam engine. I have a winch. I have a crew. We do not sail to China."

Aiden knew this boat was the only one ready to leave that day. Besides, even to his inexperienced eyes, it looked like a good ship. The decks were clean, the sails were neatly reefed, the wooden railings were recently varnished and the lumber was well stacked and secured. He had some money, almost two hundred dollars. It was a modest fortune but hard won, and he didn't want to spend it unless he had to. Fortune, for most of his life, had been a box of pennies on the shelf above the stove, saved against hard times and emptied far too often. He knew San Francisco was expensive and he had no idea what sort of work he could find there. He had no formal education and little experience. He could plow a field, skin a wolf, cut down trees and fight. He had read most of

Shakespeare, all of Dickens and the *Atlas of the World*, but he knew that didn't count for much.

"I'll give you five dollars' fare for passage, and sleep on the deck," Aiden offered.

"Your face was in a fight," the captain said, flicking a disapproving hand at Aiden's bruises. "It looks like trouble."

"Well, it never looked all that good to start with."

The captain twitched in what might have been a laugh.

"Did you win?"

"I'm here, aren't I?"

"What is this?" He tipped his prickly chin at the bundle that Aiden carried. "A gun?"

The bundle was long and narrow, wrapped in oiled cloth and tied securely with rough twine.

"Bow and arrows," Aiden answered.

"You are not the Indian."

"No," Aiden said simply. He wasn't sure what he looked like these days, but he was pretty sure he didn't look Indian.

"Where do you come from?"

"Logging camp up north."

"Before that?" the captain pressed suspiciously.

"Kansas mostly, then west. I came out with a wagon train." The facts were true, though they left out a lot. His parents had been godforsaken bog Irish who had escaped famine in the old country as indentured servants, their passage to Virginia paid for with nine years of work—the regular seven, plus two for the children they brought along, his two older brothers. After the indenture was completed, the family had worked in coal mines and rock quarries, saved every penny and bought land of their own. But that land turned out to be a barren plot of desperate Kansas, where drought and blizzard and fire made the plagues of Egypt seem like sniffles and hangnails. That land had ultimately killed most of them. A pile of woeful history, he thought, that mattered to no one.

"What is your name?"

"Aiden—Madison, sir," he said, thinking only now that he ought not use his real name. He did not imagine himself a very grand outlaw and doubted a manhunt in Seattle would chase him very far, but his real name—Aiden Lynch—might be tainted for a while in local parts and a lumber ship on regular runs might easily hear it. His sister's name had been Maddy, so Madison would be easy to remember.

"How old are you?"

"Nineteen," Aiden lied, adding on three years. He was tall and still lanky, but months of plentiful food and hard work in the logging camp had given him some muscle. His face, angular and roughened by a life outdoors, had never really looked boyish, but a close inspection would betray little need yet for shaving.

The captain frowned but didn't challenge him.

"Are you a good shot with this bow and arrow?"

"Yes," Aiden said evenly.

"What do you know about polar bears?" the captain asked abruptly.

"Um . . . they live in the Arctic," Aiden replied, quickly trying to switch his brain around. "They can weigh six hundred pounds and are solitary animals. They eat seals, which they hunt from ice floes—"

"Are you being smart?" the captain snapped.

"No, sir." Aiden flushed with confusion. Hadn't the man just asked him? Wasn't he just answering? "I had a book," he explained. "It told about all the regions of the world and their native peoples and animals and so on." The *Atlas of the World* had been nightly reading for most of his life, and the only thing that had kept him and his little sister Maddy going through the desperate last winter. He could call up most pages entirely by memory.

"So I could ask what do you know about headhunters or yaks and you would tell me that too?"

"Not yaks, sir," Aiden said. He suspected the man was now teasing him but decided to play it back straight. "They were mentioned only briefly, as Mongolia is still a largely unknown region," he said. "Though I could probably build a yurt if I had to."

"Ha!" The captain jerked his head back once, overly quick like an amateur sword swallower. He seemed too young to be captain of a ship, Aiden thought. No more than thirty, though he did have a beleaguered air of experience about him. He was shorter than Aiden and stockier. He looked like he might once have been athletic, but now had the slight softness that came from spending long periods of time on a small ship with a steam engine, a winch and a crew.

"Ha! All right, then, Mr. Atlas of the World. So you know all about polar bears! Are you afraid of polar bears?"

"I've never seen one, sir."

"Well, think! Think!" It came out *tink tink,* and Aiden, his nerves already on edge, had to work hard not to laugh. "Use your imagine! It's a bear!" He lunged at Aiden in bear pose, with curled finger-claws and toothy snarl. Two of the other sailors working on deck briefly looked up but didn't seem to think their captain's behavior all that peculiar. Aiden took some hint from that. Crazy people were in charge of lots of things in the world, he had learned, so you just had to go along with them.

"Well, if I saw one in the wild I suppose there wouldn't be much I could do," he said. "I suppose it would kill me regardless, if it wanted to, so being afraid wouldn't matter much either way." He gave a quick glance around the deck, suddenly wary that there might actually be polar bears on the loose. "But if I saw one anywhere else it would probably be in a cage." He shrugged. "So I'd be all right."

"Yes!" The captain jerked his head again in his odd way of maybe laughing. He actually had a kind face, Aiden noticed, once you got used to the twitches.

"These are in the cage." He grew still and looked at Aiden with a sudden piercing concentration. "See. Here. I have bears. For a rich man's zoo in San Francisco. Special order from Alaska. We go all the way for the special trip. It is the long trip and now mother bear is sick. We give the fish but she will not eat. My men try to kill the seals but they are not hunters. One time when they do shoot the seal, God knows by what luck, it swims away before we catch it. So here you come now with the Indian bow." He gave one tiny twitch, then went on. "This morning when we leave the harbor, we will pass by a little island full of seals. So you will put string on your arrow like the harpoon, yes? And so you can shoot the seal and pull it in." He mimed this vigorously, tugging an invisible rope hand over hand. "And then you feed the bears."

"Uh—sure," Aiden said. He doubted the string and arrow plan would work, but he certainly wasn't going to talk himself out of an opportunity.